ASTOUNDING
SEA STORIES

ASTOUNDING
SEA STORIES

FIFTEEN RIPPING
GOOD TALES

EDITED BY THOMAS P. McCARTHY

Seahorse Publishing books may be purchased in bulk at special discounts for sales promotion, corporate gifts, fund-raising, or educational purposes. Special editions can also be created to specifications. For details, contact the Special Sales Department, Skyhorse Publishing, 307 West 36th Street, 11th Floor, New York, NY 10018 or info@skyhorsepublishing.com.

Seahorse® and Seahorse Publishing® are registered trademarks of Skyhorse Publishing, Inc.®, a Delaware corporation.

Visit our website at www.skyhorsepublishing.com.

10 9 8 7 6 5 4 3 2

Library of Congress Cataloging-in-Publication Data is available on file.

Cover design by Tom Lau
Cover photo credit: Albemarle Boats

Print ISBN: 978-1-944824-24-2
Ebook ISBN: 978-1-944824-25-9

Printed in China

TABLE OF CONTENTS

INTRODUCTION

Need to escape? Want to spend an hour or two sealed off from the daily detritus that might be getting you down?

There is nothing like a sea story to help you along. It's been that way forever. Certainly even before Jason and his heroic crew of Argonauts set off to find the Golden Fleece and had an adventure or two along the way. Writers love to use the sea as a backdrop for adventure and tragedy and inspiration and elevating heart rates. Why? For one thing, using the sea as a setting is an easy first step to draw readers in. Throw in a few storms and shipwrecks and some pirates, and the rest is easy. Well, maybe not that easy, because there have certainly been some forgettable sea stories—the ones springing from the "it was a dark and stormy night" variety of pulp writing.

But not in this collection.

Here are fifteen unexpected pleasures—many that have been sitting unread for years. And that's a shame. Some are from master writers whose deserved fame rests on works and characters that lived far from the sea and might never have set foot in a boat of any kind. You'll find Jack London's first published story, written when he was seventeen, and it's miles away from the frozen north that London loved and wrote about often. You'll also discover Charles Dickens without Scrooge, Victor Hugo far from Paris, and Arthur Conan Doyle on the deck of a ship, without Sherlock or Watson. All are hidden gems that make you wish they had written more sea stories.

But fear not. There are also in this collection some wonderful stories that simply slipped away quietly. It's time to revive them.

Astounding Sea Stories also brings along some of the best writers of the sea: Herman Melville; Richard Henry Dana Jr.; and Erskine Childers, a writer who captures the sublime joyous beauty of being aboard a small sailboat better than any other author in his genre.

You will find adventure, certainly, along with drama and well-paced tales that will make you sit back in the comfort of your warm and cozy (and I hope, dry) reading chair and start turning the pages quickly—being pulled in to the story and happy you are home and safe. That's the magic of a good tale and why some of the best writers chose it as a backdrop.

This is not just a collection of stirring writing by wonderful writers. Here also are frank and—one must admit—inspiring stories of men of the sea, not writers but individuals who by luck (more often than not, bad luck), found themselves alone on a boat in devastating circumstances. Inside is William Bligh taking his small group of supporters to safety after they were thrown from the *Bounty*. In his own words, an understated firsthand account of what many consider, even today nearly 250 years later, the greatest small boat navigation ever. Here also is Elisha Kent Kane, frozen, dismal but still hopeful, looking for the lost ships of John Franklin along the Northwest Passage Franklin gave his life trying to find.

And this courage and resoluteness, of course, is not just the purview of men. Read here Charlotte-Adélaïde Dard's account of surviving the sinking of the *Medusa* and try to argue against her valor. Charlotte and her family survived only to land in a small boat with little water and food on the edge of the Sahara. But that's another journey for another time.

You will also find a tale of how a ship was holed and sunk by an angry whale (sound familiar?), written by its captain. He began by writing: "Having been requested to give an account of the sinking of the Bark *Kathleen* by a whale, I will do the best I can, though I think that those who have read the papers know as much or more about it than I do."

Ah, one wonders what a twenty-first-century publicist would have told him about marketing?

We also take a step away from literature and compelling writing to find something more practical yet as equally compelling as works in the original report of the investigation of the sinking of the *Titanic*.

It is fascinating stuff. Read. Enjoy. Stay dry.

Le Terrible Coffret

Par Conan DOYLE

J'aperçus à terre un homme étendu près du coffret, le crâne fendu d'un coup de hache!

"Le Terrible Coffret" by George Conrad, from *Journal Des Voyages*, 1906.

1.

THE STRIPED CHEST

ARTHUR CONAN DOYLE

"What do you make of her, Allardyce?" I asked.

My second mate was standing beside me upon the poop, with his short, thick legs astretch, for the gale had left a considerable swell behind it, and our two quarter-boats nearly touched the water with every roll. He steadied his glass against the mizzen-shrouds, and he looked long and hard at this disconsolate stranger every time she came reeling up on to the crest of a roller and hung balanced for a few seconds before swooping down upon the other side. She lay so low in the water that I could only catch an occasional glimpse of a pea-green line of bulwark.

She was a brig, but her mainmast had been snapped short off some ten feet above the deck, and no effort seemed to have been made to cut away the wreckage, which floated, sails and yards, like the broken wing of a wounded gull, upon the water beside her. The foremast was still standing, but the fore-topsail was flying loose, and the head-sails were streaming out in long white pennons in front of her. Never have I seen a vessel which appeared to have gone through rougher handling.

But we could not be surprised at that, for there had been times during the last three days when it was a question whether our own barque would ever see land again. For thirty-six hours we had kept her nose to it, and if the *Mary Sinclair* had not been as good a seaboat as ever left the Clyde, we could not have gone through. And yet here we were at the end of it with the loss only of our gig and of part of the starboard bulwark. It did not astonish us, however, when the smother had cleared away, to find that others had been less lucky, and that this mutilated brig, staggering about upon a blue sea, and under a cloudless sky, had been left, like a blinded man after a lightning flash, to tell of the terror which is past.

Allardyce, who was a slow and methodical Scotchman, stared long and hard at the little craft, while our seamen lined the bulwark or clustered upon the fore shrouds to have a view of the stranger. In latitude 20° and longitude 10°, which were about our bearings, one becomes a little curious as to whom one meets, for one has left the main lines of Atlantic commerce to the north. For ten days we had been sailing over a solitary sea.

"She's derelict, I'm thinking," said the second mate.

I had come to the same conclusion, for I could see no sign of life upon her deck, and there was no answer to the friendly wavings from our seamen. The crew had probably deserted her under the impression that she was about to founder.

"She can't last long," continued Allardyce, in his measured way. "She may put her nose down and her tail up any minute. The water's lipping up to the edge of her rail."

"What's her flag?" I asked.

"I'm trying to make out. It's got all twisted and tangled with the halyards. Yes, I've got it now, clear enough. It's the Brazilian flag, but it's wrong side up."

She had hoisted a signal of distress, then, before her people abandoned her. Perhaps they had only just gone. I took the mate's glass and looked round over the tumultuous face of the deep blue Atlantic, still veined and starred with white lines and spoutings of foam. But nowhere could I see anything human beyond ourselves.

"There may be living men aboard," said I.

"There may be salvage," muttered the second mate.

"Then we will run down upon her lee side, and lie to."

We were not more than a hundred yards from her when we swung our fore-yard aback, and there we were, the barque and the brig, ducking and bowing like two clowns in a dance.

"Drop one of the quarter-boats," said I. "Take four men, Mr. Allardyce, and see what you can learn of her."

But just at that moment my first officer, Mr. Armstrong, came on deck, for seven bells had struck, and it was but a few minutes off his watch. It would interest me to go myself to this abandoned vessel and to see what there might be aboard of her. So, with a word to Armstrong, I swung myself over the side, slipped down the falls, and took my place in the sheets of the boat.

It was but a little distance, but it took some time to traverse, and so heavy was the roll, that often, when we were in the trough of the sea, we could not see either the barque which we had left or the brig which we were approaching. The sinking sun did not penetrate down there, and it was cold and dark in the hollows of the waves, but each passing billow heaved us up into the warmth and the sunshine once more. At each of these moments, as we hung upon a white-capped ridge between the two dark valleys, I caught a glimpse of the long, pea-green line, and the nodding foremast of the brig, and I steered so as to come round by her stern, so that we might determine which was the best way of boarding her. As we passed her we saw the name *Nossa Sehnora da Vittoria* painted across her dripping counter.

"The weather side, sir," said the second mate. "Stand by with the boat-hook, carpenter!" An instant later we had jumped over the bulwarks, which were hardly higher than our boat, and found ourselves upon the deck of the abandoned vessel.

Our first thought was to provide for our own safety in case—as seemed very probable—the vessel should settle down beneath our feet. With this object two of our men held on to the painter of the boat, and fended her off from the vessel's side, so that she might be ready in case we had to make a hurried retreat. The carpenter was sent to find out how much water there was, and whether it was still gaining, while the other seaman, Allardyce, and myself, made a rapid inspection of the vessel and her cargo.

The deck was littered with wreckage and with hen-coops, in which the dead birds were washing about. The boats were gone, with the exception of one, the bottom of which had been stove, and it was certain that the crew had abandoned the vessel. The cabin was in a deck house, one side of which had been beaten in by a heavy sea. Allardyce and I entered it, and found the captain's table as he had left it, his books and papers—all Spanish or Portuguese—scattered over it, with piles of cigarette ash everywhere. I looked about for the log, but could not find it.

"As likely as not he never kept one," said Allardyce. "Things are pretty slack aboard a South American trader, and they don't do more than they can help. If there was one it must have been taken away with him in the boat."

"I should like to take all these books and papers," said I. "Ask the carpenter how much time we have."

His report was reassuring. The vessel was full of water, but some of the cargo was buoyant, and there was no immediate danger of her sinking. Probably she would never sink, but would drift about as one of those terrible, unmarked reefs which have sent so many stout vessels to the bottom.

"In that case there is no danger in your going below, Mr. Allardyce," said I. "See what you can make of her, and find out how much of her cargo may be saved. I'll look through these papers while you are gone."

The bills of lading, and some notes and letters which lay upon the desk, sufficed to inform me that the Brazilian brig *Nossa Sehnora da Vittoria* had cleared from Bahia a month before. The name of the captain was Texeira, but there was no record as to the number of the crew. She was bound for London, and a glance at the bills of lading was sufficient to show me that we were not likely to profit much in the way of salvage. Her cargo consisted of nuts, ginger, and wood, the latter in the shape of great logs of valuable tropical growths. It was these, no doubt, which had prevented the ill-fated vessel from going to the bottom, but they were of such a size as to make it impossible for us to extract them. Besides these, there were a few fancy goods, such as a number of ornamental birds for millinery purposes, and a hundred cases of preserved fruits. And then, as I turned over the papers, I came upon a short note in English, which arrested my attention.

"It is requested," said the note, "that the various old Spanish and Indian curiosities, which came out of the Santarem collection, and which are consigned to Prontfoot and Neuman, of Oxford Street, London, should be put in some place where there may be no danger of these very valuable and unique articles being injured or tampered with. This applies most particularly to the treasure-chest of Don Ramirez di Leyra, which must on no account be placed where any one can get at it."

The treasure-chest of Don Ramirez! Unique and valuable articles! Here was a chance of salvage after all! I had risen to my feet with the paper in my hand, when my Scotch mate appeared in the doorway.

"I'm thinking all isn't quite as it should be aboard of this ship, sir," said he. He was a hard-faced man, and yet I could see that he had been startled.

"What's the matter?"

"Murder's the matter, sir. There's a man here with his brains beaten out."

"Killed in the storm?" said I.

"May be so, sir. But I'll be surprised if you think so after you have seen him."

"Where is he, then?"

"This way, sir; here in the main-deck house."

There appeared to have been no accommodation below in the brig, for there was the afterhouse for the captain, another by the main hatchway with the cook's galley attached to it, and a third in the forecastle for the men. It was to this middle one that the mate led me. As you entered the galley, with its litter of tumbled pots and dishes, was upon the right, and upon the left was a small room with two bunks for the officers. Then beyond there was a place about twelve feet square, which was littered with flags and spare canvas.

All round the walls were a number of packets done up in coarse cloth and carefully lashed to the woodwork. At the other end was a great box, striped red and white, though the red was so faded and the white so dirty that it was only where the light fell directly upon it that one could see the colouring. The box was, by subsequent measurement, four feet three inches in length, three feet two inches in height, and three feet across—considerably larger than a seaman's chest.

But it was not to the box that my eyes or my thoughts were turned as I entered the store-room. On the floor, lying across the litter of bunting, there was stretched a small, dark man with a short, curling beard. He lay as far as it was possible from the box, with his feet towards it and his head away. A crimson patch was printed upon the white canvas on which his head was resting, and little red ribbons wreathed themselves round his swarthy neck and trailed away on to the floor, but there was no sign of a wound that I could see, and his face was as placid as that of a sleeping child.

It was only when I stooped that I could perceive his injury, and then I turned away with an exclamation of horror. He had been pole-axed; apparently by some person standing behind him. A frightful blow had smashed in the top of his head and penetrated deeply into his brain. His face might well be placid, for death must have been absolutely instantaneous, and the position of the wound showed that he could never have seen the person who had inflicted it.

"Is that foul play or accident, Captain Barclay?" asked my second mate, demurely.

"You are quite right, Mr. Allardyce. The man has been murdered, struck down from above by a sharp and heavy weapon. But who was he, and why did they murder him?"

"He was a common seaman, sir," said the mate. "You can see that if you look at his fingers." He turned out his pockets as he spoke and brought to light a pack of cards, some tarred string, and a bundle of Brazilian tobacco.

"Hullo, look at this!" said he.

It was a large, open knife with a stiff spring blade which he had picked up from the floor. The steel was shining and bright, so that we could not associate it with the crime, and yet the dead man had apparently held it in his hand when he was struck down, for it still lay within his grasp.

"It looks to me, sir, as if he knew he was in danger, and kept his knife handy," said the mate. "However, we can't help the poor beggar now. I can't make out these things that are lashed to the wall. They seem to be idols and weapons and curios of all sorts done up in old sacking."

"That's right," said I. "They are the only things of value that we are likely to get from the cargo. Hail the barque and tell them to send the other quarter-boat to help us to get the stuff aboard."

While he was away I examined this curious plunder which had come into our possession. The curiosities were so wrapped up that I could only form a general idea as to their nature, but the striped box stood in a good light where I could thoroughly examine it. On the lid, which was clamped and cornered with metal-work, there was engraved a complex coat of arms, and beneath it was a line of Spanish which I was able to decipher as meaning, "The treasure-chest of Don Ramirez di Leyra, Knight of the Order of Saint James, Governor and Captain-General of Terra Firma and of the Province of Veraquas." In one corner was the date 1606, and on the other a large white label, upon which was written in English, "You are earnestly requested, upon no account, to open this box." The same warning was repeated underneath in Spanish. As to the lock, it was a very complex and heavy one of engraved steel, with a Latin motto, which was above a seaman's comprehension.

By the time I had finished this examination of the peculiar box, the other quarter-boat with Mr. Armstrong, the first officer, had come alongside, and we began to carry out and place in her the various curiosities which appeared to be the only objects worth moving from the derelict ship. When she was full I sent her back to the barque, and then Allardyce and I, with a carpenter and one seaman, shifted the striped box, which was the only thing left, to our boat, and lowered it over, balancing it upon the two middle thwarts, for it was so heavy that it would have given the boat a dangerous tilt had we placed it at either end. As to the dead man, we left him where we had found him.

The mate had a theory that at the moment of the desertion of the ship, this fellow had started plundering, and that the captain in an attempt to preserve discipline, had struck him down with a hatchet or some other heavy weapon. It seemed more probable than any other explanation, and yet it did not entirely satisfy me either. But the ocean is full of mysteries, and we were content to leave the fate of the dead seaman of the Brazilian brig to be added to that long list which every sailor can recall.

The heavy box was slung up by ropes on to the deck of the *Mary Sinclair*, and was carried by four seamen into the cabin, where, between the table and the after-lockers, there was just space for it to stand. There it remained during supper, and after that meal the mates remained with me, and discussed over a glass of grog the event of the day. Mr. Armstrong was a long, thin, vulture-like man, an excellent seaman, but famous for his nearness and cupidity. Our treasure-trove had excited him greatly, and already he had begun with glistening eyes to reckon up how much it might be worth to each of us when the shares of the salvage came to be divided.

"If the paper said that they were unique, Mr. Barclay, then they may be worth anything that you like to name. You wouldn't believe the sums that the rich collectors give. A thousand pounds is nothing to them. We'll have something to show for our voyage, or I am mistaken."

"I don't think that," said I. "As far as I can see they are not very different from any other South American curios."

"Well, sir, I've traded there for fourteen voyages, and I have never seen anything like that chest before. That's worth a pile of money, just as it stands. But it's so heavy, that surely there must be something valuable inside it. Don't you think we ought to open it and see?"

"If you break it open you will spoil it, as likely as not," said the second mate.

Armstrong squatted down in front of it, with his head on one side, and his long, thin nose within a few inches of the lock.

"The wood is oak," said he, "and it has shrunk a little with age. If I had a chisel or a strong-bladed knife I could force the lock back without doing any damage at all."

The mention of a strong-bladed knife made me think of the dead seaman upon the brig.

"I wonder if he could have been on the job when someone came to interfere with him," said I.

"I don't know about that, sir, but I am perfectly certain that I could open the box. There's a screwdriver here in the locker. Just hold the lamp, Allardyce, and I'll have it done in a brace of shakes."

"Wait a bit," said I, for already, with eyes which gleamed with curiosity and with avarice, he was stooping over the lid. "I don't see that there is any hurry over this matter. You've read that card which warns us not to open it. It may mean anything or it may mean nothing, but somehow I feel inclined to obey it. After all, whatever is in it will keep, and if it is valuable it will be worth as much if it is opened in the owner's offices as in the cabin of the *Mary Sinclair*."

The first officer seemed bitterly disappointed at my decision.

"Surely, sir, you are not superstitious about it," said he, with a slight sneer upon his thin lips. "If it gets out of our own hands, and we don't see for ourselves what is inside it, we may be done out of our rights; besides—"

"That's enough, Mr. Armstrong," said I, abruptly. "You may have every confidence that you will get your rights, but I will not have that box opened to-night."

"Why, the label itself shows that the box has been examined by Europeans," Allardyce added. "Because a box is a treasure-box is no reason that it has treasures inside it now. A good many folk have had a peep into it since the days of the old Governor of Terra Firma."

Armstrong threw the screwdriver down upon the table and shrugged his shoulders.

"Just as you like," said he; but for the rest of the evening, although we spoke upon many subjects, I noticed that his eyes were continually coming round, with the same expression of curiosity and greed, to the old striped box.

And now I come to that portion of my story which fills me even now with a shuddering horror when I think of it. The main cabin had the rooms of the officers round it, but mine was the farthest away from it at the end of the little passage which led to the companion. No regular watch was kept by me, except in cases of emergency, and the three mates divided the watches among them. Armstrong had the middle watch, which ends at four in the morning, and he was relieved by Allardyce. For my part I have always been one of the soundest of sleepers, and it is rare for anything less than a hand upon my shoulder to arouse me.

And yet I was aroused that night, or rather in the early grey of the morning. It was just half-past four by my chronometer when something caused me to sit up in my berth wide awake and with every nerve tingling. It was a sound of some sort, a crash with a human cry at the end of it, which still jarred upon my ears. I sat listening, but all was now silent. And yet it could not have been imagination, that hideous cry, for the echo of it still rang in my head, and it seemed to have come from some place quite close to me. I sprang from my bunk, and, pulling on some clothes, I made my way into the cabin.

At first I saw nothing unusual there. In the cold, grey light I made out the red-clothed table, the six rotating chairs, the walnut lockers, the swinging barometer, and there, at the end, the big striped chest. I was turning away with the intention of going upon deck and asking the second mate if he had heard anything, when my eyes fell suddenly upon something which projected from under the table. It was the leg of a man—a leg with a long sea-boot upon it. I stooped, and there was a figure sprawling upon his face, his arms thrown forward and his body twisted. One glance told me that it was Armstrong, the first officer, and a second that he was a dead man. For a few moments I stood gasping. Then I rushed on to the deck, called Allardyce to my assistance, and came back with him into the cabin.

Together we pulled the unfortunate fellow from under the table, and as we looked at his dripping head, we exchanged glances, and I do not know which was the paler of the two.

"The same as the Spanish sailor," said I.

"The very same. God preserve us! It's that infernal chest! Look at Armstrong's hand!"

He held up the mate's right hand, and there was the screwdriver which he had wished to use the night before.

"He's been at the chest, sir. He knew that I was on deck and you asleep. He knelt down in front of it, and he pushed the lock back with that tool. Then something happened to him, and he cried out so that you heard him."

"Allardyce," I whispered, "what *could* have happened to him?"

The second mate put his hand upon my sleeve and drew me into his cabin.

"We can talk here, sir, and we don't know who may be listening to us in there. What do you suppose is in that box, Captain Barclay?"

"I give you my word, Allardyce, that I have no idea."

"Well, I can only find one theory which will fit all the facts. Look at the size of the box. Look at all the carving and metal-work which may conceal any number of holes. Look at the weight of it; it took four men to carry it. On the top of that, remember that two men have tried to open it, and both have come to their end through it. Now, sir, what can it mean except one thing?"

"You mean there is a man in it?"

"Of course there is a man in it. You know how it is in these South American States, sir. A man may be President one week and hunted like a dog the next. They are for ever flying for their lives. My idea is that there is some fellow in hiding there, who is armed and desperate, and who will fight to the death before he is taken."

"But his food and drink?"

"It's a roomy chest, sir, and he may have some provisions stowed away. As to his drink, he had a friend among the crew upon the brig who saw that he had what he needed."

"You think, then, that the label asking people not to open the box was simply written in his interest?"

"Yes, sir, that is my idea. Have you any other way of explaining the facts?"

I had to confess that I had not.

"The question is what are we to do?" I asked.

"The man's a dangerous ruffian who sticks at nothing. I'm thinking it wouldn't be a bad thing to put a rope round the chest and tow it alongside for half an hour; then we could open it at our ease. Or if we just tied the box up and kept him from getting any water maybe that would do as well. Or the carpenter could put a coat of varnish over it and stop all the blowholes."

"Come, Allardyce," said I, angrily. "You don't seriously mean to say that a whole ship's company are going to be terrorised by a single man in a box. If he's there I'll engage to fetch him out!" I went to my room and came back with my revolver in my hand. "Now, Allardyce," said I. "Do you open the lock, and I'll stand on guard."

"For God's sake, think what you are doing, sir," cried the mate. "Two men have lost their lives over it, and the blood of one not yet dry upon the carpet."

"The more reason why we should revenge him."

"Well, sir, at least let me call the carpenter. Three are better than two, and he is a good stout man."

He went off in search of him, and I was left alone with the striped chest in the cabin. I don't think that I'm a nervous man, but I kept the table between me and this solid old relic of the Spanish Main. In the growing light of morning the red and white striping was beginning to appear, and the curious scrolls and wreaths of metal and carving which showed the loving pains which cunning craftsmen had expended upon it. Presently the carpenter and the mate came back together, the former with a hammer in his hand.

"It's a bad business, this, sir," said he, shaking his head, as he looked at the body of the mate. "And you think there's someone hiding in the box?"

"There's no doubt about it," said Allardyce, picking up the screwdriver and setting his jaw like a man who needs to brace his courage. "I'll drive the lock back if you will both stand by. If he rises let him have it on the head with your hammer, carpenter! Shoot at once, sir, if he raises his hand. Now!"

He had knelt down in front of the striped chest, and passed the blade of the tool under the lid. With a sharp snick the lock flew back. "Stand by!" yelled the mate, and with a heave he threw open the massive top of the box. As it swung up, we all three sprang back, I with my pistol levelled, and the carpenter with the hammer above his head. Then, as nothing happened, we each took a step forward and peeped in. The box was empty.

Not quite empty either, for in one corner was lying an old yellow candlestick, elaborately engraved, which appeared to be as old as the box itself. Its rich yellow tone and artistic shape suggested that it was an object of value. For the rest there was nothing more weighty or valuable than dust in the old striped treasure-chest.

"Well, I'm blessed!" cried Allardyce, staring blankly into it. "Where does the weight come in, then?"

"Look at the thickness of the sides and look at the lid. Why, it's five inches through. And see that great metal spring across it."

"That's for holding the lid up," said the mate. "You see, it won't lean back. What's that German printing on the inside?"

"It means that it was made by Johann Rothstein of Augsburg, in 1606."

"And a solid bit of work, too. But it doesn't throw much light on what has passed, does it, Captain Barclay? That candlestick looks like gold. We shall have something for our trouble after all."

He leant forward to grasp it, and from that moment I have never doubted as to the reality of inspiration, for on the instant I caught him by the collar and pulled him straight again. It may have been some story of the Middle Ages which had come back to my mind, or it may have been that my eye had caught some red which was not that of rust upon the upper part of the lock, but to him and to me it will always seem an inspiration, so prompt and sudden was my action.

"There's devilry here," said I. "Give me the crooked stick from the corner."

It was an ordinary walking-cane with a hooked top. I passed it over the candlestick and gave it a pull. With a flash a row of polished steel fangs shot out from below the upper lip, and the great striped chest snapped at us like a wild animal. Clang came the huge lid into its place, and the glasses on the swinging rack sang and tinkled with the shock. The mate sat down on the edge of the table, and shivered like a frightened horse.

"You've saved my life, Captain Barclay!" said he.

So this was the secret of the striped treasure-chest of old Don Ramirez di Leyra, and this was how he preserved his ill-gotten gains from the Terra Firma and the Province of Veraquas. Be the thief ever so cunning he could not tell that golden candlestick from the other articles of value, and the instant that he laid hand upon it the terrible spring was unloosed and the murderous steel spikes were driven into his brain, while the shock of the blow sent the victim backwards and enabled the chest to automatically close itself. How many, I wondered, had fallen victims to the ingenuity of the Mechanic of Augsburg. And as I thought of the possible history of that grim striped chest my resolution was very quickly taken.

"Carpenter, bring three men and carry this on deck."

"Going to throw it overboard, sir?"

"Yes, Mr. Allardyce. I'm not superstitious as a rule, but there are some things which are more than a sailor can be called upon to stand."

"No wonder that brig made heavy weather, Captain Barclay, with such a thing on board. The glass is dropping fast, sir, and we are only just in time."

So we did not even wait for the three sailors, but we carried it out, the mate, the carpenter, and I, and we pushed it with our own hands over the bulwarks. There was a white spout of water, and it was gone. There it lies, the striped chest, a thousand fathoms deep, and if, as they say, the sea will some day be dry land, I grieve for the man who finds that old box and tries to penetrate into its secret.

2.

LOSS OF THE BRIG *TYRREL*

T. PURNELL

Steamship run ashore at the entrance to the Grey River, Greymouth, October 30, 1908. James Ring.

The following is a circumstantial account given by T. Purnell, chief mate of the brig *Tyrrel*, Arthur Cochlan, commander, and the only person among the whole crew who had the good fortune to escape, and whom claims our particular attention.

On Saturday, June 29th, 1759, they sailed from New York to Sandy Hook, and there came to an anchor, waiting for the captain's coming down with a new boat, and some other articles. Accordingly he came on board early the succeeding morning, and the boat cleared, hoisted in, stowed and lashed. At eight o'clock, A.M., they weighed anchor, sailed out of Sandy Hook, and the same day at noon, took their departure from the High Land Never Sunk, and proceeded on their passage to Antigua. As soon as they made sail, the captain ordered the boat to be cast loose, in order that she might be painted, with the oars, rudder and tiller, which job, he (Captain Cochlan) undertook to do himself.

At four P.M. they found the vessel made a little more water than usual; but as it did not cause much additional labour at the pump, nothing was thought of it. At eight, the leak did not seem to increase. At twelve it began to blow very hard in squalls, which caused the vessel to lie down very much, whereby it was apprehended she wanted more ballast. Thereupon the captain came on deck, being the starboard watch, and close reefed both top-sails.

At four A.M. the weather moderated—let out both reefs:—at eight it became still more moderate, and they made more sail, and set top-gallant-sails; the weather was still thick and hazy. There was no further observation taken at present, except that the vessel made more water. The captain was now chiefly employed in painting the boat, oars, rudder and tiller.

On Monday, June 30, at four P.M. the wind was at E. N. E. freshened very much, and blew so very hard, as occasioned the brig to lie along in such a manner as caused general alarm. The captain was now earnestly intreated to put for New York, or steer for the Capes of Virginia. At eight, took in top-gallant-sail, and close reefed both top-sails, still making more water. Afterwards the weather became still more moderate and fair, and they made more sail.

July 1, at four A.M. it began to blow in squalls very hard, took in one reef in each top-sail, and continued so until eight A.M. the weather being still thick and hazy.—No observation.

The next day she made still more water, but as every watch pumped it out, this was little regarded. At four P.M. took second reef in each top-sail,—close reefed both, and sent down top-gallant-yard; the gale still increasing.

At four A.M. the wind got round to N. and there was no appearance of its abating. At eight, the captain well satisfied that she was very crank and ought to have had more ballast, agreed to make for Bacon Island Road, in North Carolina; and in the very act of wearing her, a sudden gust of wind laid her down on her beam-end, and she never rose again!

At this time Mr. Purnell was lying in the cabin, with his clothes on, not having pulled them off since they left land.—Having been rolled out of his bed (on his chest), with great difficulty he reached the round-house door; the first salutation he met with was from the step-ladder that went from the quarter-deck to the poop, which knocked him against the companion, (a lucky circumstance for those below, as, by laying the ladder against the companion, it served both him and the rest of the people who were in the steerage, as a conveyance to windward); having transported the two after guns forward to bring her more by the head, in order to make her hold a better wind; thus they got through the aftermost gun-port on the quarter-deck, and being all on her broadside, every moveable rolled to leeward, and as the vessel overset, so did the boat, and turned bottom upwards, her lashings being cast loose, by order of the captain, and having no other prospect of saving their lives but by the boat, Purnell, with two others, and the cabin-boy (who were excellent swimmers) plunged into the water, and with difficulty righted her, when she was brim full, and washing with the water's edge. They then made fast the end of the main-sheet to the ring in her stern-post, and those who were in the fore-chains sent down the end of the boom-tackle, to which they made fast the boat's painter, and by which they lifted her a little out of the water, so that she swam about two or three inches free, but almost full.

They then put the cabin-boy into her, and gave him a bucket that happened to float by, and he bailed away as quick as he could, and soon after another person got in with another bucket, and in a short time got all the water out of her.—They then put two long oars that were stowed in the larboard-quarter of the *Tyrrel* into the boat, and pulled or rowed right to windward; for, as the wreck drifted, she made a dreadful appearance in the water, and Mr. Purnell and two of the people put off from the wreck, in search of the oars, rudder and tiller. After a long while they succeeded in picking them all up, one after another. They then returned to their wretched companions, who were all overjoyed to see them, having given them up for lost.

By this time night drew on very fast. While they were rowing in the boat, some small quantity of white biscuit (Mr. Purnell supposed about half a peck) floated in a small cask, out of the round house; but before it came to hand, it was so soaked with salt water, that it was almost in a fluid state; and about double the quantity of common ship-biscuit likewise floated, which was in like manner soaked. This was all the provision that they had; not a drop of fresh water could they get; neither could the carpenter get at any of his tools to scuttle her sides, for, could this have been accomplished, they might have saved plenty of provisions and water.

By this time it was almost dark; having got one compass, it was determined to quit the wreck, and take their chance in the boat, which was nineteen feet six inches long, and six feet four inches broad; Mr. Purnell supposes it was now about nine o'clock; it was very dark.

They had run about 360 miles by their dead reckoning, on a S. E. by E. course. The number in the boat was 17 in all; the boat was very deep, and little hopes were entertained of either seeing land or surviving long. The wind got round to westward, which was the course they wanted to steer; but it began to blow and rain so very hard, that they were obliged to keep before the wind and sea, in order to preserve her above water. Soon after they had put off from the wreck the boat shipped two heavy seas, one after another, so that they were obliged to keep her before the wind and sea; for had she shipped another sea, she certainly would have swamped with them.

By sunrise the next morning, July 3, they judged that they had been running E. S. E. which was contrary to their wishes. The wind dying away, the weather became very moderate. The compass which they had saved proved of no utility, one of the people having trod upon, and broken it; it was accordingly thrown overboard. They now proposed to make a sail of some frocks and trowsers, but they had got neither needles nor sewing twine, one of the people however, had a needle in his knife, and another several fishing lines in his pockets, which were unlaid by some, and others were employed in ripping the frocks and trowsers. By sunset they had provided a tolerable lug-sail; having split one of the boat's thwarts (which was of yellow deal) with a very large knife, which one of the crew had in his pocket, they made a yard and lashed it together by the strands of the fore-top-gallant-halyards, that were thrown into the boat promiscuously.—They also made a mast of one of the long oars, and set their sails, with sheets and tacks made out of the top-gallant-halyards. Their only guide was the North star. They had a tolerable good breeze all night; and the whole of the next day, July 4, the weather continued very moderate, and the people were in as good spirits as their dreadful situation would admit.

July 5, the wind and weather continued much the same, and they knew by the North star that they were standing in for the land. The next day Mr. Purnell observed some of the men drinking salt water, and seeming rather fatigued.—At this time they imagined the wind was got round to the southward, and they steered, as they thought by the North star, to the northwest quarter; but on the 7th, they found the wind had got back to the northward, and blew very fresh. They got their oars out the greatest part of the night, and the next day the wind still dying away, the people laboured alternately at the oars, without distinction. About noon the wind sprung up so that they laid in their oars, and, as they thought, steered about N. N. W. and continued so until about eight or nine in the morning of July 9, when they all thought they were upon soundings, by the coldness of the water.—They were, in general, in very good spirits. The weather continued still thick and hazy, and by the North star, they found that they had been steering about N. by W.

July 10.—The people had drank so much salt water, that it came from them as clear as it was before they drank it; and Mr. Purnell perceived that the second mate had lost a considerable share of his strength and spirits; and also, at noon, that the carpenter was delirious, his malady increasing every hour; about dusk he had almost overset the boat, by attempting to throw himself overboard, and otherwise behaving quite violent.

As his strength, however, failed him, he became more manageable, and they got him to lie down in the middle of the boat, among some of the people. Mr. Purnell drank once a little salt water, but could not relish it; he preferred his own urine, which he drank occasionally as he made it. Soon after sunset the second mate lost his speech. Mr. Purnell desired him to lean his head on him; he died, without a groan or struggle, on the 11th of July, being the 9th day they were in the boat. In a few minutes after, the carpenter expired almost in a similar manner. These melancholy scenes rendered the situation of the survivors more dreadful; it is impossible to describe their feelings. Despair became general; every man imagined his own dissolution was near. They all now went to prayers; some prayed in the Welch language, some in Irish, and others in English; then, after a little deliberation, they stripped the two dead men, and hove them overboard.

The weather being now very mild, and almost calm, they turned to, cleaned the boat, and resolved to make their sail larger out of the frocks and trowsers of the two deceased men. Purnell got the captain to lie down with the rest of the people, the boatswain and one man excepted, who assisted him in making the sail larger, which they had completed by six or seven o'clock in the afternoon, having made a shroud out of the boat's painter, which served as a shifting back-stay.—Purnell also fixed his red flannel waistcoat at the mast-head, as a signal the most likely to be seen.

Soon after this some of them observed a sloop at a great distance, coming, as they thought, from the land. This roused every man's spirits; they got out their oars, at which they laboured alternately, exerting all their remaining strength to come up with her; but night coming on, and the sloop getting a fresh breeze of wind, they lost sight of her, which occasioned a general consternation; however, the appearance of the North star, which they kept on their starboard-bow, gave them hopes that they stood in for land. This night one William Wathing died; he was 64 years of age, and had been to sea 50 years; quite worn out with fatigue and hunger, he earnestly prayed, to the last moment, for a drop of water to cool his tongue. Early the next morning Hugh Williams also died, and in the course of the day another of the crew: entirely exhausted,—they both expired without a groan.

Early in the morning of July 13, it began to blow very fresh, and increased so much, that they were obliged to furl their sail, and keep the boat before the wind and sea, which drove them off soundings. In the evening their gunner died. The weather now becoming moderate and the wind in the S. W. quarter, they made sail, not one being able to row or pull an oar at any rate; they ran all this night with a fine breeze.

The next morning (July 14) two more of the crew died, and in the evening they also lost the same number. They found they were on soundings again, and concluded the wind had got round to the N. W. quarter. They stood in for the land all this night, and early on July 12 two others died; the deceased were thrown overboard as soon as their breath had departed. The weather was now thick and hazy, and they were still certain that they were on soundings.

The cabin-boy was seldom required to do any thing, and as his intellects, at this time, were very good, and his understanding clear, it was the opinion of Mr. Purnell that he would survive them all, but he prudently kept his thoughts to himself. The captain seemed likewise tolerably well, and to have kept up his spirits. On account of the haziness of the weather, they could not so well know how they steered in the day time as at night; for, whenever the North star appeared, they endeavored to keep it on their starboard bow, by which means they were certain of making the land some time or other. In the evening two more of the crew died, also, before sunset, one Thomas Philpot, an old experienced seaman, and very strong; he departed rather convulsed; having latterly lost the power of articulation, his meaning could not be comprehended. He was a native of Belfast, Ireland, and had no family. The survivors found it a difficult task to heave his body overboard, as he was a very corpulent man.

About six or seven the next morning, July 16, they stood in for the land, according to the best of their judgment, the weather still thick and hazy. Purnell now prevailed upon the captain and boatswain of the boat to lie down in the fore-part of the boat, to bring her more by the head, in order to make her hold a better wind. In the evening the cabin-boy, who lately appeared so well, breathed his last, leaving behind, the captain, the boatswain and Mr. Purnell.

The next morning, July 17, Mr. Purnell asked his two companions if they thought they could eat any of the boy's flesh; and having expressed an inclination to try, and the body being quite cold, he cut the inside of his thigh, a little above his knee, and gave a piece to the captain and boatswain, reserving a small piece for himself; but so weak were their stomachs that none of them could swallow a morsel of it, the body was therefore thrown overboard.

Early in the morning of the 18th, Mr. Purnell found both of his companions dead and cold! Thus destitute, he began to think of his own dissolution; though feeble, his understanding was still clear, and his spirits as good as his forlorn situation could possibly admit. By the colour and coldness of the water, he knew he was not far from land, and still maintained hopes of making it. The weather continued very foggy. He lay to all this night, which was very dark, with the boat's head to the northward.

In the morning of the 19th, it began to rain; it cleared up in the afternoon, and the wind died away; still Mr. Purnell was convinced he was on soundings.

On the 20th, in the afternoon, he thought he saw land, and stood in for it; but night coming on, and it being now very dark, he lay to, fearing he might get on some rocks and shoals.

July 21, the weather was very fine all the morning, but in the afternoon it became thick and hazy. Mr. Purnell's spirits still remained good, but his strength was almost exhausted; he still drank his own water occasionally.

On the 22d he saw some barnacles on the boat's rudder, very similar to the spawn of an oyster, which filled him with greater hopes of being near land. He unshipped the rudder, and scraping them off with his knife, found they were of a salt fishy substance, and ate them; he was now so weak, the boat having a great motion, that he found it a difficult task to ship the rudder.

At sunrise, July 23, he became so sure that he saw land, that his spirits were considerably raised. In the middle of this day he got up, leaned his back against the mast, and received succour from the sun, having previously contrived to steer the boat in this position. The next day he saw, at a very great distance, some kind of a sail, which he judged was coming from the land, which he soon lost sight of. In the middle of the day he got up, and received warmth from the sun as before. He stood on all night for the land.

Very early in the morning of the 25th, after drinking his morning draught, to his inexpressible joy he saw, while the sun was rising, a sail, and when the sun was up, found she was a two-mast vessel. He was, however, considerably perplexed, not knowing what to do, as she was a great distance astern and to the leeward. In order to watch her motions better, he tacked about. Soon after this he perceived she was standing on her starboard tack, which had been the same he had been standing on for many hours. He saw she approached him very fast, and he lay to for some time, till he believed she was within two miles of the boat, but still to leeward; therefore he thought it best to steer larger, when he found she was a top-sail schooner, nearing him very fast.—He continued to edge down towards her, until he had brought her about two points under his lee-bow, having it in his power to spring his luff, or bear away. By this time she was within half a mile, and he saw some of her people standing forwards on her deck and waiving for him to come under their lee-bow.

At the distance of about 200 yards they hove the schooner up in the wind, and kept her so until Purnell got alongside, when they threw him a rope, still keeping the schooner in the wind. They now interrogated him very closely; by the manner the boat and oars were painted, they imagined she belonged to a man of war, and that they had run away with her from some of his Majesty's ships at Halifax, consequently that they would be liable to some punishment if they took him up; they also thought, as the captain and boatswain were lying dead in the boat, they might expose themselves to some contagious disorder. Thus they kept Purnell in suspense for some time. They told him they had made the land that morning from the mast-head, and that they were running along shore for Marblehead, to which place they belonged, and where they expected to be the next morning. At last they told him he might come on board; which as he said, he could not without assistance, the captain ordered two of his men to help him.—They conducted him aft on the quarter deck, where they left him resting on the companion.

They were now for casting the boat adrift, but Mr. Purnell told them she was not above a month old, built at New York, and if they would hoist her in, it would pay them well for their trouble. To this they agreed, and having thrown the two corpses overboard, and taken out the clothes that were left by the deceased, they hoisted her in and made sail.

Being now on board, Purnell asked for a little water, Captain Castleman (for that was his name) ordered one of his sons, (having two on board) to fetch him some; when he came with the water, his father looked to see how much he was bringing him, and thinking it too much, threw some of it away, and desired him to give the remainder, which he drank being the first fresh water he had tasted for 23 days. As he leaned all this time against the companion, he became very cold, and begged to go below; the captain ordered two men to help him down to the cabin, where they left him sitting on the cabin-deck, leaning upon the lockers, all hands being now engaged in hoisting in and securing the boat. This done, all hands went down to the cabin to breakfast, except the man at the helm. They made some soup for Purnell, which he thought very good, but at present he could eat very little, and in consequence of his late draughts, he had broke out in many parts of his body, so that he was in great pain whenever he stirred. They made a bed for him out of an old sail, and behaved very attentive. While they were at breakfast a squall of wind came on, which called them all upon deck; during their absence, Purnell took up a stone bottle, and without smelling or tasting it, but thinking it was rum, took a hearty draught of it, and found it to be sweet oil; having placed it where he found it, he lay down.

They still ran along shore with the land in sight, and were in great hopes of getting into port that night, but the wind dying away, they did not get in till nine o'clock the next night. All this time Purnell remained like a child; some one was always with him, to give him whatever he wished to eat or drink.

As soon as they came to anchor, Captain Castleman went on shore, and returned on board the next morning with the owner, John Picket, Esq. Soon after they got Purnell into a boat, and carried him on shore; but he was still so very feeble, that he was obliged to be supported by two men. Mr. Picket took a very genteel lodging for him, and hired a nurse to attend him; he was immediately put to bed, and afterwards provided with a change of clothes. In the course of the day he was visited by every doctor in the town, who all gave him hopes of recovering, but told him it would be some time, for the stronger the constitution, the longer (they said) it took to recover its lost strength. Though treated with the utmost tenderness and humanity, it was three weeks before he was able to come down stairs. He stayed in Marblehead two months, during which he lived very comfortably, and gradually recovered his strength. The brig's boat and oars were sold for 95 dollars, which paid all his expenses, and procured him a passage to Boston. The nails of his fingers and toes withered away almost to nothing, and did not begin to grow for many months after.

Fight Against the Elements, artist unknown.

3.

TYPHOON OFF THE COAST OF JAPAN

JACK LONDON

It was four bells in the morning watch. We had just finished breakfast when the order came forward for the watch on deck to stand by to heave her to and all hands stand by the boats.

"Port! hard a port!" cried our sailing-master. "Clew up the topsails! Let the flying jib run down! Back the jib over to windward and run down the foresail!" And so was our schooner *Sophie Sutherland* hove to off the Japan coast, near Cape Jerimo, on April 10, 1893.

Then came moments of bustle and confusion. There were eighteen men to man the six boats. Some were hooking on the falls, others casting off the lashings; boat-steerers appeared with boat-compasses and water-breakers, and boat-pullers with the lunch boxes. Hunters were staggering under two or three shotguns, a rifle and heavy ammunition box, all of which were soon stowed away with their oilskins and mittens in the boats.

The sailing-master gave his last orders, and away we went, pulling three pairs of oars to gain our positions. We were in the weather boat, and so had a longer pull than the others. The first, second and third lee boats soon had all sail set and were running off to the southward and westward with the wind beam, while the schooner was running off to leeward of them, so that in case of accident the boats would have fair wind home.

It was a glorious morning, but our boat steerer shook his head ominously as he glanced at the rising sun and prophetically muttered: "Red sun in the morning, sailor take warning." The sun had an angry look, and a few light, fleecy clouds in that quarter seemed abashed and frightened and soon disappeared.

Away off to the northward Cape Jerimo reared its black, forbidding head like some huge monster rising from the deep. The winter's snow, not yet entirely dissipated by the sun, covered it in patches of glistening white, over which the light wind swept on its way out to sea. Huge gulls rose slowly, fluttering their wings in the light breeze and striking their webbed feet on the surface of the water for over half a mile before they could leave it. Hardly had the patter, patter died away when a flock of sea quail rose, and with whistling wings flew away to windward, where members of a large band of whales were disporting themselves, their blowings sounding like the exhaust of steam engines. The harsh, discordant cries of a sea-parrot grated unpleasantly on the ear, and set half a dozen alert in a small band of seals that were ahead of us. Away they went, breaching and jumping entirely out of water. A sea-gull with slow, deliberate flight and long, majestic curves circled round us, and as a reminder of home a little English sparrow perched impudently on the fo'castle head, and, cocking his head on one side, chirped merrily. The boats were soon among the seals, and the bang! bang! of the guns could be heard from down to leeward.

The wind was slowly rising, and by three o'clock as, with a dozen seals in our boat, we were deliberating whether to go on or turn back, the recall flag was run up at the schooner's mizzen—a sure sign that with the rising wind the barometer was falling and that our sailing-master was getting anxious for the welfare of the boats.

Away we went before the wind with a single reef in our sail. With clenched teeth sat the boat-steerer, grasping the steering oar firmly with both hands, his restless eyes on the alert—a glance at the schooner ahead, as we rose on a sea, another at the mainsheet, and then one astern where the dark ripple of the wind on the water told him of a coming puff or a large white-cap that threatened to overwhelm us. The waves were holding high carnival, performing the strangest antics, as with wild glee they danced along in fierce pursuit—now up, now down, here, there, and everywhere, until some great sea of liquid green with its milk-white crest of foam rose from the ocean's throbbing bosom and drove the others from view. But only for a moment, for again under new forms they reappeared. In the sun's path they wandered, where every ripple, great or small, every little spit or spray looked like molten silver, where the water lost its dark green color and became a dazzling, silvery flood, only to vanish and become a wild waste of sullen turbulence, each dark foreboding sea rising and breaking, then rolling on again. The dash, the sparkle, the silvery light soon vanished with the sun, which became obscured by black clouds that were rolling swiftly in from the west, northwest; apt heralds of the coming storm.

We soon reached the schooner and found ourselves the last aboard. In a few minutes the seals were skinned, boats and decks washed, and we were down below by the roaring fo'castle fire, with a wash, change of clothes, and a hot, substantial supper before us. Sail had been put on the schooner, as we had a run of seventy-five miles to make to the southward before morning, so as to get in the midst of the seals, out of which we had strayed during the last two days' hunting.

We had the first watch from eight to midnight. The wind was soon blowing half a gale, and our sailing-master expected little sleep that night as he paced up and down the poop. The topsails were soon clewed up and made fast, then the flying jib run down and furled. Quite a sea was rolling by this time, occasionally breaking over the decks, flooding them and threatening to smash the boats. At six bells we were ordered to turn them over and put on storm lashings. This occupied us till eight bells, when we were relieved by the mid-watch. I was the last to go below, doing so just as the watch on deck was furling the spanker. Below all were asleep except our green hand, the "bricklayer," who was dying of consumption. The wildly dancing movements of the sea lamp cast a pale, flickering light through the fo'castle and turned to golden honey the drops of water on the yellow oilskins. In all the corners dark shadows seemed to come and go, while up in the eyes of her, beyond the pall bits, descending from deck to deck, where they seemed to lurk like some dragon at the cavern's mouth, it was dark as Erebus.

Now and again, the light seemed to penetrate for a moment as the schooner rolled heavier than usual, only to recede, leaving it darker and blacker than before. The roar of the wind through the rigging came to the ear muffled like the distant rumble of a train crossing a trestle or the surf on the beach, while the loud crash of the seas on her weather bow seemed almost to rend the beams and planking asunder as it resounded through the fo'castle. The creaking and groaning of the timbers, stanchions, and bulkheads, as the strain the vessel was undergoing was felt, served to drown the groans of the dying man as he tossed uneasily in his bunk. The working of the foremast against the deck beams caused a shower of flaky powder to fall, and sent another sound mingling with the tumultuous storm. Small cascades of water streamed from the pall bits from the fo'castle head above, and, joining issue with the streams from the wet oilskins, ran along the floor and disappeared aft into the main hold.

At two bells in the middle watch—that is, in land parlance one o'clock in the morning;—the order was roared out on the fo'castle: "All hands on deck and shorten sail!"

Then the sleepy sailors tumbled out of their bunk and into their clothes, oilskins and sea-boots and up on deck. 'Tis when that order comes on cold, blustering nights that "Jack" grimly mutters: "Who would not sell a farm and go to sea?"

It was on deck that the force of the wind could be fully appreciated, especially after leaving the stifling fo'castle. It seemed to stand up against you like a wall, making it almost impossible to move on the heaving decks or to breathe as the fierce gusts came dashing by. The schooner was hove to under jib, foresail and mainsail. We proceeded to lower the foresail and make it fast. The night was dark, greatly impeding our labor. Still, though not a star or the moon could pierce the black masses of storm clouds that obscured the sky as they swept along before the gale, nature aided us in a measure. A soft light emanated from the movement of the ocean. Each mighty sea, all phosphorescent and glowing with the tiny lights of myriads of animalculae, threatened to overwhelm us with a deluge of fire. Higher and higher, thinner and thinner, the crest grew as it began to curve and overtop preparatory to breaking, until with a roar it fell over the bulwarks, a mass of soft glowing light and tons of water which sent the sailors sprawling in all directions and left in each nook and cranny little specks of light that glowed and trembled till the next sea washed them away, depositing new ones in their places. Sometimes several seas following each other with great rapidity and thundering down on our decks filled them full to the bulwarks, but soon they were discharged through the lee scuppers.

To reef the mainsail we were forced to run off before the gale under the single reefed jib. By the time we had finished the wind had forced up such a tremendous sea that it was impossible to heave her to. Away we flew on the wings of the storm through the muck and flying spray. A wind sheer to starboard, then another to port as the enormous seas struck the schooner astern and nearly broached her to. As day broke we took in the jib, leaving not a sail unfurled. Since we had begun scudding she had ceased to take the seas over her bow, but amidships they broke fast and furious. It was a dry storm in the matter of rain, but the force of the wind filled the air with fine spray, which flew as high as the crosstrees and cut the face like a knife, making it impossible to see over a hundred yards ahead. The sea was a dark lead color as with long, slow, majestic roll it was heaped up by the wind into liquid mountains of foam. The wild antics of the schooner were sickening as she forged along. She would almost stop, as though climbing a mountain, then rapidly rolling to right and left as she gained the summit of a huge sea, she steadied herself and paused for a moment as though affrighted at the yawning precipice before her. Like an avalanche, she shot forward and down as the sea astern struck her with the force of a thousand battering rams, burying her bow to the cat-heads in the milky foam at the bottom that came on deck in all directions—forward, astern, to right and left, through the hawse-pipes and over the rail.

The wind began to drop, and by ten o'clock we were talking of heaving her to. We passed a ship, two schooners and a four-masted barkentine under the smallest canvas, and at eleven o'clock, running up the spanker and jib, we hove her to, and in another hour we were beating back again against the aftersea under full sail to regain the sealing ground away to the westward.

Below, a couple of men were sewing the "bricklayer's" body in canvas preparatory to the sea burial. And so with the storm passed away the "bricklayer's" soul.

4.

SEARCHING FOR FRANKLIN

ELISHA KENT KANE

The Arctic Council planning a search for Sir John Franklin, by Stephen Pearce, 1904. The National Portrait Gallery.

August 19. The wind continued freshening, the aneroid falling two tenths in the night. About eight I was called by our master, with the news that a couple of vessels were following in our wake. We were shortening sail for our consort; and by half past twelve, the larger stranger, the *Lady Franklin*, came up alongside of us. A cordial greeting, such as those only know who have been pelted for weeks in the solitudes of Arctic ice—and we learned that this was Captain Penny's squadron, bound on the same pursuit as ourselves. A hurried interchange of news followed. The ice in Melville Bay had bothered both parties alike; Commodore Austin, with his steamer tenders, was three days ago at Carey's Islands, a group nearly as high as 77° north latitude; the *North Star*, the missing provision transport of last summer, was safe somewhere in Lancaster Sound, probably at Leopold Island. For the rest, God speed!

"As she slowly forged ahead, there came over the rough sea that good old English hurrah, which we inherit on our side the water. 'Three cheers, hearty, with a will!' indicating as much of brotherhood as sympathy. 'Stand aloft, boys!' and we gave back the greeting. One cheer more of acknowledgment on each side, and the sister flags separated, each on its errand of mercy.

"8 P.M. The breeze has freshened to a gale. Fogs have closed round us, and we are driving ahead again, with look-outs on every side. We have no observation; but by estimate we must have got into Lancaster Sound.

"The sea is short and excessive. Everything on deck, even anchors and quarter-boats, have 'fetched away,' and the little cabin is half afloat. The *Rescue* is staggering under heavy sail astern of us. We are making six or seven knots an hour. Murdaugh ahead, looking out for ice and rocks; De Haven conning the ship.

"All at once a high mountain shore rises before us, and a couple of isolated rocks show themselves, not more than a quarter of a mile ahead, white with breakers. Both vessels are laid to."

The storm reminded me of a Mexican "norther." It was not till the afternoon of the next day that we were able to resume our track, under a double-reefed top-sail, stay-sail, and spencer. We were, of course, without observation still, and could only reckon that we had passed the Cunningham Mountains and Cape Warrender.

About three o'clock in the morning of the 21st, another sail was reported ahead, a top-sail schooner, towing after her what appeared to be a launch, decked over.

"When I reached the deck, we were nearly up to her, for we had shaken out our reefs, and were driving before the wind, shipping seas at every roll.

The little schooner was under a single close-reefed top-sail, and seemed fluttering over the waves like a crippled bird. Presently an old fellow, with a cloak tossed over his night gear, appeared in the lee gangway, and saluted with a voice that rose above the winds.

"It was the *Felix*, commanded by that practical Arctic veteran, Sir John Ross. I shall never forget the heartiness with which the hailing officer sang out, in the midst of our dialogue, 'You and I are ahead of them all.' It was so indeed. Austin, with two vessels, was at Pond's Bay; Penny was somewhere in the gale; and others of Austin's squadron were exploring the north side of the Sound. The *Felix* and the *Advance* were on the lead.

"Before we separated, Sir John Ross came on deck, and stood at the side of his officer. He was a square-built man, apparently very little stricken in years, and well able to bear his part in the toils and hazards of life. He has been wounded in four several engagements—twice desperately—and is scarred from head to foot. He has conducted two Polar expeditions already, and performed in one of them the unparalleled feat of wintering four years in Arctic snows. And here he is again, in a flimsy cockle-shell, after contributing his purse and his influence, embarked himself in the crusade of search for a lost comrade. We met him off Admiralty Inlet, just about the spot at which he was picked up seventeen years before."

Soon after midnight, the land became visible on the north side of the Sound. We had passed Cape Charles Yorke and Cape Crawfurd, and were fanning along sluggishly with all the sail we could crowd for Port Leopold.

It was the next day, however, before we came in sight of the island, and it was nearly spent when we found ourselves slowly approaching Whaler Point, the seat of the harbor. Our way had been remarkably clear of ice for some days, and we were vexed to find, therefore, that a firm and rugged barrier extended along the western shore of the inlet, and apparently across the entrance we were seeking.

It was a great relief to us to see, at half past six in the evening, a topsail schooner working toward us through the ice. She boarded us at ten, and proved to be Lady Franklin's own search-vessel, the *Prince Albert*.

This was a very pleasant meeting. Captain Forsyth, who commanded the *Albert*, and Mr. Snow, who acted as a sort of adjutant under him, were very agreeable gentlemen. They spent some hours with us, which Mr. Snow has remembered kindly in the journal he has published since his return to England. Their little vessel was much less perfectly fitted than ours to encounter the perils of the ice; but in one respect at least their expedition resembled our own. They had to rough it: to use a Western phrase, they had no fancy fixings—nothing but what a hasty outfit and a limited purse could supply. They were now bound for Cape Rennell, after which they proposed making a sledge excursion over the lower Boothian and Cockburne lands.

The *North Star*, they told us, had been caught by the ice last season in the neighborhood of our own first imprisonment, off the Devil's Thumb. After a perilous drift, she had succeeded in entering Wolstenholme Sound, whence, after a tedious winter, she had only recently arrived at Port Bowen.

They followed in our wake the next day as we pushed through many streams of ice across the strait. We sighted the shore about five miles to the west of Cape Hurd very closely; a miserable wilderness, rising in terraces of broken-down limestone, arranged between the hills like a vast theatre.

On the 25th, still beating through the ice off Radstock Bay, we discovered on Cape Riley two cairns, one of them, the most conspicuous, with a flag-staff and ball. A couple of hours after, we were near enough to land. The cape itself is a low projecting tongue of limestone, but at a short distance behind it the cliff rises to the height of some eight hundred feet. We found a tin canister within the larger cairn, containing the information that Captain Ommanney had been there two days before us, with the *Assistance* and *Intrepid*, belonging to Captain Austin's squadron, and had discovered traces of an encampment, and other indications "that some party belonging to her Britannic majesty's service had been detained at this spot." Similar traces, it was added, had been found also on Beechy Island, a projection on the channel side some ten miles from Cape Riley.

Our consort, the *Rescue*, as we afterward learned, had shared in this discovery, though the British commander's inscription in the cairn, as well as his official reports, might lead perhaps to a different conclusion. Captain Griffin, in fact, landed with Captain Ommanney, and the traces were registered while the two officers were in company.

I inspected these different traces very carefully, and noted what I observed at the moment. The appearances which connect them with the story of Sir John Franklin have been described by others; but there may still be interest in a description of them made while they were under my eye. I transcribe it word for word from my journal.

"On a tongue of fossiliferous limestone, fronting toward the west on a little indentation of the water, and shielded from the north by the precipitous cliffs, are five distinct remnants of habitation.

"Nearest the cliffs, four circular mounds or heapings-up of the crumbled limestone, aided by larger stones placed at the outer edge, as if to protect the leash of a tent. Two larger stones, with an interval of two feet, fronting the west, mark the places of entrance.

"Several large square stones, so arranged as to serve probably for a fireplace. These have been tumbled over by parties before us.

"More distant from the cliffs, yet in line with the four already described, is a larger inclosure; the door facing south, and looking toward the strait: this so-called door is simply an entrance made of large stones placed one above the other. The inclosure itself triangular; its northern side about eighteen inches high, built up of flat stones. Some bird bones and one rib of a seal were found exactly in the centre of this triangle, as if a party had sat round it eating; and the top of a preserved-meat case, much rusted, was found in the same place. I picked up a piece of canvas or duck on the cliff side, well worn by the weather: the sailors recognized it at once as the gore of a pair of trowsers.

"A fifth circle is discernible nearer the cliffs, which may have belonged to the same party. It was less perfect than the others, and seemed of an older date.

"On the beach, some twenty or thirty yards from the triangular inclosure, were several pieces of pine wood about four inches long, painted green, and white, and black, and, in one instance, puttied; evidently parts of a boat, and apparently collected as kindling wood."

The indications were meagre, but the conclusion they led to was irresistible. They could not be the work of Esquimaux: the whole character of them contradicted it: and the only European who could have visited Cape Riley was Parry, twenty-eight years before; and we knew from his journal that he had not encamped here. Then, again, Ommanney's discovery of like vestiges on Beechy Island, just on the track of a party moving in either direction between it and the channel: all these speak of a land party from Franklin's squadron.

The Advance near Kosoak, from Elisha Kent Kane, *Arctic Explorations, The Second Grinnell Expedition in Search of Sir John Franklin* (Philadelphia: Childs and Peterson, 1856), engraving by Van Ingen and Snyder after a sketch by Kane.

Our commander resolved to press onward along the eastern shore of Wellington Channel. We were under weigh in the early morning of the 26th, and working along with our consort toward Beechy—I drop the "Island," for it is more strictly a peninsula or a promontory of limestone, as high and abrupt as that at Cape Riley, connected with what we call the main by a low isthmus. Still further on we passed Cape Spencer; then a fine bluff point, called by Parry Point Innes; and further on again, the trend being to the east of north, we saw the low tongue, Cape Bowden. Parry merely sighted these points from a distance, so that the shore line has never been traced. I sketched it myself with some care; but the running survey of this celebrated explorer had left nothing to alter. To the north of Cape Innes, though the coast retains the same geognostical character, the bluff promontories subside into low hills, between which the beach, composed of coarse silicious limestone, sweeps in long curvilinear terraces. Measuring some of these rudely afterward, I found that the elevation of the highest plateau did not exceed forty feet.

Our way northward was along an ice channel close under the eastern shore, and bounded on the other side by the ice-pack, at a distance varying from a quarter of a mile to a mile and three quarters. Off Cape Spencer the way seemed more open, widening perhaps to two miles, and showing something like continued free water to the north and west. Here we met Captain Penny, with the *Lady Franklin* and *Sophia*. He told us that the channel was completely shut in ahead by a compact ice barrier, which connected itself with that to the west, describing a horseshoe bend. He thought a south wester was coming on, and counseled us to prepare for the chances of an impactment. The go-ahead determination which characterized our commander made us test the correctness of his advice. We pushed on, tracked the horseshoe circuit of the ice without finding an outlet, and were glad to labor back again almost in the teeth of a gale.

Captain Penny had occupied the time more profitably. In company with Dr. Goodsir, an enthusiastic explorer and highly educated gentleman, whose brother was an assistant surgeon on board the missing vessels, he had been examining the shore. On the ridge of limestone, between Cape Spencer and Point Innes, they had come across additional proofs that Sir John's party had been here—very important these proofs as extending the line along the shore over which the party must have moved from Cape Riley.

Among the articles they had found were tin canisters, with the London maker's label; scraps of newspaper, bearing the date 1844; a paper fragment,

with the words "until called" on it, seemingly part of a watch order; and two
other fragments, each with the name of one of Franklin's officers written on it
in pencil. They told us, too, that among the articles found by Captain Penny's
men was a dredge, rudely fashioned of iron hoops beat round, with spikes
inserted in them, and arranged for a long handle, as if to fish up missing
articles; besides some footless stockings, tied up at the lower end to serve as
socks, an officer's pocket, velvet-lined, torn off from the dress, &c., &c.; all of
which, they thought, spoke of a party that had suffered wreck, and were moving eastward. Acting on this impression, Captain Penny was about to proceed
toward Baffin's Bay, along the north shore of Lancaster Sound, in the hope of
encountering them, or, more probably, their bleached remains.

For myself, looking only at the facts, and carefully discarding every de-
duction that might be prompted by sympathy rather than reason, my journal
reminds me that I did not see in these signs the evidence of a lost party. The
party was evidently in motion; but it might be that it was a detachment, engaged in making observations, or in exploring with a view to the operations
of the spring, while the ships were locked in winter quarters at Cape Riley or
Beechy, which had returned on board before the opening of the ice.

I may add, as not without some bearing on the fortunes of this party,
whatever may have been its condition or purposes, that the vacant water-
spaces around us at this time were teeming with animal life. After passing
Beechy, we saw seal disporting in great flocks, rising out of the water as high
as their middle, like boys in swimming; the white whale, the first we had seen,
to the extent of thirty-eight separate shoals; the narwhal, or sea-unicorn; and,
finally, that marine pachyderm, the tusky walrus. These last were always crowded on small tongues of ice, whose purity they marred not a little—grim-looking
monsters, reminding me of the stage hobgoblins, something venerable and
semi-Egyptian withal. We passed so close as to have several shots at them. They
invariably rose after plunging, and looked snortingly around, as if to make fight.
Polar bears were numerous beyond our previous experience, and the Arctic fox
and hare abounded. If we add to these the crowding tenants of the air, the Brent
goose, which now came in great cunoid flocks from the north and north by

east, the loons, the mollemokes, and the divers, we may form an estimate of the means of human subsistence in these seas.

On the 27th, the chances of this narrow and capricious navigation had gathered five of the searching vessels, under three different commands, within the same quarter of a mile—Sir John Ross', Penny's, and our own. Both Ross and Penny had made the effort to push through the sound to the west, but found a great belt of ice, reaching in an almost regular crescent from Leopold's Island across to the northern shore, about half a mile from the entrance of the channel. Captain Ommanney, with the *Intrepid* and *Assistance*, had been less fortunate. He had attempted to break his way through the barrier, but it had closed on him, and he was now fast, within fifteen miles of us, to the west.

Graves on Beechey Island, from Elisha Kent Kane, *The US Grinnell Expedition in Search of Sir John Franklin* (New York: Harper, 1854), engraving by Hamilton after a sketch by Kane.

After breakfast, our commander and myself took a boat to visit the traces discovered yesterday by Captain Penny. Taking the *Lady Franklin* in our way, we met Sir John Ross and Commander Phillips, and a conference naturally took place upon the best plans for concerted operations. I was very much struck with the gallant disinterestedness of spirit which was shown by all the officers in this discussion. Penny, an energetic, practical fellow, sketched out at once a plan of action for each vessel of the party. He himself would take the western search; Ross should run over to Prince Regent's Sound, communicate the news to the *Prince Albert*, and so relieve that little vessel from the now unnecessary perils of her intended expedition; and we were to press through the first openings in the ice by Wellington Channel, to the north and east.

It was wisely determined by brave old Sir John that he would leave the *Mary*, his tender of twelve tons, at a little inlet near the point, to serve as a fallback in case we should lose our vessels or become sealed up in permanent ice, and De Haven and Penny engaged their respective shares of her outfit, in the shape of some barrels of beef and flour. Sir John Ross, I think, had just left us to go on board his little craft, and I was still talking over our projects with Captain Penny, when a messenger was reported, making all speed to us over the ice.

The news he brought was thrilling. "Graves, Captain Penny! Graves! Franklin's winter quarters!" We were instantly in motion. Captain De Haven, Captain Penny, Commander Phillips, and myself, joined by a party from the *Rescue*, hurried on over the ice, and, scrambling along the loose and rugged slope that extends from Beechy to the shore, came, after a weary walk, to the crest of the isthmus. Here, amid the sterile uniformity of snow and slate, were the head-boards of three graves, made after the old orthodox fashion of gravestones at home. The mounds which adjoined them were arranged with some pretensions to symmetry, coped and defended with limestone slabs. They occupied a line facing toward Cape Riley, which was distinctly visible across a little cove at the distance of some four hundred yards.

The first, or that most to the southward, is nearest to the front in the accompanying sketch. Its inscription, cut in by a chisel, ran thus;

"Sacred

to the

memory

of

W. Braine, R. M.,

H. M. S. *Erebus.*

Died April 3d, 1846,

aged 32 years.

'Choose ye this day whom ye will serve.'

Joshua, ch. xxiv., 15."

The second was:

"Sacred to the memory of

John Hartnell, A. B. of H. M. S.

Erebus,

aged 23 years.

'Thus saith the Lord, consider your ways.'

Haggai, i., 7."

The third and last of these memorials was not quite so well finished as the others. The mound was not of stone-work, but its general appearance was more grave-like, more like the sleeping-place of Christians in happier lands. It was inscribed:

"Sacred

to

the memory

of

John Torrington,

who departed this life

January 1st, A.D. 1846,

on board of

H. M. ship *Terror,*

aged 20 years."

"Departed this life *on board* the *Terror*, 1st January, 1846!" Franklin's ships, then, had not been wrecked when he occupied the encampment at Beechy!

Two large stones were imbedded in the friable limestone a little to the left of these sad records, and near them was a piece of wood, more than a foot in diameter, and two feet eight inches high, which had evidently served for an anvil-block: the marks were unmistakable. Near it again, but still more to the east, and therefore nearer the beach, was a large blackened space, covered with coal cinders, iron nails, spikes, hinges, rings, clearly the remains of the armorer's forge. Still nearer the beach, but more to the south, was the carpenter's shop, its marks equally distinctive.

Leaving "the graves," and walking toward Wellington Straits, about four hundred yards, or perhaps less, we came to a mound, or rather a series of mounds, which, considering the Arctic character of the surface at this spot, must have been a work of labor. It inclosed one nearly elliptical area, and one other, which, though separated from the first by a lesser mound, appeared to be connected with it. The spaces thus inclosed abounded in fragmentary remains. Among them I saw a stocking without a foot, sewed up at its edge, and a mitten not so much the worse for use as to have been without value to its owner. Shavings of wood were strewed freely on the southern side of the mound, as if they had been collected there by the continued labor of artificers, and not far from these, a few hundred yards lower down, was the remnant of a garden. Weighing all the signs carefully, I had no doubt that this was some central shore establishment, connected with the squadron, and that the lesser area was used as an observatory, for it had large stones fixed as if to support instruments, and the scantling props still stuck in the frozen soil.

Travelling on about a quarter of a mile further, and in the same direction, we came upon a deposit of more than six hundred preserved-meat cans, arranged in regular order. They had been emptied, and were now filled with limestone pebbles, perhaps to serve as convenient ballast on boating expeditions.

These were among the more obvious vestiges of Sir John Franklin's party. The minor indications about the ground were innumerable: fragments of canvas, rope, cordage, sail-cloth, tarpaulins; of casks, iron-work, wood, rough and carved; of clothing, such as a blanket lined by long stitches with common cotton stuff, and made into a sort of rude coat; paper in scraps, white, waste, and journal; a small key; a few odds and ends of brass-work, such as might be part of the furniture of a locker; in a word, the numberless reliquiæ of a winter resting-place. One of the papers, which I have preserved, has on it the notation of an astronomical sight, worked out to Greenwich time.

With all this, not a written memorandum, or pointing cross, or even the vaguest intimation of the condition or intentions of the party. The traces found at Cape Riley and Beechy were still more baffling. The cairn was mounted on a high and conspicuous portion of the shore, and evidently intended to attract observation; but, though several parties examined it, digging round it in every direction, not a single particle of information could be gleaned. This is remarkable; and for so able and practiced an Artic commander as Sir John Franklin, an incomprehensible omission.

In a narrow interval between the hills which come down toward Beechy Island, the searching parties of the *Rescue* and Mr. Murdaugh of our own vessel found the tracks of a sledge clearly defined, and unmistakable both as to character and direction. They pointed to the eastern shores of Wellington Sound, in the same general course with the traces discovered by Penny between Cape Spencer and Point Innes.

Similar traces were seen toward Caswell's Tower and Cape Riley, which gave additional proofs of systematic journeyings. They could be traced through the comminuted limestone shingle in the direction of Cape Spencer; and at intervals further on were scraps of paper, lucifer matches, and even the cinders of the temporary fire. The sledge parties must have been regularly organized, for their course had evidently been the subject of a previous reconnoissance. I observed their runner tracks not only in the limestone crust, but upon some snow slopes further to the north. It was startling to see the evidences of a travel nearly six years old, preserved in intaglio on a material so perishable.

The snows of the Arctic regions, by alternations of congelation and thaw, acquire sometimes an ice-like durability; but these traces had been covered by the after-snows of five winters. They pointed, like the Sastrugi, or snow-waves of the Siberians, to the marchers of the lost company.

Mr. Griffin, who performed a journey of research along this coast toward the north, found at intervals, almost to Cape Bowden, traces of a passing party. A corked bottle, quite empty, was among these. Reaching a point beyond Cape Bowden, he discovered the indentation or bay which now bears his name, and on whose opposite shores the coast was again seen.

It is clear to my own mind that a systematic reconnoissance was undertaken by Franklin of the upper waters of the Wellington, and that it had for its object an exploration in that direction as soon as the ice would permit.

There were some features about this deserted homestead inexpressibly touching. The frozen trough of an old water channel had served as the wash-house stream for the crews of the lost squadron. The tubs, such as Jack makes by sawing in half the beef barrels, although no longer fed by the melted snows, remained as the washers had left them five years ago. The little garden, too: I did not see it; but Lieutenant Osborn describes it as still showing the mosses and anemones that were transplanted by its farmers. A garden implies a purpose either to remain or to return: he who makes it is looking to the future. The same officer found a pair of cashmere gloves, carefully "laid out to dry, with two small stones upon the palms to keep them from blowing away." It would be wrong to measure the value of these gloves by the price they could be bought in Bond Street or Broadway. The Arctic traveler they belonged to intended to come back for them, and did not probably forget them in his hurry.

The facts I have mentioned, almost all of them, have been so ably analyzed already, that I might be excused from venturing any deductions of my own. But it was impossible to review the circumstances as we stood upon the ground without forming an opinion; and such as mine was, it is perhaps best that I should express it here.

In the first place, it is plain that Sir John Franklin's consort, the *Terror*, wintered in 1845-6 at or near the promontory of Beechy; that at least part of her crew remained on board of her; and that some of the crew of the flag-ship, the *Erebus*, if not the ship herself, were also there. It is also plain that a part of one or both these crews was occupied during a portion of the winter in the various pursuits of an organized squadron, at an encampment on the isthmus I have described, a position which commanded a full view of Lancaster Sound to the east of south, and of Wellington Channel extending north. It may be fairly inferred, also, that the general health of the crews had not suffered severely, three only having died out of a hundred and thirty odd; and that in addition to the ordinary details of duty, they were occupied in conducting and computing astronomical observations, making sledges, preparing their little anti-scorbutic garden patches, and exploring the eastern shore of the channel. Many facts that we ourselves observed made it seem probable that Franklin had not, in the first instance, been able to prosecute his instructions for the Western search; and the examinations made so fully since by Captain Austin's officers have proved that he never reached Cape Walker, Banks' Land, Melville Island, Prince Regent's Inlet, or any point of the sound considerably to the west or southwest. The whole story of our combined operations in and about the channel shows that it is along its eastern margin that the water-leads occur most frequently: natural causes of general application may be assigned for this, some of which will readily suggest themselves to the physicist; but I have only to do here with the recognized fact.

So far I think we proceed safely. The rest is conjectural. Let us suppose the season for renewed progress to be approaching; Franklin and his crews, with their vessels, one or both, looking out anxiously from their narrow isthmus for the first openings of the ice. They come: a gale of wind has severed the pack, and the drift begins. The first clear water that would meet his eye would be close to the shore on which he had his encampment. Would he wait till the continued drift had made the navigation practicable in Lancaster

Sound, and then retrace his steps to try the upper regions of Baffin's Bay, which he could not reach without a long circuit; or would he press to the north through the open lead that lay before him? Those who know Franklin's character, his declared opinions, his determined purpose, so well portrayed in the lately published letters of one of his officers, will hardly think the question difficult to answer: his sledges had already pioneered the way. We, the searchers, were ourselves tempted, by the insidious openings to the north in Wellington Channel, to push on in the hope that some lucky chance might point us to an outlet beyond. Might not the same temptation have had its influence for Sir John Franklin? A careful and daring navigator, such as he was, would not wait for the lead to close. I can imagine the dispatch with which the observatory would be dismantled, the armorer's establishment broken up, and the camp vacated. I can understand how the preserved-meat cans, not very valuable, yet not worthless, might be left piled upon the shore; how one man might leave his mittens, another his blanket coat, and a third hurry over the search for his lost key. And if I were required to conjecture some explanation of the empty signal cairn, I do not know what I could refer it to but the excitement attendant on just such a sudden and unexpected release from a weary imprisonment, and the instant prospect of energetic and perilous adventure.

"*August 28.* Strange enough, during the night. Captain Austin, of her majesty's search squadron, with his flag-ship the *Resolute*, entered the same little indentation in which five of us were moored before. His steam-tender, the *Pioneer*, grounded off the point of Beechy Island, and is now in sight, canted over by the ice nearly to her beam ends. He has come to us not of design, but under the irresistible guidance of the ice. We are now seven vessels within hailing distance, not counting Captain Ommanney's, imbedded in the field to the westward.

"I called this morning on Sir John Ross, and had a long talk with him. He said that, as far back as 1847, anticipating the 'detention' of Sir John Franklin—I use his own word—he had volunteered his services for an expedition of retrieve, asking for the purpose four small vessels, something like our own; but no one listened to him. Volunteering again in 1848, he was told that his nephew's claim to the service had received a recognition; whereupon his own was withdrawn. 'I told Sir John,' said Ross, 'that my own experience in these seas proved that all these sounds and inlets may, by the caprice or even the routine of seasons, be closed so as to prevent any egress, and that a missing or shut-off party must have some means of falling back. It was thus I saved myself from the abandoned *Victory* by a previously constructed house for wintering, and a boat for temporary refuge.' All this, he says, he pressed on Sir John Franklin before he set out, and he thinks that Melville Island is now the seat of such a house-asylum. 'For, depend upon it,' he added, 'Franklin will be expecting some of us to be following on his traces. Now, may it be that the party, whose winter quarters we have discovered, sent out only exploring detachments along Wellington Sound in the spring, and then, when themselves released, continued on to the west, by Cape Hotham and Barrow's Straits?' I have given this extract from my journal, though the theory it suggests has since been disproved by Lieutenant M'Clintock, because the tone and language of Sir John Ross may be regarded as characteristic of this manly old seaman.

"I next visited the *Resolute*. I shall not here say how their perfect organization and provision for winter contrasted with those of our own little expedition. I had to shake off a feeling almost of despondency when I saw how much better fitted they were to grapple with the grim enemy, Cold. Winter, if we may judge of it by the clothing and warming appliances of the British squadron, must be something beyond our power to cope with; for, in comparison with them, we have nothing, absolutely nothing.

"The officers received me, for I was alone, with the cordiality of recognized brotherhood. They are a gentlemanly, well-educated set of men, thoroughly up to the history of what has been done by others, and full of personal resource. Among them I was rejoiced to meet an old acquaintance. Lieutenant Brown, whose admirably artistic sketches I had seen in Haghe's lithotints, at Mr. Grinnell's, before leaving New York. When we were together last, it was among the tropical jungles of Luzon, surrounded by the palm, the cycas, and bamboo, in the glowing extreme of vegetable exuberance: here we are met once more, in the stinted region of lichen and mosses. He was then a junior, under Sir Edward Belcher: I—what I am yet. The lights and shadows of a naval life are nowhere better, and, alas! nowhere worse displayed, than in these remote accidental greetings.

"Returning, I paid a visit to Penny's vessels, and formed a very agreeable acquaintance with the medical officer, Dr. R. Anstruther Goodsir, a brother of assistant surgeon Goodsir of Franklin's flag-ship.

"In commemoration of the gathering of the searching squadrons within the little cove of Beechy Point, Commodore Austin has named it, very appropriately, Union Bay. It is here the *Mary* is deposited as an asylum to fall back upon in case of disaster.

"The sun is traveling rapidly to the south, so that our recently glaring midnight is now a twilight gloom. The coloring over the hills at Point Innes this evening was sombre, but in deep reds; and the sky had an inhospitable coldness. It made me thoughtful to see the long shadows stretching out upon the snow toward the isthmus of the Graves.

"The wind is from the north and westward, and the ice is so driven in around us as to grate and groan against the sides of our little vessel. The masses, though small, are very thick, and by the surging of the sea have been rubbed as round as pebbles. They make an abominable noise."

The remaining days of August were not characterized by any incident of note. We had the same alternations of progress and retreat through the ice as before, and without sensibly advancing toward the western shore, which it was now our object to reach. The next extracts from my journal are of the date of September 3.

"After floating down, warping, to avoid the loose ice, we finally cast off in comparatively open water, and began beating toward Cape Spencer to get round the field. Once there, we got along finely, sinking the eastern shore by degrees, and nearing the undelineated coasts of Cornwallis Island. White whales, narwhals, seals—among them the Phoca leonina with his puffed cheeks—and two bears, were seen.

"The ice is tremendous, far ahead of anything we have met with. The thickness of the upraised tables is sometimes fourteen feet; and the hummocks are so ground and distorted by the rude attrition of the floes, that they rise up in cones like crushed sugar, some of them forty feet high. But that the queer life we are leading—a life of constant exposure and excitement, and one that seems more like the 'roughing it' of a land party than the life of shipboard—has inured us to the eccentric fancies of the ice, our position would be a sleepless one.

"*September 4,* 2 A.M. Was awakened by Captain De Haven to look at the ice: an impressive sight. We were fast with three anchors to the main floe; and now, though the wind was still from the northward, and therefore in opposition to the drift, the floating masses under the action of the tide came with a westward trend directly past us. Fortunately, they were not borne down upon the vessels; but, as they went by in slow procession to the west, our sensations were, to say the least, sensations. It was very grand to see up-piled blocks twenty feet and more above our heads, and to wonder whether this fellow would strike our main-yard or clear our stern. Some of the moving hummocks were thirty feet high. They grazed us; but a little projection of the main field to windward shied them off.

"I killed to-day my first polar bear. We made the animal on a large floe to the northward while we were sighting the western shores of Wellington, and of course could not stop to shoot bears. But he took to the water ahead of us, and came so near that we fired at him from the bows of the vessel. Mr. Lovell and myself fired so simultaneously, that we had to weigh the ball to determine which had hit. My bullet struck exactly in the ear, the mark I had aimed at, for he had only his head above water. The young ice was forming so rapidly around us that it was hard work getting him on board. I was one of the oarsmen, and sweated rarely, with the thermometer at 25°.

"On the way back I succeeded in hitting an enormous seal; but, much to my mortification, he sunk, after floating till we nearly reached him.

"Without any organization, and with very little time for the hunt, the *Advance* now counts upon her game list two polar bears, three seals, a single goose, and a fair table allowance of loons, divers, and snipes. The *Rescue* boasts of four bears, and, in addition to the small game, a couple of Arctic hares. Our solitary goose was the Anas bernicla, crowds of which now begin to fly over the land and ice in cunoid streams to the east of south. It was killed by Mr. Murdaugh with a rifle, on the wing.

"How very much I miss my good home assortment of hunting materials! We have not a decent gun on board; as for the rifle I am now shooting, it is a flintlock concern, and half the time hangs fire."

The next morning found me at work skinning my bear, not a pleasant task with the thermometer below the freezing point. He was a noble specimen, larger than the largest recorded by Parry, measuring eight feet, eight inches and three-quarters from tip to tip. I presented the skin, on my return home, to the Academy of Natural Sciences at Philadelphia.

The carcass was larger than that of an ordinary ox fatted for market. We estimated his weight at nearly sixteen hundred pounds. In build he was very solid, and the muscles of the arms and haunch fearfully developed. I once before compared the posterior aspect of the Arctic bear to an elephant's. All my mess-mates used the same comparison. The extreme roundness of his back and haunches, with the columnar character of the legs, and the round expansion of the feet, give you the impression of a small elephant. The plantigrade base of support overlapped by long hair heightens the resemblance. The head and neck, of course, are excluded from the comparison.

At five in the afternoon we succeeded in reaching within a quarter of a mile of the shore off Barlow's Inlet, and made fast there to the floe. This inlet is but a few miles from Cape Hotham, and is marked on the charts as a mere interruption of the coast line. Parry, who named it, must have had wonderfully favoring weather to sight so accurately an insignificant cove. He was a practiced hydrographer.

The limestone cliffs rise on each side, forming stupendous piers gnarled by frost degradation, between which is the entrance, about a quarter of a mile wide. The moment our little vessel entered the shadow of these cliffs, a quiet gloom took the place of bustling movement. We ground our way into the newly-formed ice, and, after making a couple of ships' lengths, found ourselves within a sort of cape of land floe, surrounded by high hummocks and anchored bergs. It was a melancholy spot; not one warm sun tint; everything blank, repulsive sterility.

"*September 6.* The captain, Mr. Murdaugh, Mr. Carter, and myself started on a walk of exploration. The distance between the brig and the shore is not over three hundred yards, but the travel was arduous. The ice was eight and ten feet thick, studded with broken bergs and hummocks. These fragments were seldom larger than our Rensselaer dining-room, some twenty feet square, and, owing either to the rise and fall of the tides or the piling action of storms, deep crevices were formed around their edges, partially masked by the snow which had found its way into them, and by an icy crust over the surface. Alternately jumping these crevices and clambering up the hummocks between them made it a dangerous walk. We had some narrow escapes. Reaching the shore, we pushed forward about a mile and a quarter to the head of the inlet, and then crossed over on the ice to a cairn that stood near it. We found nothing but a communication from Captain Ommanney, whose vessels we saw as we entered the lead yesterday, informing the Secretary of the Admiralty that he had been off this place since the 24th, and that 'no traces are to be found on Cornwallis Island of the party under Sir John Franklin'—a somewhat too confident assertion perhaps, seeing that the island, if it be one, is more than fifty miles across, and that the observations can hardly have extended beyond the coast line.

"*September 7.* The spot at which we have been lying is in front of Barlow's Inlet. There is no barrier between it and our vessels but the young ice, which has now attained a thickness of three inches. On the east we have the drift plain of Wellington Channel, impacted with floes, hummocks, and broken bergs; and to the south we look out upon a wild aggregation of enormous hummocks. These hummocks are totally unlike anything we saw in Baffin's Bay. They seem to have been so disintegrated by the conflicting forces that raised them as to have lost altogether the character of tables. If hogshead upon hogshead of crushed sugar had been emptied out at random, two or three in

one pile, and two or three ship loads in another, and the summits of these
irregular heaps were covered over with a succession of layers of snow, and the
heaps themselves multiplied in number indefinitely, and crowded together in
a disordered phalanx, they would look a good deal like the hummock field
some twenty yards south of us. These fearful masses are all anchored, solid
hills, rising thirty feet above the level from a bottom twenty-two feet below it.

"Our situation might be regarded as an ugly one in some states of the
wind, but for the solid main floe to the north of us. This projected from the
cliff, which served as an abutment for it; and, after forming a sort of cape
outside of our position, extended with a horseshoe sweep to the northward
and eastward, as far as the eye could reach, following the trend of the shore.
It formed, of course, a reliable break-water. Commodore Austin's vessels were
made fast to it some distance to the north and east of us.

"The barometer had given us, in the early morning of the 4th, 29.90,
since when it rose steadily till the 5th, at 6 A.M., when it stood 30.38. For the
next twenty-four hours it fluctuated between .33 and .37; but at 6 A.M. of the
6th, it again began to rise; by midnight, it had reached 30.44; and before ten
o'clock P.M. of the 7th, it was at the unwonted height of 30.68. At 2 P.M. the
wind had changed from S.S.E. to N.N.E., and went on increasing to a gale.

"We were seated cosily around our little table in the cabin, imagining
our harbor of land ice perfectly secure, when we were startled by a crash.
We rushed on deck just in time to see the solid floe to windward part in the
middle, liberate itself from its attachment to the shore, and bear down upon
us with the full energy of the storm. Our lee bristled ominously half a ship's
length from us, and to the east was the main drift. The *Rescue* was first caught,
nipped astern, and lifted bodily out of water; fortunately she withstood the
pressure, and rising till she snapped her cable, launched into open water,
crushing the young ice before her. The *Advance*, by hard warping, drew a little closer to the cove; and, a moment after, the ice drove by, just clearing our
stern. Commodore Austin's vessels were imprisoned in the moving fragments,
and carried helplessly past us. In a very little while they were some four miles
off."

The summer was now leaving us rapidly. The thermometer had been at 21° and 23° for several nights, and scarcely rose above 32° in the daytime. Our little harbor at Barlow's Inlet was completely blocked in by heavy masses; the new ice gave plenty of sport to the skaters; but on shipboard it was uncomfortably cold. As yet we had no fires below; and, after drawing around me the India-rubber curtains of my berth, with my lamp burning inside, I frequently wrote my journal in a freezing temperature. "This is not very cold, no doubt"—I quote from an entry of the 8th—"not very cold to your forty-five minus men of Arctic winters; but to us poor devils from the zone of the liriodendrons and peaches, it is rather cold for the September month of water-melons. My bear with his arsenic swabs is a solid lump, and some birds that are waiting to be skinned are absolutely rigid with frost."

In the afternoon of this day, the 8th, we went to work, all hands, officers included, to cut up the young ice and tow it out into the current: once there, the drift carried it rapidly to the south. We cleared away in this manner a space of some forty yards square, and at five the next morning were rewarded by being again under weigh. We were past Cape Hotham by breakfast-time on the 9th, and in the afternoon were beating to the west in Lancaster Sound.

"The sound presented a novel spectacle to us; the young ice glazing it over, so as to form a viscid sea of sludge and *tickly-benders*, from the northern shore to the pack, a distance of at least ten miles. This was mingled with the drift floes from Wellington Channel; and in them, steaming away manfully, were the *Resolute* and *Pioneer*. The wind was dead ahead; yet, but for the new ice, there was a clear sea to the west. What, then, was our mortification, first, to see our pack-bound neighbors force themselves from their prison and steam ahead dead in the wind's eye, and, next, to be overhauled by Penny, and passed by both his brigs. We are now the last of all the searchers, except perhaps old Sir John, who is probably yet in Union Bay, or at least east of the straits.

"The shores along which we are passing are of the same configuration with the coast to the east of Beechy Island; the cliffs, however, are not so high, and their bluff appearance is relieved occasionally by terraces and shingle beach. The lithological characters of the limestone appear to be the same.

"We are all together here, on a single track but little wider than the Delaware or Hudson. There is no getting out of it, for the shore is on one side and the fixed ice close on the other. All have the lead of us, and we are working only to save a distance. Ommanney must be near Melville by this time: pleasant, very!

"Closing memoranda for the day: 1. I have the rheumatism in my knees; 2. I left a bag containing my dress suit of uniforms, and, what is worse, my winter suit of furs, and with them my double-barrel gun, on board Austin's vessel. The gale of the 7th has carried him and them out of sight.

"*September 10*. Unaccountable, most unaccountable, the caprices of this ice-locked region! Here we are again all together, even Ommanney with the rest. The *Resolute, Intrepid, Assistance, Pioneer, Lady Franklin, Sophia, Advance*, and *Rescue*; Austin, Ommanney, Penny, and De Haven, all anchored to the 'fast' off Griffith's Island. The way to the west completely shut out."

5.

THE RUBICON

ERSKINE CHILDERS

I t was a cold, vaporous dawn, the glass rising, and the wind fallen to a light air still from the north-east. Our creased and sodden sails scarcely answered to it as we crept across the oily swell to Langeoog. 'Fogs and calms,' Davies prophesied. The *Blitz* was astir when we passed her, and soon after steamed out to sea. Once over the bar, she turned westward and was lost to view in the haze. I should be sorry to have to explain how we found that tiny anchor-buoy, on the expressionless waste of grey. I only know that I hove the lead incessantly while Davies conned, till at last he was grabbing overside with the boat-hook, and there was the buoy on deck. The cable was soon following it, and finally the rusty monster himself, more loathsome than usual, after his long sojourn in the slime.

'That's all right,' said Davies. 'Now we can go anywhere.'

'Well, it's Norderney, isn't it? We've settled that.'

'Yes, I suppose we have. I was wondering whether it wouldn't be shortest to go inside Langeoog after all.'

'Surely not,' I urged. 'The tide's ebbing now, and the light's bad; it's new ground, with a "watershed" to cross, and we're safe to get aground.'

'All right—outside. Ready about.' We swung lazily round and headed for the open sea. I record the fact, but in truth Davies might have taken me where he liked, for no land was visible, only a couple of ghostly booms.

'It seems a pity to miss over that channel,' said Davies with a sigh; 'just when the *Kormoran* can't watch us.' (We had not seen her at all this morning.)

I set myself to the lead again, averse to reopening a barren argument. Grimm had done his work for the present, I felt certain, and was on his way by the shortest road to Norderney and Memmert.

We were soon outside and heading west, our boom squared away and the island sand-dunes just apparent under our lee. Then the breeze died to the merest draught, and left us rolling inert in a long swell. Consumed with impatience to get on I saw fatality in this failure of wind, after a fortnight of unprofitable meanderings, when we had generally had too much of it, and always enough for our purpose. I tried to read below, but the vile squirting of the centre-board drove me up.

'Can't we go any faster?' I burst out once. I felt that there ought to be a pyramid of gauzy canvas aloft, spinnakers, flying jibs and what not.

'I don't go in for speed,' said Davies, shortly. He loyally did his best to 'shove her' along, but puffs and calms were the rule all day, and it was only by towing in the dinghy for two hours in the afternoon that we covered the length of Langeoog, and crept before dark to an anchorage behind Baltrum, its slug-shaped neighbour on the west. Strictly, I believe, we should have kept the sea all night; but I had not the grit to suggest that course, and Davies was only too glad of an excuse for threading the shoals of the Accumer Ee on a rising tide. The atmosphere had been slowly clearing as the day wore on; but we had scarcely anchored ten minutes before a blanket of white fog, rolling in from seaward, swallowed us up. Davies was already afield in the dinghy, and I had to guide him back with a foghorn, whose music roused hosts of sea birds from the surrounding flats, and brought them wheeling and complaining round us, a weird invisible chorus to my mournful solo.

The fog hung heavy still at daybreak on the 20th, but dispersed partially under a catspaw from the south about eight o'clock, in time for us to traverse the boomed channel behind Baltrum, before the tide left the watershed.

'We shan't get far to-day,' said Davies, with philosophy. 'And this sort of thing may go on for any time. It's a regular autumn anti-cyclone—glass thirty point five and steady. That gale was the last of a stormy equinox.'

We took the inside route as a matter of course to-day. It was now the shortest to Norderney harbour, and scarcely less intricate than the Wichter Ee, which appeared to be almost totally blocked by banks, and is, in fact, the most impassable of all these outlets to the North Sea. But, as I say, this sort of navigation, always puzzling to me, was utterly bewildering in hazy weather. Any attempt at orientation made me giddy. So I slaved at the lead, varying my labour with a fierce bout of kedge-work when we grounded somewhere. I had two rests before two o'clock, one of an hour, when we ran into a patch of windless fog; another of a few moments, when Davies said, 'There's Norderney!' and I saw, surmounting a long slope of weedy sand, still wet with the receding sea, a cluster of sandhills exactly like a hundred others I had seen of late, but fraught with a new and unique interest.

The usual formula, 'What have you got now?' checked my reverie, and 'Helm's a-lee,' ended it for the time. We tacked on (for the wind had headed us) in very shoal water.

Suddenly Davies said: 'Is that a boat ahead?'

'Do you mean that galliot?' I asked. I could plainly distinguish one of those familiar craft about half a mile away, just within the limit of vision.

'The *Kormoran*, do you think?' I added. Davies said nothing, but grew inattentive to his work. 'Barely four,' from me passed unnoticed, and we

The East Frisian Islands, Germany.

touched once, but swung off under some play of the current. Then came abruptly, 'Stand by the anchor. Let go,' and we brought up in mid-stream of the narrow creek we were following. I triced up the main-tack, and stowed the headsails unaided. When I had done Davies was still gazing to windward through his binoculars, and, to my astonishment, I noticed that his hands were trembling violently. I had never seen this happen before, even at moments when a false turn of the wrist meant death on a surf-battered bank.

'What is it?' I asked; 'are you cold?'

'That little boat,' he said. I gazed to windward, too, and now saw a scrap of white in the distance, in sharp relief.

'Small standing lug and jib; it's her, right enough,' said Davies to himself, in a sort of nervous stammer.

'Who? What?'

'*Medusa*'s dinghy.'

He handed, or rather pushed, me the glasses, still gazing.

'Dollmann?' I exclaimed.

'No, it's *hers*—the one she always sails. She's come to meet m—, us.'

Through the glasses the white scrap became a graceful little sail, squared away for the light following breeze. An angle of the creek hid the hull, then it glided into view. Someone was sitting aft steering, man or woman I could not say, for the sail hid most of the figure. For full two minutes—two long, pregnant minutes—we watched it in silence. The damp air was fogging the lenses, but I kept them to my eyes; for I did not want to look at Davies. At last I heard him draw a deep breath, straighten himself up, and give one of his characteristic 'h'ms'. Then he turned briskly aft, cast off the dinghy's painter, and pulled her up alongside.

'You come too,' he said, jumping in, and fixing the rowlocks. (His hands were steady again.) I laughed, and shoved the dinghy off.

'I'd rather you did,' he said, defiantly.

'I'd rather stay. I'll tidy up, and put the kettle on.' Davies had taken a half stroke, but paused.

'She oughtn't to come aboard,' he said.

'She might like to,' I suggested. 'Chilly day, long way from home, common courtesy—'

'Carruthers,' said Davies, 'if she comes aboard, please remember that she's outside this business. There are no clues to be got from *her*.'

A little lecture which would have nettled me more if I had not been exultantly telling myself that, once and for all, for good or ill, the Rubicon was passed.

'It's your affair this time,' I said; 'run it as you please.'

He sculled away with vigorous strokes. 'Just as he is,' I thought to myself: bare head, beaded with fog-dew, ancient oilskin coat (only one button); grey jersey; grey woollen trousers (like a deep-sea fisherman's) stuffed into long boots. A vision of his antitype, the Cowes Philanderer, crossed me for a second. As to his face—well, I could only judge by it, and marvel, that he was gripping his dilemma by either horn, as firmly as he gripped his sculls.

I watched the two boats converging. They would meet in the natural course about three hundred yards away, but a hitch occurred. First, the sail-boat checked and slewed; 'aground,' I concluded. The rowboat leapt forward still; then checked, too. From both a great splashing of sculls floated across the still air, then silence. The summit of the watershed, a physical Rubicon, prosaic and slimy, had still to be crossed, it seemed. But it could be evaded. Both boats headed for the northern side of the creek: two figures were out on the brink, hauling on two painters. Then Davies was striding over the sand, and a girl—I could see her now—was coming to meet him. And then I thought it was time to go below and tidy up.

Nothing on earth could have made the *Dulcibella*'s saloon a worthy reception-room for a lady. I could only use hurried efforts to make it look its best by plying a bunch of cotton-waste and a floor-brush; by pitching into racks and lockers the litter of pipes, charts, oddments of apparel, and so on, that had a way of collecting afresh, however recently we had tidied up; by neatly arranging our demoralized library, and by lighting the stove and veiling the table under a clean white cloth.

I suppose about twenty minutes had elapsed, and I was scrubbing fruitlessly at the smoky patch on the ceiling, when I heard the sound of oars and voices outside. I threw the cotton-waste into the fo'c'sle, made an onslaught on my hands, and then mounted the companion ladder. Our own dinghy was just rounding up alongside, Davies sculling in the bows, facing him in the stern a young girl in a grey tam-o'-shanter, loose waterproof jacket and dark serge skirt, the latter, to be frigidly accurate, disclosing a pair of workman-like rubber boots which, *mutatis mutandis,* were very like those Davies was wearing. Her hair, like his, was spangled with moisture, and her rose-brown skin struck a note of delicious colour against the sullen Stygian background.

'There he is,' said Davies. Never did his 'meiner Freund, Carruthers,' sound so pleasantly in my ears; never so discordantly the 'Fräulein Dollmann' that followed it. Every syllable of the four was a lie. Two honest English eyes were looking up into mine; an honest English hand—is this insular nonsense? Perhaps so, but I stick to it—a brown, firm hand—no, not so very small, my sentimental reader—was clasping mine. Of course I had strong reasons, apart from the racial instinct, for thinking her to be English, but I believe that if I had had none at all I should at any rate have congratulated Germany on a clever bit of plagiarism. By her voice, when she spoke, I knew that she must have talked German habitually from childhood; diction and accent were faultless, at least to my English ear; but the native constitutional ring was wanting.

She came on board. There was a hollow discussion first about time and weather, but it ended as we all in our hearts wished it to end. None of us uttered our real scruples. Mine, indeed, were too new and rudimentary to be worth uttering, so I said common-sense things about tea and warmth; but I began to think about my compact with Davies.

'Just for a few minutes, then,' she said.

I held out my hand and swung her up. She gazed round the deck and rigging with profound interest—a breathless, hungry interest—touching to see.

'You've seen her before, haven't you?' I said.

'I've not been on board before,' she answered.

This struck me in passing as odd; but then I had only too few details from Davies about his days at Norderney in September.

'Of course, *that* is what puzzled me,' she exclaimed, suddenly, pointing to the mizzen. 'I knew there was something different.'

Davies had belayed the painter, and now had to explain the origin of the mizzen. This was a cumbrous process, and his hearer's attention soon wandered from the subject and became centred in him—his was already more than half in her—and the result was a golden opportunity for the discerning onlooker. It was very brief, but I made the most of it; buried deep a few regrets, did a little heartfelt penance, told myself I had been a cynical fool not to have foreseen this, and faced the new situation with a sinking heart; I am not ashamed to admit that, for I was fond of Davies, and I was keen about the quest.

She had never been a guilty agent in that attempt on Davies. Had she been an unconscious tool or only an unwilling one? If the latter, did she know the secret we were seeking? In the last degree unlikely, I decided. But, true to the compact, whose importance I now fully appreciated, I flung aside my diplomatic weapons, recoiling, as strongly, or nearly as strongly, let us say, from any effort direct or indirect to gain information from such a source. It was not our fault if by her own conversation and behaviour she gave us some idea of how matters stood. Davies already knew more than I did.

We spent a few minutes on deck while she asked eager questions about our build and gear and seaworthiness, with a quaint mixture of professional acumen and personal curiosity.

'How *did* you manage alone that day?' she asked Davies, suddenly.

'Oh, it was quite safe,' was the reply. 'But it's much better to have a friend.'

She looked at me; and—well, I would have died for Davies there and then.

'Father said you would be safe,' she remarked, with decision—a slight excess of decision, I thought. And at that turned to some rope or block and pursued her questioning. She found the compass impressive, and the trappings of that hateful centre-board had a peculiar fascination for her. Was this the way we did it in England? was her constant query.

Yet, in spite of a superficial freedom, we were all shy and constrained. The descent below was a welcome diversion, for we should have been less than human if we had not extracted some spontaneous fun from the humours of the saloon. I went down first to see about the tea, leaving them struggling for mutual comprehension over the theory of an English lifeboat. They soon followed, and I can see her now stooping in at the doorway, treading delicately, like a kitten, past the obstructive centre-board to a place on the starboard sofa, then taking in her surroundings with a timid rapture that broke into delight at all the primitive arrangements and dingy amenities of our den. She explored the cavernous recesses of the Rippingille, fingered the duck-guns and the miscellany in the racks, and peeped into the fo'c'sle with dainty awe. Everything was a source of merriment, from our cramped attitudes to the painful deficiency of spoons and the 'yachtiness' (there is no other word to describe it) of the bread, which had been bought at Bensersiel, and had suffered from incarceration and the climate. This fact came out, and led to some questions, while we waited for the water to boil, about the gale and our visit there. The topic, a pregnant one for us, appeared to have no special significance to her. At the mention of von Brüning she showed no emotion of any sort; on the contrary, she went out of her way, from an innocent motive that anyone could have guessed, to show that she could talk about him with dispassionate detachment.

'He came to see us when you were here last, didn't he?' she said to Davies. 'He often comes. He goes with father to Memmert sometimes. You know about Memmert? They are diving for money out of an old wreck.'

'Yes, we had heard about it.'

'Of course you have. Father is a director of the company, and Commander von Brüning takes great interest in it; they took me down in a diving-bell once.'

I murmured, 'Indeed!' and Davies sawed laboriously at the bread. She must have misconstrued our sheepish silence, for she stopped and drew herself up with just a touch of momentary *hauteur*, utterly lost on Davies. I could have laughed aloud at this transient little comedy of errors.

'Did you see any gold?' said Davies at last, with husky solemnity. Something had to be said or we should defeat our own end; but I let him say it. He had not my faith in Memmert.

'No, only mud and timber—oh, I forgot—'

'You mustn't betray the company's secrets,' I said, laughing; 'Commander von Brüning wouldn't tell us a word about the gold.' ('There's self-denial!' I said to myself.)

'Oh, I don't think it matters much,' she answered, laughing too. 'You are only visitors.'

'That's all,' I remarked, demurely. 'Just passing travellers.'

'You will stop at Norderney?' she said, with naïve anxiety. 'Herr Davies said—'

I looked to Davies; it was his affair. Fair and square came his answer, in blunt dog-German.

'Yes, of course, we shall. I should like to see your father again.'

Up to this moment I had been doubtful of his final decision; for ever since our explanation at Bensersiel I had had the feeling that I was holding his nose to a very cruel grindstone. This straight word, clear and direct, beyond anything I had hoped for, brought me to my senses and showed me that his mind had been working far in advance of mine; and more, shaping a double purpose that I had never dreamt of.

'My father?' said Fräulein Dollmann; 'yes, I am sure he will be very glad to see you.'

There was no conviction in her tone, and her eyes were distant and troubled.

'He's not at home now, is he?' I asked.

'How did you know?' (a little maidenly confusion). 'Oh, Commander von Brüning.'

I might have added that it had been clear as daylight all along that this visit was in the nature of an escapade of which her father might not approve. I tried to say 'I won't tell,' without words, and may have succeeded.

'I told Mr. Davies when we first met,' she went on. 'I expect him back very soon—to-morrow in fact; he wrote from Amsterdam. He left me at Hamburg and has been away since. Of course, he will not know your yacht is back again. I think he expected Mr. Davies would stay in the Baltic, as the season was so late. But—but I am sure he will be glad to see you.'

'Is the *Medusa* in harbour?' said Davies.

'Yes; but we are not living on her now. We are at our villa in the Schwan-nallée—my stepmother and I, that is.' She added some details, and Davies gravely pencilled down the address on a leaf of the log-book; a formality which somehow seemed to regularize the present position.

'We shall be at Norderney to-morrow,' he said.

Meanwhile the kettle was boiling merrily, and I made the tea—cocoa, I should say, for the menu was changed in deference to our visitor's tastes. 'This *is* fun!' she said. And by common consent we abandoned ourselves, three youthful, hungry mariners, to the enjoyment of this impromptu picnic. Such a chance might never occur again—*carpamus diem.*

But the banquet was never celebrated. As at Belshazzar's feast, there was a writing on the wall; no supernatural inscription, but just a printed name; an English surname with title and initials, in cheap gilt lettering on the back of an old book; a silent, sneering witness of our snug party. The catastrophe came and passed so suddenly that at the time I had scarcely even an inkling of what caused it; but I know now that this is how it happened. Our visitor was sitting at the forward end of the starboard sofa, close to the bulkhead. Davies and I were opposite her. Across the bulkhead, on a level with our heads, ran the bookshelf, whose contents, remember, I had carefully straightened only half an hour ago, little dreaming of the consequence. Some trifle, probably the logbook which Davies had reached down from the shelf, called her attention to the rest of our library. While busied with the cocoa I heard her spelling out some titles, fingering leaves, and twitting Davies with the little care he took of his books. Suddenly there was a silence which made me look up, to see a startled and pitiful change in her. She was staring at Davies with wide eyes and parted lips, a burning flush mounting on her forehead, and such an expression on her face as a sleep-walker might wear, who wakes in fear he knows not where.

Half her mind was far away, labouring to construe some hideous dream of the past; half was in the present, cringing before some sickening reality. She remained so for perhaps ten seconds, and then—plucky girl that she was—she mastered herself, looked deliberately round and up with a circular glance, strangely in the manner of Davies himself, and spoke. How late it was, she must be going—her boat was not safe. At the same time she rose to go, or rather slid herself along the sofa, for rising was impossible. We sat like mannerless louts, in blank amazement. Davies at the outset had said, 'What's the matter?' in plain English, and then relapsed into stupefaction. I recovered myself the first, and protested in some awkward fashion about the cocoa, the time, the absence of fog. In trying to answer, her self-possession broke down, poor child, and her retreat became a blind flight, like that of a wounded animal, while every sordid circumstance seemed to accentuate her panic.

She tilted the corner of the table in leaving the sofa and spilt cocoa over her skirt; she knocked her head with painful force against the sharp lintel of the doorway, and stumbled on the steps of the ladder. I was close behind, but when I reached the deck she was already on the counter hauling up the dinghy. She had even jumped in and laid hands on the sculls before any check came in her precipitate movements. Now there occurred to her the patent fact that the dinghy was ours, and that someone must accompany her to bring it back.

'Davies will row you over,' I said.

'Oh no, thank you,' she stammered. 'If you will be so kind, Herr Carruthers. It is your turn. No, I mean, I want—'

'Go on,' said Davies to me in English.

I stepped into the dinghy and motioned to take the sculls from her. She seemed not to see me, and pushed off while Davies handed down her jacket, which she had left in the cabin. Neither of us tried to better the situation by conventional apologies. It was left to her, at the last moment, to make a show of excusing herself, an attempt so brave and yet so wretchedly lame that I tingled all over with hot shame. She only made matters worse, and Davies interrupted her.

'*Auf Wiedersehen*,' he said, simply.

She shook her head, did not even offer her hand, and pulled away; Davies turned sharp round and went below.

There was now no muddy Rubicon to obstruct us, for the tide had risen a good deal, and the sands were covering. I offered again to take the sculls, but she took no notice and rowed on, so that I was a silent passenger on the stern seat till we reached her boat, a spruce little yacht's gig, built to the native model, with a spoon-bow and tiny lee-boards. It was already afloat, but riding quite safely to a rope and a little grapnel, which she proceeded to haul in.

'It was quite safe after all, you see,' I said.

'Yes, but I could not stay. Herr Carruthers, I want to say something to you.' (I knew it was coming; von Brüning's warning over again.) 'I made a mistake just now; it is no use your calling on us to-morrow.'

'Why not?'

'You will not see my father.'

'I thought you said he was coming back?'

'Yes, by the morning steamer; but he will be very busy.'

'We can wait. We have several days to spare, and we have to call for letters anyhow.'

'You must not delay on our account. The weather is very fine at last. It would be a pity to lose a chance of a smooth voyage to England. The season—'

'We have no fixed plans. Davies wants to get some shooting.'

'My father will be much occupied.'

'We can see *you*.'

I insisted on being obtuse, for though this fencing with an unstrung girl was hateful work, the quest was at stake. We were going to Norderney, come what might, and sooner or later we must see Dollmann. It was no use promising not to. I had given no pledge to von Brüning, and I would give none to her. The only alternative was to violate the compact (which the present fiasco had surely weakened), speak out, and try and make an ally of her. Against her own father? I shrank from the responsibility and counted the cost of failure— certain failure, to judge by her conduct. She began to hoist her lugsail in a dazed, shiftless fashion, while our two boats drifted slowly to leeward.

'Father might not like it,' she said, so low and from such tremulous lips that I scarcely caught her words. 'He does not like foreigners much. I am afraid . . . he did not want to see Herr Davies again.'

'But I thought—'

'It was wrong of me to come aboard—I suddenly remembered; but I could not tell Herr Davies.'

'I see,' I answered. 'I will tell him.'

'Yes, that he must not come near us.'

'He will understand. I know he will be very sorry, but,' I added, firmly, 'you can trust him implicitly to do the right thing.' And how I prayed that this would content her! Thank Heaven, it did.

'Yes,' she said, 'I am afraid I did not say good-bye to him. You will do so?' She gave me her hand.

'One thing more,' I added, holding it, 'nothing had better be said about this meeting?'

'No, no, nothing. It must never be known.'

I let go the gig's gunwale and watched her tighten her sheet and make a tack or two to windward. Then I rowed back to the *Dulcibella* as hard as I could.

6.

CAST ADRIFT

WILLIAM BLIGH

A re-creation of the HMS *Bounty*, built in 1960.

1789 April. Just before sun-rising, Mr. Christian, with the master at arms, gunner's mate, and Thomas Burket, seaman, came into my cabin while I was asleep, and seizing me, tied my hands with a cord behind my back, and threatened me with instant death, if I spoke or made the least noise: I, however, called so loud as to alarm every one; but they had already secured the officers who were not of their party, by placing centinels at their doors. There were three men at my cabin door, besides the four within; Christian had only a cutlass in his hand, the others had muskets and bayonets. I was hauled out of bed, and forced on deck in my shirt, suffering great pain from the tightness with which they had tied my hands. I demanded the reason of such violence, but received no other answer than threats of instant death, if I did not hold my tongue. Mr. Elphinston, the master's mate, was kept in his birth; Mr. Nelson, botanist, Mr. Peckover, gunner, Mr. Ledward, surgeon, and the master, were confined to their cabins; and also the clerk, Mr. Samuel, but he soon obtained leave to come on deck. The fore hatchway was guarded by centinels; the boatswain and carpenter were, however, allowed to come on deck, where they saw me standing abaft the mizen-mast, with my hands tied behind my back, under a guard, with Christian at their head.

The boatswain was now ordered to hoist the launch out, with a threat, if he did not do it instantly, to take care of himself.

The boat being out, Mr. Hayward and Mr. Hallet, midshipmen, and Mr. Samuel, were ordered into it; upon which I demanded the cause of such an order, and endeavoured to persuade some one to a sense of duty; but it was to no effect: "Hold your tongue, Sir, or you are dead this instant," was constantly repeated to me.

The master, by this time, had sent to be allowed to come on deck, which was permitted; but he was soon ordered back again to his cabin.

I continued my endeavours to turn the tide of affairs, when Christian changed the cutlass he had in his hand for a bayonet, that was brought to him, and, holding me with a strong gripe by the cord that tied my hands, he with many oaths threatened to kill me immediately if I would not be quiet: the villains round me had their pieces cocked and bayonets fixed. Particular people were now called on to go into the boat, and were hurried over the side: whence I concluded that with these people I was to be set adrift.

I therefore made another effort to bring about a change, but with no other effect than to be threatened with having my brains blown out.

The boatswain and seamen, who were to go in the boat, were allowed to collect twine, canvas, lines, sails, cordage, an eight and twenty gallon cask of water, and the carpenter to take his tool chest. Mr. Samuel got 150 lbs of bread, with a small quantity of rum and wine. He also got a quadrant and compass into the boat; but was forbidden, on pain of death, to touch either map, ephemeris, book of astronomical observations, sextant, time-keeper, or any of my surveys or drawings.

The mutineers now hurried those they meant to get rid of into the boat. When most of them were in, Christian directed a dram to be served to each of his own crew. I now unhappily saw that nothing could be done to effect the recovery of the ship: there was no one to assist me, and every endeavour on my part was answered with threats of death.

The officers were called, and forced over the side into the boat, while I was kept apart from every one, abaft the mizen-mast; Christian, armed with a bayonet, holding me by the bandage that secured my hands. The guard round me had their pieces cocked, but, on my daring the ungrateful wretches to fire, they uncocked them.

Isaac Martin, one of the guard over me, I saw, had an inclination to assist me, and, as he fed me with shaddock, (my lips being quite parched with my endeavours to bring about a change) we explained our wishes to each other by our looks; but this being observed, Martin was instantly removed from me; his inclination then was to leave the ship, for which purpose he got into the boat; but with many threats they obliged him to return.

The armourer, Joseph Coleman, and the two carpenters, M'Intosh and Norman, were also kept contrary to their inclination; and they begged of me, after I was astern in the boat, to remember that they declared they had no hand in the transaction. Michael Byrne, I am told, likewise wanted to leave the ship.

It is of no moment for me to recount my endeavours to bring back the offenders to a sense of their duty: all I could do was by speaking to them in general; but my endeavours were of no avail, for I was kept securely bound, and no one but the guard suffered to come near me.

To Mr. Samuel I am indebted for securing my journals and commission, with some material ship papers. Without these I had nothing to certify what I had done, and my honour and character might have been suspected, without my possessing a proper document to have defended them. All this he did with great resolution, though guarded and strictly watched. He attempted to save the time-keeper, and a box with all my surveys, drawings, and remarks for fifteen years past, which were numerous; when he was hurried away, with "Damn your eyes, you are well off to get what you have."

It appeared to me that Christian was some time in doubt whether he should keep the carpenter, or his mates; at length he determined on the latter, and the carpenter was ordered into the boat. He was permitted, but not without some opposition, to take his tool chest.

Much altercation took place among the mutinous crew during the whole business: some swore "I'll be damned if he does not find his way home, if he gets any thing with him," (meaning me); others, when the carpenter's chest was carrying away, "Damn my eyes, he will have a vessel built in a month." While others laughed at the helpless situation of the boat, being very deep, and so little room for those who were in her. As for Christian, he seemed meditating instant destruction on himself and every one.

I asked for arms, but they laughed at me, and said I was well acquainted with the people where I was going, and therefore did not want them; four cutlasses, however, were thrown into the boat, after we were veered astern.

When the officers and men, with whom I was suffered to have no communication, were put into the boat, they only waited for me, and the master at arms informed Christian of it; who then said—"Come, captain Bligh, your officers and men are now in the boat, and you must go with them; if you attempt to make the least resistance you will instantly be put to death"; and, without any farther ceremony, holding me by the cord that tied my hands, with a tribe of armed ruffians about me, I was forced over the side, where they untied my hands. Being in the boat we were veered astern by a rope. A few pieces of pork were then thrown to us, and some cloths, also the cutlasses I have already mentioned; and it was now that the armourer and carpenters called out to me to remember that they had no hand in the transaction. After having undergone a great deal of ridicule, and been kept some time to make sport for these unfeeling wretches, we were at length cast adrift in the open ocean.

Having little or no wind, we rowed pretty fast towards Tofoa, which bore N E about 10 leagues from us. While the ship was in sight she steered to the W N W, but I considered this only as a feint; for when we were sent away— "Huzza for Otaheite," was frequently heard among the mutineers.

It now remained with me to consider what was best to be done. My first determination was to seek a supply of bread-fruit and water at Tofoa, and afterwards to sail for Tongataboo; and there risk a solicitation to Poulaho, the king, to equip my boat, and grant a supply of water and provisions, so as to enable us to reach the East Indies.

The quantity of provisions I found in the boat was 150 lb. of bread, 16 pieces of pork, each piece weighing 2 lb.; 6 quarts of rum, 6 bottles of wine, with 28 gallons of water, and four empty barrecoes.

The coast of Tahiti, as Bligh may have seen it.

Wednesday, April 29. Happily the afternoon kept calm, until about 4 o'clock, when we were so far to windward, that, with a moderate easterly breeze which sprung up, we were able to sail. It was nevertheless dark when we got to Tofoa, where I expected to land; but the shore proved to be so steep and rocky, that I was obliged to give up all thoughts of it, and keep the boat under the lee of the island with two oars; for there was no anchorage. Having fixed on this mode of proceeding for the night, I served to every person half a pint of grog, and each took to his rest as well as our unhappy situation would allow.

In the morning, at dawn of day, we set off along shore in search of landing, and about ten o'clock we discovered a stony cove at the N W part of the island, where I dropt the grapnel within 20 yards of the rocks. A great deal of surf ran on the shore; but, as I was unwilling to diminish our stock of provisions, I landed Mr. Samuel, and some others, who climbed the cliffs, and got into the country to search for supplies. The rest of us remained at the cove, not discovering any way to get into the country, but that by which Mr. Samuel had proceeded. It was great consolation to me to find, that the spirits of my people did not sink, notwithstanding our miserable and almost hopeless situation. Towards noon Mr. Samuel returned, with a few quarts of water, which he had found in holes; but he had met with no spring or any prospect of a sufficient supply in that particular, and had only seen signs of inhabitants. As it was impossible to know how much we might be in want, I only issued a morsel of bread, and a glass of wine, to each person for dinner.

I observed the latitude of this cove to be 19° 41′ S.

This is the N W part of Tofoa, the north-westernmost of the Friendly Islands.

Thursday, April 30th. Fair weather, but the wind blew so violently from the E S E that I could not venture to sea. Our detention therefore made it absolutely necessary to see what we could do more for our support; for I determined, if possible, to keep my first stock entire: I therefore weighed, and rowed along shore, to see if any thing could be got; and at last discovered some cocoa-nut trees, but they were on the top of high precipices, and the surf made it dangerous landing; both one and the other we, however, got the better of. Some, with much difficulty, climbed the cliffs, and got about 20 cocoa-nuts, and others slung them to ropes, by which we hauled them through the surf into the boat. This was all that could be done here; and, as I found no place so eligible as the one we had left to spend the night at, I returned to the cove, and, having served a cocoa-nut to each person, we went to rest again in the boat.

1789. April 30. At dawn of day I attempted to get to sea; but the wind and weather proved so bad, that I was glad to return to my former station; where, after issuing a morsel of bread and a spoonful of rum to each person, we landed, and I went off with Mr. Nelson, Mr. Samuel, and some others, into the country, having hauled ourselves up the precipice by long vines, which were fixed there by the natives for that purpose; this being the only way into the country.

We found a few deserted huts, and a small plantain walk, but little taken care of; from which we could only collect three small bunches of plantains. After passing this place, we came to a deep gully that led towards a mountain, near a volcano; and, as I conceived that in the rainy season very great torrents of water must pass through it, we hoped to find sufficient for our use remaining in some holes of the rocks; but, after all our search, the whole that we found was only nine gallons, in the course of the day. We advanced within two miles of the foot of the highest mountain in the island, on which is the volcano that is almost constantly burning. The country near it is all covered with lava, and has a most dreary appearance. As we had not been fortunate in our discoveries, and saw but little to alleviate our distresses, we filled our cocoa-nut shells with the water we found, and returned exceedingly fatigued and faint. When I came to the precipice whence we were to descend into the cove, I was seized with such a dizziness in my head, that I thought it scarce possible to effect it: however, by the assistance of Mr. Nelson, and others, they at last got me down, in a weak condition. Every person being returned by noon, I gave about an ounce of pork and two plantains to each, with half a glass of wine. I again observed the latitude of this place 19° 41′ south. The people who remained by the boat I had directed to look for fish, or what they could pick up about the rocks; but nothing eatable could be found: so that, upon the whole, we considered ourselves on as miserable a spot of land as could well be imagined.

I could not say positively, from the former knowledge I had of this island, whether it was inhabited or not; but I knew it was considered inferior to the other islands, and I was not certain but that the Indians only resorted to it at particular times. I was very anxious to ascertain this point; for, in case there had only been a few people here, and those could have furnished us with but very moderate supplies, the remaining in this spot to have made preparations for our voyage, would have been preferable to the risk of going amongst multitudes, where perhaps we might lose every thing. A party, therefore, sufficiently strong, I determined should go another route, as soon as the sun became lower; and they cheerfully undertook it.

Friday, May the 1st. Stormy weather, wind E S E and S E. About two o'clock in the afternoon the party set out; but, after suffering much fatigue, they returned in the evening, without any kind of success.

At the head of the cove, about 150 yards from the water-side, was a cave; across the stony beach was about 100 yards, and the only way from the country into the cove was that which I have already described. The situation secured us from the danger of being surprised, and I determined to remain on shore for the night, with a part of my people, that the others might have more room to rest in the boat, with the master; whom I directed to lie at a grapnel, and be watchful, in case we should be attacked. I ordered one plantain for each person to be boiled; and, having supped on this scanty allowance, with a quarter of a pint of grog, and fixed the watches for the night, those whose turn it was, laid down to sleep in the cave; before which we kept up a good fire, yet notwithstanding we were much troubled with flies and musquitoes.

1789. May 1. At dawn of day the party set out again in a different route, to see what they could find; in the course of which they suffered greatly for want of water: they, however, met with two men, a woman, and a child; the men came with them to the cove, and brought two cocoa-nut shells of water. I immediately made friends with these people, and sent them away for bread-fruit, plantains, and water. Soon after other natives came to us; and by noon

I had 30 of them about me, trading with the articles we were in want of: but I could only afford one ounce of pork, and a quarter of a bread-fruit, to each man for dinner, with half a pint of water; for I was fixed in not using any of the bread or water in the boat.

No particular chief was yet among the natives: they were, notwithstanding, tractable, and behaved honestly, giving the provisions they brought for a few buttons and beads. The party who had been out, informed me of having discovered several neat plantations; so that it became no longer a doubt of there being settled inhabitants on the island; and for that reason I determined to get what I could, and sail the first moment the wind and weather would allow me to put to sea.

Saturday, May the 2d. Stormy weather, wind E S E. It had hitherto been a weighty consideration with me, how I was to account to the natives for the loss of my ship: I knew they had too much sense to be amused with a story that the ship was to join me, when she was not in sight from the hills. I was at first doubtful whether I should tell the real fact, or say that the ship had overset and sunk, and that only we were saved: the latter appeared to me to be the most proper and advantageous to us, and I accordingly instructed my people, that we might all agree in one story. As I expected, enquiries were made after the ship, and they seemed readily satisfied with our account; but there did not appear the least symptom of joy or sorrow in their faces, although I fancied I discovered some marks of surprise. Some of the natives were coming and going the whole afternoon, and we got enough of bread-fruit, plantains, and cocoa-nuts for another day; but water they only brought us about five pints. A canoe also came in with four men, and brought a few cocoa-nuts and bread-fruit, which I bought as I had done the rest. Nails were much enquired after, but I would not suffer one to be shewn, as I wanted them for the use of the boat.

Towards evening I had the satisfaction to find our stock of provisions somewhat increased: but the natives did not appear to have much to spare. What they brought was in such small quantities, that I had no reason to hope we should be able to procure from them sufficient to stock us for our voyage.

At sun-set all the natives left us in quiet possession of the cove. I thought this a good sign, and made no doubt that they would come again the next day with a larger proportion of food and water, with which I hoped to sail without farther delay: for if, in attempting to get to Tongataboo, we should be blown away from the islands altogether, there would be a larger quantity of provisions to support us against such a misfortune.

1789. May 2. At night I served a quarter of a bread-fruit and a cocoa-nut to each person for supper; and, a good fire being made, all but the watch went to sleep.

At day-break I was happy to find every one's spirits a little revived, and that they no longer regarded me with those anxious looks, which had constantly been directed towards me since we lost sight of the ship: every countenance appeared to have a degree of cheerfulness, and they all seemed determined to do their best.

As I doubted of water being brought by the natives, I sent a party among the gullies in the mountains, with empty shells, to see what they could get. In their absence the natives came about us, as I expected, but more numerous; also two canoes came in from round the north side of the island. In one of them was an elderly chief, called Maccaackavow. Soon after some of our foraging party returned, and with them came a good-looking chief, called Eegijeefow, or perhaps more properly Eefow, Egij or Eghee, signifying a chief. To both these men I made a present of an old shirt and a knife, and I soon found they either had seen me, or had heard of my being at Annamooka. They knew I had been with captain Cook, who they enquired after, and also captain Clerk. They were very inquisitive to know in what manner I had lost my ship. During this conversation a young man appeared, whom I remembered to have seen at Annamooka, called Nageete: he expressed much pleasure at seeing me. I now enquired after Poulaho and Feenow, who, they said, were at Tongataboo; and Eefow agreed to accompany me thither, if I would wait till the weather moderated. The readiness and affability of this man gave me much satisfaction.

1789. May 2. This, however, was but of short duration, for the natives began to increase in number, and I observed some symptoms of a design against us; soon after they attempted to haul the boat on shore, when I threatened Eefow with a cutlass, to induce him to make them desist; which they did, and every thing became quiet again. My people, who had been in the mountains, now returned with about three gallons of water. I kept buying up the little bread-fruit that was brought to us, and likewise some spears to arm my men with, having only four cutlasses, two of which were in the boat. As we had no means of improving our situation, I told our people I would wait until sun-set, by which time, perhaps, something might happen in our favour: that if we attempted to go at present, we must fight our way through, which we could do more advantageously at night; and that in the mean time we would endeavour to get off to the boat what we had bought. The beach was now lined with the natives, and we heard nothing but the knocking of stones together, which they had in each hand. I knew very well this was the sign of an attack. It being now noon, I served a cocoa-nut and a bread-fruit to each person for dinner, and gave some to the chiefs, with whom I continued to appear intimate and friendly. They frequently importuned me to sit down, but I as constantly refused; for it occurred both to Mr. Nelson and myself, that they intended to seize hold of me, if I gave them such an opportunity. Keeping, therefore, constantly on our guard, we were suffered to eat our uncomfortable meal in some quietness.

Sunday, 3d May. Fresh gales at S E and E S E, varying to the N E in the latter part, with a storm of wind.

After dinner we began by little and little to get our things into the boat, which was a troublesome business, on account of the surf. I carefully watched the motions of the natives, who still increased in number, and found that, instead of their intention being to leave us, fires were made, and places fixed on for their stay during the night. Consultations were also held among them, and every thing assured me we should be attacked. I sent orders to the master, that when he saw us coming down, he should keep the boat close to the shore, that we might the more readily embark.

I had my journal on shore with me, writing the occurrences in the cave, and in sending it down to the boat it was nearly snatched away, but for the timely assistance of the gunner.

The sun was near setting when I gave the word, on which every person, who was on shore with me, boldly took up his proportion of things, and carried them to the boat. The chiefs asked me if I would not stay with them all night, I said, "No, I never sleep out of my boat; but in the morning we will again trade with you, and I shall remain until the weather is moderate, that we may go, as we have agreed, to see Poulaho, at Tongataboo." Maccaackavow then got up, and said, "You will not sleep on shore? then Mattie," (which directly signifies we will kill you) and he left me. The onset was now preparing; every one, as I have described before, kept knocking stones together, and Eefow quitted me. We had now all but two or three things in the boat, when I took Nageete by the hand, and we walked down the beach, every one in a silent kind of horror.

1789. May 3. When I came to the boat, and was seeing the people embark, Nageete wanted me to stay to speak to Eefow; but I found he was encouraging them to the attack, and I determined, had it then begun, to have killed him for his treacherous behaviour. I ordered the carpenter not to quit me until the other people were in the boat. Nageete, finding I would not stay, loosed himself from my hold and went off, and we all got into the boat except one man, who, while I was getting on board, quitted it, and ran up the beach to cast the stern fast off, notwithstanding the master and others called to him to return, while they were hauling me out of the water.

I was no sooner in the boat than the attack began by about 200 men; the unfortunate poor man who had run up the beach was knocked down, and the stones flew like a shower of shot. Many Indians got hold of the stern rope, and were near hauling us on shore, and would certainly have done it if I had not had a knife in my pocket, with which I cut the rope. We then hauled off to the grapnel, every one being more or less hurt. At this time I saw five of the natives about the poor man they had killed, and two of them were beating him about the head with stones in their hands.

1789. May 3. We had no time to reflect, before, to my surprise, they filled their canoes with stones, and twelve men came off after us to renew the attack, which they did so effectually as nearly to disable all of us. Our grapnel was foul, but Providence here assisted us; the fluke broke, and we got to our oars, and pulled to sea. They, however, could paddle round us, so that we were obliged to sustain the attack without being able to return it, except with such stones as lodged in the boat, and in this I found we were very inferior to them. We could not close, because our boat was lumbered and heavy, and that they knew very well: I therefore adopted the expedient of throwing overboard some cloaths, which they lost time in picking up; and, as it was now almost dark, they gave over the attack, and returned towards the shore, leaving us to reflect on our unhappy situation.

The poor man I lost was John Norton: this was his second voyage with me as a quarter-master, and his worthy character made me lament his loss very much. He has left an aged parent, I am told, whom he supported.

1789. May 3. I once before sustained an attack of a similar nature, with a smaller number of Europeans, against a multitude of Indians; it was after the death of captain Cook, on the Morai at Owhyhee, where I was left by lieutenant King: yet, notwithstanding, I did not conceive that the power of a man's arm could throw stones, from two to eight pounds weight, with such force and exactness as these people did. Here unhappily I was without arms, and the Indians knew it; but it was a fortunate circumstance that they did not begin to attack us in the cave: in that case our destruction must have been inevitable, and we should have had nothing left for it but to die as bravely as we could, fighting close together; in which I found every one cheerfully disposed to join me. This appearance of resolution deterred them, supposing they could effect their purpose without risk after we were in the boat.

Taking this as a sample of the dispositions of the Indians, there was little reason to expect much benefit if I persevered in my intention of visiting Poulaho; for I considered their good behaviour hitherto to proceed from a dread of our fire-arms, which, now knowing us destitute of, would cease; and, even supposing our lives not in danger, the boat and every thing we had would most probably be taken from us, and thereby all hopes precluded of ever being able to return to our native country.

We were now sailing along the west side of the island Tofoa, and my mind was employed in considering what was best to be done, when I was solicited by all hands to take them towards home: and, when I told them no hopes of relief for us remained, but what I might find at New Holland, until I came to Timor, a distance of full 1,200 leagues, where was a Dutch settlement, but in what part of the island I knew not, they all agreed to live on one ounce of bread, and a quarter of a pint of water, per day. Therefore, after examining our stock of provisions, and recommending this as a sacred promise for ever to their memory, we bore away across a sea, where the navigation is but little known, in a small boat, twenty-three feet long from stern to stern, deep laden with eighteen men; without a chart, and nothing but my own recollection and general knowledge of the situation of places, assisted by a book of latitudes and longitudes, to guide us. I was happy, however, to see every one better satisfied with our situation in this particular than myself.

7.

THE WRECK ON THE ANDAMANS

JOSEPH DARVALL, ESQ.

THE DEPARTURE

The gallant Barque the *Runnymede*, of 507 tons burthen, commanded by Captain William Clement Doutty, an experienced seaman, and the property of Messrs. Hall & Co. and Ingram of Riches-court, Lime-street, London, being a remarkably staunch river-built vessel of the A 1 or first class, left Gravesend on the 20th of June, 1844, bound for Calcutta. She had on board a general cargo and a crew of twenty-eight persons, including officers. She also carried out, on account of the Honourable East India Company, thirty-eight soldiers, with two women and one child, belonging to Her Majesty's 10th Regiment of Foot, and also Captain Stapleton, Ensigns Venables, Du Vernett, and Purcell, and one hundred and five soldiers, ten women, and thirteen children, belonging to Her Majesty's 50th Regiment of Foot. The whole of the military were under the command of Captain Stapleton; the medical officer was Mr. Bell, the surgeon of the vessel.

Every thing proceeded in the same manner as is usual on voyages in the same course, till they arrived south of the Tropics. The only casualty they met with was the death of William Bryant, a private of the 10th, on the 12th of July. He had suffered from sea-sickness ever since his embarkation. His body was committed to the deep the same evening, with the customary ceremonies. The principal amusements of the officers and crew were fishing, shark-catching, booby and pigeon shooting, and playing at backgammon. There were also on board the ship, books provided for the use of those who were disposed to read. The hour of dinner was four o'clock.

On arriving south of the Tropics, the wind, instead of backing to the westward, blew almost constantly from the north-east and east-north-east; and when it occasionally got to the westward of north, it always fell light, contrary to the usual course; and so it continued until it got to the westward, and then it freshened. In consequence of the delay occasioned by this state of things, and the near approach of the north-east monsoon, the captain, on the 21st of October, resolved to call at Penang, for the purpose of taking in an additional supply of water and other necessaries. They accordingly steered their course thither. On the 24th they saw the Island of Sumatra, bearing east-north-east about eight leagues. On the 26th, in the forenoon, they saw Pulo Rondo, bearing east-south-east, and on the 29th, at half-past two o'clock in the afternoon, the ship anchored in safety off Fort Cornwallis, in the roads of Penang, or Pulo Penang, the word Pulo signifying an island. Penang is sometimes called Prince of Wales's Island. It is on the coast of Queda. Its capital is George Town. The East-India Company first formed a settlement here in 1786.

At Penang they remained till Sunday, the 3d of November, busily engaged in taking in sixty-one casks or about thirty tons of water, and other necessaries, and various articles of merchandize on account of cargo. They found lying here Her Majesty's ship *Dido*, commanded by the Honourable Captain Keppel.

The coast of Penang.

Immediately on the arrival of the *Runnymede*, Captain Doutty and Mr. Bell, together with Captain Stapleton and Ensign Du Vernett, went on shore, it being the duty of the latter to report themselves to the proper authorities.

It was agreed, that after the parties had accomplished their business, they should meet at the best hotel in the place and dine together. This understanding led to the following entertaining incidents. On landing, the parties stepped into palanquin-carriages. The Captain and the Doctor went one way, and their military friends, another. After finishing their business, the Captain and his companion went in quest of their friends, desiring the Malay boy, who had charge of their carriage, to take them to the hotel. The lad replied, "I stand," and off they set. After a number of turns and windings, amongst most beautiful scenery, they arrived in front of a very well planned house, and were told by their conductor "this was house." They thought it remarkable that a hotel should be in such a retired situation. However, upstairs they ran, and sure enough they found their military friends there.

They were congratulating them upon their good quarters, when a lady appeared, to whom they were introduced as the lady of the commandant, whose house it was, and were speedily convinced of their mistake, which produced a hearty laugh. They then, by signs, tried to make their palanquin-boys comprehend that it was a hotel they wanted, and not a private house. These said they understood "Master," and away they all four went towards the town. At a short distance from this the boys stopped at another large building, which appeared more like a hotel than the former. They questioned the lads as to this house, who replied, "All right," so they entered. They met an old gentleman, who requested them to pass into an inner room, where he introduced them to Captain Keppel, who received them most kindly. Their introducer proved to be Captain Quin, of Her Majesty's ship *Minden*, who was on his way home on sick leave in the *Dido*, and the mansion proved to be the Admiralty-house. Captain Keppel, with great kindness, invited the party to a ball and supper, to be given by him on the following evening, to the inhabitants of Penang, previously to his sailing for England.

On leaving the Admiralty-house, the party were directed to a place little better than a booth, and denominated by the natives a punch-house, a name given to all low taverns in India, but which was dignified with the name of "The Albion Hotel." In the only sitting-room of this place they found the officers of the *Dido* at dinner. Of this meal they would have been disappointed, had not those gentlemen kindly invited them to partake of their fare, which consisted principally of curries of various kinds. So poorly was the place furnished that no two articles were alike; chairs, plates, dishes, glasses, knives and forks, were all odd ones, of different colours and sizes. The badness of this accommodation arises from the circumstance that those who call at the island are hospitably entertained, during their stay, at the houses of those residents to whom they happen to be introduced. For this reason a good hotel cannot be supported. After the dinner, which went off with a good deal of fun and mirth, some of the party "chartered ponies for a cruise" in the interior of the island. Penang is remarkable for piebald ponies.

The next evening the party from the *Runnymede* repaired to the admiralty-house, pursuant to invitation, and were hospitably received by Captain Keppel and his officers. There they met the whole of the respectable inhabitants of the island, both civil and military, with their families. The rooms were handsomely decorated, and dancing was kept up with great spirit, enlivened by the harmonious strains of Captain Keppel's private band. This was succeeded, at midnight, by a champagne supper, which, for excellence, might have borne a comparison with any civic entertainment in London. Between three and four in the morning the ladies began to move off, and some of the youngsters, by way of further amusement, sat down to a second supper. At daylight the *Dido* was apeak, under all sails, and by eight o'clock, was leading down the north channel with skysails set for Old England. Her captain and officers carried with them the good wishes of all they left behind at Penang.

At 9 o'clock, A.M., of Sunday, the 3d of November, 1844, the *Runnymede* weighed from Penang-roads with a light southerly wind, and made sail through the north channel. At noon the wind came in from seaward. At midnight, on Monday the 4th, she was abreast of the Ladda Islands, with a barque in company. On Friday, the 8th, the weather was unsettled, with heavy rain. All the small sails were stored, and the royal yards sent down. At noon the sun was obscured. Saturday, the 9th, the breeze increased, with every appearance of bad weather. Took in the top-gallant sails, and reefed the topsails, and took in the jib and spanker. At noon the sun was obscured. Sunday, 10th, the barometer falling fast, with the gale increasing, close reefed the topsails. At noon heavy gusts. The courses were taken in and furled.

At 6 the fore-topsail was taken in, and the ship hove-to under the main topsail and the main trysail. All the sails were re-secured, the top-gallant yards sent down, and everything prepared for the storm, which it was evident was now approaching. At noon the sun was again obscured, the latitude being, by log, 11° 6" north, and the longitude 96° 0" east. The wind now blew a hurricane. The barometer was 29°, and falling. The main-topsail was taken in, and the ship left under the main topsail only.

At half-past three the fore and main top-gallant masts were blown away. The wind was south, and so very severe that the main trysail was blown to atoms, and the ship was lying-to under bare poles, and laying beautifully to the wind, with her helm amidship and perfectly tight. The hurricane was accompanied with a deluge of rain. At 4 P.M. the wind shifted to the south-east, and was blowing so terrifically that all the hatches were obliged to be battened down, the sea making a fair breach over the vessel. The starboard-quarter boat was washed away.

About half-past 6 P.M. there was a lull, and it was nearly calm, the wind backing to the south-west, and the sea became comparatively quiet. The barometer having fallen as low as 28° 45", the ship was kept away north by east, and the topsails re-secured, portions of them having blown adrift. At 8 P.M. the wind began to blow again, and within half an hour the hurricane was as severe as before. The larboard-quarter boat was torn from the davits and blown across the poop, carrying away the binnacle and crushing the hencoops in its passage.

At 9 P.M., the hurricane still increasing, the foremast broke into three pieces, and carried away with it the jib-boom, the main and mizen topmasts, the starboard cathead, and mainyard, the main and mizen masts alone standing. At 10 P.M. the wind and rain were so severe that the men could not hold on upon the poop. The soldiers were engaged in baling the water out of their quarters between decks, whither it had been forced down the hatches. In other respects the ship was quite tight and free from leak, proving herself to be a capital sea boat. The pumps being attended to drew out the water which was forced down the hatches, mast-coats, and topside forwards.

During the hurricane, numbers of land-birds were driven on board—a case not uncommon during storms—and an owl and a hawk were observed perched on the swinging table on the poop, without shewing any alarm at the presence of the ship's company. It was not noticed what became of them. This circumstance tended to shew the intensity of the tempest on shore, which

Ships in a Storm on a Rocky Coast, by Jan Porcellis, 1618.

must have forced these birds out to sea, a distance not much less than two hundred miles from any land.

Monday, 11th.—The hurricane was equally severe, the wind south-east, and the barometer as low as 28° 0". The gusts were so terrific, mixed with drift and rain, that none of the people could stand on the deck. Advantage was therefore taken of the lulls to draw the ship out, and clear away the wreck of the masts. As the starboard bower-anchor was hanging only by the shank-painter, and its stock, which was of iron, was working into the ship's side, the chain-cable was unshackled, and the anchor was cut away from the bows.

At noon, latitude, per log, 11° 6" north longitude 95° 20" east, the barometer apparently rose a little. No observations had been able to be made since the 7th. The hurricane was equally severe in gusts, and the ship perfectly unmanageable from her crippled state, but rode all the time like a sea-bird on the waves, notwithstanding the sea was apparently running from every point of the compass.

The crew observed a large barque ahead of them which had lost its top-mast and mainyard. They feared at first that she would not go clear of them. Happily, however, she drifted past ahead of them. This vessel afterwards proved to have been the *Briton*, of which we shall presently have occasion to speak. They also saw a brig to leeward, totally dismasted. From her appearance it was judged that she must soon have foundered, and every soul on board perished. At 4 in the afternoon the barometer fell to 27° 70", and Cummin's mineral sympiesometer left the index.

The hurricane was now most terrific; the part of the poop to leeward and the cabin-doors and the skylights were literally torn away, and every moment they expected the poop itself to be carried off. None but those who have witnessed so awful a tempest at sea could form an idea of the weight and destructive power of the wind, crushing and beating every thing to pieces, as if it had been done with a heavy metallic body. At 8 P.M. the soldiers and sailors could not stand at the pumps, but were obliged to bale out the water from between decks.

Tuesday, the 12th.—At the turn of the day the hurricane still continued, and the rudder was gone. At 1 A.M. they felt the ship strike, and gave themselves up for lost, expecting every moment to be engulphed in the depths of the ocean.

After a short time, it was discovered that the ship was thrown on a reef of rocks, and had bilged; and although the water entered her through the holes which the rocks had made, and filled her up to the lower beams, yet that it soon smothered, and, the bilge pieces keeping her upright, she lay comparatively quiet. But being fearful that she might beat over the reef into deep water, they let go the larboard bower-anchor, and shortly afterwards found the water leaving her. After this all hands fell asleep, being exhausted with fatigue and hardship. Captain Doutty and the military gentlemen were in Captain Stapleton's cabin, which was the only one habitable. Captain Doutty felt too anxious to rest long, but lay watching whilst all was still, except the beating of the waves and the rain on the poop. He then went out in front of the poop. He could discern nothing but the surf breaking heavily on and around his unfortunate vessel. He then lay down again, wishing earnestly for the break of day.

At length the morning broke, which was to introduce the ship's company, just rescued from a watery grave, to a new era in their existence. With the daybreak the hurricane also began to break, and, though it rained heavily, the barometer rose rapidly until it stood at 29° 45". The captain then beheld, to his great joy, the loom, or land-mark of the shore, to leeward, rising like a black belt, above the breakers. The land was an island, off the east coast of the Great Andaman, in latitude 12° 1" north, and longitude about 93° 14" east. The Andaman Islands, which are about eight in number, and covered with trees, form a group at the entrance of the Bay of Bengal, and are near 750 miles from the Sand Heads at Calcutta, and twelve degrees from the Equator. That on which the vessel was driven was in point of latitude about the centre, and may be easily known by a remarkable hill somewhat resembling a puritan's hat, and being placed in a hollow of the land, with much higher hills, both on the north and south of it. The anchorage is good, and a ship may be sheltered from all points.

About 60 years ago an attempt was made on the part of the East-India Company to form a settlement on the Andaman Islands for the convenience of shipping. Their first settlement was called Port Chatham, on the South Andaman. But, after about a year or two, it was removed thence, on account of its unhealthiness, to the North Andaman, where it was named Port Cornwallis, after Admiral Cornwallis, who recommended the removal, and not long after that was finally broken up, and the islands abandoned.

The ship being nearly dry aft, on the weather clearing, her crew, to their great astonishment, beheld, about a quarter of a mile inside of them, high amongst the trees, in a swamp of mangroves, whither she had forced herself a passage, a large barque, with troops on board. In consequence of this discovery, Ensign Du Vernett was, as soon as possible, lowered with ropes from the *Runnymede's* stern, with twelve soldiers, to communicate with the barque. At 7 A.M., the tide rising, orders were given to the men to prepare to land at next low water, and, if possible, get something cooked, as, during the hurricane, no fires could be kept in the ship, and, consequently, the crew and troops had not had anything but biscuit and a glass of spirits during the storm. At half-past

3 o'clock P.M. the tide having fallen sufficiently to enable the people to wade on shore, Ensign Du Vernett returned on board and reported the vessel he had visited to be the *Briton* from Sydney, bound to Calcutta, and which had sailed from the former place, in company with the ships *Royal Saxon*, *Loyds*, and *Enmore*, on the 12th of August, 1844, having on board Her Majesty's 80th regiment, 1000 strong, under the command of Lieut.-col. Baker. The companies two, three, and six were on board the *Briton*, under the orders of Major, afterwards Lieut.-col. Bunbury, and consisted of 311 soldiers, including 12 serjeants and 4 drummers, 34 women, 51 children, and the following officers, namely, Captains Best, Sayers, and Montgomery; Lieutenants Leslie and Freeman; Ensigns Hunter and Coleman; and Assistant-surgeon Gammie, medical officer in charge. The *Briton* was commanded by Captain Alexander Hall. She had a crew of 34, was a vessel of 776 tons, A 1, and was ascertained to be the same barque which had drifted a-head of the *Runnymede* in the storm, having parted with all her companions, which afterwards arrived safely at their destination. The *Briton* was so short of provisions, that twelve men were obliged to be satisfied with the ordinary allowance of four.

By dusk, all hands, including soldiers, women, and children, had left the wreck of the *Runnymede*, and were accommodated on board the *Briton*. They were received by Captain Hall, Colonel Bunbury, and the officers of the 80th, with the greatest kindness, although they were enduring very great privations themselves. The crew of the *Briton* were delighted to hear of there being a fair stock of stores on board the *Runnymede*, particularly as regarded biscuit and flour, which, if moderate weather continued, would be landed for the benefit of both ships' companies.

In the morning after the wreck, a seaman of the *Runnymede* lost his life by the following piece of disobedience and fool-hardy temerity. Captain Doutty was sitting in Captain Stapleton's cabin, consulting with the military officers as to the best mode of getting the women and children on shore, when it was perceived that one of the seamen had placed himself by the cabin windows, apparently dressed for a swim. Captain Doutty enquired what brought him there: he instantly replied, "We are all alike now." Captain Doutty told him he was mistaken if he thought so, for that whilst two planks of the ship held together, he was determined to keep the command, and ordered him to leave the cabin. As he appeared unwilling to go, the chief officer was desired to send him forward. Being called accordingly, he refused, with an oath, to go, and immediately threw himself from the cabin window, and swam towards the shore, which he never reached, as the receding waves kept him out until he was exhausted, and the ship's company saw him sink without being able to assist him. This man's fate had the effect of keeping the others quiet until the water had fallen sufficiently to enable them to wade through it to the shore.

After the landing Colonel Bunbury took the chief command of all parties.

We shall now find it most convenient to ourselves, as well as entertaining to our readers, to continue our narrative in the shape of a journal, only noticing those days on which any circumstances worth recording occurred.

Wednesday, 13th.—At daybreak, nearly low water, all hands returned on board and commenced getting up provisions for landing. All more or less damaged.

The *Briton* had lost all her boats, and the *Runnymede's* long boat was the only one they had, and that was badly stove, so that the water had run through her, and thereby prevented her being washed off the deck by the waves; and she eventually became the means, by God's blessing, of obtaining that assistance which saved the sufferers from perishing on a desert island.

The carpenters, therefore, of both ships were ordered to report how long a time it would take to put this boat into a state fit to proceed to sea to seek assistance. They reported eight days. After a personal communication, Captains Doutty and Hall received from Captain Sayers, of the 80th regt. the following order, putting their ships' crews under martial law, which was twice read to each crew.

Troop Ship Briton,
12th Nov. 1844.
Dear Sir,

In consequence of the wreck of the troop ships "Briton" and "Runnymede," Major Bunbury calls on Captains Hall and Doutty to explain to the crews of their respective ships that they are from this moment under military law, and feeling it to be most essential for the well-being of the service that the strictest order and discipline be preserved by every one under his command, declares it to be his determination to punish, with the utmost severity, any act of insubordination and drunkenness.
By Order, H. T. Sayers,
Capt. 80th Regt.
To Capt. Doutty.

This day were landed from the *Runnymede* at low water, 37 bags and 6 half-bags of biscuit, 3 and a half bags of flour, and 9 baskets of plums. In consequence of information that the crew of the *Runnymede* meant to help themselves to the beer which formed part of the cargo, and had laid a plan to plunder the ship, they were in the evening all ordered on board the *Briton*. The only persons who remained on board the *Runnymede* were Captain Doutty and his officers, and a few steady soldiers of the 50th, and watches were regularly kept throughout the night.

There appears to be a very prevalent opinion amongst common sailors and private soldiers, that when a vessel is wrecked, all control over private property is from that moment lost too, and that it is not stealing to lay hands on all they can take. Numerous instances of this kind took place on the present occasion. And this crime, as well as that of drunkenness, were scarcely checked by severe corporeal punishment. Some of the men attempted thefts at the risk of their lives; and, in one instance, a cask of bottled beer having been landed too late to be got into store, was placed, by a serjeant's tent, in care of a sentry, whose musket was known to be loaded with ball. During the night two fellows attempted to get at it, and being discovered were fired at, which so alarmed them, that one of them, in his hurry to escape, fell into a mangrove swamp, which caused him so much pain that he was easily captured. He proved to be a man of bad character.

Thursday, 14th.—Weather moderate, wind east, barometer 29° 55". The crew employed this day landing stores, cleansing the decks from the accumulated filth and rubbish. The carpenters employed on the long boat. The stores landed were 3 baskets of sugar, 2 barrels of flour, 7 tierces and 1 barrel of salt provisions, 1 cask of vinegar, 1 puncheon of arrack, 2 cases of bottled fruits, 2 boxes of pickles, 6 barrels of pale ale, and 1 cask of sherry. The soldiers were employed on shore clearing the ground of trees, many having been thrown down by the hurricane, some of them very large, and apparently of the growth of a century. They were also employed in erecting tents and making roads and bridges. The tents were made of the sails of both ships, and the flags or camp-colours used to distinguish the companies, were Marryat's signals, also from the ships.

Friday, 15th.—Wind east and moderate. Weather fine. Continued landing provisions consisting of soap, preserved potatoes, biscuit, flour, sugar, dholl or split peas, rice, pale ale, port wine, and sherry. Finished the long boat's bottom, turned her up, and commenced raising her two streaks. Employed drying damaged provisions. Water discovered in the island; and a number of crabs, prawns, and other shell fish picked up at low water. Several indications of other wrecks were seen, but exploring parties had not yet straggled far from the encampment.

Saturday, 16th.—More provisions were landed this day. In the evening, large fires were seen on the island to the north, and as several muskets were discharged on shore away from the camp, and the people fancied they saw natives, they were hailed and a volley of musketry discharged, so no more of them were seen. But double watches were set at night with loaded arms.

La Balsa de la Medusa, by Théodore Géricault, 1818-9. Louvre.

8.

ESCAPING THE SINKING *MEDUSA*

CHARLOTTE-ADÉLAÏDE DARD

At noon, on the 2d of July, soundings were taken. M. Maudet, ensign of the watch, was convinced we were upon the edge of the Arguin Bank. The Captain said to him, as well as to every one, that there was no cause of alarm. In the mean while, the wind blowing with great violence, impelled us nearer and nearer to the danger which menaced us. A species of stupor overpowered all our spirits, and every one preserved a mournful silence, as if they were persuaded we would soon touch the bank.

The colour of the water entirely changed, a circumstance even remarked by the ladies. About three in the afternoon, being in 19° 30' north latitude, and 19° 45' west longitude, a universal cry was heard upon deck. All declared they saw sand rolling among the ripple of the sea. The Captain in an instant ordered to sound. The line gave eighteen fathoms; but on a second sounding it only gave six. He at last saw his error, and hesitated no longer on changing the route, but it was too late. A strong concussion told us the frigate had struck. Terror and consternation were instantly depicted on every face. The crew stood motionless; the passengers in utter despair.

In the midst of this general panic, cries of vengeance were heard against the principal author of our misfortunes, wishing to throw him overboard; but some generous persons interposed, and endeavoured to calm their spirits, by diverting their attention to the means of our safety. The confusion was already so great, that M. Poinsignon, commandant of a troop, struck my sister Caroline a severe blow, doubtless thinking it was one of his soldiers. At this crisis my father was buried in profound sleep, but he quickly awoke, the cries and the tumult upon deck having informed him of our misfortunes.

He poured out a thousand reproaches on those whose ignorance and boasting had been so disastrous to us. However, they set about the means of averting our danger. The officers, with an altered voice, issued their orders, expecting every moment to see the ship go in pieces. They strove to lighten her, but the sea was very rough and the current strong. Much time was lost in doing nothing; they only pursued half measures, and all of them unfortunately failed.

When it was discovered that the danger of the *Medusa* was not so great as was at first supposed, various persons proposed to transport the troops to the island of Arguin, which was conjectured to be not far from the place where we lay aground. Others advised to take us all successively to the coast of the desert of Sahara, by the means of our boats, and with provisions sufficient to form a caravan, to reach the island of Saint Louis, at Senegal. The events which afterwards ensued proved this plan to have been the best, and which would have been crowned with success; unfortunately it was not adopted. M. Schmaltz, the governor, suggested the making of a raft of a sufficient size to carry two hundred men, with provisions: which latter plan was seconded by the two officers of the frigate, and put in execution.

The fatal raft was then begun to be constructed, which would, they said, carry provisions for every one. Masts, planks, boards, cordage, were thrown over board. Two officers were charged with the framing of these together. Large barrels were emptied and placed at the angles of the machine, and the workmen were taught to say, that the passengers would be in greater security there, and more at their ease, than in the boats. However, as it was forgotten to erect rails, every one supposed, and with reason, that those who had given the plan of the raft, had had no design of embarking upon it themselves.

When it was completed, the two chief officers of the frigate publicly promised, that all the boats would tow it to the shore of the Desert; and, when there, stores of provisions and fire-arms would be given us to form a caravan to take us all to Senegal. Why was not this plan executed? Why were these promises, sworn before the French flag, made in vain? But it is necessary to draw a veil over the past. I will only add, that if these promises had been fulfilled, every one would have been saved, and that, in spite of the detestable egotism of certain personages, humanity would not now have had to deplore the scenes of horror consequent on the wreck of the *Medusa*!

On the 3d of July, the efforts were renewed to disengage the frigate, but without success. We then prepared to quit her. The sea became very rough, and the wind blew with great violence. Nothing now was heard but the plaintive and confused cries of a multitude, consisting of more than four hundred persons, who, seeing death before their eyes, deplored their hard fate in bitter lamentations.

On the 4th, there was a glimpse of hope. At the hour the tide flowed, the frigate, being considerably lightened by all that had been thrown over board, was found nearly afloat; and it is very certain, if on that day they had thrown the artillery into the water, the *Medusa* would have been saved; but M. Lachaumareys said, he could not thus sacrifice the King's cannon, as if the frigate did not belong to the King also. However, the sea ebbed, and the ship sinking into the sand deeper than ever, made them relinquish that on which depended our last ray of hope.

On the approach of night, the fury of the winds redoubled, and the sea became very rough. The frigate then received some tremendous concussions, and the water rushed into the hold in the most terrific manner, but the pumps would not work. We had now no alternative but to abandon her for the frail boats, which any single wave would overwhelm. Frightful gulfs environed us; mountains of water raised their liquid summits in the distance. How were we to escape so many dangers? Whither could we go? What hospitable land would receive us on its shores? My thoughts, then reverted to our beloved country. I did not regret Paris, but I could have esteemed myself happy to have been yet in the marshes on the road to Rochefort. Then starting suddenly from my reverie, I exclaimed: "O terrible condition! that black and boundless sea resembles the eternal night which will ingulf us! All those who surround me seem yet tranquil; but that fatal calm will soon be succeeded by the most frightful torments. Fools, what had we to find in Senegal, to make us trust to the most perfidious of elements! Did France not afford every necessary for our happiness? Happy! yes, thrice happy, they who never set foot on a foreign soil! Great God! succour all these unfortunate beings; save our unhappy family!"

My father perceived my distress, but how could he console me? What words could calm my fears, and place me above the apprehension of those dangers to which we were exposed? How, in a word, could I assume a serene appearance, when friends, parents, and all that was most dear to me were, in all human probability, on the very verge of destruction? Alas! my fears were but too well founded. For I soon perceived that, although we were the only ladies, besides the Misses Schmaltz, who formed a part of the Governor's suit, they had the barbarity of intending our family to embark upon the raft, where were only soldiers, sailors, planters of Cape Verd, and some generous officers who had not the honour (if it could be accounted one) of being considered among the ignorant confidents of MM. Schmaltz and Lachaumareys.

My father, indignant at a proceeding so indecorous, swore we would not embark upon the raft, and that, if we were not judged worthy of a place in one of the six boats, he would himself, his wife, and children, remain on board the wrecks of the frigate. The tone in which he spoke these words, was that of a man resolute to avenge any insult that might be offered to him. The governor of Senegal, doubtless fearing the world would one day reproach him for his inhumanity, decided we should have a place in one of the boats. This having in some measure quieted our fears concerning our unfortunate situation, I was desirous of taking some repose, but the uproar among the crew was so great I could not obtain it.

Aftercastle of Méduse, by Ambrose-Louis Garneray, 1816.

Towards midnight, a passenger came to inquire at my father if we were disposed to depart; he replied, we had been forbid to go yet. However, we were soon convinced that a great part of the crew and various passengers were secretly preparing to set off in the boats. A conduct so perfidious could not fail to alarm us, especially as we perceived among those so eager to embark unknown to us, several who had promised, but a little while before, not to go without us.

M. Schmaltz, to prevent that which was going on upon deck, instantly rose to endeavour to quiet their minds; but the soldiers had already assumed a threatening attitude, and, holding cheap the words of their commander, swore they would fire upon whosoever attempted to depart in a clandestine manner. The firmness of these brave men produced the desired effect, and all was restored to order. The governor returned to his cabin; and those who were desirous of departing furtively were confused and covered with shame. The governor, however, was ill at ease; and as he had heard very distinctly certain energetic words which had been addressed to him, he judged it proper to assemble a council. All the officers and passengers being collected, M. Schmaltz there solemnly swore before them not to abandon the raft, and a second time promised, that all the boats would tow it to the shore of the Desert, where they would all be formed into a caravan. I confess this conduct of the governor greatly satisfied every member of our family; for we never dreamed he would deceive us, nor act in a manner contrary to what he had promised.

About three in the morning, some hours after the meeting of the council, a terrible noise was heard in the powder room; it was the helm which was broken. All who were sleeping were roused by it. On going on deck every one was more and more convinced that the frigate was lost beyond all recovery. Alas! the wreck was for our family the commencement of a horrible series of misfortunes. The two chief officers then decided with one accord, that all should embark at six in the morning, and abandon the ship to the mercy of the waves. After this decision, followed a scene the most whimsical, and at the same time the most melancholy that can be well conceived. To have a more distinct idea of it, let the reader transport himself in imagination to the midst of the liquid plains of the ocean; then let him picture to himself a multitude of all classes, of every age, tossed about at the mercy of the waves upon a dismasted vessel, foundered, and half submerged; let him not forget these are thinking beings with the certain prospect before them of having reached the goal of their existence.

Separated from the rest of the world by a boundless sea, and having no place of refuge but the wrecks of a grounded vessel, the multitude addressed at first their vows to heaven, and forgot, for a moment, all earthly concerns. Then, suddenly starting from their lethargy, they began to look after their wealth, the merchandise they had in small ventures, utterly regardless of the elements which threatened them. The miser, thinking of the gold contained in his coffers, hastening to put it in a place of safety, either by sewing it into the lining of his clothes, or by cutting out for it a place in the waistband of his trousers.

The smuggler was tearing his hair at not being able to save a chest of contraband which he had secretly got on board, and with which he had hoped to have gained two or three hundred per cent. Another, selfish to excess, was throwing over board all his hidden money, and amusing himself by burning all his effects. A generous officer was opening his portmanteau, offering caps, stockings, and shirts, to any who would take them. These had scarcely gathered together their various effects, when they learned that they could not take any thing with them; those were searching the cabins and store-rooms to carry away every thing that was valuable.

Ship-boys were discovering the delicate wines and fine liqueurs, which a wise foresight had placed in reserve. Soldiers and sailors were penetrating even into the spirit-room, broaching casks, staving others, and drinking till they fell exhausted. Soon the tumult of the inebriated made us forget the roaring of the sea which threatened to ingulf us. At last the uproar was at its height; the soldiers no longer listened to the voice of their captain. Some knit their brows and muttered oaths; but nothing could be done with those whom wine had rendered furious. Next, piercing cries mixed with doleful groans were heard—this was the signal of departure.

At six o'clock on the morning of the 5th, a great part of the military were embarked upon the raft, which was already covered with a large sheet of foam. The soldiers were expressly prohibited from taking their arms. A young officer of infantry, whose brain seemed to be powerfully affected, put his horse beside the barricadoes of the frigate, and then, armed with two pistols, threatened to fire upon any one who refused to go upon the raft. Forty men had scarcely descended when it sunk to the depth of about two feet. To facilitate the embarking of a greater number, they were obliged to throw over several barrels of provisions which had been placed upon it the day before. In this manner did this furious officer get about one hundred and fifty heaped upon that floating tomb; but he did not think of adding one more to the number by descending himself, as he ought to have done, but went peaceably away, and placed himself in one of the best boats. There should have been sixty sailors upon the raft, and there were but about ten. A list had been made out on the 4th, assigning each his proper place; but this wise precaution being disregarded, every one pursued the plan he deemed the best for his own preservation. The precipitation with which they forced one hundred and fifty unfortunate beings upon the raft was such that they forgot to give them one morsel of biscuit. However, they threw towards them twenty-five pounds in a sack, whilst they were not far from the frigate; but it fell into the sea, and was with difficulty recovered.

During this disaster, the governor of Senegal, who was busied in the care of his own dear self, effeminately descended in an arm-chair into the barge, where were already various large chests, all kinds of provisions, his dearest friends, his daughter and his wife. Afterwards the captain's boat received twenty-seven persons, amongst whom were twenty-five sailors, good rowers. The shallop, commanded by M. Espiau, ensign of the ship, took forty-five passengers, and put off. The boat, called the *Senegal*, took twenty-five; the pinnace thirty-three; and the yawl, the smallest of all the boats, took only ten.

Almost all the officers, the passengers, the mariners and supernumeraries, were already embarked—all, but our weeping family, who still remained upon the boards of the frigate, till some charitable souls would kindly receive us into a boat. Surprised at this abandonment, I instantly felt myself roused, and, calling with all my might to the officers of the boats, besought them to take our unhappy family along with them. Soon after, the barge, in which were the governor of Senegal and all his family, approached the *Medusa*, as if still to take some passengers, for there were but few in it. I made a motion to descend, hoping that the Misses Schmaltz, who had, till that day, taken a great interest in our family, would allow us a place in their boat; but I was mistaken: those ladies, who had embarked in a mysterious incognito, had already forgotten us; and M. Lachaumareys, who was still on the frigate, positively told me they would not embark along with us.

Nevertheless I ought to tell, what we learned afterwards, that that officer who commanded the pinnace had received orders to take us in, but, as he was already a great way from the frigate, we were certain he had abandoned us. My father however hailed him, but he persisted on his way to gain the open sea. A short while afterwards we perceived a small boat among the waves, which seemed desirous to approach the *Medusa*; it was the yawl.

When it was sufficiently near, my father implored the sailors who were in it to take us on board, and to carry us to the pinnace, where our family ought to be placed. They refused. He then seized a firelock, which lay by chance upon deck, and swore he would kill every one of them if they refused to take us into the yawl, adding that it was the property of the king, and that he would have advantage from it as well as another.

The sailors murmured, but durst not resist, and received all our family, which consisted of nine persons, viz. Four children, our stepmother, my cousin, my sister Caroline, my father, and myself. A small box, filled with valuable papers, which we wished to save, some clothes, two bottles of ratafia, which we had endeavoured to preserve amidst our misfortunes, were seized and thrown over board by the sailors of the yawl, who told us we would find in the pinnace every thing which we could wish for our voyage.

We had then only the clothes which covered us, never thinking of dressing ourselves in two suits; but the loss which affected us most was that of several MSS. at which my father had been labouring for a long while. Our trunks, our linen, and various chests of merchandise of great value, in a word, every thing we possessed, was left in the *Medusa*. When we boarded the pinnace, the officer who commanded it began excusing himself for having set off without forewarning us, as he had been ordered, and said a thousand things in his justification. But without believing the half of his fine protestations, we felt very happy in having overtaken him; for it is most certain they had had no intention of encumbering themselves with our unfortunate family. I say encumber, for it is evident that four children, one of whom was yet at the breast, were very indifferent beings to people who were actuated by a selfishness without all parallel.

When we were seated in the long-boat, my father dismissed the sailors with the yawl, telling them he would ever gratefully remember their services. They speedily departed, but little satisfied with the good action they had done. My father hearing their murmurs and the abuse they poured out against us, said, loud enough for all in the boat to hear: "We are not surprised sailors are destitute of shame, when their officers blush at being compelled

to do a good action." The commandant of the boat feigned not to understand the reproaches conveyed in these words, and, to divert our minds from
brooding over our wrongs, endeavoured to counterfeit the man of gallantry.

All the boats were already far from the *Medusa*, when they were brought
to, to form a chain in order to tow the raft. The barge, in which was the
governor of Senegal, took the first tow, then all the other boats in succession
joined themselves to that. M. Lachaumareys embarked, although there yet
remained upon the *Medusa* more than sixty persons. Then the brave and
generous M. Espiau, commander of the shallop, quitted the line of boats, and
returned to the frigate, with the intention of saving all the wretches who had
been abandoned. They all sprung into the shallop; but as it was very much
overloaded, seventeen unfortunates preferred remaining on board, rather
than expose themselves as well as their companions to certain death. But,
alas! the greater part afterwards fell victims to their fears or their devotion.

Fifty-two days after they were abandoned, no more than three of them
were alive, and these looked more like skeletons than men. They told that
their miserable companions had gone afloat upon planks and hen-coops, after having waited in vain forty-two days for the succour which had been
promised them, and that all had perished.

The shallop, carrying with difficulty all those she had saved from the
Medusa, slowly rejoined the line of boats which towed the raft. M. Espiau
earnestly besought the officers of the other boats to take some of them along
with them; but they refused, alleging to the generous officer that he ought
to keep them in his own boat, as he had gone for them himself. M. Espiau,
finding it impossible to keep them all without exposing them to the utmost
peril, steered right for a boat which I will not name.

Immediately a sailor sprung from the shallop into the sea, and endeavoured to reach it by swimming; and when he was about to enter it, an officer who possessed great influence, pushed him back, and, drawing his sa-
bre, threatened to cut off his hands, if he again made the attempt. The poor
wretch regained the shallop, which was very near the pinnace, where we were.
Various friends of my father supplicated M. Lapérère, the officer of our boat,

to receive him on board. My father had his arms already out to catch him, when M. Lapérère instantly let go the rope which attached us to the other boats, and tugged off with all his force. At the same instant every boat imitated our execrable example; and wishing to shun the approach of the shallop, which sought for assistance, stood off from the raft, abandoning in the midst of the ocean, and to the fury of the waves, the miserable mortals whom they had sworn to land on the shores of the Desert.

Scarcely had these cowards broken their oath, when we saw the French flag flying upon the raft. The confidence of these unfortunate persons was so great, that when they saw the first boat which had the tow removing from them, they all cried out, the rope is broken! the rope is broken! but when no attention was paid to their observation they instantly perceived the treachery of the wretches who had left them so basely. Then the cries of *Vive le Roi* arose from the raft, as if the poor fellows were calling to their father for assistance; or, as if they had been persuaded that, at that rallying word, the officers of the boats would return, and not abandon their countrymen. The officers repeated the cry of *Vive le Roi*, without a doubt, to insult them; but, more particularly, M. Lachaumareys, who, assuming a martial attitude, waved his hat in the air. Alas! what availed these false professions?

Frenchmen, menaced with the greatest peril, were demanding assistance with the cries of *Vive le Roi*; yet none were found sufficiently generous, nor sufficiently French, to go to aid them. After a silence of some minutes, horrible cries were heard; the air resounded with the groans, the lamentations, the imprecations of these wretched beings, and the echo of the sea frequently repeated, Alas! how cruel you are to abandon us!!! The raft already appeared to be buried under the waves, and its unfortunate passengers immersed.

The fatal machine was drifted by currents far behind the wreck of the Frigate; without cable, anchor, mast, sail, oars; in a word, without the smallest means of enabling them to save themselves. Each wave that struck it, made them stumble in heaps on one another. Their feet getting entangled among the cordage, and between the planks, bereaved them of the faculty of moving. Maddened by these misfortunes, suspended, and adrift upon a merciless ocean, they were soon tortured between the pieces of wood which formed the scaffold on which they floated. The bones of their feet and their legs were bruised and broken, every time the fury of the waves agitated the raft; their flesh covered with contusions and hideous wounds, dissolved, as it were, in the briny waves, whilst the roaring flood around them was coloured with their blood.

As the raft, when it was abandoned, was nearly two leagues from the frigate, it was impossible these unfortunate persons could return to it: they were soon after far out at sea. These victims still appeared above their floating tomb; and, stretching out their supplicating hands towards the boats which fled from them, seemed yet to invoke, for the last time, the names of the wretches who had deceived them. O horrid day! a day of shame and reproach! Alas! that the hearts of those who were so well acquainted with misfortune, should have been so inaccessible to pity!

After witnessing that most inhuman scene, and seeing they were insensible to the cries and lamentations of so many unhappy beings, I felt my heart bursting with sorrow. It seemed to me that the waves would overwhelm all these wretches, and I could not suppress my tears. My father, exasperated to excess, and bursting with rage at seeing so much cowardice and inhumanity among the officers of the boats, began to regret he had not accepted the place which had been assigned for us upon the fatal raft. "At least," said he, "we would have died with the brave, or we would have returned to the wreck of the *Medusa*; and not have had the disgrace of saving ourselves with cowards." Although this produced no effect upon the officers, it proved very fatal to us afterwards; for, on our arrival at Senegal, it was reported to the Governor, and very probably was the principal cause of all those evils and vexations which we endured in that colony.

Let us now turn our attention to the several situations of all those who were endeavouring to save themselves in the different boats, as well as to those left upon the wreck of the *Medusa*.

We have already seen, that the frigate was half sunk when it was deserted, presenting nothing but a hulk and wreck. Nevertheless, seventeen still remained upon it, and had food, which, although damaged, enabled them to support themselves for a considerable time; whilst the raft was abandoned to float at the mercy of the waves, upon the vast surface of the ocean. One hundred and fifty wretches were embarked upon it, sunk to the depth of at least three feet on its fore part, and on its poop immersed even to the middle. What victuals they had were soon consumed, or spoiled by the salt water; and perhaps some, as the waves hurried them along, became food for the monsters of the deep.

Two only of all the boats which left the *Medusa,* and these with very few people in them, were provisioned with every necessary; these struck off with security and despatch. But the condition of those who were in the shallop was but little better than those upon the raft; their great number, their scarcity of provisions, their great distance from the shore, gave them the most melancholy anticipations of the future. Their worthy commander, M. Espiau, had no other hope but of reaching the shore as soon as possible.

The other boats were less filled with people, but they were scarcely better provisioned; and, as by a species of fatality, the pinnace, in which were our family, was destitute of every thing. Our provisions consisted of a barrel of biscuit, and a tierce of water; and, to add to our misfortunes, the biscuit being soaked in the sea, it was almost impossible to swallow one morsel of it. Each passenger in our boat was obliged to sustain his wretched existence with a glass of water, which he could get only once a day. To tell how this happened, how this boat was so poorly supplied, whilst there were abundance left upon the *Medusa,* is far beyond my power. But it is at least certain, that the greater part of the officers commanding the boats, the shallop, the pinnace, the Senegal boat, and the yawl, were persuaded, when they quitted the frigate, that they would not abandon the raft, but that all the expedition would sail together to the coast of Sahara; that when there, the boats would be again sent to the *Medusa* to take provisions, arms, and those who were left there; but it appears the chiefs had decided otherwise.

After abandoning the raft, although scattered, all the boats formed a little fleet, and followed the same route. All who were sincere hoped to arrive the same day at the coast of the Desert, and that every one would get on shore; but MM. Schmaltz and Lachaumareys gave orders to take the route for Senegal. This sudden change in the resolutions of the chiefs was like a thunderbolt to the officers commanding the boats. Having nothing on board but what was barely necessary to enable us to allay the cravings of hunger for one day, we were all sensibly affected. The other boats, which, like ourselves, hoped to have got on shore at the nearest point, were a little better provisioned than we were; they had at least a little wine, which supplied the place of other necessaries.

We then demanded some from them, explaining our situation, but none would assist us, not even Captain Lachaumareys, who, drinking to a kept mistress, supported by two sailors, swore he had not one drop on board. We were next desirous of addressing the boat of the Governor of Senegal, where we were persuaded were plenty of provisions of every kind, such as oranges, biscuits, cakes, comfits, plumbs, and even the finest liqueurs; but my father opposed it, so well was he assured we would not obtain any thing.

We will now turn to the condition of those on the raft, when the boats left them to themselves.

If all the boats had continued dragging the raft forward, favoured as we were by the breeze from the sea, we would have been able to have conducted them to the shore in less than two days. But an inconceivable fatality caused the generous plan to be abandoned which had been formed.

When the raft had lost sight of the boats, a spirit of sedition began to manifest itself in furious cries. They then began to regard one another with ferocious looks, and to thirst for one another's flesh. Some one had already whispered of having recourse to that monstrous extremity, and of commencing with the fattest and youngest. A proposition so atrocious filled the brave Captain Dupont and his worthy lieutenant M. L'Heureux with horror; and that courage which had so often supported them in the field of glory, now forsook them.

Among the first who fell under the hatchets of the assassins, was a young woman who had been seen devouring the body of her husband. When her turn was come, she sought a little wine as a last favour, then rose, and without uttering one word, threw herself into the sea. Captain Dupont being proscribed for having refused to partake of the sacrilegious viands with which the monsters were feeding on, was saved as by a miracle from the hands of the butchers. Scarcely had they seized him to lead him to the slaughter, when a large pole, which served in place of a mast, fell upon his body; and believing that his legs were broken, they contented themselves by throwing him into the sea. The unfortunate captain plunged, disappeared, and they thought him already in another world.

Providence, however, revived the strength of the unfortunate warrior. He emerged under the beams of the raft, and clinging with all his might, holding his head above water, he remained between two enormous pieces of wood, whilst the rest of his body was hid in the sea. After more than two hours of suffering, Captain Dupont spoke in a low voice to his lieutenant, who by chance was seated near the place of his concealment. The brave L'Heureux, with eyes glistening with tears, believed he heard the voice, and saw the shade of his captain; and trembling, was about to quit the place of horror; but, O wonderful! he saw a head which seemed to draw its last sigh, he recognised it, he embraced it, alas! it was his dear friend! Dupont was instantly drawn from the water, and M. L'Heureux obtained for his unfortunate comrade again a place upon the raft. Those who had been most inveterate against him, touched at what Providence had done for him in so miraculous a manner, decided with one accord to allow him entire liberty upon the raft.

The sixty unfortunates who had escaped from the first massacre, were soon reduced to fifty, then to forty, and at last to twenty-eight. The least murmur, or the smallest complaint, at the moment of distributing the provisions, was a crime punished with immediate death. In consequence of such a regulation, it may easily be presumed the raft was soon lightened. In the meanwhile the wine diminished sensibly, and the half rations very much displeased a certain chief of the conspiracy. On purpose to avoid being reduced to that extremity, the *executive power* decided it was much wiser to *drown thirteen people,* and to get full rations, than that twenty-eight should have half rations. Merciful Heaven! what shame! After the last catastrophe, the chiefs of the conspiracy, fearing doubtless of being assassinated in their turn, threw all the arms into the sea, and swore an inviolable friendship with the heroes which the hatchet had spared.

On the 17th of July, in the morning, Captain Parnajon, commandant of the *Argus* brig, still found fifteen men on the raft. They were immediately taken on board, and conducted to Senegal. Four of the fifteen are yet alive, viz. Captain Dupont, residing in the neighbourhood of Maintenon, Lieutenant L'Heureux, since Captain, at Senegal, Savigny, at Rochefort, and Corréard, I know not where.

On the 5th of July, at ten in the morning, one hour after abandoning the raft, and three after quitting the *Medusa*, M. Lapérère, the officer of our boat, made the first distribution of provisions. Each passenger had a small glass of water and nearly the fourth of a biscuit. Each drank his allowance of water at one draught, but it was found impossible to swallow one morsel of our biscuit, it being so impregnated with sea-water. It happened, however, that some was found not quite so saturated. Of these we eat a small portion, and put back the remainder for a future day. Our voyage would have been sufficiently agreeable, if the beams of the sun had not been so fierce. On the evening we perceived the shores of the Desert; but as the two chiefs (MM. Schmaltz and Lachaumareys) wished to go right for Senegal, notwithstanding we were still one hundred leagues from it, we were not allowed to land.

Several officers remonstrated, both on account of our want of provisions and the crowded condition of the boats, for undertaking so dangerous a voyage. Others urged with equal force, that it would be dishonouring the French name, if we were to neglect the unfortunate people on the raft, and insisted we should be set on shore, and whilst we waited there, three boats should return to look after the raft, and three to the wrecks of the frigate, to take up the seventeen who were left there, as well as a sufficient quantity of provisions to enable us to go to Senegal by the way of Barbary. But MM. Schmaltz and Lachaumareys, whose boats were sufficiently well provisioned, scouted the advice of their subalterns, and ordered them to cast anchor till the following morning.

They were obliged to obey these orders, and to relinquish their designs. During the night, a certain passenger, who was doubtless no doctor, and who believed in ghosts and witches, was suddenly frightened by the appearance of flames, which he thought he saw in the waters of the sea, a little way from where our boat was anchored. My father, and some others, who were aware that the sea is sometimes phosphorated, confirmed the poor credulous man in his belief, and added several circumstances which fairly turned his brain. They persuaded him the Arabic sorcerers had fired the sea to prevent us from travelling along their deserts.

On the morning of the 6th of July, at five o'clock, all the boats were under way on the route to Senegal. The boats of MM. Schmaltz and Lachaumareys took the lead along the coast, and all the expedition followed. About eight, several sailors in our boat, with threats, demanded to be set on shore; but M. Lapérère, not acceding to their request, the whole were about to revolt and seize the command; but the firmness of this officer quelled the mutineers.

In a spring which he made to seize a firelock which a sailor persisted in keeping in his possession, he almost tumbled into the sea. My father fortunately was near him, and held him by his clothes, but he had instantly to quit him, for fear of losing his hat, which the waves were floating away. A short while after this slight accident, the shallop, which we had lost sight of since the morning, appeared desirous of rejoining us. We plied all hands to avoid her, for we were afraid of one another, and thought that that boat, encumbered with so many people, wished to board us to oblige us to take some of its passengers, as M. Espiau would not suffer them to be abandoned like those upon the raft.

That officer hailed us at a distance, offering to take our family on board, adding, he was anxious to take about sixty people to the Desert. The officer of our boat, thinking that this was a pretence, replied, we preferred suffering where we were. It even appeared to us that M. Espiau had hid some of his people under the benches of the shallop. But, alas! in the end we deeply deplored being so suspicious, and of having so outraged the devotion of the most generous officer of the *Medusa*.

Our boat began to leak considerably, but we prevented it as well as we could, by stuffing the largest holes with oakum, which an old sailor had had the precaution to take before quitting the frigate. At noon the heat became so strong—so intolerable, that several of us believed we had reached our last moments. The hot winds of the Desert even reached us; and the fine sand with which they were loaded, had completely obscured the clearness of the atmosphere. The sun presented a reddish disk; the whole surface of the ocean became nebulous, and the air which we breathed, depositing a fine sand, an impalpable powder, penetrated to our lungs, already parched with a burning thirst.

In this state of torment we remained till four in the afternoon, when a breeze from the north-west brought us some relief. Notwithstanding the privations we felt, and especially the burning thirst which had become intolerable, the cool air which we now began to breathe, made us in part forget our sufferings. The heavens began again to resume the usual serenity of those latitudes, and we hoped to have passed a good night. A second distribution of provisions was made; each received a small glass of water, and about the eighth part of a biscuit. Notwithstanding our meagre fare, every one seemed content, in the persuasion we would reach Senegal by the morrow. But how vain were all our hopes, and what sufferings had we yet to endure!

At half past seven, the sky was covered with stormy clouds. The serenity we had admired a little while before, entirely disappeared, and gave place to the most gloomy obscurity. The surface of the ocean presented all the signs of a coming tempest. The horizon on the side of the Desert had the appearance of a long hideous chain of mountains piled on one another, the summits of which seemed to vomit fire and smoke. Bluish clouds, streaked with a dark copper colour, detached themselves from that shapeless heap, and came and joined with those which floated over our heads. In less than half an hour the ocean seemed confounded with the terrible sky which canopied us. The stars were hid. Suddenly a frightful noise was heard from the west, and all the waves of the sea rushed to founder our frail bark.

A fearful silence succeeded to the general consternation. Every tongue was mute; and none durst communicate to his neighbour the horror with which his mind was impressed. At intervals the cries of the children rent our hearts. At that instant a weeping and agonized mother bared her breast to her dying child, but it yielded nothing to appease the thirst of the little innocent who pressed it in vain. O night of horrors! what pen is capable to paint thy terrible picture! How describe the agonizing fears of a father and mother, at the sight of their children tossed about and expiring of hunger in a small boat, which the winds and waves threatened to ingulf at every instant! Having full before our eyes the prospect of inevitable death, we gave ourselves up to our unfortunate condition, and addressed our prayers to Heaven. The winds growled with the utmost fury; the tempestuous waves arose exasperated. In their terrific encounter a mountain of water was precipitated into our boat, carrying away one of the sails, and the greater part of the effects which the sailors had saved from the *Medusa*. Our bark was nearly sunk; the females and the children lay rolling in its bottom, drinking the waters of bitterness; and their cries, mixed with the roaring of the waves and the furious north wind, increased the horrors of the scene. My unfortunate father then experienced the most excruciating agony of mind. The idea of the loss which the shipwreck had occasioned to him, and the danger which still menaced all he held dearest in the world, plunged him into a deep swoon. The tenderness of his wife and children recovered him; but alas! his recovery was to still more bitterly to deplore the wretched situation of his family. He clasped us to his bosom; he bathed us with his tears, and seemed as if he was regarding us with his last looks of love.

Every soul in the boat were seized with the same perturbation, but it manifested itself in different ways. One part of the sailors remained motionless, in a bewildered state; the other cheered and encouraged one another; the children, locked in the arms of their parents, wept incessantly. Some demanded drink, vomiting the salt water which choked them; others, in short, embraced as for the last time, intertwining their arms, and vowing to die together.

In the meanwhile the sea became rougher and rougher. The whole surface of the ocean seemed a vast plain furrowed with huge blackish waves fringed with white foam. The thunder growled around us, and the lightning discovered to our eyes all that our imagination could conceive most horrible. Our boat, beset on all sides by the winds, and at every instant tossed on the summit of mountains of water, was very nearly sunk in spite of our every effort in baling it, when we discovered a large hole in its poop. It was instantly stuffed with every thing we could find;—old clothes, sleeves of shirts, shreds of coats, shawls, useless bonnets, every thing was employed, and secured us as far as it was possible. During the space of six hours, we rowed suspended alternately between hope and fear, between life and death. At last towards the middle of the night, Heaven, which had seen our resignation, commanded the floods to be still. Instantly the sea became less rough, the veil which covered the sky became less obscure, the stars again shone out, and the tempest seemed to withdraw. A general exclamation of joy and thankfulness issued at one instant from every mouth. The winds calmed, and each of us sought a little sleep, whilst our good and generous pilot steered our boat on a still very stormy sea.

The day at last, the day so desired, entirely restored the calm; but it brought no other consolation. During the night, the currents, the waves, and the winds had taken us so far out to sea, that, on the dawning of the 7th of July, we saw nothing but sky and water, without knowing whether to direct our course; for our compass had been broken during the tempest. In this hopeless condition, we continued to steer sometimes to the right and sometimes to the left, until the sun arose, and at last showed us the east.

On the morning of the 7th of July, we again saw the shores of the Desert, notwithstanding we were yet a great distance from it. The sailors renewed their murmurings, wishing to get on shore, with the hope of being able to get some wholesome plants, and some more palatable water than that of the sea; but as we were afraid of the Moors, their request was opposed. However, M. Lapérère proposed to take them as near as he could to the first breakers on the coast; and when there, those who wished to go on shore should throw themselves into the sea, and swim to land. Eleven accepted the proposal; but when we had reached the first waves, none had the courage to brave the mountains of water which rolled between them and the beach.

Our sailors then betook themselves to their benches and oars, and promised to be more quiet for the future. A short while after, a third distribution was made since our departure from the *Medusa*; and nothing more remained than four pints of water, and one half dozen biscuits. What steps were we to take in this cruel situation? We were desirous of going on shore, but we had such dangers to encounter. However, we soon came to a decision, when we saw a caravan of Moors on the coast. We then stood a little out to sea. According to the calculation of our commanding officer, we would arrive at Senegal on the morrow.

Deceived by that false account, we preferred suffering one day more, rather than to be taken by the Moors of the Desert, or perish among the breakers. We had now no more than a small half glass of water, and the seventh of a biscuit. Exposed as we were to the heat of the sun, which darted its rays perpendicularly on our heads, that ration, though small, would have been a great relief to us; but the distribution was delayed to the morrow. We were then obliged to drink the bitter sea-water, ill as it was calculated to quench our thirst.

Must I tell it! thirst had so withered the lungs of our sailors, that they drank water salter than that of the sea! Our numbers diminished daily, and nothing but the hope of arriving at the colony on the following day sustained our frail existence. My young brothers and sisters wept incessantly for water. The little Laura, aged six years, lay dying at the feet of her mother. Her mournful cries so moved the soul of my unfortunate father, that he was on the eve of opening a vein to quench the thirst which consumed his child; but a wise person opposed his design, observing that all the blood in his body would not prolong the life of his infant one moment.

The freshness of the night-wind procured us some respite. We anchored pretty near to the shore, and, though dying of famine, each got a tranquil sleep. On the morning of the 8th of July at break of day, we took the route for Senegal. A short while after the wind fell, and we had a dead calm. We endeavoured to row, but our strength was exhausted. A fourth and last distribution was made, and, in the twinkling of an eye, our last resources were consumed. We were forty-two people who had to feed upon *six biscuits* and about *four pints* of water, with no hope of a farther supply.

Then came the moment for deciding whether we were to perish among the breakers, which defended the approach to the shores of the Desert, or to die of famine in continuing our route. The majority preferred the last species of misery. We continued our progress along the shore, painfully pulling our oars. Upon the beach were distinguished several downs of white sand, and some small trees. We were thus creeping along the coast, observing a mournful silence, when a sailor suddenly exclaimed, Behold the Moors! We did, in fact, see various individuals upon the rising ground, walking at a quick pace, and whom we took to be the Arabs of the Desert. As we were very near the shore, we stood farther out to sea, fearing that these pretended Moors, or Arabs, would throw themselves into the sea, swim out, and take us. Some hours after, we observed several people upon an eminence, who seemed to make signals to us. We examined them attentively, and soon recognised them to be our companions in misfortune. We replied to them by attaching a white handkerchief to the top of our mast.

Then we resolved to land, at the risk of perishing among the breakers, which were very strong towards the shore, although the sea was calm. On approaching the beach, we went towards the right, where the waves seemed less agitated, and endeavoured to reach it, with the hope of being able more easily to land. Scarcely had we directed our course to that point, when we perceived a great number of people standing near to a little wood surrounding the sand-hills. We recognised them to be the passengers of that boat, which, like ourselves, were deprived of provisions.

Meanwhile we approached the shore, and already the foaming surge filled us with terror. Each wave that came from the open sea, each billow that swept beneath our boat, made us bound into the air; so we were sometimes thrown from the poop to the prow, and from the prow to the poop. Then, if our pilot had missed the sea, we would have been sunk; the waves would have thrown us aground, and we would have been buried among the breakers. The helm of the boat was again given to the old pilot, who had already so happily steered us through the dangers of the storm. He instantly threw into the sea the mast, the sails, and every thing that could impede our proceedings. When we came to the first landing point, several of our shipwrecked companions, who had reached the shore, ran and hid themselves behind the hills, not to see us perish; others made signs not to approach at that place; some covered their eyes with their hands; others, at last despising the danger, precipitated themselves into the waves to receive us in their arms.

We then saw a spectacle that made us shudder. We had already doubled two ranges of breakers; but those which we had still to cross raised their foaming waves to a prodigious height, then sunk with a hollow and monstrous sound, sweeping along a long line of the coast. Our boat sometimes greatly elevated, and sometimes ingulfed between the waves, seemed, at the moment, of utter ruin. Bruised, battered, tossed about on all hands, it turned of itself, and refused to obey the kind hand which directed it. At that instant a huge wave rushed from the open sea, and dashed against the poop; the boat plunged, disappeared, and we were all among the waves. Our sailors, whose strength had returned at the presence of danger, redoubled their efforts, uttering mournful sounds.

Our bark groaned, the oars were broken; it was thought aground, but it was stranded; it was upon its side. The last sea rushed upon us with the impetuosity of a torrent. We were up to the neck in water; the bitter sea-froth choked us. The grapnel was thrown out. The sailors threw themselves into the sea; they took the children in their arms; returned, and took us upon their shoulders; and I found myself seated upon the sand on the shore, by the side of my step-mother, my brothers and sisters, almost dead. Every one was upon the beach except my father and some sailors; but that good man arrived at last, to mingle his tears with those of his family and friends.

Instantly our hearts joined in addressing our prayers and praises to God. I raised my hands to heaven, and remained some time immoveable upon the beach. Every one also hastened to testify his gratitude to our old pilot, who, next to God, justly merited the title of our preserver. M. Dumège, a naval surgeon, gave him an elegant gold watch, the only thing he had saved from the *Medusa*.

Let the reader now recollect all the perils to which we had been exposed in escaping from the wreck of the frigate to the shores of the Desert—all that we had suffered during our four days' voyage—and he will perhaps have a just notion of the various sensations we felt on getting on shore on that strange and savage land. Doubtless the joy we experienced at having escaped, as by a miracle, the fury of the floods, was very great; but how much was it lessened by the feelings of our horrible situation!

Without water, without provisions, and the majority of us nearly naked, was it to be wondered at that we should be seized with terror on thinking of the obstacles which we had to surmount, the fatigues, the privations, the pains and the sufferings we had to endure, with the dangers we had to encounter in the immense and frightful Desert we had to traverse before we could arrive at our destination? Almighty Providence! it was in Thee alone I put my trust.

Relation complète du naufrage de la frégate La Méduse faisant partie de l'expédition du Sénégal en 1816, by Jean-Jérôme Baugean, 1816.

9.

LOSS OF THE *TITANIC*: THE OFFICIAL REPORT

A FORMAL INVESTIGATION INTO THE CIRCUMSTANCES ATTENDING THE FOUNDERING ON APRIL 15, 1912, OF THE BRITISH STEAMSHIP *TITANIC*, AS CONDUCTED BY THE BRITISH GOVERNMENT

The *Titanic* departing Southampton on April 10, 1912.

THE SAILING ORDER

The masters of vessels belonging to the White Star Line are not given any special "sailing orders" before the commencement of any particular voyage. It is understood, however, that the "tracks" or "lane routes" proper to the particular time of the year, and agreed upon by the great steamship companies, are to be generally adhered to. Should any master see fit during this passage to deviate from his route he has to report on and explain this deviation at the end of his voyage. When such deviation has been in the interests of safety, and not merely to shorten his passage, his action has always been approved of by the company.

A book of general ship's rules and uniform regulations is also issued by the company as a guide; there are in this book no special instructions in regard to ice, but there is a general instruction that the safety of the lives of the passengers and ship are to be the first consideration.

Besides the book of ship's rules, every master when first appointed to command a ship is addressed by special letter from the company, of which the following passage is an extract:

You are to dismiss all idea of competitive passages with other vessels and to concentrate your attention upon a cautious, prudent, and ever-watchful system of navigation, which shall lose time or suffer any other temporary inconvenience rather than incur the slightest risk which can be avoided.

Mr. Sanderson, one of the directors, in his evidence says with reference to the above letter:

We never fail to tell them in handing them these letters that we do not wish them to take it as a mere matter of form; that we wish them to read these letters, and to write an acknowledgment to us that they have read them, and that they will be influenced by what we have said in those letters.

THE ROUTE FOLLOWED

The *Titanic* left Southampton on Wednesday, April 10, and after calling at Cherbourg, proceeded to Queenstown, from which port she sailed on the afternoon of Thursday, April 11, following what was at that time the accepted outward-bound route for mail steamers from the Fastnet Light, off the southwest coast of Ireland, to the Nantucket Shoal light vessel, off the coast of the United States. It is desirable here to explain that it has been, since 1899, the practice, by common agreement between the great North Atlantic steamship companies, to follow lane routes, to be used by their ships at the different seasons of the year. Speaking generally, it may be said that the selection of these routes has hitherto been based on the importance of avoiding as much as possible the areas where fog and ice are prevalent at certain seasons, without thereby unduly lengthening the passage across the Atlantic, and also with the view of keeping the tracks of "outward" and "homeward" bound mail steamers well clear of one another. A further advantage is that, in case of a breakdown, vessels are likely to receive timely assistance from other vessels following the same route. The decisions arrived at by the steamship companies referred to above have, from time to time, been communicated to the Hydrographic Office, and the routes have there been marked on the North Atlantic route charts printed and published by the Admiralty; and they have also been embodied in the sailing directions.

Before the *Titanic* disaster the accepted mail steamers outward track between January 15 and August 14 followed the arc of a great circle between the Fastnet Light and a point in latitude 42° N. and 47° W. (sometimes termed the "turning point"), and from thence by Rhumb Line so as to pass just south of the Nantucket Shoal light vessel, and from this point on to New York. This track, usually called the outward southern track, was that followed by the *Titanic* on her journey.

An examination of the North Atlantic route chart shows that this track passes about 25 miles south (that is outside) of the edge of the area marked "field ice between March and July," but from 100 to 300 miles to the northward (that is inside) of the dotted line on the chart marked, "Icebergs have been seen within this line in April, May, and June."

That is to say, assuming the areas indicated to be based on the experience of many years, this track might be taken as passing clear of field ice under the usual conditions of that time of year, but well inside the area in which icebergs might be seen.

It is instructive here to remark that had the "turning point" been in longitude 45° W. and latitude 38° N., that is some 240 miles to the south-eastward, the total distance of the passage would only have been increased by about 220 miles, or some 10 hours' steaming for a 22-knot ship. This is the route which was provisionally decided on by the great trans-Atlantic companies subsequent to the *Titanic* disaster.

It must not be supposed that the lane routes referred to had never been changed before. Owing to the presence of ice in 1903, 1904, and 1905 from about early in April to mid-June or early in July, westward-bound vessels crossed the meridian of 47° W. in latitude 41° N., that is 60 miles further south than the then accepted track.

The publications known as "Sailing Directions," compiled by the hydrographic office at the Admiralty, indicate the caution which it is necessary to use in regions where ice is likely to be found.

The following is an extract from one of these books, named "United States Pilot (East Coast)," Part I (second edition, 1909, p. 34), referring to the ocean passages of the large trans-Atlantic mail and passenger steamers:

To these vessels one of the chief dangers in crossing the Atlantic lies in the probability of encountering masses of ice, both in the form of bergs and of extensive fields of solid compact ice, released at the breaking up of winter in the Arctic regions, and drifted down by the Labrador current across their direct route. Ice is more likely to be encountered in this route between April and August, both months inclusive, than at other times, although icebergs have been seen at all seasons northward of the parallel of 43° N., but not often so far south after August.

These icebergs are sometimes over 200 feet in height and of considerable extent. They have been seen as far south as latitude 39° N., to obtain which position they must have crossed the Gulf Stream impelled by the cold Arctic current underrunning the warm waters of the Gulf Stream. That this should happen is not to be wondered at when it is considered that the specific gravity of fresh-water ice, of which these bergs are composed, is about seven-eighths that of sea water; so that, however vast the berg may appear to the eye of the observer, he can in reality see one-eighth of its bulk, the remaining seven-eighths being submerged and subject to the deep-water currents of the ocean. The track of an iceberg is indeed directed mainly by current, so small a portion of its surface being exposed to the action of the winds that its course is but slightly retarded or deflected by moderate breezes. On the Great Bank of Newfoundland bergs are often observed to be moving south or southeast; those that drift westward of Cape Race usually pass between Green and St. Pierre Banks.

The route chart of the North Atlantic, No. 2058, shows the limits within which both field ice and icebergs may be met with, and where it should be carefully looked out for at all times, but especially during the spring and summer seasons. From this chart it would appear that whilst the southern and eastern limits of field ice are about latitude 42° N., and longitude 45° W., icebergs may be met with much farther from Newfoundland; in April, May, and June they have been seen as far south as latitude 39° N. and as far east as longitude 38° 30′ W."

And again, on page 35:

It is, in fact, impossible to give, within the outer limits named, any distinct idea of where ice may be expected, and no rule can be laid down to insure safe navigation, as its position and the quantity met with differs so greatly in different seasons. Everything must depend upon the vigilance, caution, and skill with which a vessel is navigated when crossing the dangerous ice-bearing regions of the Atlantic Ocean.

Similar warnings as to ice are also given in the "Nova Scotia (Southeast Coast) and Bay of Fundy Pilot" (sixth edition, 1911), which is also published by the hydrographic office.

Both the above quoted books were supplied to the master of the *Titanic* (together with other necessary charts and books) before that ship left Southampton.

The above extracts show that it is quite incorrect to assume that icebergs had never been encountered or field ice observed so far south, at the particular time of year when the *Titanic* disaster occurred; but it is true to say that the field ice was certainly at that time farther south than it has been seen for many years.

It may be useful here to give some definitions of the various forms of ice to be met with in these latitudes, although there is frequently some confusion in their use.

An iceberg may be defined as a detached portion of a polar glacier carried out to sea. The ice of an iceberg formed from a glacier is of quite fresh water. Only about an eighth of its mass floats above the surface of sea water.

A "growler" is a colloquial term applied to icebergs of small mass, which therefore only show a small portion above the surface. It is not infrequently a berg which has turned over, and is therefore showing what has been termed "black ice" or, more correctly, dark-blue ice.

Pack ice is the floating ice which covers wide areas of the polar seas, broken into large pieces, which are driven ("packed") together by wind and current, so as to form a practically continuous sheet. Such ice is generally frozen from sea water, and not derived from glaciers.

Field ice is a term usually applied to frozen sea water floating in much looser form than pack ice.

An icefloe is the term generally applied to the same ice (i.e., field ice) in a smaller quantity.

A floe berg is a stratified mass of floe ice (i.e., sea-water ice).

ICE MESSAGES RECEIVED

The *Titanic* followed the outward southern track until Sunday, April 14, in the usual way. At 11.40 P.M. on that day she struck an iceberg and at 2.20 A.M. on the next day she foundered.

At 9 A.M. (*Titanic* time) on that day a wireless message from the steamship *Caronia* was received by Capt. Smith. It was as follows:

A photograph of an iceberg floating near the site of the *Titanic* sinking, December 14, 1912.

CAPTAIN, *Titanic*:

West-bound steamers report bergs, growlers, and field ice in 42° N., from 49° to 51° W., April 12. Compliments.

BARR.

It will be noticed that this message referred to bergs, growlers, and field ice sighted on April 12—at least 48 hours before the time of the collision. At the time this message was received the *Titanic's* position was about latitude 43° 35′ N. and longitude 43° 50′ W. Capt. Smith acknowledged the receipt of this message.

At 1.42 P.M., a wireless message from the steamship *Baltic* was received by Capt. Smith. It was as follows:

Capt. SMITH, *Titanic*:

Have had moderate, variable winds and clear, fine weather since leaving. Greek steamer *Athenai* reports passing icebergs and large quantities of field ice to-day in latitude 41° 51′ N., longitude 49° 52′ W. Last night we spoke German oiltank steamer *Deutschland*, Stettin to Philadelphia, not under control, short of coal, latitude 40° 42′ N., longitude 55° 11′ W. Wishes to be reported to New York and other steamers. Wish you and *Titanic* all success.

COMMANDER.

At the time this message was received the *Titanic* position was about 42° 35′ N., 45° 50′ W. Capt. Smith acknowledged the receipt of this message also.

Mr. Ismay, the managing director of the White Star Line, was on board the *Titanic*, and it appears that the master handed the *Baltic*'s message to Mr. Ismay almost immediately after it was received. This no doubt was in order that Mr. Ismay might know that ice was to be expected. Mr. Ismay states that he understood from the message that they would get up to the ice "that night." Mr. Ismay showed this message to two ladies, and it is therefore probable that many persons on board became aware of its contents. This message ought in my opinion to have been put on the board in the chart room as soon as it was received. It remained, however, in Mr. Ismay's possession until 7.15 P.M., when the master asked Mr. Ismay to return it. It was then that it was first posted in the chart room.

This was considerably before the time at which the vessel reached the position recorded in the message. Nevertheless, I think it was irregular for the master to part with the document, and improper for Mr. Ismay to retain it, but the incident had, in my opinion, no connection with or influence upon the manner in which the vessel was navigated by the master.

It appears that about 1.45 P.M. (*Titanic* time) on the 14th a message was sent from the German steamer *Amerika* to the Hydrographic Office in Washington, which was in the following terms:

Amerika passed two large icebergs in 41° 27′ N., 50° 8′ W., on April 14.

This was a position south of the point of the *Titanic's* disaster. The message does not mention at what hour the bergs had been observed. It was a private message for the hydrographer at Washington, but it passed to the *Titanic* because she was nearest to Cape Race, to which station it had to be sent in order to reach Washington. Being a message affecting navigation, it should in the ordinary course have been taken to the bridge. So far as can be ascertained, it was never heard of by anyone on board the *Titanic* outside the Marconi room. There were two Marconi operators in the Marconi room, namely, Phillips, who perished, and Bride, who survived and gave evidence. Bride did not receive the *Amerika* message nor did Phillips mention it to him, though the two had much conversation together after it had been received. I am of opinion that when this message reached the Marconi room it was put aside by Phillips to wait until the *Titanic* would be within call of Cape Race (at about 8 or 8.30 P.M.), and that it was never handed to any officer of the *Titanic*.

At 5.50 P.M. the *Titanic's* course (which had been S. 62° W.) was changed to bring her on a westerly course for New York. In ordinary circumstances this change in her course should have been made about half an hour earlier, but she seems on this occasion to have continued for about 10 miles longer on her southwesterly course before turning, with the result that she found herself, after altering course at 5.50 P.M., about 4 or 5 miles south of the customary route on a course S. 86° W. true. Her course, as thus set, would bring her at the time of the collision to a point about 2 miles to the southward of the customary route and 4 miles south and considerably to the westward of the indicated position of the *Baltic's* ice. Her position at the time of the collision would also be well to the southward of the indicated position of the ice mentioned in the *Caronia* message. This change of course was so insignificant that in my opinion it can not have been made in consequence of information as to ice.

In this state of things, at 7.30 P.M. a fourth message was received, and is said by the Marconi operator Bride to have been delivered to the bridge. This message was from the steamship *Californian* to the steamship *Antillian*, but was picked up by the *Titanic*. It was as follows:

To CAPTAIN, *Antillian*:
Six-thirty P.M., apparent ship's time; latitude 42° 3′ N., longitude 49° 9′ W. Three large bergs 5 miles to southward of us. Regards.
LORD

Bride does not remember to what officer he delivered this message.

By the time the *Titanic* reached the position of the collision (11.40 P.M.) she had gone about 50 miles to the westward of the indicated position of the ice mentioned in this fourth message. Thus it would appear that before the collision she had gone clear of the indicated positions of ice contained in the messages from the *Baltic* and *Californian*. As to the ice advised by the *Caronia* message, so far as it consisted of small bergs and field ice, it had before the time of the collision possibly drifted with the Gulf Stream to the eastward; and so far as it consisted of large bergs (which would be deep enough in the water to reach the Labrador current) it had probably gone to the southward. It was urged by Sir Robert Finlay, who appeared for the owners, that this is strong evidence that the *Titanic* had been carefully and successfully navigated so as to avoid the ice of which she had received warning. Mr. Ismay, however, stated that he understood from the *Baltic* message that "we would get up to the ice that night."

There was a fifth message received in the Marconi room of the *Titanic* at 9.40 P.M. This was from a steamer called the *Mesaba*. It was in the following terms:

From "Mesaba" to "Titanic" and all east-bound ships:
Ice report in latitude 42° N. to 41° 25′ N., longitude 49° to longitude 50° 30′ W. Saw much heavy pack ice and great number large icebergs. Also field ice. Weather good, clear.

This message clearly indicated the presence of ice in the immediate vicinity of the *Titanic*, and if it had reached the bridge would perhaps have affected the navigation of the vessel. Unfortunately, it does not appear to have been delivered to the master or to any of the officers. The Marconi operator was very busy from 8 o'clock onward transmitting messages via Cape Race for passengers on board the *Titanic*, and the probability is that he failed to grasp the significance and importance of the message, and put it aside until he should be less busy. It was never acknowledged by Capt. Smith, and I am satisfied that it was not received by him. But, assuming Sir Robert Finlay's contentions to be well founded that the Titanic had been navigated so as to avoid the *Baltic* and the *Californian* ice, and that the *Caronia* ice had drifted to the eastward and to the southward, still there can be no doubt, if the evidence of Mr. Lightoller, the second officer, is to be believed, that both he and the master knew that the danger of meeting ice still existed. Mr. Lightoller says that the master showed him the *Caronia* message about 12.45 P.M. on April 14, when he was on the bridge. He was about to go off watch, and he says he made a rough calculation in his head which satisfied him that the *Titanic* would not reach the position mentioned in the message until he came on watch again at 6 P.M. At 6 P.M. Mr. Lightoller came on the bridge again to take over the ship from Mr. Wilde, the chief officer (dead).

He does not remember being told anything about the *Baltic* message, which had been received at 1.42 P.M. Mr. Lightoller then requested Mr. Moody, the sixth officer (dead), to let him know "at what time we should reach the vicinity of ice," and says that he thinks Mr. Moody reported "about 11 o'clock." Mr. Lightoller says that 11 o'clock did not agree with a mental calculation he himself had made and which showed 9.30 as the time. This mental calculation he at first said he had made before Mr. Moody gave him 11 o'clock as the time, but later on he corrected this, and said his mental calculation was made between 7 and 8 o'clock, and after Mr. Moody had mentioned 11. He did not point out the difference to him, and thought that perhaps Mr. Moody had made his calculations on the basis of some "other" message.

Mr. Lightoller excuses himself for not pointing out the difference by saying that Mr. Moody was busy at the time, probably with stellar observations. It is, however, an odd circumstance that Mr. Lightoller, who believed that the vicinity of ice would be reached before his watch ended at 10 P.M., should not have mentioned the fact to Mr. Moody, and it is also odd that if he thought that Mr. Moody was working on the basis of some "other" message, he did not ask what the other message was or where it came from.

The point, however, of Mr. Lightoller's evidence is that they both thought that the vicinity of ice would be reached before midnight. When he was examined as to whether he did not fear that on entering the indicated ice region he might run foul of a growler (a low-lying berg) he answers: "No, I judged I should see it with 'sufficient distinctness' and at a distance of a 'mile and a half, more probably 2 miles.'" He then adds:

> In the event of meeting ice there are many things we look for. In the first place, a slight breeze. Of course, the stronger the breeze the more visible will the ice be, or, rather, the breakers on the ice.

He is then asked whether there was any breeze on this night, and he answers:

> When I left the deck at 10 o'clock there was a slight breeze. Oh, pardon me, no; I take that back. No, it was calm, perfectly calm—

And almost immediately afterwards he describes the sea as "absolutely flat." It appeared, according to this witness, that about 9 o'clock the master came on the bridge and that Mr. Lightoller had a conversation with him which lasted half an hour. This conversation, so far as it is material, is described by Mr. Lightoller in the following words:

We commenced to speak about the weather. He said, "there is not much wind." I said, "No, it is a flat calm," as a matter of fact. He repeated it, he said, "A flat calm." I said, "Quite flat; there is no wind." I said something about it was rather a pity the breeze had not kept up whilst we were going through the ice region. Of course, my reason was obvious: he knew I meant the water ripples breaking on the base of the berg.

We then discussed the indications of ice. I remember saying, "In any case, there will be a certain amount of reflected light from the bergs." He said, "Oh, yes, there will be a certain amount of reflected light." I said or he said—blue was said between us—that even though the blue side of the berg was towards us, probably the outline, the white outline, would give us sufficient warning, that we should be able to see it at a good distance, and as far as we could see, we should be able to see it. Of course, it was just with regard to that possibility of the blue side being toward us, and that if it did happen to be turned with the purely blue side toward us, there would still be the white outline.

Further on Mr. Lightoller says that he told the master nothing about his own calculation as to coming up with the ice at 9.30 or about Mr. Moody's calculation as to coming up with it at 11.

The conversation with the master ended with the master saying, "If it becomes at all doubtful let me know at once; I will be just inside." This remark Mr. Lightoller says undoubtedly referred to ice.

At 9.30 the master went to his room, and the first thing that Mr. Lightoller did afterwards was to send a message to the crow's nest "to keep a sharp lookout for ice, particularly small ice and growlers," until daylight. There seems to be no doubt that this message was in fact sent, and that it was passed on to the next lookouts when they came on watch. Hitchins, the quartermaster, says he heard Mr. Lightoller give the message to Mr. Moody, and both the men in the crow's nest at the time (Jewell and Symons) speak to having received it. From 9.30 to 10 o'clock, when his watch ended, Mr. Lightoller remained on the bridge "looking out for ice." He also said that the night order book for the 14th had a footnote about keeping a sharp lookout for ice, and that this note was "initialed by every officer." At 10 o'clock Mr. Lightoller handed over the watch to Mr. Murdoch, the first officer (dead), telling him that "we might be up around the ice any time now." That Mr. Murdoch knew of the danger of meeting ice appears from the evidence of Hemming, a lamp trimmer, who says that about 7.15 P.M. Mr. Murdoch told him to go forward and see the forescuttle hatch closed—as we are in the vicinity of ice and there is a glow coming from that, and I want everything dark before the bridge.

The foregoing evidence establishes quite clearly that Capt. Smith, the master; Mr. Murdoch, the first officer; Mr. Lightoller, the second officer; and Mr. Moody, the sixth officer, all knew on the Sunday evening that the vessel was entering a region where ice might be expected; and this being so, it seems to me to be of little importance to consider whether the master had by design or otherwise succeeded in avoiding the particular ice indicated in the three messages received by him.

SPEED OF THE SHIP

The entire passage had been made at high speed, though not at the ship's maximum, and this speed was never reduced until the collision was unavoidable. At 10 P.M. the ship was registering 45 knots every two hours by the Cherub log.

The quartermaster on watch aft when the *Titanic* struck states that the log, reset at noon, then registered 260 knots, and the fourth officer, when working up the position from 7.30 P.M. to the time of the collision, states he estimated the *Titanic*'s speed as 22 knots, and this is also borne out by evidence that the engines were running continuously at 75 revolutions.

THE WEATHER CONDITIONS

From 6 P.M. onward to the time of the collision the weather was perfectly clear and fine. There was no moon, the stars were out, and there was not a cloud in the sky. There was, however, a drop in temperature of 10° in slightly less than two hours, and by about 7.30 P.M. the temperature was 33° F., and it eventually fell to 32° F. That this was not necessarily an indication of ice is borne out by the sailing directions. The Nova Scotia (S. E. Coast) and Bay of Fundy Pilot (sixth edition, 1911, p. 16) says:

No reliance can be placed on any warning being conveyed to a mariner by a fall of temperature, either of the air or sea, on approaching ice. Some decrease in temperature has occasionally been recorded, but more often none has been observed.

Sir Ernest Shackleton was, however, of opinion that—if there was no wind and the temperature fell abnormally for the time of the year, I would consider that I was approaching an area which might have ice in it.

ACTION THAT SHOULD HAVE BEEN TAKEN

The question is what ought the master to have done. I am advised that with the knowledge of the proximity of ice which the master had, two courses were open to him: The one was to stand well to the southward instead of turning up to a westerly course; the other was to reduce speed materially as night approached. He did neither. The alteration of the course at 5.50 P.M. was so insignificant that it can not be attributed to any intention to avoid ice. This deviation brought the vessel back to within about 2 miles of the customary route before 11.30 P.M. And there was certainly no reduction of speed. Why, then, did the master persevere in his course and maintain his speed? The answer is to be found in the evidence. It was shown that for many years past, indeed, for a quarter of a century or more, the practice of liners using this track when in the vicinity of ice at night had been in clear weather to keep the course, to maintain the speed and to trust to a sharp lookout to enable them to avoid the danger. This practice, it was said, had been justified by experience, no casualties having resulted from it. I accept the evidence as to the practice and as to the immunity from casualties which is said to have accompanied it.

But the event has proved the practice to be bad. Its root is probably to be bound in competition and in the desire of the public for quick passages rather than in the judgment of navigators. But unfortunately experience appeared to justify it. In these circumstances I am not able to blame Capt. Smith. He had not the experience which his own misfortune has afforded to those whom he has left behind, and he was doing only that which other skilled men would have done in the same position. It was suggested at the bar that he was yielding to influences which ought not to have affected him; that the presence of Mr. Ismay on board and the knowledge which he perhaps had of a conversation between Mr. Ismay and the chief engineer at Queenstown about the speed of the ship and the consumption of coal probably induced him to neglect precautions which he would otherwise have taken.

But I do not believe this. The evidence shows that he was not trying to make any record passage or indeed any exceptionally quick passage. He was not trying to please anybody, but was exercising his own discretion in the way he thought best. He made a mistake, a very grievous mistake, but one in which, in face of the practice and of past experience, negligence can not be said to have had any part; and in the absence of negligence it is, in my opinion, impossible to fix Capt. Smith with blame. It is, however, to be hoped that the last has been heard of the practice and that for the future it will be abandoned for what we now know to be more prudent and wiser measures. What was a mistake in the case of the *Titanic* would without doubt be negligence in any similar case in the future.

THE COLLISION

Mr. Lightoller turned over the ship to Mr. Murdoch, the first officer, at 10 o'clock, telling him that the ship was within the region where ice had been reported. He also told him of the message he had sent to the crow's nest, and of his conversation with the master, and of the latter's orders.

The ship appears to have run on, on the same course, until, at a little before 11.40, one of the lookouts in the crow's nest struck three blows on the gong, which was the accepted warning for something ahead, following this immediately afterward by a telephone message to the bridge "Iceberg right ahead." Almost simultaneously with the three-gong signal Mr. Murdoch, the officer of the watch, gave the order "Hard-a-starboard," and immediately telegraphed down to the engine room "Stop. Full speed astern." The helm was already "hard over," and the ship's head had fallen off about two points to port, when she collided with an iceberg well forward on her starboard side.

Mr. Murdoch at the same time pulled the lever over which closed the water-tight doors in the engine and boiler rooms.

The master "rushed out" onto the bridge and asked Mr. Murdoch what the ship had struck.

Mr. Murdoch replied:

An iceberg, sir. I hard-a-starboarded and reversed the engines, and I was going to hard-a-port round it, but she was too close. I could not do any more. I have closed the water-tight doors.

From the evidence given it appears that the *Titanic* had turned about two points to port before the collision occurred. From various experiments subsequently made with the steamship *Olympic*, a sister ship to the *Titanic*, it was found that traveling at the same rate as the *Titanic*, about 37 seconds would be required for the ship to change her course to this extent after the helm had been put hard-a-starboard. In this time the ship would travel about 466 yards, and allowing for the few seconds that would be necessary for the order to be given, it may be assumed that 500 yards was about the distance at which the iceberg was sighted either from the bridge or crow's nest.

That it was quite possible on this night, even with a sharp lookout at the stemhead, crow's nest, and on the bridge, not to see an iceberg at this distance is shown by the evidence of Capt. Rostron, of the *Carpathia*.

The injuries to the ship, which are described in the next section, were of such a kind that she foundered in 2 hours and 40 minutes.

DAMAGE

The collision with the iceberg, which took place at 11.40 P.M., caused damage to the bottom of the starboard side of the vessel at about 10 feet above the level of the keel, but there was no damage above this height. There was damage in—The forepeak, No. 1 hold, No. 2 hold, No. 3 hold, No. 6 boiler room, No. 5 boiler room.

The damage extended over a length of about 300 feet.

TIME IN WHICH THE DAMAGE WAS DONE

As the ship was moving at over 20 knots, she would have passed through 300 feet in less than 10 seconds, so that the damage was done in about this time.

THE FLOODING IN FIRST TEN MINUTES

At first it is desirable to consider what happened in the first 10 minutes.

The forepeak was not flooded above the orlop deck—i.e., the peak tank top, from the hole in the bottom of the peak tank.

In No. 1 hold there was 7 feet of water.

In No. 2 hold five minutes after the collision water was seen rushing in at the bottom of the firemen's passage on the starboard side, so that the ship's side was damaged abaft of bulkhead B sufficiently to open the side of the firemen's passage, which was 3-1/2 feet from the outer skin of the ship, thereby flooding both the hold and the passage.

In No. 3 hold the mail room was filled soon after the collision. The floor of the mail room is 24 feet above the keel.

In No. 6 boiler room, when the collision took place, water at once poured in at about 2 feet above the stokehold plates, on the starboard side, at the after end of the boiler room. Some of the firemen immediately went through the water-tight door opening to No. 5 boiler room because the water was flooding the place. The water-tight doors in the engine rooms were shut from the bridge almost immediately after the collision. Ten minutes later it was found that there was water to the height of 8 feet above the double bottom in No. 6 boiler room.

No. 5 boiler room was damaged at the ship's side in the starboard forward bunker at a distance of 2 feet above the stokehold plates, at 2 feet from the water-tight bulkhead between Nos. 5 and 6 boiler rooms. Water poured in at that place as it would from an ordinary fire hose. At the time of the collision this bunker had no coal in it. The bunker door was closed when water was seen to be entering the ship.

In No. 4 boiler room there was no indication of any damage at the early stages of the sinking.

GRADUAL EFFECT OF THE DAMAGE

It will thus be seen that all the six compartments forward of No. 4 boiler room were open to the sea by damage which existed at about 10 feet above the keel. At 10 minutes after the collision the water seems to have risen to about 14 feet above the keel in all these compartments except No. 5 boiler room. After the first ten minutes the water rose steadily in all these six compartments. The forepeak above the peak tank was not filled until an hour after the collision, when the vessel's bow was submerged to above C deck. The water then flowed in from the top through the deck scuttle forward of the collision bulkhead. It was by this scuttle that access was obtained to all the decks below C down to the peak tank top on the orlop deck.

At 12 o'clock water was coming up in No. 1 hatch. It was getting into the firemen's quarters and driving the firemen out. It was rushing round No. 1 hatch on G deck and coming mostly from the starboard side, so that in 20 minutes the water had risen above G deck in No. 1 hold.

In No. 2 hold about 40 minutes after the collision the water was coming in to the seamen's quarters on E deck through a burst fore and aft wooden bulkhead of a third-class cabin opposite the seamen's wash place. Thus, the water had risen in No. 2 hold to about 3 feet above E deck in 40 minutes.

In No. 3 hold the mail room was afloat about 20 minutes after the collision. The bottom of the mail room which is on the orlop deck, is 24 feet above the keel.

The water-tight doors on F deck at the fore and after ends of No. 3 compartment were not closed then.

The mail room was filling and water was within 2 feet of G deck, rising fast when the order was given to clear the boats.

There was then no water on F deck.

There is a stairway on the port side on G deck which leads down to the first-class baggage room on the orlop deck immediately below. There was water in this baggage room 25 minutes after the collision. Half an hour after the collision water was up to G deck in the mail room.

Thus the water had risen in this compartment to within 2 feet of G deck in 20 minutes, and above G deck in 25 to 30 minutes.

No. 6 boiler room was abandoned by the men almost immediately after the collision. Ten minutes later the water had risen to 8 feet above the top of the double bottom, and probably reached the top of the bulkhead at the after end of the compartment, at the level of E deck, in about one hour after the collision.

In No. 5 boiler room there was no water above the stokehold plates, until a rush of water came through the pass between the boilers from the forward end, and drove the leading stoker out.

It has already been shown in the description of what happened in the first 10 minutes, that water was coming into No. 5 boiler room in the forward starboard bunker at 2 feet above the plates in a stream about the size of a deck hose. The door in this bunker had been dropped probably when water was first discovered, which was a few minutes after the collision. This would cause the water to be retained in the bunker until it rose high enough to burst the door which was weaker than the bunker bulkhead. This happened about an hour after the collision.

No. 4 boiler room.—One hour and 40 minutes after the collision water was coming in forward, in No. 4 boiler room, from underneath the floor in the forward part, in small quantities. The men remained in that stokehold till ordered on deck.

Nos. 3, 2, and 1 boiler rooms.—When the men left No. 4 some of them went through Nos. 3, 2, and 1 boiler rooms into the reciprocating engine room, and from there on deck. There was no water in the boiler rooms abaft No. 4 one hour 40 minutes after the collision (1.20 A.M.), and there was then none in the reciprocating and turbine engine rooms.

Electrical engine room and tunnels.—There was no damage to these compartments.

From the foregoing it follows that there was no damage abaft No. 4 boiler room.

All the water-tight doors aft of the main engine room were opened after the collision.

Half an hour after the collision the water-tight doors from the engine room to the stokehold were opened as far forward as they could be to No. 4 boiler room.

FINAL EFFECT OF THE DAMAGE

The later stages of the sinking can not be stated with any precision, owing to a confusion of the times which was natural under the circumstances.

The forecastle deck was not under water at 1.35 A.M. Distress signals were fired until two hours after the collision (1.45 A.M.). At this time the fore deck was under water. The forecastle head was not then submerged though it was getting close down to the water, about half an hour before she disappeared (1.50 A.M.).

When the last boat, lowered from davits (D), left the ship, A deck was under water, and water came up the stairway under the boat deck almost immediately afterwards. After this the other port collapsible (B), which had been stowed on the officers' house, was uncovered, the lashings cut adrift, and she was swung round over the edge of the coamings of the deckhouse on to the boat deck.

Very shortly afterwards the vessel, according to Mr. Lightoller's account, seemed to take a dive, and he just walked into the water. When he came to the surface all the funnels were above the water.

Her stern was gradually rising out of the water, and the propellers were clear of the water. The ship did not break in two, and she did, eventually, attain the perpendicular, when the second funnel from aft about reached the water. There were no lights burning then, though they kept alight practically until the last.

Before reaching the perpendicular, when at an angle of 50° or 60°, there was a rumbling sound which may be attributed to the boilers leaving their beds and crashing down on to or through the bulkheads. She became more perpendicular and finally absolutely perpendicular, when she went slowly down.

After sinking as far as the after part of the boat deck she went down more quickly. The ship disappeared at 2.20 A.M.

OBSERVATIONS

I am advised that the *Titanic* as constructed could not have remained afloat long with such damage as she received. Her bulkheads were spaced to enable her to remain afloat with any two compartments in communication with the sea. She had a sufficient margin of safety with any two of the compartments flooded which were actually damaged.

In fact, any three of the four forward compartments could have been flooded by the damage received without sinking the ship to the top of her bulkheads.

Even if the four forward compartments had been flooded the water would not have got into any of the compartments abaft of them though it would have been above the top of some of the forward bulkheads. But the ship, even with these four compartments flooded, would have remained afloat. But she could not remain afloat with the four compartments and the forward boiler room (No. 6) also flooded.

The flooding of these five compartments alone would have sunk the ship sufficiently deep to have caused the water to rise above the bulkhead at the after end of the forward boiler room (No. 6) and to flow over into the next boiler room (No. 5), and to fill it up until in turn its after bulkhead would be overwhelmed and the water would thereby flow over and fill No. 4 boiler room, and so on in succession to the other boiler rooms till the ship would ultimately fill and sink.

It has been shown that water came into the five forward compartments to a height of about 14 feet above the keel in the first 10 minutes. This was at a rate of inflow with which the ship's pumps could not possibly have coped, so that the damage done to these five compartments alone inevitably sealed the doom of the ship.

The damage done in the boiler rooms Nos. 4 and 5 was too slight to have hastened appreciably the sinking of the ship, for it was given in evidence that no considerable amount of water was in either of these compartments for an hour after the collision. The rate at which water came into No. 6 boiler room makes it highly probable that the compartment was filled in not more than an hour, after which the flow over the top of the bulkhead between 5 and 6 began and continued till No. 5 was filled.

It was shown that the leak in No. 5 boiler room was only about equal to the flow of a deck hose pipe about 3 inches in diameter.

The leak in No. 4, supposing that there was one, was only enough to admit about 3 feet of water in that compartment in 1 hour 40 minutes.

Hence the leaks in Nos. 4 and 5 boiler rooms did not appreciably hasten the sinking of the vessel.

The evidence is very doubtful as to No. 4 being damaged. The pumps were being worked in No. 5 soon after the collision. The 10-inch leather special suction pipe which was carried from aft is more likely to have been carried for use in No. 5 than No. 4 because the doors were ordered to be opened probably soon after the collision when water was known to be coming into No. 5. There is no evidence that the pumps were being worked in No. 4.

The only evidence possibly favorable to the view that the pipe was required for No. 4, and not for No. 5, is that Scott, a greaser, says that he saw engineers dragging the suction pipe along one hour after the collision. But even as late as this it may have been wanted for No. 5 only.

The importance of the question of the damage to No. 5 is small because the ship as actually constructed was doomed as soon as the water in No. 6

boiler room and all compartments forward of it entered in the quantities it actually did.

It is only of importance in dealing with the question of what would have happened to the ship had she been more completely subdivided.

It was stated in evidence that if No. 4 had not been damaged or had only been damaged to an extent within the powers of the pumps to keep under, then, if the bulkheads had been carried to C deck, the ship might have been saved. Further methods of increased subdivision and their effect upon the fate of the ship are discussed later.

Evidence was given showing that after the water-tight doors in the engine and boiler rooms had been all closed, except those forward of No. 4 group of boilers, they were opened again, and there is no evidence to show that they were again closed. Though it is probable that the engineers who remained below would have closed these doors as the water rose in the compartments, yet it was not necessary for them to do this, as each door had an automatic closing arrangement which would have come into operation immediately a small amount of water came through the door.

It is probable, however, that the life of the ship would have been lengthened somewhat if these doors had been left open, for the water would have flowed through them to the after part of the ship, and the rate of flow of the water into the ship would have been for a time reduced as the bow might have been kept up a little by the water which flowed aft.

It is thus seen that the efficiency of the automatic arrangements for the closing of the water-tight doors, which was questioned during the inquiry, had no important bearing on the question of hastening the sinking of the ship, except that, in the case of the doors not having been closed by the engineers, it might have retarded the sinking of the ship if they had not acted. The engineers would not have prevented the doors from closing unless they had been convinced that the ship was doomed. There is no evidence that they did prevent the doors from closing.

The engineers were applying the pumps when Barrett, leading stoker, left No. 5 boiler room, but even if they had succeeded in getting all the pumps in the ship to work they could not have saved the ship or prolonged her life to any appreciable extent.

EFFECT OF SUGGESTED ADDITIONAL SUBDIVISION UPON FLOTATION

Water-tight decks.—It is in evidence that advantage might be obtained from the point of view of greater safety in having a water-tight deck.

Without entering into the general question of the advantage of water-tight decks for all ships, it is desirable to form an opinion in the case of the *Titanic* as to whether making the bulkhead deck water-tight would have been an advantage in the circumstances of the accident, or in case of accident to ships of this class.

I am advised that it is found that with all the compartments certainly known to have been flooded, viz., those forward of No. 4 boiler room, the ship would have remained afloat if the bulkhead deck had been a water-tight deck. If, however, No. 4 boiler room had also been flooded the ship would not have remained afloat unless, in addition to making the bulkhead deck water-tight, the transverse bulkhead abaft of No. 4 boiler room had been carried up to D deck.

To make the bulkhead deck effectively water-tight for this purpose it would have been necessary to carry water-tight trunks round all the openings in the bulkhead deck up to C deck.

It has been shown that with the bulkhead abaft No. 5 boiler room carried to C deck the ship would have remained afloat if the compartments certainly known to have been damaged had been flooded.

I do not desire to express an opinion upon the question whether it would have conduced to safety in the case of the *Titanic* if a water-tight deck had been fitted below the water line, as there may be some objections to such a deck. There are many considerations involved, and I think that the matter should be dealt with by the bulkhead committee for ships in general.

Longitudinal subdivision.—The advantages and disadvantages of longitudinal subdivision by means of water-tight bunker bulkheads were pointed out in evidence.

While not attempting to deal with this question generally for ships, I am advised that if the *Titanic* had been divided in the longitudinal method, instead of in the transverse method only, she would have been able, if damaged as supposed, to remain afloat, though with a list which could have been corrected by putting water ballast into suitable places.

This subject is one, however, which again involves many considerations, and I think that for ships generally the matter should be referred to the bulkhead committee for their consideration and report.

Extending double bottom up the sides.—It was shown in evidence that there would be increased protection in carrying the double bottom higher up the side than was done in the *Titanic*, and that some of the boiler rooms would probably not then have been flooded, as water could not have entered the ship except in the double bottom.

In the case of the *Titanic* I am advised that this would have been an advantage, but it was pointed out in evidence that there are certain disadvantages which in some ships may outweigh the advantages.

In view of what has already been said about the possible advantages of longitudinal subdivision, it is unnecessary further to discuss the question of carrying up the double bottom in ships generally. This matter should also be dealt with by the bulkhead committee.

Water-tight doors.—With reference to the question of the water-tight doors of the ship, there does not appear to have been any appreciable effect upon the sinking of the ship caused by either shutting or not shutting the doors. There does not appear to have been any difficulty in working the water-tight doors. They appear to have been shut in good time after the collision.

But in other cases of damage in ships constructed like the *Titanic*, it is probable that the efficiency of the closing arrangement of the water-tight doors may exert a vital influence on the safety of the ship. It has been represented that in future consideration should be given to the question—as to how far bulkhead should be solid bulkheads, and how far there should be water-tight doors, and, if there should be water-tight doors, how far they may or may not be automatically operated.

This again is a question on which it is not necessary here to express any general opinion, for there are conflicting considerations which vary in individual cases. The matter, however, should come under the effective supervision of the board of trade much more than it seems to come at present, and should be referred to the bulkhead committee for their consideration with a view to their suggesting in detail where doors should or should not be allowed, and the type of door which should be adopted in the different parts of ships.

ACCOUNT OF THE SAVING AND RESCUE OF THOSE WHO SURVIVED

The last lifeboat successfully launched from the HMS *Titanic*, April 15, 1912.

The *Titanic* was provided with 20 boats. They were all on the boat deck. Fourteen were lifeboats. These were hung inboard in davits, 7 on the starboard side and 7 on the port side, and were designed to carry 65 persons each. Two were emergency boats. These were also in davits, but were hung outboard, one on the starboard side and one on the port side, and were designed to carry 40 persons each. The remaining 4 boats were Engelhardt or collapsible boats. Two of these were stowed on the boat deck and 2 on the roof of the officers' quarters, and were designed to carry 47 persons each. Thus the total boat accommodation was for 1,178 persons. The boats in davits were numbered, the odd numbers being on the starboard side and the even numbers on the port side. The numbering began with the emergency boats, which were forward, and ran aft. Thus the boats on the starboard side were numbered 1 (an emergency boat), 3, 5, 7, 9, 11, 13, and 15 (lifeboats), and those on the port side 2 (an emergency boat), 4, 6, 8, 10, 12, 14, and 16 (lifeboats). The collapsible boats were lettered, A and B being on the roof of the officers' quarters and C and D being on the boat deck; C was abreast of No. 1 (emergency boat) and D abreast of No. 2 (emergency boat). Further particulars as to the boats will be found on page 18.

In ordinary circumstances all these boats (with the exception of 1 and 2) were kept covered up, and contained only a portion of their equipment, such as oars, masts, and sails, and water; some of the remaining portion, such as lamps, compasses, and biscuits being stowed in the ship in some convenient place, ready for use when required. Much examination was directed at the hearing to showing that some boats left the ship without a lamp and others without a compass, and so on, but in the circumstances of confusion and excitement which existed at the time of the disaster this seems to me to be excusable.

Each member of the crew had a boat assigned to him in printed lists, which were posted up in convenient places for the men to see; but it appeared that in some cases the men had not looked at these lists and did not know their respective boats.

There had been no proper boat drill nor a boat muster. It was explained that great difficulty frequently exists in getting firemen to take part in a boat drill. They regard it as no part of their work. There seem to be no statutory requirements as to boat drills or musters, although there is a provision (sec. 9

of the merchant shipping act of 1906) that when a boat drill does take place the master of the vessel is, under a penalty, to record the fact in his log. I think it is desirable that the board of trade should make rules requiring boat drills and boat musters to be held of such a kind and at such times as may be suitable to the ship and to the voyage on which she is engaged. Boat drill, regulated according to the opportunities of the service, should always be held.

It is perhaps worth recording that there was an inspection of the boats themselves at Southampton by Mr. Clarke, the emigration officer, and that, as a result, Mr. Clarke gave his certificate that the boats were satisfactory. For the purpose of this inspection two of the boats were lowered to the water and crews exercised in them.

The collision took place at 11.40 P.M. (ship's time). About midnight it was realized that the vessel could not live, and at about 12.05 the order was given to uncover the 14 boats under davits. The work began on both sides of the ship under the superintendence of five officers. It did not proceed quickly at first; the crew arrived on the boat deck only gradually, and there was an average of not more than three deck hands to each boat. At 12.20 the order was given to swing out the boats, and this work was at once commenced. There were a few passengers on the deck at this time. Mr. Lightoller, who was one of the officers directing operations, says that the noise of the steam blowing off was so great that his voice could not be heard, and that he had to give directions with his hands.

Before this work had been begun, the stewards were rousing the passengers in their different quarters, helping them to put on life-belts and getting them up to the boat deck. At about 12.30 the order was given to place women and children in the boats. This was proceeded with at once and at about 12.45 Mr. Murdoch gave the order to lower No. 7 boat (on the starboard side) to the water. The work of uncovering, filling, and lowering the boats was done under the following supervision: Mr. Lowe, the fifth officer, saw to Nos. 1, 3, 5, and 7; Mr. Murdoch (lost) saw also to 1 and 7 and to A and C. Mr. Moody (lost) looked after Nos. 9, 11, 13, and 15. Mr. Murdoch also saw to 9 and 11. Mr. Lightoller saw to Nos. 4, 6, 8, B, and D. Mr. Wilde (lost) also saw to 8 and D. Mr. Lightoller and Mr. Moody saw to 10 and 16 and Mr. Lowe to 12 and 14. Mr. Wilde also assisted at No. 14, Mr. Boxall helping generally.

The evidence satisfies me that the officers did their work very well and without any thought of themselves. Capt. Smith, the master, Mr. Wilde, the chief officer, Mr. Murdoch, the first officer, and Mr. Moody, the sixth officer, all went down with the ship while performing their duties. The others, with the exception of Mr. Lightoller, took charge of boats and thus were saved. Mr. Lightoller was swept off the deck as the vessel went down and was subsequently picked up.

So far as can be ascertained the boats left the ship at the following times, but I think it is necessary to say that these, and, indeed, all the times subsequent to the collision which are mentioned by the witnesses, are unreliable.

As regards the collapsible boats, C and D were properly lowered; as to A and B, which were on the roof of the officers' house, they were left until the last. There was difficulty in getting these boats down to the deck, and the ship had at this time a list. Very few of the deck hands were left in the ship, as they had nearly all gone to man the lifeboats, and the stewards and firemen were unaccustomed to work the collapsible boats. Work appears to have been going on in connection with these two boats at the time that the ship sank. The boats seem to have floated from the deck and to have served in the water as rafts.

There were in all 107 men of the crew, 43 male passengers, and 704 women and children, or a total of 854 in 18 boats. In addition, about 60 persons, two of whom were women, were said to have been transferred, subsequently, from A and B collapsible boats to other boats, or rescued from the water, making a total of 914 who escaped with their lives. It is obvious that these figures are quite unreliable, for only 712 were in fact saved by the *Carpathia*, the steamer which came to the rescue at about 4 A.M., and all the boats were accounted for.

Another remarkable discrepancy is that, of the 712 saved, 189 were in fact men of the crew, 129 were male passengers, and 394 were women and children. In other words, the real proportion of women to men saved was much less than the proportion appearing in the evidence from the boats. Allowing for those subsequently picked up, of the 712 persons saved only 652 could have left the *Titanic* in boats, or an average of about 36 per boat. There was a tendency in the evidence to exaggerate the numbers in each boat, to exaggerate the proportion of women to men, and to diminish the number of crew.

I do not attribute this to any wish on the part of the witnesses to mislead the court, but to a natural desire to make the best case for themselves and their ship. The seamen who gave evidence were too frequently encouraged when under examination in the witness box to understate the number of crew in the boats. The number of crew actually saved was 189, giving an average of 10 per boat, and if from this figure the 58 men of the 60 persons above mentioned be deducted the average number of crew leaving the ship in the boats must still have been at least 7. The probability, however, is that many of the 60 picked up were passengers.

The discipline both among passengers and crew during the lowering of the boats was good, but the organization should have been better, and if it had been it is possible that more lives would have been saved.

The real difficulty in dealing with the question of the boats is to find the explanation of so many of them leaving the ship with comparatively few persons in them. No. 1 certainly left with only 12; this was an emergency boat with a carrying capacity of 40. No. 7 left with only 27, and No. 6 with only 28; these were lifeboats with a carrying capacity of 65 each; and several of the others, according to the evidence, and certainly according to the truth, must have left only partly filled. Many explanations are forthcoming, one being that the passengers were unwilling to leave the ship. When the earlier boats left, and before the *Titanic* had begun materially to settle down, there was a drop of 65 feet from the boat deck to the water, and the women feared to get into the boats. Many people thought that the risk in the ship was less than the risk in the boats. This explanation is supported by the evidence of Capt. Rostron, of the *Carpathia*. He says that after those who were saved got on board his ship he was told by some of them that when the boats first left the *Titanic* the people "really would not be put in the boats; they did not want to go in."

There was a large body of evidence from the *Titanic* to the same effect, and I have no doubt that many people, particularly women, refused to leave the deck for the boats. At one time the master appears to have had the intention of putting the people into the boats from the gangway doors in the side of the ship. This was possibly with a view to allay the fears of the passengers, for from these doors the water could be reached by means of ladders, and the lowering of some of the earlier boats when only partly filled may be accounted for in this way.

There is no doubt that the master did order some of the partly filled boats to row to a position under one of the doors with the object of taking in passengers at that point. It appears, however, that these doors were never opened. Another explanation is that some women refused to leave their husbands. It is said further that the officers engaged in putting the people into the boats feared that the boats might buckle if they were filled; but this proved to be an unfounded apprehension, for one or more boats were completely filled and then successfully lowered to the water.

At 12.35 the message from the *Carpathia* was received announcing that she was making for the *Titanic*. This probably became known and may have tended to make the passengers still more unwilling to leave the ship, and the lights of a ship (the *Californian*) which were seen by many people may have encouraged the passengers to hope that assistance was at hand. These explanations are perhaps sufficient to account for so many of the lifeboats leaving without a full boat load; but I think, nevertheless, that if the boats had been kept a little longer before being lowered, or if the after gangway doors had been opened, more passengers might have been induced to enter the boats.

And if women could not be induced to enter the boats, the boats ought then to have been filled up with men. It is difficult to account for so many of the lifeboats being sent from the sinking ship, in a smooth sea, far from full. These boats left behind them many hundreds of lives to perish. I do not, however, desire these observations to be read as casting any reflection on the officers of the ship or on the crew who were working on the boat deck. They all worked admirably, but I think that if there had been better organization the results would have been more satisfactory.

I heard much evidence as to the conduct of the boats after the *Titanic* sank and when there must have been many struggling people in the water, and I regret to say that in my opinion some, at all events, of the boats failed to attempt to save lives when they might have done so, and might have done so successfully. This was particularly the case with boat No. 1. It may reasonably have been thought that the risk of making the attempt was too great; but it seems to me that if the attempt had been made by some of these boats it might have been the means of saving a few more lives. Subject to these few adverse comments, I have nothing but praise for both passengers and crew. All the witnesses speak well of their behavior. It is to be remembered that the night was dark, the noise of the escaping steam was terrifying, the peril, though perhaps not generally recognized, was imminent and great, and many passengers who were unable to speak or to understand English were being collected together and hurried into the boats.

CONDUCT OF SIR C. DUFF GORDON AND MR. ISMAY

An attack was made in the course of the inquiry on the moral conduct of two of the passengers, namely, Sir Cosmo Duff Gordon and Mr. Bruce Ismay. It is no part of the business of the court to inquire into such matters, and I should pass them by in silence if I did not fear that my silence might be misunderstood. The very gross charge against Sir Cosmo Duff Gordon that, having got into No. 1 boat, he bribed the men in it to row away from drowning people is unfounded. I have said that the members of the crew in that boat might have made some attempt to save the people in the water, and that such an attempt would probably have been successful; but I do not believe that the men were deterred from making the attempt by any act of Sir Cosmo Duff Gordon's. At the same time I think that if he had encouraged the men to return to the position where the *Titanic* had foundered they would probably have made an effort to do so and could have saved some lives.

As to the attack on Mr. Bruce Ismay, it resolved itself into the suggestion that, occupying the position of managing director of the steamship company, some moral duty was imposed upon him to wait on board until the vessel foundered. I do not agree. Mr. Ismay, after rendering assistance to many passengers, found C collapsible, the last boat on the starboard side, actually being lowered. No other people were there at the time. There was room for him and he jumped in. Had he not jumped in he would merely have added one more life, namely, his own, to the number of those lost.

THE THIRD-CLASS PASSENGERS

It had been suggested before the inquiry that the third-class passengers had been unfairly treated; that their access to the boat deck had been impeded, and that when at last they reached that deck the first and second class passengers were given precedence in getting places in the boats. There appears to have been no truth in these suggestions. It is no doubt true that the proportion of third-class passengers saved falls far short of the proportion of the first and second class, but this is accounted for by the greater reluctance of the third-class passengers to leave the ship, by their unwillingness to part with their baggage, by the difficulty of getting them up from their quarters, which were at the extreme ends of the ship, and by other similar causes. The interests of the relatives of some of the third-class passengers who had perished were in the hands of Mr. Harbinson, who attended the inquiry on their behalf. He said at the end of his address to the court:

I wish to say distinctly that no evidence has been given in the course of this case which would substantiate a charge that any attempt was made to keep back the third-class passengers. I desire further to say that there is no evidence that when they did reach the boat deck there was any discrimination practiced either by the officers or the sailors in putting them into the boats.

I am satisfied that the explanation of the excessive proportion of third-class passengers lost is not to be found in the suggestion that the third-class passengers were in any way unfairly treated. They were not unfairly treated.

MEANS TAKEN TO PROCURE ASSISTANCE

As soon as the dangerous condition of the ship was realized, messages were sent by the master's orders to all steamers within reach. At 12.15 A.M. the distress signal CQD was sent. This was heard by several steamships and by Cape Race. By 12.25 Mr. Boxall, the fourth officer, had worked out the correct position of the *Titanic*, and then another message was sent: "Come at once, we have struck a berg." This was heard by the Cunard steamer *Carpathia*, which was at this time bound from New York to Liverpool and 58 miles away. The *Carpathia* answered, saying that she was coming to the assistance of the *Titanic*. This was reported to Capt. Smith on the boat deck. At 12.26 a message was sent out, "Sinking; can not hear for noise of steam." Many other messages were also sent, but as they were only heard by steamers which were too far away to render help, it is not necessary to refer to them. At 1.45 a message was heard by the *Carpathia*, "Engine-room full up to boilers." The last message sent out was "CQ" which was faintly heard by the steamer *Virginian*. This message was sent at 2.17. It thus appears that the Marconi apparatus was at work until within a few minutes of the foundering of the *Titanic*.

Meanwhile Mr. Boxall was sending up distress signals from the deck. These signals (rockets) were sent off at intervals from a socket by No. 1 emergency boat on the boat deck. They were the ordinary distress signals, exploding in the air and throwing off white stars. The firing of these signals began about the time that No. 7 boat was lowered (12.45 A.M.), and it continued until Mr. Boxall left the ship at about 1.45.

Mr. Boxall was also using a Morse light from the bridge in the direction of a ship whose lights he saw about half a point on the port bow of the *Titanic* at a distance, as he thought, of about 5 or 6 miles. He got no answer. In all, Mr. Boxall fired about eight rockets. There appears to be no doubt that the vessel whose lights he saw was the *Californian*. The evidence from the *Californian* speaks of eight rockets having been seen between 12.30 and 1.40. The *Californian* heard none of the *Titanic's* messages; she had only one Marconi operator on board and he was asleep.

THE RESCUE BY THE STEAMSHIP *CARPATHIA*

On the 15th of April the steamship *Carpathia*, 13,600 tons gross, of the Cunard Line, Mr. Arthur Henry Rostron, master, was on her passage to Liverpool from New York. She carried some 740 passengers and 325 crew.

On receipt of the *Titanic's* first distress message the captain immediately ordered the ship to be turned around and driven at her highest speed (17-1/2 knots) in the direction of the *Titanic*. He also informed the *Titanic* by wireless that he was coming to her assistance, and he subsequently received various messages from her. At about 2.40 A.M. he saw a green flare which, as the evidence shows, was being sent up by Mr. Boxall in No. 2 boat. From this time until 4 A.M. Capt. Rostron was altering his course continually in order to avoid icebergs. He fired rockets in answer to the signals he saw from Boxall's boat. At 4 o'clock he considered he was practically up to the position given and he stopped his ship at 4.05. He sighted the first boat (No. 2) and picked her up at 4.10. There was then a large number of icebergs around him, and it was just daylight. Eventually he picked up in all 13 lifeboats, two emergency boats, and two collapsible boats, all of which were taken on board the *Carpathia*, the other boats being abandoned as damaged or useless. From these boats he took on board 712 persons, one of whom died shortly afterwards. The boats were scattered over an area of 4 or 5 miles, and it was 8 A.M. before they had all been picked up. He saw very little wreckage when he got near to the scene of the disaster, only a few deck chairs, cork life belts, etc., and only one body. The position was then 41° 46′ N., 50° 14′ W.

The *Carpathia* subsequently returned to New York with the passengers and crew she had rescued.

The court desires to record its great admiration of Capt. Rostron's conduct. He did the very best that could be done.

NUMBERS SAVED

The following were the numbers saved:

First Class		
Adult males	57	out of 175, or 32.57 per cent.
Adult females	140	out of 144, or 97.22 per cent.
Male children (all saved)	5	
Female children (all saved)	1	
Total:	203	out of 325, or 62.46 per cent.
Second Class		
Adult Males	14	out of 168, or 8.33 per cent.
Adult females	80	out of 93, or 86.02 per cent.
Male children (all saved)	11	
Female children (all saved)	13	
Total:	118	out of 285, or 41.40 per cent.
Third Class		
Adult males	75	out of 462, or 16.23 per cent.
Adult females	76	out of 165, or 46.06 per cent.
Male children	13	out of 48, or 27.08 per cent.
Female children	14	out of 31, or 45.16 per cent.
Total	178	out of 706, or 25.21 per cent.
Total:	499	out of 1,316, or 37.94 per cent.

Crew Saved		
Deck department	43	out of 66, or 65.15 per cent.
Engine-room department	72	out of 325, or 22.15 per cent.
Victualing department (including 20 women out of 23)	97	out of 494, or 19.63 per cent.
Total	212	out of 885, or 23.95 per cent.
Total on board saved	711	out of 2,201, or 32.30 per cent.

Passengers and Crew		
Adult males	338	out of 1,667, or 20.27 per cent.
Adult females	316	out of 425, or 74.35 per cent.
Children	57	out of 109, or 52.29 per cent.
Total	711	out of 2,201, or 32.30 per cent.

THE CIRCUMSTANCES IN CONNECTION WITH THE STEAMSHIP *CALIFORNIAN*

It is here necessary to consider the circumstances relating to the steamship *Californian*.

On the 14th of April the steamship *Californian*, of the Leyland Line, Mr. Stanley Lord, master, was on her passage from London, which port she left on April 5, to Boston, United States, where she subsequently arrived on April 19. She was a vessel of 6,223 tons gross and 4,038 net. Her full speed was 12-1/2 to 13 knots. She had a passenger certificate, but was not carrying any passengers at the time. She belonged to the International Mercantile Marine Co., the owners of the *Titanic*.

At 7.30 P.M., ship's time, on April 14, a wireless message was sent from this ship to the *Antillian*:

> To CAPTAIN, *Antillian*:
> Six thirty P.M., apparent ship's time, latitude 42° 3′ N., longitude 49° 9′ W. Three large bergs, 5 miles to southward of us. Regards.
> LORD

The message was intercepted by the *Titanic*, and when the Marconi operator (Evans) of the *Californian* offered this ice report to the Marconi operator of the *Titanic*, shortly after 7.30 P.M., the latter replied:

> It is all right. I heard you sending it to the *Antillian*, and I have got it.

The *Californian* proceeded on her course S. 89° W. true until 10.20
P.M., ship's time, when she was obliged to stop and reverse engines because
she was running into field ice, which stretched as far as could then be seen to
the northward and southward.

The master told the court that he made her position at that time to
be 42° 5′ N., 57° 7′ W. This position is recorded in the log book, which
was written up from the scrap log book by the chief officer. The scrap log
is destroyed. It is a position about 19 miles N. by E. of the position of the
Titanic when she foundered, and is said to have been fixed by dead reckoning
and verified by observations. I am satisfied that this position is not accurate.
The master "twisted her head" to E. N. E. by the compass and she remained
approximately stationary until 5.15 A.M. on the following morning. The ship
was slowly swinging around to starboard during the night.

At about 11 P.M. a steamer's light was seen approaching from the eastward. The master went to Evans's room and asked what ships he had. The
latter replied: "I think the *Titanic* is near us. I have got her." The master
said: "You had better advise the *Titanic* we are stopped and surrounded with
ice." This Evans did, calling up the *Titanic* and sending: "We are stopped
and surrounded by ice." The *Titanic* replied: "Keep out." The *Titanic* was in
communication with Cape Race, which station was then sending messages to
her. The reason why the *Titanic* answered "keep out" was that her Marconi
operator could not hear what Cape Race was saying, as from her proximity
the message from the *Californian* was much stronger than any message being
taken in by the *Titanic* from Cape Race, which was much farther off. Evans
heard the *Titanic* continuing to communicate with Cape Race up to the time
he turned in at 11.30 P.M.

The master of the *Californian* states that when observing the approaching steamer as she got nearer he saw more lights, a few deck lights, and also
her green side light. He considered that at 11 o'clock she was approximately
6 or 7 miles away, and at some time between 11 and 11.30 he first saw her
green light; she was then about 5 miles off. He noticed that about 11.30 she

stopped. In his opinion this steamer was of about the same size as the *Californian*—a medium-sized steamer, "something like ourselves."

From the evidence of Mr. Groves, third officer of the *Californian*, who was the officer of the first watch, it would appear that the master was not actually on the bridge when the steamer was sighted.

Mr. Groves made out two masthead lights; the steamer was changing her bearing slowly as she got closer, and as she approached he went to the chart room and reported this to the master; he added, "She is evidently a passenger steamer." In fact, Mr. Groves never appears to have had any doubt on this subject. In answer to a question during his examination, "Had she much light?" he said, "Yes, a lot of light. There was absolutely no doubt of her being a passenger steamer, at least in my mind."

Gill, the assistant donkey man of the *Californian*, who was on deck at midnight, said, referring to this steamer: "It could not have been anything but a passenger boat, she was too large."

By the evidence of Mr. Groves, the master, in reply to his report, said: "Call her up on the Morse lamp, and see if you can get any answer." This he proceeded to do. The master came up and joined him on the bridge and remarked: "That does not look like a passenger steamer." Mr. Groves replied: "It is, sir. When she stopped her lights seemed to go out, and I suppose they have been put out for the night." Mr. Groves states that these lights went out at 11.40, and remembers that time because "one bell was struck to call the middle watch." The master did not join him on the bridge until shortly afterwards, and consequently after the steamer had stopped.

In his examination Mr. Groves admitted that if this steamer's head was turning to port after she stopped, it might account for the diminution of lights, by many of them being shut out. Her steaming lights were still visible and also her port side light.

The captain only remained upon the bridge for a few minutes. In his evidence he stated that Mr. Groves had made no observations to him about the steamer's deck lights going out. Mr. Groves's Morse signaling appears to have been ineffectual (although at one moment he thought he was being answered), and he gave it up. He remained on the bridge until relieved by Mr. Stone, the second officer, just after midnight. In turning the *Californian* over to him, he pointed out the steamer and said: "She has been stopped since 11.40; she is a passenger steamer. At about the moment she stopped she put her lights out." When Mr. Groves was in the witness box the following questions were put to him by me:

Speaking as an experienced seaman and knowing what you do know now, do you think that steamer that you know was throwing up rockets, and that you say was a passenger steamer, was the *Titanic*?—Do I think it? Yes. From what I have heard subsequently? Yes. Most decidedly I do, but I do not put myself as being an experienced man. But that is your opinion as far as your experience goes?—Yes, it is, my lord.

Mr. Stone states that the master, who was also up (but apparently not on the bridge), pointed out the steamer to him with instructions to tell him if her bearings altered or if she got any closer; he also stated that Mr. Groves had called her up on the Morse lamp and had received no reply.

Mr. Stone had with him during the middle watch an apprentice named Gibson, whose attention was first drawn to the steamer's lights at about 12.20 A.M. He could see a masthead light, her red light (with glasses), and a "glare of white lights on her afterdeck." He first thought her masthead light was flickering and next thought it was a Morse light, "calling us up." He replied, but could not get into communication, and finally came to the conclusion that it was, as he had first supposed, the masthead light flickering. Sometime after 12.30 A.M., Gill, the donkey man, states that he saw two rockets fired from the ship which he had been observing, and about 1.10 A.M., Mr. Stone reported to the captain by voice pipe, that he had seen five white rockets from the direction of the steamer. He states that the master answered, "Are they company's signals?" and that he replied, "I do not know, but they appear to me to be white rockets." The master told him to "go on Morsing," and, when he received any information, to send the apprentice down to him with it. Gibson states that Mr. Stone informed him that he had reported to the master, and that the master had said the steamer was to be called up by Morse light. This witness thinks the time was 12.55; he at once proceeded again to call the steamer up by Morse. He got no reply, but the vessel fired three more white rockets; these rockets were also seen by Mr. Stone.

Both Mr. Stone and the apprentice kept the steamer under observation, looking at her from time to time with their glasses. Between 1 o'clock and 1.40 some conversation passed between them. Mr. Stone remarked to Gibson: "Look at her now, she looks very queer out of water, her lights look queer." He also is said by Gibson to have remarked, "A ship is not going to fire rockets at sea for nothing"; and admits himself that he may possibly have used that expression.

Mr. Stone states that he saw the last of the rockets fired at about 1.40, and after watching the steamer for some 20 minutes more he sent Gibson down to the master.

I told Gibson to go down to the master, and be sure and wake him, and tell him that altogether we had seen eight of these white lights like white rockets in the direction of this other steamer; that this steamer was disappearing in the southwest, that we had called her up repeatedly on the Morse lamp and received no information whatsoever.

Gibson states that he went down to the chart room and told the master; that the master asked him if all the rockets were white, and also asked him the time. Gibson stated that at this time the master was awake. It was five minutes past two, and Gibson returned to the bridge to Mr. Stone and reported. They both continued to keep the ship under observation until she disappeared. Mr. Stone describes this as "A gradual disappearing of all her lights, which would be perfectly natural with a ship steaming away from us."

At about 2.40 A.M. Mr. Stone again called up the master by voice pipe and told him that the ship from which he had seen the rockets come had disappeared bearing SW. 1/2 W., the last he had seen of the light; and the master again asked him if he was certain there was no color in the lights. "I again assured him they were all white, just white rockets." There is considerable discrepancy between the evidence of Mr. Stone and that of the master. The latter states that he went to the voice pipe at about 1.15, but was told then of a white rocket (not five white rockets). Moreover, between 1.30 and 4.30, when he was called by the chief officer (Mr. Stewart), he had no recollection of anything being reported to him at all, although he remembered Gibson opening and closing the chart-room door.

Mr. Stewart relieved Mr. Stone at 4 A.M. The latter told him he had seen a ship 4 or 5 miles off when he went on deck at 12 o'clock, and at 1 o'clock he had seen some white rockets, and that the moment the ship started firing them she started to steam away. Just at this time (about 4 A.M.) a steamer came in sight with two white masthead lights and a few lights amidships. He asked Mr. Stone whether he thought this was the steamer which had fired rockets, and Mr. Stone said he did not think it was. At 4.30 he called the master and informed him that Mr. Stone had told him he had seen rockets in the middle watch. The master said, "Yes, I know; he has been telling me." The master came at once on to the bridge, and apparently took the fresh steamer for the one which had fired rockets, and said, "She looks all right; she is not making any signals now." This mistake was not corrected. He, however, had the wireless operator called.

At about 6 A.M. Capt. Lord heard from the *Virginian* that the "*Titanic* had struck a berg, passengers in boats, ship sinking"; and he at once started through the field ice at full speed for the position given.

Capt. Lord stated that about 7.30 A.M. he passed the *Mount Temple*, stopped, and that she was in the vicinity of the position given him as where the *Titanic* had collided (lat. 41° 46′ N.; long. 50° 14′ W.). He saw no wreckage there, but did later on near the *Carpathia*, which ship he closed soon afterwards, and he stated that the position where he subsequently left this wreckage was 41° 33′ N.; 50° 1′ W. It is said in the evidence of Mr. Stewart that the position of the *Californian* was verified by stellar observations at 7.30 P.M. on the Sunday evening, and that he verified the captain's position given when the ship stopped (42° 5′ N.; 50° 7′ W.) as accurate on the next day. The position in which the wreckage was said to have been seen on the Monday morning was verified by sights taken on that morning.

All the officers are stated to have taken sights, and Mr. Stewart in his evidence remarks that they all agreed. If it is admitted that these positions were correct, then it follows that the *Titanic*'s position as given by that ship when making the CQD signal was approximately S. 16° W. (true), 19 miles from the *Californian*; and further that the position in which the *Californian* was stopped during the night was 30 miles away from where the wreckage was seen by her in the morning, or that the wreckage had drifted 11 miles in a little more than five hours.

There are contradictions and inconsistencies in the story as told by the different witnesses. But the truth of the matter is plain. The *Titanic* collided with the berg at 11.40. The vessel seen by the *Californian* stopped at this time. The rockets sent up from the *Titanic* were distress signals. The *Californian* saw distress signals. The number sent up by the *Titanic* was about eight. The *Californian* saw eight. The time over which the rockets from the *Titanic* were sent up was from about 12.45 to 1.45 o'clock. It was about this time that the *Californian* saw the rockets. At 2.40 Mr. Stone called to the master that the ship from which he had seen the rockets had disappeared. At 2.20 A.M. the *Titanic* had foundered. It was suggested that the rockets seen by the *Californian* were from some other ship, not the *Titanic*. But no other ship to fit this theory has ever been heard of.

These circumstances convince me that the ship seen by the *Californian* was the *Titanic*, and if so, according to Capt. Lord, the two vessels were about 5 miles apart at the time of the disaster. The evidence from the *Titanic* corroborates this estimate, but I am advised that the distance was probably greater, though not more than 8 to 10 miles. The ice by which the *Californian* was surrounded was loose ice extending for a distance of not more than 2 or 3 miles in the direction of the *Titanic*. The night was clear and the sea was smooth. When she first saw the rockets, the *Californian* could have pushed through the ice to the open water without any serious risk and so have come to the assistance of the *Titanic*. Had she done so she might have saved many if not all of the lives that were lost.

10.

WINTER IN THE ARCTIC

REV. LEWIS HOLMES

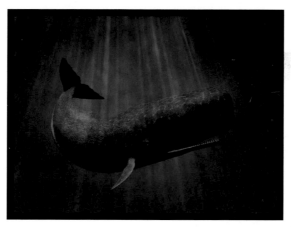

The Arctic whaleman; or, Winter in the Arctic Ocean:
being a narrative of the wreck of the whale ship Citizen,
by Lewis Holmes, 1857. Smithsonian Library.

On the 21st of September, we finished cutting in a whale, about twelve o'clock, midnight, wind high from the north-east. The northern lights were uncommonly brilliant, which prognosticated a storm; and the broken water and flying spray round the vessel seemed as if composed of an infinite number of diamonds glistening in the rays of the sun.

The season of the year had now arrived in which, in those high latitudes, sudden changes and violent storms were expected. At three o'clock on the morning of the 22d, the ship was put under short sail; rough; unable to keep fires in the furnace; ship heading to the south-east. We spoke with Captain Clough, who had just taken in a "raft" of blubber. We took a whale; and for a little time the wind moderated, which gave us hope that we should have favorable weather some time longer. Captain Clough left us that day, and turned his ship towards the straits, saying, "I am bound out of the ocean, and have enough." His ship was full; he had thirty-two hundred barrels of oil on board.

We concluded to remain on the ground a while longer, in lat. 68° N. The wind, which had in a measure subsided, now began to rise and increase, until it had reached a heavy gale. We saw in the distance several ships steering for the straits, and bound for the islands. On the 23d, it blew hard, and we were unable to boil.

We judged we were, at this time, about one hundred and fifty miles from land. The weather had been thick for several days past, and therefore we were unable to get an observation. We saw several ships lying to, and heading some one way and some another. The water, we perceived, was very much colored, which indicated that we were drifting towards the eastern shore of the Arctic. At twelve o'clock, wore ship, heading north-west by north. At the same hour that night, wore ship again, heading north-east.

We passed a ship, within the distance of half a mile, under bare poles, laboring very hard. On the 24th, four o'clock, wore ship north-north-west, wind blowing very heavily from the north-east. We saw great quantities of drift stuff, such as barrels, wood, &c., probably the deck load of some ship swept by the sea. At twelve o'clock, wore ship again; the wind appeared to lull somewhat, but the sea was very rugged; we judged we were about one hundred or one hundred and twenty miles distant from land; weather thick, with rain, sleet, and fog. About one o'clock, on the morning of the 25th, the wind increased, and swept over the ocean with the violence of a hurricane. The darkness of the night added to the tumultuous and mountainous waves that were running at that time; the surface of the ocean lashed into fury by the thickening storm, still gathering its strength; the noble ship now rising the crested billow, and then sinking into the watery valley beneath, and pressed down by the beating and overwhelming elements, made the scene one of indescribable grandeur and awfulness. With the return of morning light, an ugly sea struck the ship, and took her spars from the bow, and carried away one of the starboard boats.

The mate immediately reported to the captain, who was below at the time, that the ship was in shoal water. As soon as he reached the deck, he ordered to set the fore and mizzen topsails. About the same time, the fourth mate reported that there were rocks and breakers just before and under the bows of the ship. From the house, the captain saw projecting rocks through the opening waters, and land all around to the leeward, while the sea was breaking with tremendous violence between the ship and shore.

It now became a certainty, which no earthly power could change, that the ship must go ashore; and the only hope for any one on board was to avoid, if possible, the fatal reef, which appeared to extend out some distance from the land. To strike upon that reef was certain destruction; we saw no way of escape.

The man at the wheel was ordered to put the helm hard up, and at the same time command was given to the seamen to sheet home the fore topsail. The ship immediately paid off two or three points, when she was struck again by another sea, that threw her round on the other tack.

The ship was now in the midst of the rollers, pitching and laboring dreadfully, while the sea was flying all over her deck, and the spray reaching nearly or quite to her fore and main yards. She was utterly unmanageable; and, at this instant, another sea boarded her, and took off three boats. The yards were ordered to be braced round as soon as possible; but, in the act of bracing them, a terrible blast of wind struck and carried away the fore and mizzen topsails, half-sheeted home. The foresail was now ordered to be set, the ship still pitching, tumbling, and rolling frightfully, and tossed about as a mere plaything at the mercy of winds and waves. In the act of setting the foresail, the weather clew was carried away, and with the next sea the ship struck aft very heavily, and knocked her rudder off, and sent the wheel up through the house. From five to eight minutes she struck forward with such stunning and overwhelming effect that the try-works started three or four feet from the deck, and opened a hole so large in her starboard bow that the largest casks came out.

About this time, the foremast was cut away, with the hope of temporarily relieving the foundering vessel. Shortly after this, the ship struck midships; and the dreadful crash which followed showed that her entire framework was shattered, while the standing masts bent to and fro like slender reeds when shaken by the wind. This was in effect the finishing blow; and what was to be done towards rescuing any thing below deck must be done soon or never.

The captain, at this critical juncture, went into the cabin to secure what articles he could, such as clothes, nautical instruments, money, &c. While there, the stern burst in, and the water came in between the opening timbers in such torrents as to send him backward and headlong with the few articles he had hastily gathered, and scattered them in every direction. The floor of the cabin opened beneath his feet. There was no time for delay. His life was in imminent peril. He at once started for the deck, but was unable to reach it on account of the house having been thrown down upon the gangway, and the mizzenmast having gone by the board, one part of which rested upon the rail. All access to the deck by the cabin doors was thus cut off.

Mr. Fisher became aware of the condition of the captain in the cabin, and called to him to come to the skylight; and as he jumped, he was caught by his arms, and drawn up by several who had come to his rescue. On reaching the deck, the captain saw at once the sad condition of his men. The sea was making a clear breach over the vessel, and they were huddled together round the forecastle and forward part of the ship, amazed, stupefied, cold, and shivering, and had apparently given themselves up to the fate which awaited them.

The fog having in a measure cleared away, the land was more plainly seen, and just at hand—not more than three hundred yards distant. The mainmast was still standing; and there was every indication that the entire top of the vessel, including the first and second decks, had become separated from her bottom, and was drifting in towards the shore. This proved to be the case. The standing mast was now inclining towards the shore, which seemed to present the only way to deliverance and life. The captain, therefore, encouraged his men to seize the first opportunity which should occur, and escape to land, and the sooner they did so the safer and better.

As the ship changed her position by the action of the waves, which swept over and around her with resistless fury, the end of the flying jib boom, at one time, was brought quite near the shore. The seamen were again urged to make an effort to save themselves. It was, indeed, a most desperate chance to venture an escape even from a present danger, with the liability of falling into another, unknown, and perhaps more to be dreaded. Though so near the solid land, towards which every eye looked and every heart panted, still the surging billows and receding undertow around the bow of the ship, were sufficient to appall the most courageous mind.

About this time, as near as can be recollected, the cooper and one of the boat steerers, having dropped themselves from the bow, reached land in safety. The captain, having observed that two had gained the shore, and knowing the utter impossibility of getting fire ashore if it was deferred until the breaking up of the ship, and without it all must unavoidably perish, even if they were saved from a watery grave, held up the lantern keg to attract their attention, and, making signs to them as far he was able for them to look after and save it, tossed the keg overboard. It was borne on the advancing and retreating waves back and forth for more than a quarter of a mile, before it was finally secured. In this keg, which was air-tight, there were candles, matches, tinder, and other combustible materials. It was indeed a most timely and fortunate rescue.

An effort was now made to get a line ashore. One of the crew fastened a line round his body, and attempted to reach the shore, the captain paying out the warp as was necessary. But in consequence of the great force of the current and undertow around the bow of the ship, the line swayed out so far that the man was compelled to let it go in order to save his life. It was with the greatest difficulty he reached the shore.

As the only and last resort which remained, offering reasonable prospect of deliverance, the mainmast was cut away. The ship was now lying nearly broadside to the shore, with her deck inboard, and so much heeled that it required the greatest attention to prevent one from falling off. The mast fell in the direction of the shore, and nearly reached land. The sea was still breaking with fearful power over the vessel, and its spray flying in dense masses over every thing around us, and the din of the thundering billows, as they beat upon the wreck and upon the shore, drowned all human voices to silence.

Again the captain passed along to the forward part of the ship, and once more remonstrated, urged and entreated his men to exert themselves for their safety and lives, as they had now the same means of getting ashore that the officers had; and, furthermore, that in a short time the deck would go to pieces, and then there would be but little, if any hope of their being saved. He resolved he would not leave the wreck until he saw his men in a fair way of escape. Up to this time, no one, it is supposed, had been lost; several had reached land in safety, but those still on the wreck were exposed every moment to a watery grave.

At length, the steerage boy lowered himself down from the bow, and with manly efforts sought to gain the land. He was immediately swept away, and was never seen after. About this time, many began to crawl down on the mainmast, still lying in the direction of the shore. In working their way along on the mast, their progress was not only slow, but they were chilled, benumbed with cold, their clothes thoroughly wet to their backs, and the sea at the same time flying over them. It was with the greatest difficulty they could hold on. The sight was a most affecting one. It was a period of painful anxiety. How many of these seamen will be saved?—how many will be lost?

While attempting thus to escape upon the mast, the advancing or the returning waves would frequently wash numbers off, and then they would struggle with all their energies to regain the mast or the rigging; while those who were more fortunate, and had retained their hold, would aid them as far as possible in getting on to the mast again. It was a most trying and heart-rending scene.

WRECK OF THE *CITIZEN*

The captain and Mr. Fisher were on the quarter deck, and observed a part of a boat hanging by the side of the ship; and they proposed to get into it, and, if possible, reach the land. Their purpose was to hold on to the boat, and thus be borne by the sea towards the shore. They did get into it; but whether it was carried towards the shore or not, or what became of the piece of the boat, they have no recollection. They were struck by a sea, and probably stunned. The first returning consciousness the captain had, he found himself floating alongside of the ship. He knew not what had become of Mr. Fisher until some time after. He regained a foothold on the quarter deck again, and seemed awakened more fully than ever to the conviction that he must do something, and that soon, in order to save his own life. He was chilled, benumbed, and exhausted; chances of escape appearing less and less probable, as a last resort, said Captain Norton, "I threw myself into the water, among casks, broken pieces of the wreck, and, besides, my own men floating all around me, that I might, if possible, gain the shore. I was probably insensible for some time. I knew nothing of what took place around me. When I came to myself, I found I was lying near the edge of the water, having been cast ashore by some friendly wave. I looked around, and the first man I saw was the fourth mate, floating about in the water a short distance from me. Mr. Fisher was washed ashore about the same time I was. We hastened to the fourth mate as soon as we were able; and one held on to the hand of the other, and hauled him ashore, supposing him to be dead. He, however, revived."

A heavy sea came along, and washed a number from the mast, and brought them ashore; but one man was carried off by the undertow outside the ship. The next sea brought him near to the shore again; and four of those on shore took hold of each other's hands, and ventured as far as safety would allow into the water, and succeeded in drawing him safe to land.

The condition of the carpenter was painful and distressing in the highest degree; yet no one could help him—no earthly power could afford him any assistance. He was plainly seen by those on shore. He was probably washed from the mast, with some others, and carried out to the deck again; and while there, he was doubtless caught in between the opening planks and timbers, and held fast by his legs; and it may be he was otherwise injured. He answered no signs made to him from the shore; he made no effort to free himself or to escape; and, in his case, an escape was an impossibility. In that position, his head dropped upon his breast, and there he died. Soon after, another sea struck the deck, and broke it all to pieces. The largest part that could be seen was that from the bow to the fore chains.

Another painful occurrence was witnessed by those on the shore. A Portuguese sailor was discovered floating about among the broken pieces of the wreck, among casks, barrels, &c. His efforts for self-preservation were remarkable. His shipmates would most gladly have given him a helping hand, but it was impossible to do so. Every heart was moved with sympathy for him. As the towering wave would hurl towards him some piece of the wreck, or a cask or barrel, he was seen to dive, and thus avoid being crushed by it. This he did repeatedly, until, from exhaustion or injury, or both, he sunk to rise no more.

We had three dogs on board, but they were all either killed or drowned; and of three hogs, only one got ashore alive. Within two hours from the time the ship first struck, the wreck was piled up on shore, opposite to where the disaster occurred, to the height of ten feet or more. Spars, timbers, planks, casks both whole and broken, shooks, &c., were thrown together in frightful confusion; and in this promiscuous mass we saw what was once our home and hope on the deep. Here we saw before our eyes a striking illustration of the feebleness of man's frail bark, and with what ease it is torn to pieces, and scattered far and wide, by the resistless power of the elements.

All who were living of our number had reached the shore. Those that were saved had become greatly chilled, and some were nearly perishing. Notwithstanding it was storming at the time, one of the first efforts of a part of our men was to make a fire over a cliff some little distance from the shore, affording a partial protection from the wind and rain.

In searching for articles as they came ashore, we discovered a small keg of spirits, which, in our condition of cold and destitution, was somewhat reviving to all our minds. Five casks of bread, also, were cast upon the beach; but neither beef nor pork was found. The latter probably sunk where the ship left her bottom.

The whole company was soon gathered round the fire, in order to dry our clothes, and, if possible, to obtain some additional warmth. All, however, of our former number were not there; it was a solemn gathering, and the appearance of all of us indicated that we had a narrow escape. Alas! some of our comrades and fellow-seamen were left behind in the surges of the deep, or mingled with the floating wreck, or cast with it upon the shore. The roll was called by the captain, and thirty-three answered to their names; five were numbered with the dead.

The few hours of the past had been full of painful and distressing interest. The majority of our number had been mercifully rescued; but we were cast shelterless, with a small supply of provisions, with no clothing, only what was upon our backs, upon the most barren and desolate region of the earth.

What were our present prospects? They were dark and ominous indeed. A new voyage, in effect, was just opening before us, with diminished numbers, of the progress and termination of which we could not even entertain a reasonable conjecture; yet one thing was certain—its commencement was inauspicious. And, though hope might measurably sustain our minds, still the prospective view before this company of castaway seamen—the rigors of the arctic winter before us, wholly unprepared with clothing to withstand the merciless and long-continued cold of the north, uncertain whether there would be any deliverance for us by any friendly sail, or what would be our reception among the natives,—indeed, the prospect before us was any thing but cheering and encouraging.

But here we were, in the providence of God, vessel and boats gone, at an unknown distance from civilized life and from the settlements of the natives; this was our present lot. Self-preservation, therefore, prompted us to make immediate efforts, in anticipation of what we might need in the future. A common misfortune united all our interests and exertions.

The captain ordered that every thing of value to them in their present circumstances found among the wreck—such as provisions, casks of sails, pieces of canvas, ropes, broken spars, tools, whale gearing, &c.—should be selected, and brought out of the reach of the surf and the accumulation of ice upon the shore. More than a thousand barrels of oil had drifted ashore, and could have been saved had some vessel arrived about that time. A temporary tent was erected as soon as possible, in which various articles could be stored, as well as afford some protection to us from the inclemency of the weather.

There were two circumstances exceedingly favorable in our disaster. It might have been much worse, and no one might have lived to relate the sad event. We realized, upon the review, that this would have been our certain fate, had the ship gone ashore in the night time. It was, however, daylight, and thus we had a clearview of our condition, danger, and prospects. Had it been otherwise, and the same general features of the wreck been transferred to the darkness of night, we do not believe that one soul of us would have been saved.

The other favorable circumstance was, we were not cast upon a rocky part of the coast, or against some high and precipitous cliffs, which lift their bold and defiant fronts against the surges of the ocean far into deep water; to strike against such as we saw, would, at the first concussion, have been the last of the ship and of all on board.

In the good providence of God, however, we drifted upon a part of the coast which presented, for half of a mile or more, quite a plain, sandy beach. We were, therefore, wrecked in the most fortunate spot. On both sides of us, to the west and south-east, cliffs began to rise, and broken and abrupt ledges extended some distance into the sea. Though five of our number found a watery grave, yet the fact that so many of us reached the shore was a matter of profound gratitude to that God who controls the elements, and before whom the sparrow does not fall to the ground without his notice.

11.

SUNK BY A WHALE

CAPTAIN THOMAS H. JENKINS

Having been requested to give an account of the sinking of the Bark *Kathleen* by a whale I will do the best I can, though I think that those who have read the papers know as much or more about it than I do.

We sailed from New Bedford the 22d October, 1901, and with the exception of three weeks of the worst weather I have ever had on leaving home, everything went fairly well till we arrived out on the 12-40 ground.

The day we arrived there we raised a large whale and chased him most all day but could not seem to get any aim of him. We lost the run of him at last in a rain squall.

A few days after, the 17th of March, 1902, was one of the finest whaling days I have ever seen, smooth water and a clear sky. When they were going up to masthead I told them to look sharp for some one was going to raise a whale before night.

We steered different courses during the fore-noon and at 1 P.M. the man aloft raised a white water which proved to be sperm whales, and there was a lot of them, some heading one way, some another.

When we got within a mile of them we lowered four boats, and soon after Mr. Nichols, the first mate, struck a whale, the other whales went to leeward and I followed them with the ship till I was sure the boats saw them.

Mr. Nichols then had his whale dead about one mile to windward, so I came to wind on the port tack, but it took us some time to get up to the mate, as we could not carry any foretopsail or flying jibs as the topmast had given out.

SPERM WHALING—THE CHASE

I stood on the port tack a while and then tacked. When we got braced up the dead whale was one point off the lee bow. I saw we were going to fetch him all right. Mr. Nichols had wafted his whale and was chasing some more. By that time, about 3 P.M., the lookout called out that the three boats to leeward were all fast. Of course we were all glad to hear that. I ran the ship alongside of the dead whale and after darting at him two or three times managed to get fast and get him alongside. Just then it was reported that the boats to leeward were out of sight. That worried me some so I told the cooper to get the fluke chain on the whale and I would go aloft and see if I could see the boats.

At this time Mr. Nichols had given up chasing and was coming on board. I got up to the topmast crosstrees and sat down. I then heard a whale spout off the weather beam and glancing that way, saw sure enough a large whale not more than five hundred feet from us, coming directly for the ship.

Mr. Nichols was then alongside, just going to hoist his boat. I told him there was a whale, a big fellow, trying to get alongside and to go and help him along and he did help him along. He took him head and head and did not get fast. I don't know why. He certainly was near enough, the boatsteerer said too near, and did not have a chance to swing his iron.

Instead of that whale going down or going to windward as they most always do, he kept coming directly for the ship, only much faster than he was coming before he was darted at. When he got within thirty feet of the ship he saw or heard something and tried to go under the ship but he was so near and was coming so fast he did not have room enough to get clear of her.

He struck the ship forward of the mizzen rigging and about five or six feet under water. It shook the ship considerably when he struck her, then he tried to come up and he raised the stern up some two or three feet so when she came down her counters made a big splash. The whale came up on the other side of the ship and laid there and rolled, did not seem to know what to do. I asked the cooper if he thought the whale had hurt the ship any and he said he did not think so for he had not heard anything crack.

SPERM WHALING—THE CAPTURE

The Whale in a Flurry, Lithograph by F. Martens, Detail, After Louis Ambroise Garneray, mid-nineteenth century.

Mr. Nichols was still trying to get to the whale when I thought we had no business fooling with that whale any more that day as the other three boats were out of sight and fast to whales and night coming on, so I told him to come alongside. "What for?" asked Mr. Nichols, "the whale is laying there." I said, "Never mind the whale but come alongside and hoist the boat up as soon as you can." He did so and I told him to get his glasses and come up to masthead and see if he could see the boats. His eyes were younger than mine and he soon raised them. Just at this time one of the men went to the forecastle to get some dry clothes and he found the floor covered with water. He cried out and then I knew the ship must have quite a hole in her. I immediately ordered flags set at all three mastheads, a signal for all boats to come on board under any and all circumstances.

Mr. Viera was then not more than a mile and a half from the ship and I knew he could not but help seeing the flags, but it was no use, he would not let go that whale he was fast to. If he had only come to the ship they could have got some more water and bread. I set two gangs at work right away, one getting water and the other getting bread. The cask of bread was between decks and three men staid with that cask till the water came in and floated the cask away from them.

I then went to the cabin and found Mrs. Jenkins reading. She did not know that there was anything the matter with the ship. I told her the ship was sinking and to get some warm clothing as soon as she could but not to try to save anything else. Well, the first thing she did was to go for the parrot and take him on deck. Then she got a jacket and an old shawl.

By that time it was time to take to the boat, which we did without any confusion whatever.

There were twenty-one of us in the boat and with the water and bread and some old clothes she was pretty near the water, so deep that the water came over the centre board, so that some of us had to keep bailing all the time, while the rest were paddling down to the boat that was still laying by the whale.

The ship rolled over to windward five minutes after we got clear of her. Well, we got to Mr. Viera at last and divided the men and give him his share of bread and water. Then it was dark and very necessary that we should find the other boats, for I knew they did not see the ship capsize and they would be looking for her for a day or so with no water to drink. Well, we set our sails and steered as near as we could where we thought the boats ought to be and about nine o'clock we raised them.

They were very much surprised to hear that the *Kathleen* was gone. I gave them some bread and water and divided the men up again, so three boats had ten men each and one boat nine men. I told them all to keep in sight of me and that I would keep a lantern burning all night. We then started for the island of Barbados, distant 1,060 miles. It was a beautiful moonlight night with a smooth sea. When morning came there was not a boat to be seen so I came to the wind and laid with the sheet slacked off over an hour and raised a boat to windward steering for us. It was the third mate and he wanted some water. The water we gave him the night before was all salt. Well, we divided with him again and again started on our journey with five gallons of water. I told the third mate to keep up with me if he could but I should not stop for him or any one else again. About nine o'clock A.M. some one said he saw something off the port bow. We all looked and made it out to be smoke from a steamer and soon saw she was coming right for us, so we knew we were saved.

When she got near we saw she had a whale boat on her davits. They had picked up our second mate an hour before and he had told the captain that there were three other boats adrift and one of them had the captain and wife on board, so he was steaming around with two men at the masthead with glasses looking for us. We got alongside and she was way out of water. I asked Mrs. Jenkins if she could get up on a rope ladder they had put over the side and she said yes, she could get up if it was twice as high and she was not long in getting on deck.

Captain Dalton met us and welcomed us on board of the *Borderer of Glasgow*. He was very kind to us and did everything possible for us for the nine days we were on board his steamer, gave up his room to Mrs. Jenkins and myself even.

In nine days we were landed at Pernambuco and from there we came to Philadelphia on steamer *Pydna*, Captain Crossley.

We found friends everywhere we went; even in Philadelphia I had telegrams asking me to telegraph them if I needed any assistance. We arrived at New Bedford in due time and even Mr. Wing, (the agent of the Bark *Kathleen*), met me smilingly and seemed glad to see me. Everything seemed to work our way after the accident. When we were leaving the *Borderer* Capt. Dalton gave me thirty dollars in American bills, all he had with him.

He told me to take it and if I felt able when I got home to send the amount to his wife in England. It seems that Capt. Dalton had been running down this way for some years and having met head currents decided *this* trip to make a passage three or four degrees to the eastward to see if he couldn't get out of it.

Owing to this fact we were picked up as we were.

As we had not seen a sail of any description for some time we might have been days in our boat before seeing any vessel.

The other boat containing one of the mates and 9 seamen landed safely at the Barbados after being in the boat 9 days with but 5 gallons of water and a little ship bread.

Cases of whales rushing head on are very rare. One instance which will be remembered by some of the older residents of the city was in 1851, when the ship *Ann Alexander* was sunk in the Pacific ocean by a maddened whale.

In the Whaleman's Shipping List of Nov. 4, 1851, is a very full account of that occurrence. The story, which is substantially as follows, first appeared in the *Panama Herald*, as told by Captain John S. Deblois, follows:

The ship *Ann Alexander* sailed from New Bedford, June 1st, 1850, for a cruise in the South Pacific. Having taken 500 barrels of sperm oil in the Atlantic, Captain Deblois proceeded on the voyage to the Pacific.

On the 20th of August, 1851, while cruising on the "Off Shore grounds," at 9 o'clock in the morning, whales were discovered, and at noon of the same day succeeded in making fast to one.

The mate's boat made fast to the whale, which ran with the boat for some time, and then suddenly turning about rushed at the boat with open jaws, crushing the little craft into splinters. Captain Deblois rescued the boat's crew.

Later the waist boat was lowered from the ship and another attack made upon the leviathan. The mate again in charge of the attacking boat experienced another smashup, for in the battle the whale again turned on the boat's crew and crushed the second boat. The crew was saved and all hands returned to the ship, which proceeded after the whale.

The ship passed on by him, and immediately after it was discovered that the whale was making for the ship. As he came up near her they hauled on the wind and suffered the monster to pass her.

After he had fairly passed they kept off to overtake and attack him again. When the ship had reached within about 50 rods of him the crew discovered that the whale had settled down deep below the surface of the water, and as it was near sundown, it was decided to give up the pursuit.

The ship was moving about five knots, and while Captain Deblois stood at the rail he suddenly saw the whale rushing at the ship at the rate of 15 knots. In an instant the monster struck the ship with tremendous violence, shaking her from stem to stern. She quivered under the violence of the shock as if she had struck upon a rock.

The whale struck the ship about two feet from the keel, abreast the foremast, knocking a great hole entirely through her bottom, through which the water roared and rushed in impetuously. The anchors and cables were thrown overboard, as she had a large quantity of pig iron aboard. The ship sank rapidly, all effort to keep her afloat proving futile.

Captain Deblois ordered all hands to take to the boats and was the last to leave the ship, doing so by jumping from the vessel into the sea and swimming to the nearest boat. The ship was on her beam end, her topgallant yards under water.

They hung around in the vicinity of the *Ann Alexander* all that night, and the next day the captain boarded his vessel and cutting away the masts she righted, when they succeeded in getting stores from her hold, with which to supply their boats, should it become necessary to make a boat voyage to land.

On August 22 ship *Nantucket*, Captain Gibbs, cruising in that vicinity, discovered the imperiled sailors and taking them in charge landed them at Paita, September 15th. The *Ann Alexander* was hopelessly wrecked and left to her fate on August 23.

Five months after this disaster this pugnacious whale was captured by the *Rebecca Simms* of this port. Two of the *Ann Alexander's* harpoons were found in him and his head had sustained serious injuries, pieces of the ship's timbers being imbedded in it. The whale yielded 70 to 80 barrels of oil.

The only other known case of a like nature occurred to the ship *Essex* of Nantucket, commanded by Captain George Pollard, Jr.

She sailed from Nantucket, August 12, 1819, for a cruise in the Pacific ocean. On the morning of November 20, 1819, latitude 0.40 south and longitude 119 west, whales were discovered and all three boats lowered in pursuit.

The mate's boat soon struck a whale, but a blow of the animal's tail opening a bad hole in the boat, the crew was obliged to cut from him.

In the meantime, the captain's and second mate's boats had fastened to another whale, and the mate, heading the ship for the other boats, set about overhauling his boat preparatory to lowering again.

While doing this he saw a large sperm whale break water about 20 rods from the ship. The whale disappeared, but immediately came up again about a ship's length off, and made directly for the vessel, going at a velocity of about three miles an hour, and the *Essex* was advancing at about the same rate of speed.

Scarcely had the mate ordered the boy at the helm to put it hard up, when the whale, with greatly accelerated speed, struck the ship with his head just forward of the forechains.

The ship brought up suddenly and violently and trembled like a leaf. The whale passed under the vessel, scraping her keel as he went, came up on the leeward side, and lay apparently stunned for a moment.

The vessel began to settle at the head with the whale 100 yards off thrashing the water violently with his tail and opening and closing his jaws with great fury.

While the mate was thinking of getting the two extra boats clear, as the vessel had begun to settle rapidly, the cry was started by a sailor: "Here he is; he is making for us again!"

The whale came down for the ship with twice his ordinary speed and a line of foam about a rod in width, made with his tail, which he continually thrashed from side to side, marked his coming.

The whale crashed into the bows of the *Essex*, staving them completely in directly under the cathead. The whale after the second assault passed under the ship and out of sight to the leeward.

The crew were in a fix, in mid-ocean, a thousand miles from the nearest land and nothing but the frail whaleboat to save them.

The lashings of the spare boat were cut and she was launched with the ship falling on her beam ends. The ship hung together for three days. Provisions were taken from her and the whaleboats strengthened.

The boats started for the coast of Chile or Peru and after a hard time they landed at Ducies island. Unable to find subsistence there they again started, Dec. 27th, after leaving three of their number, of their own desire, and commenced to make the perilous voyage to the island of Juan Fernandez.

Many of the boats' crew died and the recital states that the flesh of a dead comrade was eaten by members of the mate's boat.

On Feb. 17th the surviving crew of the mate's boat were picked up by brig *Indian*. Captain Pollard and Charles Ramsdale, the sole survivors of the captain's boat, were picked up Feb. 23d by a Nantucket whaler, and the third boat was never heard from.

West India Docks by Pugin and Rowlandson from Ackermann's *Microcosm of London*, or, *London in Miniature* (1808-11)

12.

THE STORM

CHARLES DICKENS

For years after it occurred, I dreamed of it often. I have started up so vividly impressed by it, that its fury has yet seemed raging in my quiet room, in the still night. I dream of it sometimes, though at lengthened and uncertain intervals, to this hour. I have an association between it and a stormy wind, or the lightest mention of a sea-shore, as strong as any of which my mind is conscious. As plainly as I behold what happened, I will try to write it down. I do not recall it, but see it done; for it happens again before me.

The time drawing on rapidly for the sailing of the emigrant-ship, my good old nurse (almost broken-hearted for me, when we first met) came up to London. I was constantly with her, and her brother, and the Micawbers (they being very much together); but Emily I never saw.

One evening when the time was close at hand, I was alone with Peggotty and her brother. Our conversation turned on Ham. She described to us how tenderly he had taken leave of her, and how manfully and quietly he had borne himself. Most of all, of late, when she believed he was most tried. It was a subject of which the affectionate creature never tired; and our interest in hearing the many examples which she, who was so much with him, had to relate, was equal to hers in relating them.

My aunt and I were at that time vacating the two cottages at Highgate; I intending to go abroad, and she to return to her house at Dover. We had a temporary lodging in Covent Garden. As I walked home to it, after this evening's conversation, reflecting on what had passed between Ham and myself when I was last at Yarmouth, I wavered in the original purpose I had formed, of leaving a letter for Emily when I should take leave of her uncle on board the ship, and thought it would be better to write to her now. She might desire, I thought, after receiving my communication, to send some parting word by me to her unhappy lover. I ought to give her the opportunity.

I therefore sat down in my room, before going to bed, and wrote to her. I told her that I had seen him, and that he had requested me to tell her what I have already written in its place in these sheets. I faithfully repeated it. I had no need to enlarge upon it, if I had had the right. Its deep fidelity and goodness were not to be adorned by me or any man. I left it out, to be sent round in the morning; with a line to Mr. Peggotty, requesting him to give it to her; and went to bed at daybreak.

I was weaker than I knew then; and, not falling asleep until the sun was up, lay late, and unrefreshed, next day. I was roused by the silent presence of my aunt at my bedside. I felt it in my sleep, as I suppose we all do feel such things.

'Trot, my dear,' she said, when I opened my eyes, 'I couldn't make up my mind to disturb you. Mr. Peggotty is here; shall he come up?'

I replied yes, and he soon appeared.

'Mas'r Davy,' he said, when we had shaken hands, 'I giv Em'ly your letter, sir, and she writ this heer; and begged of me fur to ask you to read it, and if you see no hurt in't, to be so kind as take charge on't.'

'Have you read it?' said I.

He nodded sorrowfully. I opened it, and read as follows:

'I have got your message. Oh, what can I write, to thank you for your good and blessed kindness to me!

'I have put the words close to my heart. I shall keep them till I die. They are sharp thorns, but they are such comfort. I have prayed over them, oh, I have prayed so much. When I find what you are, and what uncle is, I think what God must be, and can cry to him.

'Good-bye for ever. Now, my dear, my friend, good-bye for ever in this world. In another world, if I am forgiven, I may wake a child and come to you. All thanks and blessings. Farewell, evermore.'

This, blotted with tears, was the letter.

'May I tell her as you doen't see no hurt in't, and as you'll be so kind as take charge on't, Mas'r Davy?' said Mr. Peggotty, when I had read it. 'Unquestionably,' said I—'but I am thinking—'

'Yes, Mas'r Davy?'

'I am thinking,' said I, 'that I'll go down again to Yarmouth. There's time, and to spare, for me to go and come back before the ship sails. My mind is constantly running on him, in his solitude; to put this letter of her writing in his hand at this time, and to enable you to tell her, in the moment of parting, that he has got it, will be a kindness to both of them. I solemnly accepted his commission, dear good fellow, and cannot discharge it too completely. The journey is nothing to me. I am restless, and shall be better in motion. I'll go down tonight.'

Though he anxiously endeavoured to dissuade me, I saw that he was of my mind; and this, if I had required to be confirmed in my intention, would have had the effect. He went round to the coach office, at my request, and took the box-seat for me on the mail.

In the evening I started, . . . down the road I had traversed under so many vicissitudes.

"Don't you think that," I asked the coachman, in the first stage out of London, "a very remarkable sky? I don't remember to have seen one like it."

"Nor I—not equal to it," he replied. "That's wind, sir. There'll be mischief done at sea, I expect, before long."

It was a murky confusion—here and there blotted with a color like the color of the smoke from damp fuel—of flying clouds tossed up into most remarkable heaps, suggesting greater heights in the clouds than there were depths below them to the bottom of the deepest hollows in the earth, through which the wild moon seemed to plunge headlong, as if, in a dread disturbance of the laws of nature, she had lost her way and were frightened. There had been a wind all day; and it was rising then, with an extraordinary great sound. In another hour it had much increased, and the sky was more overcast, and it blew hard.

But, as the night advanced, the clouds closing in and densely overspreading the whole sky, then very dark, it came on to blow, harder and harder. It still increased, until our horses could scarcely face the wind. Many times, in the dark part of the night (it was then late in September, when the nights were not short), the leaders turned about, or came to a dead stop; and we were often in serious apprehension that the coach would be blown over. Sweeping gusts of rain came up before this storm like showers of steel; and at those times, when there was any shelter of trees or lee walls to be got, we were fain to stop, in a sheer impossibility of continuing the struggle.

When the day broke, it blew harder and harder. I had been in Yarmouth when the seamen said it blew great guns, but I had never known the like of this, or anything approaching to it. We came to Ipswich—very late, having had to fight every inch of ground since we were ten miles out of London; and found a cluster of people in the market-place, who had risen from their beds in the night, fearful of falling chimneys. Some of these, congregating about the inn-yard while we changed horses, told us of great sheets of lead having been ripped off a high church-tower, and flung into a by-street, which they then blocked up. Others had to tell of country people, coming in from neighboring villages, who had seen great trees lying torn out of the earth, and whole ricks scattered about the roads and fields. Still, there was no abatement in the storm, but it blew harder.

As we struggled on, nearer and nearer to the sea, from which this mighty wind was blowing dead on shore, its force became more and more terrific. Long before we saw the sea, its spray was on our lips, and showered salt rain upon us. The water was out, over miles and miles of the flat country adjacent to Yarmouth; and every sheet and puddle lashed its banks, and had its stress of little breakers setting heavily towards us. When we came within sight of the sea, the waves on the horizon, caught at intervals above the rolling abyss, were like glimpses of another shore with towers and buildings. When at last we got into the town, the people came out to the doors, all aslant, and with streaming hair, making a wonder of the mail that had come through such a night.

I put up at the old inn, and went down to look at the sea; staggering along the street, which was strewn with sand and sea-weed, and with flying blotches of sea-foam; afraid of falling slates and tiles; and holding by people I met at angry corners. Coming near the beach, I saw, not only the boatmen, but half the people of the town, lurking behind buildings; some, now and then braving the fury of the storm to look away to sea, and blown sheer out of their course in trying to get zigzag back.

Joining these groups, I found bewailing women whose husbands were away in herring or oyster boats, which there was too much reason to think might have foundered before they could run in anywhere for safety. Grizzled old sailors were among the people, shaking their heads as they looked from water to sky, and muttering to one another; shipowners, excited and uneasy; children huddling together, and peering into older faces; even stout mariners, disturbed and anxious, levelling their glasses at the sea from behind places of shelter, as if they were surveying an enemy.

The tremendous sea itself, when I could find sufficient pause to look at it, in the agitation of the blinding wind, the flying stones and sand, and the awful noise, confounded me. As the high watery walls came rolling in, and, at their highest tumbled into surf, they looked as if the least would ingulf the town. As the receding wave swept back with a hoarse roar, it seemed to scoop out deep caves in the beach, as if its purpose were to undermine the earth. When some white-headed billows thundered on, and dashed themselves to pieces before they reached the land, every fragment of the late whole seemed possessed by the full might of its wrath, rushing to be gathered to the composition of another monster.

Undulating hills were changed to valleys, undulating valleys (with a solitary storm-bird sometimes skimming through them) were lifted up to hills; masses of water shivered and shook the beach with a booming sound; every shape tumultuously rolled on, as soon as made, to change its shape and place, and beat another shape and place away; the ideal shore on the horizon, with its towers and buildings, rose and fell; the clouds flew fast and thick; I seemed to see a rending and upheaving of all nature.

Not finding Ham among the people whom this memorable wind—for it is still remembered down there as the greatest ever known to blow upon that coast—had brought together, I made my way to his house. It was shut; and as no one answered to my knocking, I went by back ways and by-lanes, to the yard where he worked. I learned, there, that he had gone to Lowestoft, to meet some sudden exigency of ship-repairing in which his skill was required; but that he would be back to-morrow morning, in good time.

I went back to the inn; and when I had washed and dressed, tried to sleep, but in vain, it was five o'clock in the afternoon. I had not sat five min-utes by the coffee-room fire, when the waiter coming to stir it, as an excuse for talking, told me that two colliers had gone down, with all hands, a few miles away; and that some other ships had been seen laboring hard in the Roads, and trying in great distress, to keep off shore. Mercy on them, and on all poor sailors, said he, if we had another night like the last!

I was very much depressed in spirits; very solitary; and felt an uneasiness in Ham's not being there, disproportionate to the occasion. I was seriously affected, without knowing how much, by late events; and my long exposure to the fierce wind had confused me. There was that jumble in my thoughts and recollections, that I had lost the clear arrangement of time and distance. Thus, if I had gone out into the town, I should not have been surprised, I think, to encounter some one who I knew must be then in London. So to speak, there was in these respects a curious inattention in my mind. Yet it was busy, too, with all the remembrances the place naturally awakened; and they were particularly distinct and vivid.

In this state, the waiter's dismal intelligence about the ships immedi-ately connected itself, without any effort of my volition, with my uneasiness about Ham. I was persuaded that I had an apprehension of his returning from Lowestoft by sea, and being lost. This grew so strong with me, that I resolved to go back to the yard before I took my dinner, and ask the boat-builder if he thought his attempting to return by sea at all likely? If he gave me the least reason to think so, I would go over to Lowestoft and prevent it by bringing him with me.

I hastily ordered my dinner, and went back to the yard. I was none too soon; for the boat-builder, with a lantern in his hand, was locking the yard-gate. He quite laughed, when I asked him the question, and said there was no fear; no man in his senses, or out of them, would put off in such a gale of wind, least of all Ham Peggotty, who had been born to seafaring.

So sensible of this, beforehand, that I had really felt ashamed of doing what I was nevertheless impelled to do, I went back to the inn. If such a wind could rise, I think it was rising. The howl and roar, the rattling of the doors and windows, the rumbling in the chimneys, the apparent rocking of the very house that sheltered me, and the prodigious tumult of the sea, were more fearful than in the morning. But there was now a great darkness besides; and that invested the storm with new terrors, real and fanciful.

I could not eat, I could not sit still, I could not continue steadfast to anything. Something within me, faintly answering to the storm without, tossed up the depths of my memory, and made a tumult in them. Yet, in all the hurry of my thoughts, wild running with the thundering sea,—the storm and my uneasiness regarding Ham, were always in the foreground.

My dinner went away almost untasted, and I tried to refresh myself with a glass or two of wine. In vain. I fell into a dull slumber before the fire, without losing my consciousness, either of the uproar out of doors, or of the place in which I was. Both became overshadowed by a new and indefinable horror; and when I awoke—or rather when I shook off the lethargy that bound me in my chair—my whole frame thrilled with objectless and unintelligent fear.

I walked to and fro, tried to read an old gazetteer, listened to the awful noises: looked at faces, scenes, and figures in the fire. At length, the steady ticking of the undisturbed clock on the wall, tormented me to that degree that I resolved to go to bed.

It was reassuring, on such a night, to be told that some of the inn-servants had agreed together to sit up until morning. I went to bed, exceedingly weary and heavy; but, on my lying down, all such sensations vanished, as if by magic, and I was broad awake, with every sense refined.

For hours I lay there, listening to the wind and water; imagining, now, that I heard shrieks out at sea; now, that I distinctly heard the firing of signal guns; and now, the fall of houses in the town. I got up, several times, and looked out; but could see nothing, except the reflection in the window-panes of the faint candle I had left burning, and of my own haggard face looking in at me from the black void.

At length, my restlessness attained to such a pitch, that I hurried on my clothes, and went down stairs. In the large kitchen, where I dimly saw bacon and ropes of onions hanging from the beams, the watchers were clustered together, in various attitudes, about a table, purposely moved away from the great chimney, and brought near the door. A pretty girl, who had her ears stopped with her apron, and her eyes upon the door, screamed when I appeared, supposing me to be a spirit; but the others had more presence of mind, and were glad of an addition to their company. One man, referring to the topic they had been discussing, asked me whether I thought the souls of the collier-crews who had gone down, were out in the storm?

I remained there, I dare say, two hours. Once, I opened the yard-gate, and looked into the empty street. The sand, the sea-weed, and the flakes of foam, were driving by, and I was obliged to call for assistance before I could shut the gate again, and make it fast against the wind.

There was a dark gloom in my solitary chamber, when I at length returned to it; but I was tired now, and, getting into bed again, fell—off a tower and down a precipice—into the depths of sleep. I have an impression that, for a long time, though I dreamed of being elsewhere and in a variety of scenes, it was always blowing in my dream. At length, I lost that feeble hold upon reality, and was engaged with two dear friends, but who they were I don't know, at the siege of some town in a roar of cannonading.

The thunder of the cannon was so loud and incessant, that I could not hear something I much desired to hear, until I made a great exertion and awoke. It was broad day—eight or nine o'clock; the storm raging, in lieu of the batteries; and some one knocking and calling at my door.

"What is the matter?" I cried.

"A wreck! Close by!"

I sprung out of bed, and asked what wreck?

"A schooner, from Spain or Portugal, laden with fruit and wine. Make haste, sir, if you want to see her! It's thought down on the beach, she'll go to pieces every moment."

The excited voice went clamoring along the staircase; and I wrapped myself in my clothes as quickly as I could, and ran into the street.

Numbers of people were there before me, all running in one direction, to the beach. I ran the same way, outstripping a good many, and soon came facing the wild sea.

The wind might by this time have lulled a little, though not more sensibly than if the cannonading I had dreamed of, had been diminished by the silencing of half-a-dozen guns out of hundreds. But, the sea, having upon it the additional agitation of the whole night, was infinitely more terrific than when I had seen it last. Every appearance it had then presented, bore the expression of being *swelled*; and the height to which the breakers rose, and, looking over one another, bore one another down, and rolled in, in interminable hosts, was most appalling.

In the difficulty of hearing anything but winds and waves, and in the crowd, and the unspeakable confusion, and my first breathless efforts to stand against the weather, I was so confused that I looked out to sea for the wreck, and saw nothing but the foaming heads of the great waves. A half-dressed boatman, standing next me, pointed with his bare arm (a tattoo'd arrow on it, pointing in the same direction) to the left. Then, O great Heaven, I saw it, close in upon us!

One mast was broken short off, six or eight feet from the deck, and lay over the side, entangled in a maze of sail and rigging; and all that ruin, as the ship rolled and beat—which she did without a moment's pause, and with a violence quite inconceivable—beat the side as if it would stave it in. Some efforts were even then being made, to cut this portion of the wreck away; for, as the ship, which was broadside on, turned towards us in her rolling, I plainly descried her people at work with axes, especially one active figure with long curling hair, conspicuous among the rest. But, a great cry, which was audible even above the wind and water, rose from the shore at this moment; the sea, sweeping over the rolling wreck, made a clean breach, and carried men, spars, casks, planks, bulwarks, heaps of such toys, into the boiling surge.

The full-rigged Lord Ashburton foundering in a hurricane off Grand Manan Island, New Brunswick, 19th January 1857, by Joseph Heard, 1858.

The second mast was yet standing, with the rags of a rent sail, and a wild confusion of broken cordage flapping to and fro. The ship had struck once, the same boatman hoarsely said in my ear, and then lifted in and struck again. I understood him to add that she was parting amidships, and I could readily suppose so, for the rolling and beating were too tremendous for any human work to suffer long. As he spoke, there was another great cry of pity from the beach; four men arose with the wreck out of the deep, clinging to the rigging of the remaining mast; uppermost, the active figure with the curling hair.

There was a bell on board; and as the ship rolled and dashed, like a desperate creature driven mad, now showing us the whole sweep of her deck, as she turned on her beam-ends towards the shore, now nothing but her keel, as she sprung wildly over and turned towards the sea, the bell rang; and its sound, the knell of those unhappy men, was borne towards us on the wind. Again we lost her, and again she rose. Two men were gone. The agony on shore increased. Men groaned, and clasped their hands; women shrieked, and turned away their faces. Some ran wildly up and down along the beach, crying for help where no help could be. I found myself one of these, frantically imploring a knot of sailors whom I knew, not to let those two lost creatures perish before our eyes.

They were making out to me, in an agitated way—I don't know how, for the little I could hear I was scarcely composed enough to understand—that the life-boat had been bravely manned an hour ago, and could do nothing; and that as no man would be so desperate as to attempt to wade off with a rope, and establish a communication with the shore, there was nothing left to try; when I noticed that some new sensation moved the people on the beach, and saw them part, and Ham came breaking through them to the front.

I ran to him—as well as I know, to repeat my appeal for help. But, distracted though I was, by a sight so new to me and terrible, the determination in his face, and his look, out to sea—exactly the same look as I remembered in connection with the morning after Emily's flight—awoke me to a knowledge of his danger. I held him back with both arms; and implored the men with whom I had been speaking, not to listen to him, not to do murder, not to let him stir from off that sand!

Another cry arose on shore; and looking to the wreck, we saw the cruel sail, with blow on blow, beat off the lower of the two men, and fly up in triumph round the active figure left alone upon the mast.

Against such a sight, and against such determination as that of the calmly desperate man who was already accustomed to lead half the people present,

I might as hopefully have entreated the wind. "Mas'r Davy," he said, cheerily grasping me by both hands, "if my time is come, 'tis come. If 'tan't, I'll bide it. Lord above bless you, and bless all! Mates, make me ready! I'm a going off!"

I was swept away, but not unkindly, to some distance, where the people around me made me stay; urging, as I confusedly perceived, that he was bent on going, with help or without, and that I should endanger the precautions for his safety by troubling those with whom they rested. I don't know what I answered, or what they rejoined; but, I saw hurry on the beach, and men running with ropes from a capstan that was there, and penetrating into a circle of figures that hid him from me. Then I saw him standing alone, in a seaman's frock and trousers: a rope in his hand, or slung to his wrist: another round his body: and several of the best men holding, at a little distance, to the latter, which he laid out himself, slack upon the shore, at his feet.

The wreck, even to my unpractised eye, was breaking up. I saw that she was parting in the middle, and that the life of the solitary man upon the mast hung by a thread. Still, he clung to it. He had a singular red cap on,—not like a sailor's cap, but of a finer color; and as the few yielding planks between him and destruction rolled and bulged, and his anticipative death-knell rung, he was seen by all of us to wave it. I saw him do it now, and thought I was going distracted, when his action brought an old remembrance to my mind of a once dear friend.

Ham watched the sea, standing alone, with the silence of suspended breath behind him, and the storm before, until there was a great retiring wave, when, with a backward glance at those who held the rope which was made fast round his body, he dashed in after it, and in a moment was buffeting with the water; rising with the hills, falling with the valleys, lost beneath the foam; then drawn again to land. They hauled in hastily.

He was hurt. I saw blood on his face, from where I stood; but he took no thought of that. He seemed hurriedly to give them some directions for leaving him more free—or so I judged from the motion of his arm—and was gone as before.

And now he made for the wreck, rising with the hills, falling with the valleys, lost beneath the rugged foam, borne in towards the shore, borne on towards the ship, striving hard and valiantly. The distance was nothing, but the power of the sea and wind made the strife deadly. At length he neared the wreck. He was so near, that with one more of his vigorous strokes he would be clinging to it,—when, a high, green, vast hillside of water, moving on shoreward, from beyond the ship, he seemed to leap up into it with a mighty bound, and the ship was gone!

Some eddying fragments I saw in the sea, as if a mere cask had been broken, in running to the spot where they were hauling in. Consternation was in every face. They drew him to my very feet—insensible—dead. He was carried to the nearest house; and, no one preventing me now, I remained near him, busy, while every means of restoration were tried; but he had been beaten to death by the great wave, and his generous heart was stilled forever.

13.

A STRUGGLE WITH THE DEVIL-FISH

VICTOR HUGO

When he awakened he was hungry.

The sea was growing calmer. But there was still a heavy swell, which made his departure, for the present at least, impossible. The day, too, was far advanced. For the sloop with its burden to get to Guernsey before midnight, it was necessary to start in the morning.

Although pressed by hunger, Gilliatt began by stripping himself, the only means of getting warmth. His clothing was saturated by the storm, but the rain had washed out the sea-water, which rendered it possible to dry them.

He kept nothing on but his trousers, which he turned up nearly to the knees.

His overcoat, jacket, overalls, and sheepskin he spread out and fixed with large round stones here and there.

Then he thought of eating.

He had recourse to his knife, which he was careful to sharpen, and to keep always in good condition; and he detached from the rock a few limpets, similar in kind to the *clonisses* of the Mediterranean. It is well known that these are eaten raw; but after so many labors, so various and so rude, the pittance was meagre. His biscuit was gone; but of water he had now abundance.

He took advantage of the receding tide to wander among the rocks in search of crayfish.

A rocky cave on a coastal inlet.

He wandered, not in the gorge of the rocks, but outside among the smaller breakers. It was there that the *Durande*, ten weeks previously, had struck upon the sunken reef.

For the search that Gilliatt was prosecuting, this part was more favorable than the interior. At low water the crabs are accustomed to crawl out into the air. They seem to like to warm themselves in the sun, where they swarm sometimes to the disgust of the loiterers, who recognize in these creatures, with their awkward sidelong gait, climbing clumsily from crack to crack the lower stages of the rocks like the steps of a staircase, a sort of sea vermin.

For two months Gilliatt had lived upon these vermin of the sea.

On this day, however, the crayfish and crabs were both wanting. The tempest had driven them into their solitary retreats; and they had not yet mustered courage to venture abroad. Gilliatt held his open knife in his hand, and from time to time scraped a cockle from under the bunches of sea-weed, which he ate while still walking.

He could not have been far from the very spot where Sieur Clubin had perished.

As Gilliatt was determining to content himself with the sea-urchins and the *chataignes de mer*, a little clattering noise at his feet aroused his attention. A large crab, startled by his approach, had just dropped into a pool. The water was shallow, and he did not lose sight of it.

He chased the crab along the base of the rock; the crab moved fast.

Suddenly it was gone.

It had buried itself in some crevice under the rock.

Gilliatt clutched the protections of the rock, and stretched out to observe where it shelved away under the water.

As he suspected, there was an opening there in which the creature had evidently taken refuge. It was more than a crevice; it was a kind of porch.

The sea entered beneath it, but was not deep. The bottom was visible, covered with large pebbles. The pebbles were green and clothed with *confervæ*, indicating that they were never dry. They were like the tops of a number of heads of infants, covered with a kind of green hair.

Holding his knife between his teeth, Gilliatt descended, by the help of feet and hands, from the upper part of the escarpment, and leaped into the water. It reached almost to his shoulders.

He made his way through the porch, and found himself in a blind passage, with a roof in the form of a rude arch over his head.

The walls were polished and slippery. The crab was nowhere visible. He gained his feet and advanced in daylight growing fainter, so that he began to lose the power to distinguish objects.

At about fifteen paces the vaulted roof ended overhead. He had penetrated beyond the blind passage. There was here more space, and consequently more daylight. The pupils of his eyes, moreover, had dilated; he could see pretty clearly. He was taken by surprise.

He had made his way again into the singular cavern which he had visited in the previous month. The only difference was that he had entered by the way of the sea.

His eyes became more accustomed to the place. His vision became clearer and clearer. He was astonished. He found, above the level of the water, and within reach of his hand, a horizontal fissure. It seemed to him probable that the crab had taken refuge there, and he plunged his hand in as far as he was able, and groped about in that dusky aperture.

Suddenly he felt himself seized by the arm. A strange indescribable horror thrilled through him.

Some living thing, thin, rough, flat, cold, slimy, had twisted itself round his naked arm, in the dark depth below. It crept upward toward his chest. Its pressure was like a tightening cord, its steady persistence like that of a screw. In less than a moment some mysterious spiral form had passed round his wrist and elbow, and had reached his shoulder. A sharp point penetrated beneath the armpit.

Gilliatt recoiled; but he had scarcely power to move! He was, as it were, nailed to the place. With his left hand, which was disengaged, he seized his knife, which he still held between his teeth, and with that hand, holding the knife, he supported himself against the rocks, while he made a desperate effort to withdraw his arm. He succeeded only in disturbing his persecutor, which wound itself still tighter. It was supple as leather, strong as steel, cold as night.

A second form, sharp, elongated, and narrow, issued out of the crevice, like a tongue out of monstrous jaws. It seemed to lick his naked body. Then suddenly stretching out, it became longer and thinner, as it crept over his skin, and wound itself round him. At the same time a terrible sense of pain, comparable to nothing he had ever known, compelled all his muscles to contract. He felt upon his skin a number of flat rounded points. It seemed as if innumerable suckers had fastened to his flesh and were about to drink his blood.

A third long undulating shape issued from the hole in the rock; and seemed to feel its way about his body; lashed round his ribs like a cord, and fixed itself there.

Agony when at its height is mute. Gilliatt uttered no cry. There was sufficient light for him to see the repulsive forms which had entangled themselves about him. A fourth ligature, but this one swift as an arrow, darted toward his stomach, and wound around him there.

It was impossible to sever or tear away the slimy bands which were twisted tightly round his body, and were adhering by a number of points. Each of the points was the focus of frightful and singular pangs. It was as if numberless small mouths were devouring him at the same time.

A fifth long, slimy, riband-shaped strip issued from the hole. It passed over the others, and wound itself tightly around his chest. The compression increased his sufferings. He could scarcely breathe.

These living thongs were pointed at their extremities, but broadened like the blade of a sword toward its hilt. All belonged evidently to the same centre. They crept and glided about him; he felt the strange points of pressure, which seemed to him like mouths, change their places from time to time.

Suddenly a large, round, glutinous mass issued from beneath the crevice. It was the centre; the five thongs were attached to it like spokes to the nave of a wheel. On the opposite side of this disgusting monster appeared the commencement of three other tentacles, the ends of which remained under the rock. In the middle of this slimy mass appeared two eyes.

The eyes were fixed on Gilliatt.

He recognized the devil-fish.

It is difficult for those who have not seen it to believe in the existence of the devil-fish.

Compared to this creature, the ancient hydras are insignificant.

If terror were the object of its creation, nothing could be imagined more perfect than the devil-fish.

The devil-fish has no muscular organization, no menacing cry, no breastplate, no horn, no dart, no claw, no tail with which to hold or bruise; no cutting fins, or wings with nails, no prickles, no sword, no electric discharge, no poison, no talons, no beak, no teeth. Yet he is of all creatures the most formidably armed.

What, then, is the devil-fish? It is the sea vampire.

This frightful apparition, which is always possible among the rocks in the open sea, is a grayish form, which undulates in the water. It is of the thickness of a man's arm, and in length nearly five feet. Its outline is ragged. Its form resembles an umbrella closed, and without a handle. This irregular mass advances slowly toward you. Suddenly it opens, and eight radii issue abruptly from around a face with two eyes. These radii are alive; their undulation is like lambent flames; they resemble, when opened, the spokes of a wheel, of four or five feet in diameter. A terrible expansion! It springs upon its prey.

The devil-fish harpoons its victim.

It winds around the sufferer, covering and entangling him in its long folds. Underneath it is yellow; above a dull, earthy hue; nothing could render that inexplicable shade dust-colored. Its form is spider-like, but its tints are like those of the chameleon. When irritated, it becomes violet. Its most horrible characteristic is its softness.

Its folds strangle, its contact paralyzes.

It has an aspect like gangrened or scabrous flesh. It is a monstrous embodiment of disease.

It adheres closely to its prey, and cannot be torn away; a fact which is due to its power of exhausting air. The eight antennæ, large at their roots, diminish gradually, and end in needle-like points. Underneath each of these feelers range two rows of pustules, decreasing in size, the largest ones near the head, the smaller at the extremities. Each row contains twenty-five of these. There are, therefore, fifty pustules to each feeler, and the creature possesses in the whole four hundred. These pustules are capable of acting like cupping-glasses. They are cartilaginous substances, cylindrical, horny, and livid. Upon the large species they diminish gradually from the diameter of a five-franc piece to the size of a split pea. These small tubes can be thrust out and withdrawn by the animal at will. They are capable of piercing to a depth of more than an inch.

This sucking apparatus has all the regularity and delicacy of a key-board. It stands forth at one moment and disappears the next. The most perfect sensitiveness cannot equal the contractibility of these suckers; always proportioned to the internal movement of the animal, and its exterior circumstances. The monster is endowed with the qualities of the sensitive plant.

When swimming, the devil-fish rests, so to speak, in its sheath. It swims with all its parts drawn close. It may be likened to a sleeve sewn up with a closed fist within. The protuberance, which is the head, pushes the water aside and advances with a vague undulatory movement. Its two eyes, though large, are indistinct, being of the color of the water.

The devil-fish not only swims, it walks. It is partly fish, partly reptile. It crawls upon the bed of the sea. At these times, it makes use of its eight feelers, and creeps along in the fashion of a species of swift-moving caterpillar.

It has no blood, no bones, no flesh. It is soft and flabby; a skin with nothing inside. Its eight tentacles may be turned inside out like the fingers of a glove.

It has a single orifice in the centre of its radii, which appears at first to be neither the vent nor the mouth. It is, in fact, both one and the other. The orifice performs a double function. The entire creature is cold.

The jelly-fish of the Mediterranean is repulsive. Contact with that animated gelatinous substance which envelopes the bather, in which the hands sink, and the nails scratch ineffectively; which can be torn without killing it, and which can be plucked off without entirely removing it—that fluid and yet tenacious creature which slips through the fingers, is disgusting; but no horror can equal the sudden apparition of the devil-fish, that *Medusa* with its eight serpents.

It is with the sucking apparatus that it attacks. The victim is oppressed by a vacuum drawing at numberless points; it is not a clawing or a biting, but an indescribable scarification. A tearing of the flesh is terrible, but less terrible than a sucking of the blood. Claws are harmless compared with the horrible action of these natural air-cups. The muscles swell, the fibres of the body are contorted, the skin cracks under the loathsome oppression, the blood spurts out and mingles horribly with the lymph of the monster, which clings to its victim by innumerable hideous mouths. The hydra incorporates itself with the man; the man becomes one with the hydra. The spectre lies upon you; the tiger can only devour you; the devil-fish, horrible, sucks your life-blood away.

He draws you to him, and into himself; while bound down, glued to the ground, powerless, you feel yourself gradually emptied into this horrible pouch, which is the monster itself.

Such was the creature in whose power Gilliatt had fallen for some minutes.

The monster was the inhabitant of the grotto; the terrible genii of the place. A kind of sombre demon of the water.

All the splendors of the cavern existed for it alone.

On the day of the previous month when Gilliatt had first penetrated into the grotto, the dark outline, vaguely perceived by him in the ripples of the secret waters, was this monster. It was here in its home.

When entering for the second time into the cavern in pursuit of the crab, he had observed the crevice in which he supposed that the crab had taken refuge, the *pieuvre* was there lying in wait for prey.

Gilliatt had thrust his arm deep into the opening; the monster had snapped at it. It held him fast, as the spider holds the fly.

He was in the water up to his belt; his naked feet clutching the slippery roundness of the huge stones at the bottom; his right arm bound and rendered powerless by the flat coils of the long tentacles of the creature, and his body almost hidden under the folds and cross folds of this horrible bandage.

Of the eight arms of the devil-fish three adhered to the rock, while five encircled Gilliatt. In this way, clinging to the granite on the one hand, and with the other to its human prey, it enchained him to the rock. Two hundred and fifty suckers were upon him, tormenting him with agony and loathing. He was grasped by gigantic hands, the fingers of which were each nearly a yard long, and furnished inside with living blisters eating into the flesh.

It is impossible to tear one's self from the folds of the devil-fish. The attempt ends only in a firmer grasp. The monster clings with more determined force. Its effort increases with that of its victim; every struggle produces a tightening of its ligatures.

Gilliatt had but one resource, his knife.

His left hand only was free; but the reader knows with what power he could use it. It might have been said that he had two right hands.

His open knife was in his hand.

The antennæ of the devil-fish cannot be cut; it is a leathery substance impossible to divide with the knife, it slips under the edge; its position in attack also is such that to cut it would be to wound the victim's own flesh.

The creature is formidable, but there is a way of resisting it. The fishermen of Sark know this, as does any one who has seen them execute certain abrupt movements in the sea. The porpoises know it also; they have a way of biting the cuttle-fish which decapitates it. Hence the frequent sight on the sea of pen-fish, poulps, and cuttle-fish without heads.

The devil-fish, in fact, is only vulnerable through the head.

Gilliatt was not ignorant of this fact.

With the devil-fish, as with a furious bull, there is a certain moment in the conflict which must be seized. It is the instant when the devil-fish advances its head. The movement is rapid. He who loses that moment is destroyed.

The things we have described occupied only a few moments. Gilliatt, however, felt the increasing power of its innumerable suckers.

The monster is cunning; it tries first to stupefy its prey. It seizes and then pauses a while.

Gilliatt grasped his knife; the sucking increased.

He looked at the monster, which seemed to look at him.

Suddenly it loosened from the rock its sixth antenna, and darting it at him, seized him by the left arm.

At the same moment it advanced its head with a violent movement. In one second more its mouth would have fastened on his breast. Bleeding in the sides, and with his two arms entangled, he would have been a dead man.

But Gilliatt was watchful. He avoided the antenna, and at the moment when the monster darted forward to fasten on his breast, he struck it with the knife clenched in his left hand. There were two convulsions in opposite directions; that of the devil-fish and that of its prey. The movement was rapid as a double flash of lightning.

He had plunged the blade of his knife into the flat, slimy substance, and by a rapid movement, like the flourish of a whip in the air, describing a circle around the two eyes, he wrenched the head off as a man would draw a tooth.

The struggle was ended. The folds relaxed. The monster dropped away, like the slow detaching of bands. The four hundred suckers, deprived of their sustaining power, dropped at once from the man and the rock. The mass sank to the bottom of the water.

Breathless with the struggle, Gilliatt could perceive upon the stones at his feet two shapeless, slimy heaps, the head on one side, the remainder of the monster on the other.

Fearing, nevertheless, some convulsive return of his agony he recoiled to avoid the reach of the dreaded tentacles.

But the monster was quite dead.

Gilliatt closed his knife.

It was time that he killed the devil-fish. He was almost suffocated. His right arm and his chest were purple. Numberless little swellings were distinguishable upon them; the blood flowed from them here and there.

The remedy for these wounds is sea-water. Gilliatt plunged into it, rubbing himself at the same time with the palms of his hands. The swellings disappeared under the friction.

14.

MY FIRST VOYAGE

RICHARD HENRY DANA JR.

The American clipper ship Flying Cloud at sea under full sail by
Antonio Jacobesen, 1913.

The fourteenth day of August was the day fixed upon for the sailing of
the brig *Pilgrim* on her voyage from Boston round Cape Horn to the
western coast of North America. As she was to get under way early in
the afternoon, I made my appearance on board at twelve o'clock in full sea-rig,
and with my chest, containing an outfit for a two or three years' voyage, which
I had undertaken from a determination to cure, if possible, by an entire change
of life, and by a long absence from books and study, a weakness of the eyes,

which had obliged me to give up my pursuits, and which no medical aid seemed likely to cure.

The change from the tight dress-coat, silk cap and kid gloves of an undergraduate at Cambridge, to the loose duck trousers, checked shirt and tarpaulin hat of a sailor, though somewhat of a transformation, was soon made, and I supposed that I should pass very well for a jack tar. But it is impossible to deceive the practised eye in these matters; and while I supposed myself to be looking as salt as Neptune himself, I was, no doubt, known for a landsman by every one on board as soon as I hove in sight.

A sailor has a peculiar cut to his clothes, and a way of wearing them which a green hand can never get. The trousers, tight round the hips, and thence hanging long and loose round the feet, a superabundance of checked shirt, a low-crowned, well-varnished black hat, worn on the back of the head, with half a fathom of black ribbon hanging over the left eye, and a peculiar tie to the black silk neckerchief, with sundry other minutiæ, are signs, the want of which betrayed the beginner, at once. Besides the points in my dress which were out of the way, doubtless my complexion and hands were enough to distinguish me from the regular *salt*, who, with a sunburnt cheek, wide step, and rolling gait, swings his broad and toughened hands athwart-ships, half open, as though just ready to grasp a rope.

"With all my imperfections on my head," I joined the crew, and we hauled out into the stream, and came to anchor for the night. The next day we were employed in preparations for sea, reeving studding-sail gear, crossing royal-yards, putting on chafing gear, and taking on board our powder. On the following night, I stood my first watch. I remained awake nearly all the first part of the night from fear that I might not hear when I was called; and when I went on deck, so great were my ideas of the importance of my trust, that I walked regularly fore and aft the whole length of the vessel, looking out over the bows and taffrail at each turn, and was not a little surprised at the coolness of the old salt whom I called to take my place, in stowing himself snugly away under the long-boat, for a nap. That was a sufficient lookout, he thought, for a fine night, at anchor in a safe harbor.

The next morning was Saturday, and a breeze having sprung up from the southward, we took a pilot on board, hove up our anchor, and began beating down the bay. I took leave of those of my friends who came to see me off, and had barely opportunity to take a last look at the city and well-known objects, as no time is allowed on board ship for sentiment.

As we drew down into the lower harbor, we found the wind ahead in the bay, and we were obliged to come to anchor in the roads. We remained there through the day and a part of the night. My watch began at eleven o'clock at night, and I received orders to call the captain if the wind came out from the westward. About midnight the wind became fair, and having called the captain, I was ordered to call all hands. How I accomplished this I do not know, but I am quite sure that I did not give the true hoarse boatswain call of "A-a-ll ha-a-a-nds! up anchor, a ho-oy!" In a short time every one was in motion, the sails loosed, the yards braced, and we began to heave up the anchor, which was our last hold upon Yankee land.

I could take but little part in all these preparations. My little knowledge of a vessel was all at fault. Unintelligible orders were so rapidly given and so immediately executed; there was such a hurrying about, and such an intermingling of strange cries and strange actions, that I was completely bewildered. There is not so helpless and pitiable an object in the world as a landsman beginning a sailor's life.

At length those peculiar, long-drawn sounds, which denote that the crew are heaving at the windlass, began, and in a few moments we were under way. The noise of the water thrown from the bows began to be heard, the vessel leaned over from the damp night breeze, and rolled with a heavy ground swell, and we had actually begun our long, long journey. This was literally bidding "good-night" to my native land.

The first day we passed at sea was the Sabbath. As we were just from port, and there was a great deal to be done on board, we were kept at work all day, and at night the watches were set, and everything put into sea order. When we were called aft to be divided into watches, I had a good specimen of the manner of a sea captain. After the division had been made, he gave a short characteristic speech, walking the quarter-deck with a cigar in his mouth, and dropping the words out between the puffs:

"Now, my men, we have begun a long voyage. If we get along well together, we shall have a comfortable time; if we don't, we shall have hell afloat. All you've got to do is to obey your orders and do your duty like men,—then you'll fare well enough;—if you don't, you'll fare hard enough,—I can tell you. If we pull together, you'll find me a clever fellow; if we don't, you'll find me a *bloody* rascal. That's all I've got to say. Go below, the larboard watch!"

I being in the starboard, or second mate's watch, had the opportunity of keeping the first watch at sea. S——, a young man, making, like myself, his first voyage, was in the same watch, and as he was the son of a professional man, and had been in a counting-room in Boston, we found that we had many friends and topics in common. We talked these matters over:—Boston, what our friends were probably doing, our voyage, etc., until he went to take his turn at the lookout, and left me to myself.

I had now a fine time for reflection. I felt for the first time the perfect silence of the sea. The officer was walking the quarter-deck, where I had no right to go, one or two men were talking on the forecastle, whom I had little inclination to join, so that I was left open to the full impression of everything about me. However much I was affected by the beauty of the sea, the bright stars, and the clouds driven swiftly over them, I could not but remember that I was separating myself from all the social and intellectual enjoyments of life. Yet, strange as it may seem, I did then and afterward take pleasure in these reflections, hoping by them to prevent my becoming insensible to the value of what I was leaving.

But all my dreams were soon put to flight by an order from the officer to trim the yards, as the wind was getting ahead; and I could plainly see by the looks the sailors occasionally cast to windward, and by the dark clouds that were fast coming up, that we had bad weather to prepare for, and had heard the captain say that he expected to be in the Gulf Stream by twelve o'clock. In a few minutes eight bells were struck, the watch called, and we went below.

I now began to feel the first discomforts of a sailor's life. The steerage in which I lived was filled with coils of rigging, spare sails, old junk, and ship stores, which had not been stowed away. Moreover, there had been no berths built for us to sleep in, and we were not allowed to drive nails to hang our clothes upon. The sea, too, had risen, the vessel was rolling heavily, and every-thing was pitched about in grand confusion. There was a complete "hurrah's nest," as the sailors say, "everything on top and nothing at hand." A large hawser had been coiled away upon my chest; my hats, boots, mattress and blankets had all *fetched away* and gone over leeward, and were jammed and broken under the boxes and coils of rigging. To crown all, we were allowed no light to find anything with, and I was just beginning to feel strong symptoms of sea-sickness, and that listlessness and inactivity which accompany it.

Giving up all attempts to collect my things together, I lay down upon the sails, expecting every moment to hear the cry of "All hands ahoy," which the approaching storm would soon make necessary. I shortly heard the rain-drops falling on deck, thick and fast, and the watch evidently had their hands full of work, for I could hear the loud and repeated orders of the mate, the trampling of feet, the creaking of blocks, and all the accompaniments of a coming storm. In a few minutes the slide of the hatch was thrown back, which let down the noise and tumult of the deck still louder, the loud cry of "All hands, ahoy! tumble up here and take in sail!" saluted our ears, and the hatch was quickly shut again.

When I got upon deck, a new scene and a new experience was before me. The little brig was close-hauled upon the wind, and lying over, as it then seemed to me, nearly upon her beam ends. The heavy head sea was beating against her bows with the noise and force almost of a sledge-hammer, and flying over the deck, drenching us completely through. The topsail halyards had been let go, and the great sails were filling out and backing against the masts with a noise like thunder. The wind was whistling through the rigging, loose ropes flying about; loud and, to me, unintelligible orders constantly given and rapidly executed, and the sailors "singing out" at the ropes in their hoarse and peculiar strains. In addition to all this, I had not got my "sea legs" on, was dreadfully sick, with hardly strength enough to hold on to anything, and it was "pitch dark." This was my state when I was ordered aloft, for the first time, to reef topsails.

How I got along, I cannot now remember. I "laid out" on the yards and held on with all my strength. I could not have been of much service, for I remember having been sick several times before I left the topsail yard. Soon all was snug aloft, and we were again allowed to go below. This I did not consider much of a favor, for the confusion of everything below, and the inexpressible sickening smell, caused by the shaking up of the bilge-water in the hold, made the steerage but an indifferent refuge from the cold wet decks.

I had often read of the nautical experiences of others, but I felt as though there could be none worse than mine; for in addition to every other evil, I could not but remember that this was only the first night of a two years' voyage. When we were on deck we were not much better off, for we were continually ordered about by the officer, who said that it was good for us to be in motion. Yet anything was better than the horrible state of things below. I remember very well going to the hatchway and putting my head down, when I was oppressed by *nausea*, and always being relieved immediately. It was as good as an emetic.

This state of things continued for two days.

Wednesday, Aug. 20th. We had the watch on deck from four till eight, this morning. When we came on deck at four o'clock, we found things much changed for the better. The sea and wind had gone down, and the stars were out bright. I experienced a corresponding change in my feelings; yet continued extremely weak from my sickness. I stood in the waist on the weather side, watching the gradual breaking of the day, and the first streaks of the early light. Much has been said of the sunrise at sea; but it will not compare with the sunrise on shore. It wants the accompaniments of the songs of birds, the awakening hum of men, and the glancing of the first beams upon trees, hills, spires, and house-tops, to give it life and spirit. But though the actual *rise of the sun* at sea is not so beautiful, yet nothing will compare with the *early breaking of day* upon the wide ocean.

There is something in the first gray streaks stretching along the eastern horizon and throwing an indistinct light upon the face of the deep, which combines with the boundlessness and unknown depth of the sea round you, and gives one a feeling of loneliness, of dread, and of melancholy foreboding, which nothing else in nature can give. This gradually passes away as the light grows brighter, and when the sun comes up, the ordinary monotonous sea day begins.

From such reflections as these, I was aroused by the order from the officer, "Forward there! rig the head-pump!" I found that no time was allowed for day-dreaming, but that we must "turn to" at the first light. Having called up the "idlers," namely carpenter, cook, steward, etc., and rigged the pump, we commenced washing down the decks. This operation, which is performed every morning at sea, takes nearly two hours; and I had hardly strength enough to get through it.

After we had finished, swabbed down, and coiled up the rigging, I sat down on the spars, waiting for seven bells, which was the sign for breakfast. The officer, seeing my lazy posture, ordered me to slush the main-mast, from the royal-mast-head down. The vessel was then rolling a little, and I had taken no sustenance for three days, so that I felt tempted to tell him that I had rather wait till after breakfast; but I knew that I must "take the bull by the horns," and that if I showed any sign of want of spirit or of backwardness, that I should be ruined at once. So I took my bucket of grease and climbed up to the royal-mast-head. Here the rocking of the vessel, which increases the higher you go from the foot of the mast, which is the fulcrum of the lever, and the smell of the grease, which offended my fastidious senses, upset my stomach again, and I was not a little rejoiced when I got upon the comparative *terra firma* of the deck. In a few minutes seven bells were struck, the log hove, the watch called, and we went to breakfast.

Here I cannot but remember the advice of the cook, a simple-hearted African.

"Now," said he, "my lad, you are well cleaned out; you haven't got a drop of your 'long-shore *swash* aboard of you. You must begin on a new tack—

pitch all your sweetmeats overboard, and turn-to upon good hearty salt beef and sea bread, and I'll promise you, you'll have your ribs well sheathed, and be as hearty as any of 'em, afore you are up to the Horn."

This would be good advice to give passengers, when they speak of the little niceties which they have laid in, in case of sea-sickness.

I cannot describe the change which half a pound of cold salt beef and a biscuit or two produced in me. I was a new being. We had a watch below until noon, so that I had some time to myself; and getting a huge piece of strong, cold salt beef from the cook, I kept gnawing upon it until twelve o'clock. When we went on deck I felt somewhat like a man, and could begin to learn my sea duty with considerable spirit.

At about two o'clock we heard the loud cry of "Sail ho!" from aloft, and soon saw two sails to windward, going directly athwart our hawse. This was the first time that I had seen a sail at sea. I thought then, and have always since, that it exceeds every other sight in interest and beauty. They passed to leeward of us, and out of hailing distance; but the captain could read the names on their sterns with the glass. They were the ship *Helen Mar*, of New York, and the brig *Mermaid*, of Boston. They were both steering westward, and were bound in for our "dear native land."

Thursday, Aug. 21st. This day the sun rose clear, we had a fine wind, and everything was bright and cheerful. I had now got my sea legs on, and was beginning to enter upon the regular duties of a sea-life. About six bells, that is, three o'clock, P.M., we saw a sail on our larboard bow. I was very anxious, like every new sailor, to speak her. She came down to us, backed her main topsail and the two vessels stood "head on," bowing and curvetting at each other like a couple of war-horses reined in by their riders. It was the first vessel that I had seen near, and I was surprised to find how much she rolled and pitched in so quiet a sea. She plunged her head into the sea, and then, her stern settling gradually down, her huge bows rose up, showing the bright copper, and her stern, and breast-hooks dripping, like old Neptune's locks, with the brine. Her decks were filled with passengers who had come up at the cry of "Sail ho," and who by their dress and features appeared to be Swiss and

French emigrants. She hailed us in French, but receiving no answer, she tried us in English. She was the ship *La Carolina*, from Havre, for New York. We desired her to report the brig *Pilgrim*, from Boston, for the northwest coast of America, five days out. She then filled away and left us to plough on through our waste of waters. This day ended pleasantly; we had got into regular and comfortable weather, and into that routine of sea-life which is only broken by a storm, a sail, or the sight of land.

As we had now a long "spell" of fine weather, without any incident to break the monotony of our lives, there can be no better place to describe the duties, regulations, and customs of an American merchantman, of which ours was a fair specimen.

The captain, in the first place, is lord paramount. He stands no watch, comes and goes when he pleases, and is accountable to no one, and must be obeyed in everything, without a question, even from his chief officer. He has the power to turn his officers off duty, and even to break them and make them do duty as sailors in the forecastle. Where there are no passengers and no supercargo, as in our vessel, he has no companion but his own dignity, and no pleasures, unless he differs from most of his kind, but the consciousness of possessing supreme power and, occasionally, the exercise of it.

The prime minister, the official organ, and the active and superintending officer, is the chief mate. He is first lieutenant, boatswain, sailing-master, and quartermaster. The captain tells him what he wishes to have done, and leaves to him the care of overseeing, of allotting the work, and also the responsibility of its being well done. *The* mate (as he is always called, *par excellence*) also keeps the logbook, for which he is responsible to the owners and insurers, and has the charge of the stowage, safe-keeping, and delivery of the cargo. He is also *ex-officio*, the wit of the crew; for the captain does not condescend to joke with the men, and the second mate no one cares for; so that when "the mate" thinks fit to entertain "the people" with a coarse joke or a little practical wit, every one feels bound to laugh.

The second mate's is proverbially a dog's berth. He is neither officer nor man. The men do not respect him as an officer, and he is obliged to go aloft to reef and furl the topsails, and to put his hands into the tar and slush, with the rest. The crew call him the "sailor's waiter," as he has to furnish them with spun-yarn, marline, and all other stuffs that they need in their work, and has charge of the boatswain's locker, which includes serving-boards, marline-spikes, etc. He is expected to maintain his dignity and to enforce obedience, and still is kept at a great distance from the mate, and obliged to work with the crew. He is one to whom little is given and of whom much is required. His wages are usually double those of a common sailor, and he eats and sleeps in the cabin; but he is obliged to be on deck nearly all his time, and eats at the second table, that is, makes a meal out of what the captain and chief mate leave.

The steward is the captain's servant, and has charge of the pantry, from which every one, even the mate himself, is excluded. These distinctions usually find him an enemy in the mate, who does not like to have any one on board who is not entirely under his control; the crew do not consider him as one of their number, so he is left to the mercy of the captain.

The cook is the patron of the crew, and those who are in his favor can get their wet mittens and stockings dried, or light their pipes at the galley in the nightwatch. These two worthies, together with the carpenter and sail-maker, if there be one, stand no watch, but, being employed all day, are allowed to "sleep in" at night unless all hands are called.

The crew are divided into two divisions, as equally as may be, called the watches. Of these the chief mate commands the larboard, and the second mate the starboard. They divide the time between them, being on and off duty, or, as it is called, on deck and below, every other four hours. If, for instance, the chief mate with the larboard watch have the first night-watch from eight to twelve; at the end of the four hours the starboard watch is called, and the second mate takes the deck while the larboard watch and the first mate go below until four in the morning, when they come on deck again and remain until eight; having what is called the morning watch. As they will have been on deck eight hours out of the twelve, while those who had the middle watch—from twelve to four—will only have been up four hours, they have what is called a "forenoon watch below," that is, from eight A.M. till twelve A.M. In a man-of-war, and in some merchantmen, this alternation of watches is kept up throughout the twenty-four hours; but our ship, like most merchantmen, had "all hands" from twelve o'clock to dark, except in bad weather, when we had "watch and watch."

An explanation of the "dog-watches" may, perhaps, be of use to one who has never been at sea. They are to shift the watches each night, so that the same watch need not be on deck at the same hours. In order to effect this, the watch from four to eight A.M. is divided into two half, or dog-watches, one from four to six; and the other from six to eight. By this means they divide the twenty-four hours into seven watches instead of six, and thus shift the hours every night. As the dog-watches come during twilight, after the day's work is done, and before the night-watch is set, they are the watches in which everybody is on deck. The captain is up, walking on the weather side of the quarter-deck, the chief mate on the lee side, and the second mate about the weather gangway. The steward has finished his work in the cabin, and has come up to smoke his pipe with the cook in the galley. The crew are sitting on the windlass or lying on the forecastle, smoking, singing, or telling long yarns. At eight o'clock, eight bells are struck, the log is hove, the watch set, the wheel relieved, the galley shut up, and the other watch goes below.

The morning commences with the watch on deck "turning-to" at daybreak and washing down, scrubbing, and swabbing the decks. This together with filling the "scuttled butt" with fresh water, and coiling up the rigging, usually occupies the time until seven bells (half after seven), when all hands get breakfast. At eight, the day's work begins, and lasts until sundown, with the exception of an hour for dinner.

Before I end my explanations, it may be well to define a *day's work*, and to correct a mistake prevalent among landsmen about a sailor's life. Nothing is more common than to hear people say—"Are not sailors very idle at sea? what can they find to do?" This is a very natural mistake, and being very frequently made, it is one which every sailor feels interested in having corrected. In the first place, then, the discipline of the ship requires every man to be at work upon *something* when he is on deck, except at night and on Sundays. Except at these times, you will never see a man, on board a well-ordered vessel, standing idle on deck, sitting down, or leaning over the side. It is the officer's duty to keep every one at work, even if there is nothing to be done but to scrape the rust from the cabin cables. In no state prison are the convicts more regularly set to work, and more closely watched. No conversation is allowed among the crew at their duty, and though they frequently do talk when aloft, or when near one another, yet they always stop when an officer is nigh.

With regard to the work upon which the men are put, it is a matter which probably would not be understood by one who has not been at sea. When I first left port, and found that we were kept regularly employed for a week or two, I supposed that we were getting the vessel into sea trim and that it would soon be over, and we should have nothing to do but to sail the ship; but I found that it continued so for two years, and at the end of the two years there was as much to be done as ever. As has often been said, a ship is like a lady's watch, always out of repair. When first leaving port, studding-sail gear is to be rove, all the running rigging to be examined, that which is unfit for use to be got down, and new rigging rove in its place; then the standing rigging is to be overhauled, replaced, and repaired, in a thousand different ways; and wherever any of the numberless ropes or the yards are chafing or wearing upon it, there "chafing gear," as it is called, must be put on. This chafing gear consists of worming, parcelling, roundings, battens, and service of all kinds—both rope-yarns, spun-yarn, marline, and seizing-stuffs. Taking off, putting on, and mending the chafing gear alone, upon a vessel, would find constant employment for two or three men, during working hours, for a whole voyage.

The next point to be considered is, that all the "small stuffs" which are used on board a ship—such as spun-yarn, marline, seizing-stuff, etc.—are made on board. The owners of a vessel buy up incredible quantities of "old junk," which the sailors unlay after drawing out the yarns, knot them together and roll them up in balls. These "rope-yarns" are constantly used for various purposes, but the greater part is manufactured into spun yarn. For this purpose every vessel is furnished with a "spun-yarn winch"; which is very simple, consisting of a wheel and spindle. This may be heard constantly going on deck in pleasant weather; and we had employment, during a great part of the tune, for three hands in drawing and knotting yarns, and making spun-yarn.

Another method of employing the crew is "setting up" rigging. Wherever any of the standing rigging becomes slack (which is continually happening), the seizing and coverings must be taken off, tackles got up, and after the rigging is bowsed well taut, the seizings and coverings replaced; which is a very nice piece of work.

There is also such a connection between different parts of a vessel, that one rope can seldom be touched without altering another. You cannot stay a mast aft by the back-stays without slacking up the head-stays, etc. If we add to this all the tarring, greasing, oiling, varnishing, painting, scraping, and scrubbing which is required in the course of a long voyage, and also remember this is all to be done in *addition to* watching at night, steering, reefing, furling, bracing, making and setting sail, and pulling, hauling, and climbing in every direction, one will hardly ask, "What can a sailor find to do at sea?"

If, after all this labor—after exposing their lives and limbs in storms, wet and cold, the merchants and captains think that they have not earned their twelve dollars a month (out of which they clothe themselves), and their salt beef and hard bread, they keep them picking oakum—*ad infinitum*.

This is the usual resource upon a rainy day, for then it will not do to work upon rigging; and when it is pouring down in floods, instead of letting the sailors stand about in sheltered places, and talk, and keep themselves comfortable, they are separated to different parts of the ship and kept at work picking oakum. I have seen oakum stuff placed about in different parts of the ship, so that the sailors might not be idle in the *snatches* between the frequent squalls upon crossing the equator.

Some officers have been so driven to find work for the crew in a ship ready for sea, that they have set them to pounding the anchors (often done) and scraping the chain cables. The "Philadelphia Catechism" is, "Six days shalt thou labor and do all that thou art able, And on the seventh—holystone the decks and scrape the cable." This kind of work, of course, is not kept up

off Cape Horn, Cape of Good Hope, and in extreme north and south latitudes; but I have seen the decks washed down and scrubbed, when the water
would have frozen if it had been fresh; and all hands kept at work upon the
rigging, when we had on our pea-jackets, and our hands so numb that we
could hardly hold our marline-spikes.

I have here gone out of my narrative course in order that any who read
this may form as correct an idea of a sailor's life and duty as possible. I have
done it in this place because, for some time, our life was nothing but the
unvarying repetition of these duties which can be better described together.

Before leaving this description, however, I would state, in order to show
landsmen how little they know of the nature of a ship, that a *ship carpenter* is
kept in constant employ during good weather on board vessels which are in,
what is called, perfect sea order.

After speaking the *Carolina*, on the 21st August, nothing occurred to
break the monotony of our life until—

Friday, Sept. 5th, when we saw a sail on our weather (starboard) beam.
She proved to be a brig under English colors, and passing under our stern,
reported herself as forty-nine days from Buenos Ayres, bound to Liverpool.
Before she had passed us, "Sail ho!" was cried again and we made another sail,
far on our weather bow, and steering athwart our hawse. She passed out of
hail, but we made her out to be an hermaphrodite brig, with Brazilian colors
in her main rigging. By her course, she must have been bound from Brazil to
the south of Europe, probably Portugal.

Sunday, Sept. 7th. Fell in with the northeast trade winds. This morning
we caught our first dolphin, which I was very eager to see. I was disappointed
in the colors of this fish when dying. They were certainly very beautiful, but
not equal to what has been said of them. They are too indistinct. To do the
fish justice, there is nothing more beautiful than the dolphin when swimming
a few feet below the surface, on a bright day. It is the most elegantly formed,
and also the quickest fish, in salt water; and the rays of the sun striking upon
it, in its rapid and changing motions, reflected from the water, make it look
like a stray beam from a rainbow.

This day was spent like all pleasant Sabbaths at sea. The decks are washed down, the rigging coiled up, and everything put in order; and throughout the day, only one watch is kept on deck at a time. The men are all dressed in their best white duck trousers, and red or checked shirts, and have nothing to do but to make the necessary changes in the sails. They employ themselves in reading, talking, smoking, and mending their clothes. If the weather is pleasant, they bring their work and their books upon deck, and sit down upon the forecastle and windlass. This is the only day on which these privileges are allowed them. When Monday comes, they put on their tarry trousers again, and prepare for six days of labor.

To enhance the value of the Sabbath to the crew, they are allowed on that day a pudding, or as it is called a "duff." This is nothing more than flour boiled with water, and eaten with molasses. It is very heavy, dark, and clammy, yet it is looked upon as a luxury, and really forms an agreeable variety with salt beef and pork. Many a rascally captain has made friends of his crew by allowing them duff twice a week on the passage home.

On board some vessels this is made a day of instruction and of religious exercises; but we had a crew of swearers, from the captain to the smallest boy; and a day of rest, and of something like quiet social enjoyment, was all that we could expect.

We continued running large before the northeast trade winds for several days, until Monday—

Sept. 22d., when, upon coming on deck at seven bells in the morning we found the other watch aloft throwing water upon the sails, and looking astern we saw a small clipper-built brig with a black hull heading directly after us. We went to work immediately, and put all the canvas upon the brig which we could get upon her, rigging out oars for studding-sail yards; and continued wetting down the sails by buckets of water whipped up to the mast-head, until about nine o'clock, when there came on a drizzling rain.

The vessel continued in pursuit, changing her course as we changed ours, to keep before the wind. The captain, who watched her with his glass, said that she was armed, and full of men, and showed no colors. We continued running dead before the wind, knowing that we sailed better so, and that clippers are fastest *on* the wind. We had also another advantage. The wind was light, and we spread more canvas than she did, having royals and sky-sails fore and aft, and ten studding sails, while she, being an hermaphrodite brig, had only a gaff-top-sail aft. Early in the morning she was overhauling us a little, but after the rain came on and the wind grew lighter, we began to leave her astern.

All hands remained on deck throughout the day, and we got our arms in order; but we were too few to have done anything with her, if she had proved to be what we feared. Fortunately there was no moon, and the night which followed was exceeding dark, so that by putting out all the lights on board and altering her course four points, we hoped to get out of her reach. We had no light in the binnacle, but steered by the stars, and kept perfect silence through the night. At daybreak there was no sign of anything in the horizon, and we kept the vessel off to her course.

Wednesday, Oct. 1st. Crossed the equator in long. 24° 24' W. I now, for the first time, felt at liberty, according to the old usage, to call myself a son of Neptune, and was very glad to be able to claim the title without the disagreeable initiation which so many have to go through. After once crossing the line you can never be subjected to the process, but are considered as a son of Neptune, with full powers to play tricks upon others. This ancient custom is now seldom allowed, unless there are passengers on board, in which case there is always a good deal of sport.

It had been obvious to all hands for some time that the second mate, whose name was Foster, was an idle, careless fellow, and not much of a sailor, and that the captain was exceedingly dissatisfied with him. The power of the captain in these cases was well known, and we all anticipated a difficulty.

Foster (called *Mr.* by virtue of his office) was but half a sailor, having always been short voyages and remained at home a long time between them. His father was a man of some property, and intended to have given his son a liberal education; but he, being idle and worthless, was sent off to sea, and succeeded no better there; for, unlike many scamps, he had none of the qualities of a sailor—he was "not of the stuff that they make sailors of." He was one of the class of officers who are disliked by their captain and despised by the crew. He used to hold long yarns with the crew, and talk about the captain, and play with the boys, and relax discipline in every way.

This kind of conduct always makes the captain suspicious, and is never pleasant in the end, to the men; they preferring to have an officer active, vigilant, and distant as may be, with kindness. Among other bad practices, he frequently slept on his watch, and having been discovered asleep by the captain, he was told that he would be turned off duty if he did it again. To prevent it in every way possible, the hen-coops were ordered to be knocked up, for the captain never sat down on deck himself, and never permitted an officer to do so.

The second night after crossing the equator, we had the watch from eight till twelve, and it was "my helm" for the last two hours. There had been light squalls through the night, and the captain told Mr. Foster, who commanded our watch, to keep a bright lookout. Soon after I came to the helm, I found that he was quite drowsy, and at last he stretched himself on the companion and went fast asleep.

Soon afterward, the captain came very quietly on deck, and stood by me for some time looking at the compass. The officer at length became aware of the captain's presence, but pretending not to know it, began humming and whistling to himself, to show that he was not asleep, and went forward, without looking behind him, and ordered the main-royal to be loosed. On turning round to come aft, he pretended surprise at seeing the master on deck.

This would not do. The captain was too "wide awake" for him, and beginning upon him at once, gave him a grand blow-up, in true nautical style— "You're a lazy good-for-nothing rascal; you're neither man, boy, *soger*, nor sailor! you're no more than a *thing* aboard a vessel! you don't earn your salt! you're worse than a *Mahon soger!*" and other still more choice extracts from the sailor's vocabulary. After the poor fellow had taken this harangue, he was sent into his stateroom, and the captain stood the rest of the watch himself.

At seven bells in the morning, all hands were called aft and told that Foster was no longer an officer on board, and that we might choose one of our number for second mate. It is usual for the captain to make this offer, and it is very good policy, for the crew think themselves the choosers and are flattered by it, but have to obey, nevertheless.

Our crew, as is usual, refused to take the responsibility of choosing a man of whom we would never be able to complain, and left it to the captain. He picked out an active and intelligent young sailor born near the Kennebec, who had been several Canton voyages, and proclaimed him in the following manner:

"I choose Jim Hall—he's your second mate. All you've got to do is, to obey him as you would me; and remember that he is *Mr.* Hall." Foster went forward into the forecastle as a common sailor, and lost *the handle to his name*, while young foremast Jim became Mr. Hall, and took up his quarters in the land of knives and forks and tea-cups.

The Mellish in Sydney Harbour, W. J. Huggins, 1830. National Library of Australia.

Sunday, Oct. 5th. It was our morning watch; when, soon after day began to break, a man on the forecastle called out, "Land ho!" I had never heard the cry before, and did not know what it meant (and few would suspect what the words were, when hearing the strange sound for the first time), but I soon found, by the direction of all eyes, that there was land stretching along on our weather beam. We immediately took in the studding sails and hauled our wind, running for the land. This was done to determine our longitude; for by the captain's chronometer we were in 25° W., but by his observations we were much further, and he had been for some time in doubt whether it was his chronometer or his sextant which was out of order. This landfall settled the matter, and the former instrument was condemned, and becoming still worse, was never afterwards used.

As we ran in toward the coast, we found that we were directly off the port of Pernambuco, and could see with the telescope the roofs of the houses, and one large church, and the town of Olinda. We ran along by the mouth of the harbor, and saw a full-rigged brig going in. At two P.M., we again kept off before the wind, leaving the land on our quarter, and at sundown it was out of sight.

It was here that I first saw one of those singular things called catamarans. They are composed of logs lashed together upon the water; have one large sail, are quite fast, and, strange as it may seem, are trusted as good sea boats. We saw several, with from one to three men in each, boldly putting out to sea, after it had become almost dark. The Indians go out in them after fish, and as the weather is regular in certain seasons, they have no fear. After taking a new departure from Olinda, we kept off on our way to Cape Horn.

We met with nothing remarkable until we were in the latitude of the river La Plata. Here there are violent gales from the southwest called Pamperos, which are very destructive to the shipping in the river, and are felt for many leagues at sea. They are usually preceded by lightning. The captain told the mates to keep a bright lookout, and if they saw lightning at the southwest, to take in sail at once. We got the first touch of one during my watch on deck. I was walking in the lee gangway, and thought that I saw lightning on the bow. I told the second mate, who came over and looked out for some time. It was very black in the southwest, and in about ten minutes we saw a distinct flash. The wind, which had been southeast, had now left us, and it was dead calm. We sprang aloft immediately and furled the royals and top-gallant-sails, and took in the flying-jib, hauled up the mainsail and trysail, squared the after yards and awaited the attack. A huge mist capped with black cloud came driving towards us, extending over that quarter of the horizon, and covering the stars, which shone brightly in the other part of the heavens. It came upon us at once with a blast, and a shower of hail and rain, which almost took our breath from us. The hardiest was obliged to turn his back. We let the halyards run, and fortunately were not taken aback. The little vessel "paid off" from the wind, and ran on for some time directly before it, tearing through the water with everything flying. Having called all hands, we close reefed the topsails and trysail, furled the courses and jib, set the foretopmast staysail, and brought her up nearly to her course, with the weather braces hauled in a little, to ease her.

This was the first blow, that I have seen, which could really be called a gale. We had reefed our topsails in the Gulf Stream, and I thought it something serious, but an older sailor would have thought nothing of it. As I had now become used to the vessel and to my duty, I was of some service on a yard, and could knot my reef-point as well as anybody. I obeyed the order to lay aloft with the rest, and found the reefing a very exciting scene; for one watch reefed the foretopsail, and the other the main, and every one did his utmost to get his topsail hoisted first. We had a great advantage over the larboard watch, because the chief mate never goes aloft, while our new second mate used to jump into the rigging as soon as we began to haul out the reef-tackle, and have the weather earing passed before there was a man upon the yard. In this way we were almost always able to raise the cry of "Haul out to leeward" before them, and having knotted our points, would slide down the shrouds and back-stays, and sing out at the topsail halyards to let it be known that we were ahead of them.

Reefing is the most exciting part of a sailor's duty. All hands are engaged upon it, and after the halyards are let go, there is no time to be lost—no "sogering," or hanging back, then. If one is not quick enough, another runs over him. The first on the yard goes to the weather earing, the second to the lee, and the next two to the dog's ears, while the others lay along the bunt, just giving each other elbow-room. In reefing, the yard-arms (the extremes of the yards), are the posts of honor; but in furling, the strongest and most experienced stand in the slings (or, middle of the yard), to make up the bunt. If the second mate is a smart fellow, he will never let any one take either of these posts from him; for if he is wanting either in seamanship, strength, or activity, some better man will get the bunt and earings from him; which immediately brings him into disrepute.

We remained for the rest of the night, and throughout the next day, under the same close sail, for it continued to blow very fresh; and though we had no more hail, yet there was a soaking rain, and it was quite cold and uncomfortable; the more so, because we were not prepared for cold weather, but had on our thin clothes. We were glad to get a watch below, and put on our thick clothing, boots, and southwesters. Toward sundown the gale moderated a little, and it began to clear off in the southwest. We shook our reefs out, one by one, and before midnight had topgallant-sails upon her.

We had now made up our minds for Cape Horn and cold weather, and entered upon every necessary preparation.

Tuesday Nov. 4th. At daybreak, saw land upon our larboard quarter. There were two islands, of different size, but of the same shape; rather high, beginning low at the water's edge, and running with a curved ascent to the middle. They were so far off as to be of a deep blue color, and in a few hours we *sunk* them in the northeast. These were the Falkland Islands. We had run between them and the main land of Patagonia. At sunset the second mate, who was at the masthead, said that he saw land on the starboard bow. This must have been the island of Staten Land; and we were now in the region of Cape Horn, with a fine breeze from the northward, topmast and topgallant-studding-sails set, and every prospect of a speedy and pleasant passage round.

The bucolic coast of the Falkland Islands.

End of the Pier, New York Harbor by John Henry Twachtman, 1879.

15.

REDBURN

HERMAN MELVILLE

It was now getting dark, when all at once the sailors were ordered on the quarter-deck, and of course I went along with them.

What is to come now, thought I; but I soon found out. It seemed we were going to be divided into watches. The chief mate began by selecting a stout good-looking sailor for his watch; and then the second mate's turn came to choose, and he also chose a stout good-looking sailor. But it was not me;—no; and *I* noticed, as they went on choosing, one after the other in regular rotation, that both of the mates never so much as looked at me, but kept going round among the rest, peering into their faces, for it was dusk, and telling them not to hide themselves away so in their jackets. But the sailors, especially the stout good-looking ones, seemed to make a point of lounging as much out of the way as possible, and slouching their hats over their eyes; and although it may only be a fancy of mine, *I* certainly thought that they affected a sort of lordly indifference as to whose watch they were going to be in; and did not think it worth while to look any way anxious about the matter. And the very men who, a few minutes before, had showed the most alacrity and promptitude in jumping into the rigging and running aloft at the word of command, now lounged against the bulwarks and most lazily; as if they were quite sure, that by this time the officers must know who the best men were, and they valued themselves well enough to be willing to put the officers to the trouble of searching them out; for if they were worth having, they were worth seeking.

At last they were all chosen but me; and it was the chief mate's next turn to choose; though there could be little choosing in my case, since *I* was a thirteener, and must, whether or no, go over to the next column, like the odd figure you carry along when you do a sum in addition.

"Well, Buttons," said the chief mate, "I thought I'd got rid of you. And as it is, Mr. Rigs," he added, speaking to the second mate, "I guess you had better take him into your watch;—there, I'll let you have him, and then you'll be one stronger than me."

"No, I thank you," said Mr. Rigs.

"You had better," said the chief mate—"see, he's not a bad looking chap—he's a little green, to be sure, but you were so once yourself, you know, Rigs."

"No, I thank you," said the second mate again. "Take him yourself—he's yours by good rights—I don't want him." And so they put me in the chief mate's division, that is the larboard watch.

While this scene was going on, I felt shabby enough; there I stood, just like a silly sheep, over whom two butchers are bargaining. Nothing that had yet happened so forcibly reminded me of where I was, and what I had come to. I was very glad when they sent us forward again.

As we were going forward, the second mate called one of the sailors by name:—"You, Bill?" and Bill answered, "Sir?" just as if the second mate was a born gentleman. It surprised me not a little, to see a man in such a shabby, shaggy old jacket addressed so respectfully; but I had been quite as much surprised when I heard the chief mate call him *Mr.* Rigs during the scene on the quarter-deck; as if this *Mr. Rigs* was a great merchant living in a marble house in Lafayette Place. But I was not very long in finding out, that at sea all officers are *Misters,* and would take it for an insult if any seaman presumed to omit calling them so. And it is also one of their rights and privileges to be called *sir* when addressed—Yes, *sir*; No, *sir*; Ay, ay, *sir*; and they are as particular about being sirred as so many knights and baronets; though their titles are not hereditary, as is the case with the Sir Johns and Sir Joshuas in England. But so far as the second mate is concerned, his titles are the only dignities he enjoys; for, upon the whole, he leads a puppyish life indeed. He is not deemed company at any time for the captain, though the chief mate occasionally is, at least deck-company, though not in the cabin; and besides this, the second mate has to breakfast, lunch, dine, and sup off the leavings of the cabin table, and even the steward, who is accountable to nobody but the captain, sometimes treats him cavalierly; and he has to run aloft when topsails are reefed; and put his hand a good way down into the tar-bucket; and keep the key of the boatswain's locker, and fetch and carry balls of marline and seizing-stuff for the sailors when at work in the rigging; besides doing many other things, which a true-born baronet of any spirit would rather die and give up his title than stand.

Having been divided into watches we were sent to supper; but I could not eat any thing except a little biscuit, though I should have liked to have some good tea; but as I had no pot to get it in, and was rather nervous about asking the rough sailors to let me drink out of theirs; I was obliged to go without a sip. I thought of going to the black cook and begging a tin cup; but he looked so cross and ugly then, that the sight of him almost frightened the idea out of me.

When supper was over, for they never talk about going to *tea* aboard of a ship, the watch to which I belonged was called on deck; and we were told it was for us to stand the first night watch, that is, from eight o'clock till midnight.

I now began to feel unsettled and ill at ease about the stomach, as if matters were all topsy-turvy there; and felt strange and giddy about the head; and so I made no doubt that this was the beginning of that dreadful thing, the sea-sickness. Feeling worse and worse, I told one of the sailors how it was with me, and begged him to make my excuses very civilly to the chief mate, for I thought I would go below and spend the night in my bunk. But he only laughed at me, and said something about my mother not being aware of my being out; which enraged me not a little, that a man whom I had heard swear so terribly, should dare to take such a holy name into his mouth. It seemed a sort of blasphemy, and it seemed like dragging out the best and most cherished secrets of my soul, for at that time the name of mother was the center of all my heart's finest feelings, which ere that, I had learned to keep secret, deep down in my being.

But I did not outwardly resent the sailor's words, for that would have only made the matter worse.

Now this man was a Greenlander by birth, with a very white skin where the sun had not burnt it, and handsome blue eyes placed wide apart in his head, and a broad good-humored face, and plenty of curly flaxen hair. He was not very tall, but exceedingly stout-built, though active; and his back was as broad as a shield, and it was a great way between his shoulders. He seemed to be a sort of lady's sailor, for in his broken English he was always talking about the nice ladies of his acquaintance in Stockholm and Copenhagen and a place he called the Hook, which at first I fancied must be the place where lived the hook-nosed men that caught fowling-pieces and every other article that came along. He was dressed very tastefully, too, as if he knew he was a good-looking fellow. He had on a new blue woolen Havre frock, with a new silk handkerchief round his neck, passed through one of the vertebral bones of a shark, highly polished and carved. His trowsers were of clear white duck, and he sported a handsome pair of pumps, and a tarpaulin hat bright as a looking-glass, with a long black ribbon streaming behind, and getting entangled every now and then in the rigging; and he had gold anchors in his ears, and a silver ring on one of his fingers, which was very much worn and bent from pulling ropes and other work on board ship. I thought he might better have left his jewelry at home.

It was a long time before I could believe that this man was really from Greenland, though he looked strange enough to me, then, to have come from the moon; and he was full of stories about that distant country; how they passed the winters there; and how bitter cold it was; and how he used to go to bed and sleep twelve hours, and get up again and run about, and go to bed again, and get up again—there was no telling how many times, and all in one night; for in the winter time in his country, he said, the nights were so many weeks long, that a Greenland baby was sometimes three months old, before it could properly be said to be a day old.

I had seen mention made of such things before, in books of voyages; but that was only reading about them, just as you read the *Arabian Nights*, which no one ever believes; for somehow, when I read about these wonderful countries, I never used really to believe what I read, but only thought it very strange, and a good deal too strange to be altogether true; though I never thought the men who wrote the book meant to tell lies. But I don't know exactly how to explain what I mean; but this much I will say, that I never believed in Greenland till I saw this Greenlander. And at first, hearing him talk about Greenland, only made me still more incredulous. For what business had a man from Greenland to be in my company? Why was he not at home among the icebergs, and how could he stand a warm summer's sun, and not be melted away? Besides, instead of icicles, there were ear-rings hanging from his ears; and he did not wear bear-skins, and keep his hands in a huge muff; things, which I could not help connecting with Greenland and all Greenlanders.

But I was telling about my being sea-sick and wanting to retire for the night. This Greenlander seeing I was ill, volunteered to turn doctor and cure me; so going down into the forecastle, he came back with a brown jug, like a molasses jug, and a little tin cannikin, and as soon as the brown jug got near my nose, I needed no telling what was in it, for it smelt like a still-house, and sure enough proved to be full of Jamaica spirits.

"Now, Buttons," said he, "one little dose of this will be better for you than a whole night's sleep; there, take that now, and then eat seven or eight biscuits, and you'll feel as strong as the mainmast."

But I felt very little like doing as I was bid, for I had some scruples about drinking spirits; and to tell the plain truth, for I am not ashamed of it,

I was a member of a society in the village where my mother lived, called the Juvenile Total Abstinence Association, of which my friend, Tom Legare, was president, secretary, and treasurer, and kept the funds in a little purse that his cousin knit for him. There was three and sixpence on hand, I believe, the last time he brought in his accounts, on a May day, when we had a meeting in a grove on the river-bank. Tom was a very honest treasurer, and never spent the Society's money for peanuts; and besides all, was a fine, generous boy, whom I much loved. But I must not talk about Tom now.

When the Greenlander came to me with his jug of medicine, I thanked him as well as I could; for just then I was leaning with my mouth over the side, feeling ready to die; but I managed to tell him I was under a solemn ob-ligation never to drink spirits upon any consideration whatever; though, as I had a sort of presentiment that the spirits would now, for once in my life, do me good, I began to feel sorry, that when I signed the pledge of abstinence, I had not taken care to insert a little clause, allowing me to drink spirits in case of sea-sickness. And I would advise temperance people to attend to this matter in future; and then if they come to go to sea, there will be no need of breaking their pledges, which I am truly sorry to say was the case with me. And a hard thing it was, too, thus to break a vow before unbroken; especially as the Jamaica tasted any thing but agreeable, and indeed burnt my mouth so, that I did not relish my meals for some time after. Even when I had become quite well and strong again, I wondered how the sailors could really like such stuff; but many of them had a jug of it, besides the Greenlander, which they brought along to sea with them, *to taper off with,* as they called it. But this tapering off did not last very long, for the Jamaica was all gone on the second day, and the jugs were tossed overboard. I wonder where they are now?

But to tell the truth, I found, in spite of its sharp taste, the spirits I drank was just the thing I needed; but I suppose, if I could have had a cup of nice hot coffee, it would have done quite as well, and perhaps much better. But that was not to be had at that time of night, or, indeed, at any other time; for the thing they called *coffee,* which was given to us every morning at breakfast, was the most curious tasting drink I ever drank, and tasted as little like coffee,

as it did like lemonade; though, to be sure, it was generally as cold as lemonade, and I used to think the cook had an icehouse, and dropt ice into his
coffee. But what was more curious still, was the different quality and taste of
it on different mornings. Sometimes it tasted fishy, as if it was a decoction of
Dutch herrings; and then it would taste very salty, as if some *old horse,* or sea-
beef, had been boiled in it; and then again it would taste a sort of cheesy, as
if the captain had sent his cheese-parings forward to make our coffee of; and
yet another time it would have such a very bad flavor, that I was almost ready
to think some old stocking-heels had been boiled in it. What under heaven
it was made of, that it had so many different bad flavors, always remained a
mystery; for when at work at his vocation, our old cook used to keep himself
close shut-up in his caboose, a little cook-house, and never told any of his
secrets.

It was Though a very serious character, as I shall hereafter show, he was for
all that, and perhaps for that identical reason, a very suspicious looking sort
of a cook, that I don't believe would ever succeed in getting the cooking at
Delmonico's in New York. It was well for him that he was a black cook, for
I have no doubt his color kept us from seeing his dirty face! I never saw him
wash but once, and that was at one of his own soup pots one dark night when
he thought no one saw him. What induced him to be washing his face then,
I never could find out; but I suppose he must have suddenly waked up, after
dreaming about some real estate on his cheeks. As for his coffee, notwithstanding the disagreeableness of its flavor, I always used to have a strange curiosity every morning, to see what new taste it was going to have; and though,
sure enough, I never missed making a new discovery, and adding another
taste to my palate, I never found that there was any change in the badness of
the beverage, which always seemed the same in that respect as before.

It may well be believed, then, that now when I was seasick, a cup of such
coffee as our old cook made would have done me no good, if indeed it would
not have come near making an end of me. And bad as it was, and since it was
not to be had at that time of night, as I said before, I think I was excusable
in taking something else in place of it, as I did; and under the circumstances,

it would be unhandsome of them, if my fellow-members of the Temperance Society should reproach me for breaking my bond, which I would not have done except in case of necessity. But the evil effect of breaking one's bond upon any occasion whatever, was witnessed in the present case; for it insidiously opened the way to subsequent breaches of it, which though very slight, yet carried no apology with them.

The latter part of this first long watch that we stood was very pleasant, so far as the weather was concerned. From being rather cloudy, it became a soft moonlight; and the stars peeped out, plain enough to count one by one; and there was a fine steady breeze; and it was not very cold; and we were going through the water almost as smooth as a sled sliding down hill. And what was still better, the wind held so steady, that there was little running aloft, little pulling ropes, and scarcely any thing disagreeable of that kind.

The chief mate kept walking up and down the quarter-deck, with a lighted long-nine cigar in his mouth by way of a torch; and spoke but few words to us the whole watch. He must have had a good deal of thinking to attend to, which in truth is the case with most seamen the first night out of port, especially when they have thrown away their money in foolish dissipation, and got very sick into the bargain. For when ashore, many of these sea-officers are as wild and reckless in their way, as the sailors they command.

While I stood watching the red cigar-end promenading up and down, the mate suddenly stopped and gave an order, and the men sprang to obey it. It was not much, only something about hoisting one of the sails a little higher up on the mast. The men took hold of the rope, and began pulling upon it; the foremost man of all setting up a song with no words to it, only a strange musical rise and fall of notes. In the dark night, and far out upon the lonely sea, it sounded wild enough, and made me feel as I had sometimes felt, when in a twilight room a cousin of mine, with black eyes, used to play some old German airs on the piano. I almost looked round for goblins, and felt just a little bit afraid. But I soon got used to this singing; for the sailors never touched a rope without it. Sometimes, when no one happened to strike up, and the pulling, whatever it might be, did not seem to be getting forward very well, the mate would always say, *"Come, men, can't any of you sing? Sing now, and raise the dead."* And then some one of them would begin, and if every man's arms were as much relieved as mine by the song, and he could pull as much better as I did, with such a cheering accompaniment, I am sure the song was well worth the breath expended on it. It is a great thing in a sailor to know how to sing well, for he gets a great name by it from the officers, and a good deal of popularity among his shipmates. Some sea-captains, before shipping a man, always ask him whether he can sing out at a rope.

During the greater part of the watch, the sailors sat on the windlass and told long stories of their adventures by sea and land, and talked about Gibraltar, and Canton, and Valparaiso, and Bombay, just as you and I would about Peck Slip and the Bowery. Every man of them almost was a volume of Voyages and Travels round the World. And what most struck me was that like books of voyages they often contradicted each other, and would fall into long and violent disputes about who was keeping the Foul Anchor tavern in Portsmouth at such a time; or whether the King of Canton lived or did not live in Persia; or whether the bar-maid of a particular house in Hamburg had black eyes or blue eyes; with many other mooted points of that sort.

At last one of them went below and brought up a box of cigars from his chest, for some sailors always provide little delicacies of that kind, to break off the first shock of the salt water after laying idle ashore; and also by way of *tapering off,* as I mentioned a little while ago. But I wondered that they never carried any pies and tarts to sea with them, instead of spirits and cigars.

Ned, for that was the man's name, split open the box with a blow of his fist, and then handed it round along the windlass, just like a waiter at a party, every one helping himself. But I was a member of an Anti-Smoking Society that had been organized in our village by the Principal of the Sunday School there, in conjunction with the Temperance Association. So I did not smoke any then, though I did afterward upon the voyage, I am sorry to say. Notwithstanding I declined; with a good deal of unnecessary swearing, Ned assured me that the cigars were real genuine Havannas; for he had been in Havanna, he said, and had them made there under his own eye. According to his account, he was very particular about his cigars and other things, and never made any importations, for they were unsafe; but always made a voyage himself direct to the place where any foreign thing was to be had that he wanted. He went to Havre for his woolen shirts, to Panama for his hats, to China for his silk handkerchiefs, and direct to Calcutta for his cheroots; and as a great joker in the watch used to say, no doubt he would at last have occasion to go to Russia for his halter; the wit of which saying was presumed to be in the fact, that the Russian hemp is the best; though that is not wit which needs explaining.

By dint of the spirits which, besides stimulating my fainting strength, united with the cool air of the sea to give me an appetite for our hard biscuit; and also by dint of walking briskly up and down the deck before the windlass, I had now recovered in good part from my sickness, and finding the sailors all very pleasant and sociable, at least among themselves, and seated smoking together like old cronies, and nothing on earth to do but sit the watch out, I began to think that they were a pretty good set of fellows after all, barring their swearing and another ugly way of talking they had; and I thought I had misconceived their true characters; for at the outset I had deemed them such a parcel of wicked hard-hearted rascals that it would be a severe affliction to associate with them.

Yes, I now began to look on them with a sort of incipient love; but more with an eye of pity and compassion, as men of naturally gentle and kind dispositions, whom only hardships, and neglect, and ill-usage had made outcasts from good society; and not as villains who loved wickedness for the sake of it, and would persist in wickedness, even in Paradise, if they ever got there. And I called to mind a sermon I had once heard in a church in behalf of sailors, when the preacher called them strayed lambs from the fold, and compared them to poor lost children, babes in the wood, orphans without fathers or mothers.

And I remembered reading in a magazine, called the *Sailors' Magazine*, with a sea-blue cover, and a ship painted on the back, about pious seamen who never swore, and paid over all their wages to the poor heathen in India;

and how that when they were too old to go to sea, these pious old sailors found a delightful home for life in the Hospital, where they had nothing to do, but prepare themselves for their latter end. And I wondered whether there were any such good sailors among my ship-mates; and observing that one of them laid on deck apart from the rest, I thought to be sure he must be one of them: so I did not disturb his devotions: but I was afterward shocked at discovering that he was only fast asleep, with one of the brown jugs by his side.

I forgot to mention by the way, that every once in a while, the men went into one corner, where the chief mate could not see them, to take a "swig at the halyards," as they called it; and this swigging at the halyards it was, that enabled them "to taper off" handsomely, and no doubt it was this, too, that had something to do with making them so pleasant and sociable that night, for they were seldom so pleasant and sociable afterward, and never treated me so kindly as they did then. Yet this might have been owing to my being something of a stranger to them, then; and our being just out of port. But that very night they turned about, and taught me a bitter lesson; but all in good time.

I have said, that seeing how agreeable they were getting, and how friendly their manner was, I began to feel a sort of compassion for them, grounded on their sad conditions as amiable outcasts; and feeling so warm an interest in them, and being full of pity, and being truly desirous of benefiting them to the best of my poor powers, for I knew they were but poor indeed, I made bold to ask one of them, whether he was ever in the habit of going to church, when he was ashore, or dropping in at the Floating Chapel I had seen lying off the dock in the East River at New York; and whether he would think it too much of a liberty, if I asked him, if he had any good books in his chest. He stared a little at first, but marking what good language I used, seeing my civil bearing toward him, he seemed for a moment to be filled with a certain involuntary respect for me, and answered, that he had been to church once, some ten or twelve years before, in London, and on a week-day had helped to move the Floating Chapel round the Battery, from the North River; and that was the only time he had seen it. For his books, he said he did not know what

I meant by good books; but if I wanted the Newgate Calendar, and Pirate's Own, he could lend them to me.

When I heard this poor sailor talk in this manner, showing so plainly his ignorance and absence of proper views of religion, I pitied him more and more, and contrasting my own situation with his, I was grateful that I was different from him; and I thought how pleasant it was, to feel wiser and better than he could feel; though I was willing to confess to myself, that it was not altogether my own good endeavors, so much as my education, which I had received from others, that had made me the upright and sensible boy I at that time thought myself to be. And it was now, that I began to feel a good degree of complacency and satisfaction in surveying my own character; for, before this, I had previously associated with persons of a very discreet life, so that there was little opportunity to magnify myself, by comparing myself with my neighbors.

Thinking that my superiority to him in a moral way might sit uneasily upon this sailor, I thought it would soften the matter down by giving him a chance to show his own superiority to me, in a minor thing; for I was far from being vain and conceited.

Having observed that at certain intervals a little bell was rung on the quarter-deck by the man at the wheel; and that as soon as it was heard, some one of the sailors forward struck a large bell which hung on the forecastle; and having observed that how many times soever the man astern rang his bell, the man forward struck his—tit for tat,—I inquired of this Floating Chapel sailor, what all this ringing meant; and whether, as the big bell hung right over the scuttle that went down to the place where the watch below were sleeping, such a ringing every little while would not tend to disturb them and beget unpleasant dreams; and in asking these questions I was particular to address him in a civil and condescending way, so as to show him very plainly that I did not deem myself one whit better than he was, that is, taking all things together, and not going into particulars. But to my great surprise and mortification, he in the rudest land of manner laughed aloud in my face, and called me a "Jimmy Dux," though that was not my real name, and he must have known it;

and also the "son of a farmer," though as I have previously related, my father was a great merchant and French importer in Broad-street in New York. And then he began to laugh and joke about me, with the other sailors, till they all got round me, and if I had not felt so terribly angry, I should certainly have felt very much like a fool. But my being so angry prevented me from feeling foolish, which is very lucky for people in a passion.

While the scene last described was going on, we were all startled by a horrid groaning noise down in the forecastle; and all at once some one came rushing up the scuttle in his shirt, clutching something in his hand, and trembling and shrieking in the most frightful manner, so that I thought one of the sailors must be murdered below.

But it all passed in a moment; and while we stood aghast at the sight, and almost before we knew what it was, the shrieking man jumped over the bows into the sea, and we saw him no more. Then there was a great uproar; the sailors came running up on deck; and the chief mate ran forward, and learning what had happened, began to yell out his orders about the sails and yards; and we all went to pulling and hauling the ropes, till at last the ship lay almost still on the water. Then they loosed a boat, which kept pulling round the ship for more than an hour, but they never caught sight of the man. It seemed that he was one of the sailors who had been brought aboard dead drunk, and tumbled into his bunk by his landlord; and there he had lain till now. He must have suddenly waked up, I suppose, raging mad with the delirium tremens, as the chief mate called it, and finding himself in a strange silent place, and knowing not how he had got there, he rushed on deck, and so, in a fit of frenzy, put an end to himself.

This event, happening at the dead of night, had a wonderfully solemn and almost awful effect upon me. I would have given the whole world, and the sun and moon, and all the stars in heaven, if they had been mine, had I been safe back at Mr. Jones', or still better, in my home on the Hudson River. I thought it an ill-omened voyage, and railed at the folly which had sent me to sea, sore against the advice of my best friends, that is to say, my mother and sisters.

Alas! poor Wellingborough, thought I, you will never see your home any more. And in this melancholy mood I went below, when the watch had expired, which happened soon after. But to my terror, I found that the suicide had been occupying the very bunk which I had appropriated to myself, and there was no other place for me to sleep in. The thought of lying down there now, seemed too horrible to me, and what made it worse, was the way in which the sailors spoke of my being frightened. And they took this opportunity to tell me what a hard and wicked life I had entered upon, and how that such things happened frequently at sea, and they were used to it. But I did not believe this; for when the suicide came rushing and shrieking up the scuttle, they looked as frightened as I did; and besides that, and what makes their being frightened still plainer, is the fact, that if they had had any presence of mind, they could have prevented his plunging overboard, since he brushed right by them. However, they lay in their bunks smoking, and kept talking on some time in this strain, and advising me as soon as ever I got home to pin my ears back, so as not to hold the wind, and sail straight away into the interior of the country, and never stop until deep in the bush, far off from the least running brook, never mind how shallow, and out of sight of even the smallest puddle of rainwater.

This kind of talking brought the tears into my eyes, for it was so true and real, and the sailors who spoke it seemed so false-hearted and insincere; but for all that, in spite of the sickness at my heart, it made me mad, and stung me to the quick, that they should speak of me as a poor trembling coward, who could never be brought to endure the hardships of a sailor's life; for I felt myself trembling, and knew that I was but a coward then, well enough, without their telling me of it. And they did not say I was cowardly, because they perceived it in me, but because they merely supposed I must be, judging, no doubt, from their own secret thoughts about themselves; for I felt sure that the suicide frightened them very badly. And at last, being provoked to desperation by their taunts, I told them so to their faces; but I might better have kept silent; for they now all united to abuse me. They asked me what business I, a boy like me, had to go to sea, and take the bread out of the mouth of honest sailors, and fill a good seaman's place; and asked me whether I ever dreamed of becoming a captain, since I was a gentleman with white hands; and if I ever *should* be, they would like nothing better than to ship aboard my vessel and stir up a mutiny. And one of them, whose name was Jackson, of whom I shall have a good deal more to say by-and-by, said, I had better steer clear of him ever after, for if ever I crossed his path, or got into his way, he would be the death of me, and if ever I stumbled about in the rigging near *him,* he would make nothing of pitching me overboard; and that he swore too, with an oath. At first, all this nearly stunned me, it was so unforeseen; and then I could not believe that they meant what they said, or that they could be so cruel and black-hearted. But how could I help seeing, that the men who could thus talk to a poor, friendless boy, on the very first night of his voyage to sea, must be capable of almost any enormity. I loathed, detested, and hated them with all that was left of my bursting heart and soul, and I thought myself the most forlorn and miserable wretch that ever breathed. May I never be a man, thought I, if to be a boy is to be such a wretch. And I wailed and wept, and my heart cracked within me, but all the time I defied them through my teeth, and dared them to do their worst.

At last they ceased talking and fell fast asleep, leaving me awake, seated on a chest with my face bent over my knees between my hands. And there I sat, till at length the dull beating against the ship's bows, and the silence around soothed me down, and I fell asleep as I sat.

The next thing I knew, was the loud thumping of a handspike on deck as the watch was called again. It was now four o'clock in the morning, and when we got on deck the first signs of day were shining in the east. The men were very sleepy, and sat down on the windlass without speaking, and some of them nodded and nodded, till at last they fell off like little boys in church during a drowsy sermon. At last it was broad day, and an order was given to wash down the decks. A great tub was dragged into the waist, and then one of the men went over into the chains, and slipped in behind a band fastened to the shrouds, and leaning over, began to swing a bucket into the sea by a long rope; and in that way with much expertness and sleight of hand, he managed to fill the tub in a very short time. Then the water began to splash about all over the decks, and I began to think I should surely get my feet wet, and catch my death of cold. So I went to the chief mate, and told him I thought I would just step below, till this miserable wetting was over; for I did not have any water-proof boots, and an aunt of mine had died of consumption. But he only roared out for me to get a broom and go to scrubbing, or he would prove a worse consumption to me than ever got hold of my poor aunt. So I scrubbed away fore and aft, till my back was almost broke, for the brooms had uncommon short handles, and we were told to scrub hard.

At length the scrubbing being over, the mate began heaving buckets of water about, to wash every thing clean, by way of finishing off. He must have thought this fine sport, just as captains of fire engines love to point the tube of their hose; for he kept me running after him with full buckets of water, and sometimes chased a little chip all over the deck, with a continued flood, till at last he sent it flying out of a scupper-hole into the sea; when if he had only given me permission, I could have picked it up in a trice, and dropped it overboard without saying one word, and without wasting so much water. But he said there was plenty of water in the ocean, and to spare; which was true enough, but then I who had to trot after him with the buckets, had no more legs and arms than I wanted for my own use.

I thought this washing down the decks was the most foolish thing in the world, and besides that it was the most uncomfortable. It was worse than my mother's house-cleanings at home, which I used to abominate so.

At eight o'clock the bell was struck, and we went to breakfast. And now some of the worst of my troubles began. For not having had any friend to tell me what I would want at sea, I had not provided myself, as I should have done, with a good many things that a sailor needs; and for my own part, it had never entered my mind, that sailors had no table to sit down to, no cloth, or napkins, or tumblers, and had to provide every thing themselves. But so it was.

The first thing they did was this. Every sailor went to the cook-house with his tin pot, and got it filled with coffee; but of course, having no pot, there was no coffee for me. And after that, a sort of little tub called a "kid," was passed down into the forecastle, filled with something they called "burgoo." This was like mush, made of Indian corn, meal, and water. With the "kid," a little tin cannikin was passed down with molasses. Then the Jackson that I spoke of before, put the kid between his knees, and began to pour in the molasses, just like an old landlord mixing punch for a party. He scooped out a little hole in the middle of the mush, to hold the molasses; so it looked for all the world like a little black pool in the Dismal Swamp of Virginia.

Then they all formed a circle round the kid; and one after the other, with great regularity, dipped their spoons into the mush, and after stirring them round a little in the molasses-pool, they swallowed down their mouthfuls, and smacked their lips over it, as if it tasted very good; which I have no doubt it did; but not having any spoon, I wasn't sure.

I sat some time watching these proceedings, and wondering how polite they were to each other; for, though there were a great many spoons to only one dish, they never got entangled. At last, seeing that the mush was getting thinner and thinner, and that it was getting low water, or rather low molasses in the little pool, I ran on deck, and after searching about, returned with a bit of stick; and thinking I had as good a right as any one else to the mush and molasses, I worked my way into the circle, intending to make one of the party. So I shoved in my stick, and after twirling it about, was just managing to carry a little *burgoo* toward my mouth, which had been for some time standing ready open to receive it, when one of the sailors perceiving what I was about, knocked the stick out of my hands, and asked me where I learned my manners; Was that the way gentlemen eat in my country? Did they eat their victuals with splinters of wood, and couldn't that wealthy gentleman my father afford to buy his gentlemanly son a spoon?

All the rest joined in, and pronounced me an ill-bred, coarse, and unmannerly youngster, who, if permitted to go on with such behavior as that, would corrupt the whole crew, and make them no better than swine.

As I felt conscious that a stick was indeed a thing very unsuitable to eat with, I did not say much to this, though it vexed me enough; but remembering that I had seen one of the steerage passengers with a pan and spoon in his hand eating his breakfast on the fore hatch, I now ran on deck again, and to my great joy succeeded in borrowing his spoon, for he had got through his meal, and down I came again, though at the eleventh hour, and offered myself once more as a candidate.

But alas! there was little more of the Dismal Swamp left, and when I reached over to the opposite end of the kid, I received a rap on the knuckles from a spoon, and was told that I must help myself from my own side, for that was the rule. But *my* side was scraped clean, so I got no *burgoo* that morning.

But I made it up by eating some salt beef and biscuit, which I found to be the invariable accompaniment of every meal; the sailors sitting cross-legged on their chests in a circle, and breaking the hard biscuit, very sociably, over each other's heads, which was very convenient indeed, but gave me the headache, at least for the first four or five days till I got used to it; and then I did not care much about it, only it kept my hair full of crumbs; and I had forgot to bring a fine comb and brush, so I used to shake my hair out to windward over the bulwarks every evening.

While we sat eating our beef and biscuit, two of the men got into a dispute, about who had been sea-faring the longest; when Jackson, who had mixed the *burgoo,* called upon them in a loud voice to cease their clamor, for he would decide the matter for them. Of this sailor, I shall have something more to say, as I get on with my narrative; so, I will here try to describe him a little.

Did you ever see a man, with his hair shaved off, and just recovered from the yellow fever? Well, just such a looking man was this sailor. He was as yellow as gamboge, had no more whisker on his cheek, than I have on my elbows. His hair had fallen out, and left him very bald, except in the nape of his neck, and just behind the ears, where it was stuck over with short little tufts, and looked like a worn-out shoe-brush. His nose had broken down in the middle, and he squinted with one eye, and did not look very straight out of the other. He dressed a good deal like a Bowery boy; for he despised the ordinary sailor-rig; wearing a pair of great over-all blue trowsers, fastened with suspenders, and three red woolen shirts, one over the other; for he was subject to the rheumatism, and was not in good health, he said; and he had a large white wool hat, with a broad rolling brim. He was a native of New York city, and had a good deal to say about *highlanders,* and *rowdies,* whom he denounced as only good for the gallows; but I thought he looked a good deal like a *highlander* himself.

His name, as I have said, was Jackson; and he told us, he was a near relation of General Jackson of New Orleans, and swore terribly, if any one ventured to question what he asserted on that head. In fact he was a great bully, and being the best seaman on board, and very overbearing every way, all the men were afraid of him, and durst not contradict him, or cross his path in any thing. And what made this more wonderful was, that he was the weakest man, bodily, of the whole crew; and I have no doubt that young and small as I was then, compared to what I am now, I could have thrown him down. But he had such an overawing way with him; such a deal of brass and impudence, such an unflinching face, and withal was such a hideous looking mortal, that Satan himself would have run from him. And besides all this, it was quite plain, that he was by nature a marvelously clever, cunning man, though without education; and understood human nature to a kink, and well knew whom he had to deal with; and then, one glance of his squinting eye, was as good as a knock-down, for it was the most deep, subtle, infernal looking eye, that I ever saw lodged in a human head. I believe, that by good rights it must have belonged to a wolf, or starved tiger; at any rate, I would defy any oculist, to turn out a glass eye, half so cold, and snaky, and deadly. It was a horrible thing; and I would give much to forget that I have ever seen it; for it haunts me to this day.

It was impossible to tell how old this Jackson was; for he had no beard, and no wrinkles, except small crowsfeet about the eyes. He might have seen thirty, or perhaps fifty years. But according to his own account, he had been to sea ever since he was eight years old, when he first went as a cabin-boy in an Indiaman, and ran away at Calcutta. And according to his own account, too, he had passed through every kind of dissipation and abandonment in the worst parts of the world. He had served in Portuguese slavers on the coast of Africa; and with a diabolical relish used to tell of the *middle-passage,* where the slaves were stowed, heel and point, like logs, and the suffocated and dead were unmanacled, and weeded out from the living every morning, before washing down the decks; how he had been in a slaving schooner, which being chased by an English cruiser off Cape Verde, received three shots in her hull, which raked through and through a whole file of slaves, that were chained.

He would tell of lying in Batavia during a fever, when his ship lost a man every few days, and how they went reeling ashore with the body, and got still more intoxicated by way of precaution against the plague. He would talk of finding a cobra-di-capello, or hooded snake, under his pillow in India, when he slept ashore there. He would talk of sailors being poisoned at Canton with drugged *"shampoo,"* for the sake of their money; and of the Malay ruffians, who stopped ships in the straits of Caspar, and always saved the captain for the last, so as to make him point out where the most valuable goods were stored.

His whole talk was of this land; full of piracies, plagues and poisonings. And often he narrated many passages in his own individual career, which were almost incredible, from the consideration that few men could have plunged into such infamous vices, and clung to them so long, without paying the death-penalty.

But in truth, he carried about with him the traces of these things, and the mark of a fearful end nigh at hand; like that of King Antiochus of Syria, who died a worse death, history says, than if he had been stung out of the world by wasps and hornets.

Nothing was left of this Jackson but the foul lees and dregs of a man; he was thin as a shadow; nothing but skin and bones; and sometimes used to complain, that it hurt him to sit on the hard chests. And I sometimes fancied, it was the consciousness of his miserable, broken-down condition, and the prospect of soon dying like a dog, in consequence of his sins, that made this poor wretch always eye me with such malevolence as he did. For I was young and handsome, at least my mother so thought me, and as soon as I became a little used to the sea, and shook off my low spirits somewhat, I began to have my old color in my cheeks, and, spite of misfortune, to appear well and hearty; whereas *he* was being consumed by an incurable malady, that was eating up his vitals, and was more fit for a hospital than a ship.

As I am sometimes by nature inclined to indulge in unauthorized surmisings about the thoughts going on with regard to me, in the people I meet; especially if I have reason to think they dislike me; I will not put it down for a certainty that what I suspected concerning this Jackson relative to his thoughts of me, was really the truth. But only state my honest opinion, and how it struck me at the time; and even now, I think I was not wrong. And indeed, unless it was so, how could I account to myself, for the shudder that would run through me, when I caught this man gazing at me, as I often did; for he was apt to be dumb at times, and would sit with his eyes fixed, and his teeth set, like a man in the moody madness.

I well remember the first time I saw him, and how I was startled at his eye, which was even then fixed upon me. He was standing at the ship's helm, being the first man that got there, when a steersman was called for by the pilot; for this Jackson was always on the alert for easy duties, and used to plead his delicate health as the reason for assuming them, as he did; though I used to think, that for a man in poor health, he was very swift on the legs; at least when a good place was to be jumped to; though that might only have been a sort of spasmodic exertion under strong inducements, which every one knows the greatest invalids will sometimes show.

And though the sailors were always very bitter against any thing like *sogering*, as they called it; that is, any thing that savored of a desire to get rid of downright hard work; yet, I observed that, though this Jackson was a notorious old *soger* the whole voyage (I mean, in all things not perilous to do, from which he was far from hanging back), and in truth was a great veteran that way, and one who must have passed unhurt through many campaigns; yet, they never presumed to call him to account in any way; or to let him so much as think, what they thought of his conduct. But I often heard them call him many hard names behind his back; and sometimes, too, when, perhaps, they had just been tenderly inquiring after his health before his face. They all stood in mortal fear of him; and cringed and fawned about him like so many spaniels; and used to rub his back, after he was undressed and lying in his bunk; and used to run up on deck to the cook-house, to warm some cold coffee for him; and used to fill his pipe, and give him chews of tobacco, and mend his jackets and trowsers; and used to watch, and tend, and nurse him every way. And all the time, he would sit scowling on them, and found fault with what they did; and I noticed, that those who did the most for him, and cringed the most before him, were the very ones he most abused; while two or three who held more aloof, he treated with a little consideration.

It is not for me to say, what it was that made a whole ship's company submit so to the whims of one poor miserable man like Jackson. I only know that so it was; but I have no doubt, that if he had had a blue eye in his head, or had had a different face from what he did have, they would not have stood in such awe of him. And it astonished me, to see that one of the seamen, a remarkably robust and good-humored young man from Belfast in Ireland, was a person of no mark or influence among the crew; but on the contrary was hooted at, and trampled upon, and made a butt and laughing-stock; and more than all, was continually being abused and snubbed by Jackson, who seemed to hate him cordially, because of his great strength and fine person, and particularly because of his red cheeks.

But then, this Belfast man, although he had shipped for an *able-seaman*, was not much of a sailor; and that always lowers a man in the eyes of a ship's company; I mean, when he ships for an *able-seaman*, but is not able to do the duty of one. For sailors are of three classes—*able-seaman*, *ordinary-seaman*, and *boys*; and they receive different wages according to their rank. Generally, a ship's company of twelve men will only have five or six able seamen, who if they prove to understand their duty every way (and that is no small matter either, as I shall hereafter show, perhaps), are looked up to, and thought much of by the ordinary-seamen and boys, who reverence their very pea-jackets, and lay up their sayings in their hearts.

But you must not think from this, that persons called *boys* aboard merchant-ships are all youngsters, though to be sure, I myself was called a *boy*, and
a boy I was. No. In merchant-ships, a *boy* means a green-hand, a landsman on
his first voyage. And never mind if he is old enough to be a grandfather, he is
still called a *boy*; and boys' work is put upon him.

But I am straying off from what I was going to say about Jackson's
putting an end to the dispute between the two sailors in the forecastle after
breakfast. After they had been disputing some time about who had been to
sea the longest, Jackson told them to stop talking; and then bade one of them
open his mouth; for, said he, I can tell a sailor's age just like a horse's—by his
teeth. So the man laughed, and opened his mouth; and Jackson made him
step out under the scuttle, where the light came down from deck; and then
made him throw his head back, while he looked into it, and probed a little
with his jackknife, like a baboon peering into a junk-bottle. I trembled for
the poor fellow, just as if I had seen him under the hands of a crazy barber,
making signs to cut his throat, and he all the while sitting stock still, with the
lather on, to be shaved. For I watched Jackson's eye and saw it snapping, and
a sort of going in and out, very quick, as if it were something like a forked
tongue; and somehow, I felt as if he were longing to kill the man; but at last
he grew more composed, and after concluding his examination, said, that the
first man was the oldest sailor, for the ends of his teeth were the evenest and
most worn down; which, he said, arose from eating so much hard sea-biscuit;
and this was the reason he could tell a sailor's age like a horse's.

At this, everybody made merry, and looked at each other, as much as to
say—*come, boys, let's laugh*; and they did laugh; and declared it was a rare joke.

This was always the way with them. They made a point of shouting out,
whenever Jackson said any thing with a grin; that being the sign to them that
he himself thought it funny; though I heard many good jokes from others
pass off without a smile; and once Jackson himself (for, to tell the truth, he
sometimes had a comical way with him, that is, when his back did not ache)
told a truly funny story, but with a grave face; when, not knowing how he
meant it, whether for a laugh or otherwise, they all sat still, waiting what to

do, and looking perplexed enough; till at last Jackson roared out upon them for a parcel of fools and idiots; and told them to their beards, how it was; that he had purposely put on his grave face, to see whether they would not look grave, too; even when he was telling something that ought to split their sides. And with that, he flouted, and jeered at them, and laughed them all to scorn; and broke out in such a rage, that his lips began to glue together at the corners with a fine white foam.

He seemed to be full of hatred and gall against every thing and everybody in the world; as if all the world was one person, and had done him some dreadful harm, that was rankling and festering in his heart. Sometimes I thought he was really crazy; and often felt so frightened at him, that I thought of going to the captain about it, and telling him Jackson ought to be confined, lest he should do some terrible thing at last. But upon second thoughts, I always gave it up; for the captain would only have called me a fool, and sent me forward again.

But you must not think that all the sailors were alike in abasing themselves before this man. No: there were three or four who used to stand up sometimes against him; and when he was absent at the wheel, would plot against him among the other sailors, and tell them what a shame and ignominy it was, that such a poor miserable wretch should be such a tyrant over much better men than himself. And they begged and conjured them as men, to put up with it no longer, but the very next time, that Jackson presumed to play the dictator, that they should all withstand him, and let him know his place. Two or three times nearly all hands agreed to it, with the exception of those who used to slink off during such discussions; and swore that they would not any more submit to being ruled by Jackson. But when the time came to make good their oaths, they were mum again, and let every thing go on the old way; so that those who had put them up to it, had to bear all the brunt of Jackson's wrath by themselves. And though these last would stick up a little at first, and even mutter something about a fight to Jackson; yet in the end, finding themselves unbefriended by the rest, they would gradually become silent, and leave the field to the tyrant, who would then fly out worse than ever, and dare them to do their worst, and jeer at them for white-livered poltroons, who did not have a mouthful of heart in them. At such times, there were no bounds to his contempt; and indeed, all the time he seemed to have even more contempt than hatred, for every body and every thing.

As for me, I was but a boy; and at any time aboard ship, a boy is expected to keep quiet, do what he is bid, never presume to interfere, and seldom to talk, unless spoken to. For merchant sailors have a great idea of their dignity, and superiority to *greenhorns* and *landsmen,* who know nothing about a ship; and they seem to think, that an *able seaman* is a great man; at least a much greater man than a little boy. And the able seamen in the Highlander had such grand notions about their seamanship, that I almost thought that able seamen received diplomas, like those given at colleges; and were made a sort *A.M.S,* or *Masters of Arts.*

But though I kept thus quiet, and had very little to say, and well knew that my best plan was to get along peaceably with every body, and indeed endure a good deal before showing fight, yet I could not avoid Jackson's evil eye, nor escape his bitter enmity. And his being my foe, set many of the rest against me; or at least they were afraid to speak out for me before Jackson; so that at last I found myself a sort of Ishmael in the ship, without a single friend or companion; and I began to feel a hatred growing up in me against the whole crew—so much so, that I prayed against it, that it might not master my heart completely, and so make a fiend of me, something like Jackson.

The second day out of port, the decks being washed down and breakfast over, the watch was called, and the mate set us to work.

It was a very bright day. The sky and water were both of the same deep hue; and the air felt warm and sunny; so that we threw off our jackets. I could hardly believe that I was sailing in the same ship I had been in during the night, when every thing had been so lonely and dim; and I could hardly imagine that this was the same ocean, now so beautiful and blue, that during part of the night-watch had rolled along so black and forbidding.

There were little traces of sunny clouds all over the heavens; and little fleeces of foam all over the sea; and the ship made a strange, musical noise under her bows, as she glided along, with her sails all still. It seemed a pity to go to work at such a time; and if we could only have sat in the windlass again; or if they would have let me go out on the bowsprit, and lay down between the *manropes* there, and look over at the fish in the water, and think of home, I should have been almost happy for a time.

I had now completely got over my sea-sickness, and felt very well; at least in my body, though my heart was far from feeling right; so that I could now look around me, and make observations.

And truly, though we were at sea, there was much to behold and wonder at; to me, who was on my first voyage. What most amazed me was the sight of the great ocean itself, for we were out of sight of land. All round us, on both sides of the ship, ahead and astern, nothing was to be seen but water-water— water; not a single glimpse of green shore, not the smallest island, or speck of moss any where. Never did I realize till now what the ocean was: how grand and majestic, how solitary, and boundless, and beautiful and blue; for that day it gave no tokens of squalls or hurricanes, such as I had heard my father tell of; nor could I imagine, how any thing that seemed so playful and placid, could be lashed into rage, and troubled into rolling avalanches of foam, and great cascades of waves, such as I saw in the end.

As I looked at it so mild and sunny, I could not help calling to mind my little brother's face, when he was sleeping an infant in the cradle. It had just such a happy, careless, innocent look; and every happy little wave seemed gamboling about like a thoughtless little kid in a pasture; and seemed to look up in your face as it passed, as if it wanted to be patted and caressed. They seemed all live things with hearts in them, that could feel; and I almost felt grieved, as we sailed in among them, scattering them under our broad bows in sun-flakes, and riding over them like a great elephant among lambs. But what seemed perhaps the most strange to me of all, was a certain wonderful rising and falling of the sea; I do not mean the waves themselves, but a sort of wide heaving and swelling and sinking all over the ocean. It was something I can not very well describe; but I know very well what it was, and how it affected me. It made me almost dizzy to look at it; and yet I could not keep my eyes off it, it seemed so passing strange and wonderful.

I felt as if in a dream all the time; and when I could shut the ship out, almost thought I was in some new, fairy world, and expected to hear myself called to, out of the clear blue air, or from the depths of the deep blue sea. But I did not have much leisure to indulge in such thoughts; for the men were now getting some *stun'-sails* ready to hoist aloft, as the wind was getting fairer and fairer for us; and these stun'-sails are light canvas which are spread at such times, away out beyond the ends of the yards, where they overhang the wide water, like the wings of a great bird.

For my own part, I could do but little to help the rest, not knowing the name of any thing, or the proper way to go about aught. Besides, I felt very dreamy, as I said before; and did not exactly know where, or what I was; every thing was so strange and new.

While the stun'-sails were lying all tumbled upon the deck, and the sailors were fastening them to the booms, getting them ready to hoist, the mate ordered me to do a great many simple things, none of which could I comprehend, owing to the queer words he used; and then, seeing me stand quite perplexed and confounded, he would roar out at me, and call me all manner of names, and the sailors would laugh and wink to each other, but durst not go farther than that, for fear of the mate, who in his own presence would not let any body laugh at me but himself.

However, I tried to wake up as much as I could, and keep from dreaming with my eyes open; and being, at bottom, a smart, apt lad, at last I managed to learn a thing or two, so that I did not appear so much like a fool as at first.

People who have never gone to sea for the first time as sailors, can not imagine how puzzling and confounding it is. It must be like going into a barbarous country, where they speak a strange dialect, arid dress in strange clothes, and live in strange houses. For sailors have their own names, even for things that are familiar ashore; and if you call a thing by its shore name, you are laughed at for an ignoramus and a landlubber. This first day I speak of, the mate having ordered me to draw some water, I asked him where I was to get the pail; when I thought I had committed some dreadful crime; for he flew into a great passion, and said they never had any *pails* at sea, and then I learned that they were always called *buckets*. And once I was talking about sticking a little wooden peg into a bucket to stop a leak, when he flew out again, and said there were no *pegs* at sea, only *plugs*. And just so it was with every thing else.

But besides all this, there is such an infinite number of totally new names of new things to learn, that at first it seemed impossible for me to master them all. If you have ever seen a ship, you must have remarked what a thicket of ropes there are; and how they all seemed mixed and entangled together like a great skein of yarn. Now the very smallest of these ropes has its own proper name, and many of them are very lengthy, like the names of young royal princes, such as the *starboard-main-top-gallant-bow-line,* or the *larboard-fore-top-sail-clue-line.*

I think it would not be a bad plan to have a grand new naming of a ship's ropes, as I have read, they once had a simplifying of the classes of plants in Botany. It is really wonderful how many names there are in the world. There is no counting the names, that surgeons and anatomists give to the various parts of the human body; which, indeed, is something like a ship; its bones being the stiff standing-rigging, and the sinews the small running ropes, that manage all the motions.

I wonder whether mankind could not get along without all these names, which keep increasing every day, and hour, and moment; till at last the very air will be full of them; and even in a great plain, men will be breathing each other's breath, owing to the vast multitude of words they use, that consume all the air, just as lamp-burners do gas. But people seem to have a great love for names; for to know a great many names, seems to look like knowing a good many things; though I should not be surprised, if there were a great many more names than things in the world. But I must quit this rambling, and return to my story.

At last we hoisted the stun'-sails up to the top-sail yards, and as soon as the vessel felt them, she gave a sort of bound like a horse, and the breeze blowing more and more, she went plunging along, shaking off the foam from her bows, like foam from a bridle-bit. Every mast and timber seemed to have a pulse in it that was beating with life and joy; and I felt a wild exulting in my own heart, and felt as if I would be glad to bound along so round the world.

Then was I first conscious of a wonderful thing in me, that responded to all the wild commotion of the outer world; and went reeling on and on with the planets in their orbits, and was lost in one delirious throb at the center of the All. A wild bubbling and bursting was at my heart, as if a hidden spring had just gushed out there; and my blood ran tingling along my frame, like mountain brooks in spring freshets.

Yes! yes! give me this glorious ocean life, this salt-sea life, this briny, foamy life, when the sea neighs and snorts, and you breathe the very breath that the great whales respire! Let me roll around the globe, let me rock upon the sea; let me race and pant out my life, with an eternal breeze astern, and an endless sea before!

But how soon these raptures abated, when after a brief idle interval, we were again set to work, and I had a vile commission to clean out the chicken coops, and make up the beds of the pigs in the long-boat.

Miserable dog's life is this of the sea! commanded like a slave, and set to work like an ass! vulgar and brutal men lording it over me, as if I were an African in Alabama. Yes, yes, blow on, ye breezes, and make a speedy end to this abominable voyage!

SOURCES

"The Striped Chest," from *The Dealings of Captain Sharkey and Other Tales of Pirates*, Arthur Conan Doyle, 1905.

"Loss of the Brig *Tyrrel*," from *Thrilling Narratives: Tales of Shipwreck and Disaster*, T. Purnell, 1913.

"Typhoon Off the Coast of Japan," from *Stories of Ships and the Sea*, Jack London, 1922.

"Searching for Franklin," from *Adrift in the Arctic Pack Ice*, Elisha Kent Kane, 1918.

"The Rubicon," from *The Riddle of the Sands*, Erskine Childers, 1903.

"Cast Adrift," from *A Narrative of the Mutiny on Board His Majesty's Ship Bounty*, William Bligh, 1790.

"The Wreck on the Andamans," from *The Wreck on the Andamans*, Joseph Darvall, Esq., 1845.

"Escaping the Sinking *Medusa*," from *Perils and Captivity*, Charlotte-Adélaïde Dard, 1827.

"Loss of the Titanic: The Official Report," from *Loss of the Steamship "Titanic": Report of a Formal Investigation into the Circumstances Surrounding the Foundering on April 15, 1912, of the British Steamship "Titanic" of Liverpool*, The British Government, *1912*.

"Winter in the Arctic," from *The Arctic Whaleman*, Rev. Lewis Holmes, 1857.

"Sunk by a Whale," from *Bark* Kathleen *Sunk by a Whale,* Captain Thomas H. Jenkins,1902.

"The Storm," from *David Copperfield*, Charles Dickens, 1850.

"A Struggle with the Devil-Fish," from *Toilers of the Sea,* Victor Hugo, 1866.

"My First Voyage," from *Two Years Before the Mast,* Richard Henry Dana Jr., 1840.

"Redburn," from *Redburn: Being the Sailor Boy, Confessions and Reminiscences of the Son-Of-A-Gentleman In the Merchant Navy,* Herman Melville, 1849.